WOLF IN SHADOW

Baen Books
by John Lambshead

Lucy's Blade

Into the Hinterlands
(with David Drake)

WOLF IN SHADOW

JOHN LAMBSHEAD

WOLF IN SHADOW

A Baen Books Original

Baen Publishing Enterprises
P.O. Box 1403
Riverdale, NY 10471
www.baen.com

ISBN: 978-1-4516-3910-0

Cover art by Dave Seeley

First printing, July 2013

Distributed by Simon & Schuster
1230 Avenue of the Americas
New York, NY 10020

Library of Congress Cataloging-in-Publication Data

Lambshead, John.
 Wolf in shadow / John Lambshead.
    pages cm
  ISBN 978-1-4516-3910-0 (trade pb)
 I. Title.
 PR6112.A53W65 2013
 823'.92--dc23

                              2013005979

Printed in the United States of America

10 9 8 7 6 5 4 3 2 1

Acknowledgements

I would like to thank David Drake for his invaluable help and many kindnesses and Fred Kiesche for reading through the manuscript for typos. Finally, I must thank Toni Weisskopf for whipping the novel into shape.

Note

Everything you read in this novel about London from this point on is true, except for the bits I have exaggerated, distorted, or completely fabricated.

—John Lambshead

CONTENTS

WOLF IN SHADOW

"He's mad that trusts in the tameness of a wolf."
—Shakespeare, King Lear

CHAPTER 1
SAYING GOODBYE

Saying goodbye is the defining moment between ending an old life and starting anew. Without that terminal farewell, shadows and regrets of the past hang around like a bunch of distant relatives who have learned of your lottery win. They tended to haunt Rhian no matter how far she ran so she wanted to say goodbye.

She had never moved into the flat properly, just kept a spare washbag and a change of clothes there. So it would always be James' flat in her head, not their flat.

Somehow the door looked shabbier than she remembered, the paint peeling from around the wooden panels. She turned her key in the Yale lock noting the scratches where tired and drunken tenants had marked the paint. One gouge looked new suggesting that James himself must have caused it—James or her.

She pushed the door and walked in, dropping her heavy shoulder bag to the floor. The tiny flat was exactly the same even though everything was different. James had gone and the life of the flat had departed with him. It had always been a warm place, a welcoming place, but now it smelled cold and stale. It had not taken long for the damp to get a grip. Like her life, she thought. The decay mirrored her life.

The front door opened straight into a living room with a kitchenette in the corner. She slipped her rucksack off and sat on the arm of the old, stained sofa to catch her breath. An unwashed plate encrusted with the dried remains of a meal was discarded carelessly on the floor beside a knocked-over coffee mug. She picked them up, putting them on the side for washing. The mug had a picture of a superhero on the side. James had been into comics. She had often scolded him about his untidiness. How could she have wasted her time with him on such trivia?

James' computer was still where he always kept it, on a cheap self-assembly office table against the wall. She used to sit just where she sat now, watching while he worked. He was completely unaware of her presence when he concentrated with that terrible male focus. Then she felt that she saw into the real James and she liked what she observed.

Rhian unzipped her coat, allowing the silver Celtic brooch hung around her neck to swing free on its chain. The stylised wolf head on the brooch glinted in the light from the window, catching her eye. Worn letters picked out the word *Morgana*.

James had looked up the British goddess on the internet and read off her list of attributes. To the English she was Morgan le Fay, Goddess of fate and sister and sworn enemy to King Arthur. In the Welsh tradition she was the goddess of death, the Moon, lakes and rivers. James had been puzzled why the brooch was shaped like a wolf's head when Morgana's symbol was the raven, until he discovered she was the queen of shape shifters.

Rhian could still hear James' voice in the empty flat, could picture him standing over her.

"Shapeshifters, you know, weres." He growled and clawed his hand at her. "Werewolves, Rhian. Haven't you ever met a wolf?"

He had jumped on her theatrically and she had fallen over with a shriek, his heavy body pinning her down.

"It's getting late," he said. "I had better walk you back to your bed-sit."

"I've some things in my bag. I could stay here tonight," she replied.

"It's a small flat. I only have one bed."

"I know," Rhian said, raising her lips to his.

She smiled, recalling what a bad girl she had been, and regretting not a moment. Then the numbness came down like the curtain falling for the last time on a cancelled play and Rhian went back into robotic mode. She couldn't bear to feel, to let herself hurt.

She slipped into the bathroom, retrieving her washbag from under the sink. The area was surprisingly spacious with room for a full-sized bath. It had probably served a much bigger living area before the building had been subdivided into the largest possible number of flats.

The bedroom, in contrast, was minute. Nevertheless, the landlord had squeezed in a single bed, side table, and wardrobe. Rhian opened the wardrobe, removing the few things that she kept there. All James' clothes were still hung on hangers or crammed into carrier bags, waiting to be washed. She pulled a shirt out of a bag and lifted it to her face, smelling his scent.

She almost broke down then but she held it together. She had promised herself she would not cry. She froze her feelings until she felt hollow. Inside her head was a vacuum, a cold emptiness like the center of a bronze-cast statue.

Rhian put the garment down and was businesslike again. She gathered up everything—her clothes, her washbag—what else was there? She wanted to leave no sign of her presence in the flat. She opened the drawer under the side table. Inside was a bad photograph of a girl sitting on James' knee. She remembered the picture being taken in the passport booth at Victoria Station. They were waiting for a train to the coast for a day trip. It rained the whole day and she had a wonderful time. She put the photo in her pocket.

Rhian looked into the bedroom mirror. The face that looked back at her was near identical to the girl in the photo. Both girls had the same short-cut dark hair, the same petite bone structure but the eyes were different. The girl in the mirror had eyes that were a thousand years older.

She put the photo carefully in her coat pocket and turned away. She was about to leave when a thought struck her, so she reopened the drawer and pulled it completely out. Feeling under the lid, she found an envelope taped out of sight. She slipped open the flap to reveal a slim stack of ten- and twenty-pound notes. She placed the envelope in her coat pocket next to the photo.

She put her rucksack back on, loaded her bag upon her shoulder and placed her key firmly down on the computer table. She would not be coming back, ever. The door closed with a click of the Yale lock when she let herself out. She went down the stairs and out of the front door onto the street. Rhian walked along the pavement for a few meters then stopped.

"I wonder," she said, "where I should go?"

CHAPTER 2
THE TUBE

Outside Ealing Broadway tube station, a large schematic map showed the various bus routes into the outer West London suburbs, Hounslow, Uxbridge, and Heathrow. Coaches ventured further west down the M4 to Slough, Reading, or even Wales.

Return to Wales? That thought concentrated her mind. Return to her mother and the endless stream of transient "uncles" that passed through her house; uncles with greedy eyes and wandering hands. She came to a decision not to go west. She would go east, as far to the east as she could. Rhian was running away all over again.

She punched pound coins into the vending machine on the wall. It refused to accept her two-pound coin so she resorted to the old trick of licking one side, disgusting but effective. The machine disgorged a single one-way ticket to Upminster on the end of the District Line. Rhian had absolutely no idea what it was like, but it fulfilled her two vital criteria: it was not in Ealing and it was a long way from Wales.

The automatic barrier fought to strip her of her bags but she triumphed and after a brief struggle walked down onto the platform. A bored London Transport official studied the bare-breasted page three girl in *The Sun*. The tube station was above ground so she could look up at the grey sky. It was one of those dreary London days where the clouds refused to rain but still hung around, like anxious parents at a teenage party.

It almost never rained in London. At this rate they would be declaring another drought and banning hosepipes and car washes. She glanced every few minutes at the electronic board, watching the marker count out the minutes to the arrival of the Upminster train.

A deep male voice boomed over the speakers in a Jamaican accent. "Stand clear of the platform."

She obediently moved two paces backward, and an empty train with its lights off rattled through.

"The Upminster train has been taken out of service. The next one is due . . . ," there was a pause. "Sometime soon."

Rhian sighed and searched for a seat unmarked by chewing gum or unmentionable stains in shades of brown.

Oddly enough, the train did arrive shortly afterwards. Rhian climbed into an empty carriage and slipped between the arms of a seat. The interior stank of the sharp tang of ozone from the powered rail pickups mixed with the musty smell of ancient upholstery. The doors slid shut with a solid thump, and they were off. Rhian leaned back against the seat and closed her eyes. She dozed fitfully, a watchful part of her mind noting the automatic opening and closing of the sliding doors as the tube train ground its way through the western suburbs.

A sudden surge in noise woke her up. The train dived into the network of tunnels under central London and sound reverberated off the walls. She was no longer alone in the carriage. On the seat opposite, a thin youth in dirty jeans looked away a little too quickly when her eyes met his. She put a protective arm across her luggage. Bag snatching had the status of a cottage industry in London. The youth leaned forward, lank, greasy hair hiding his face. Rhian picked up one of the free newspapers that littered the floor and leafed through the pages, more to occupy her hands than because she was interested in reading the articles.

The carriage filled as the train ran towards the West End, so she moved her bags onto her lap. Eventually, all the seats were taken and people were obliged to strap-hang. The youth slouched off at South Kensington. Maybe he had promised himself an improving day at the museums thought Rhian sourly. Once the train left the City of Westminster for the City of London, the original Roman London, the carriage began to empty. The last two occupants, a couple of elderly tourists instantly recognizable as American by the man's baseball hat, got off at Tower Hill and Rhian was left on her own.

The tube wound under Charles Dickens' old East London.

The carriage swayed backwards and forwards over a hidden set of points, throwing her against the arm rests and causing her rucksack to fall onto the floor. She brushed muck off the bottom and put it beside her on the empty seat. At this time of day the trains outside the tourist areas were little used. The massed lemminglike hordes of commuters had thundered into their offices earlier and would not reappear until the evening. More than three million people used London's tube trains every day.

"Tickets, please?" A young man stood in front of her with his hand out.

He had come out of nowhere. She was sure that he had not been there earlier. They never usually checked the tickets on the tube once you were through the automatic barriers. Wordlessly, she fished around in her pocket for the ticket and handed it over to the man. He examined it casually. He was dressed in a T-shirt and cargo trousers, showing a superbly fit, muscled body. He had a bag slung on a strap over his shoulder.

He looked unlike any London Transport official or policeman that Rhian had ever seen. She wondered if the government was putting SAS troopers back on the trains again. There might be some sort of terrorist panic on and the authorities were trying to reassure the public. Rhian did not own a TV and hardly ever read a paper, so she was rarely aware of national events.

The man's eyes flicked up and down her body in that characteristic male once-over that every woman between the age of fifteen and fifty got used to receiving. He was clearly bored. No doubt he would prefer to be doing something more masculine and exciting like abseiling down embassy walls or running around Dartmoor waving a machine gun, but here he was, checking girlys' train tickets as a public relations stunt for the government. He handed her ticket back and passed on down the carriage, letting himself into the next one by the interconnecting door. That was highly unusual in itself as those doors were not usually used when the train was in service.

The train screeched to a halt without warning, the carriages lurching and bumping as the multiple brakes bit differentially. Rhian sighed. London had the oldest and largest underground railway system in the world, two hundred and seventy-five stations connected by two hundred and fifty miles of track. Rhian had chosen the history of the London Underground as her special topic at school so she had a fund of pointless information about the system stored up in her head. The idea of a giant underground railway had seemed romantic to a girl growing up in a Welsh valley.

The problem with being the oldest and biggest was that the system was out of date and impossibly expensive to modernize. When she came to London she discovered that the tubes might be impressive but were hardly glamorous. They were an example of archaic heavy engineering. Some of the power wiring was fifty years old and had a habit of cutting out at inconvenient moments.

Half the system ran underground in tight tunnels. There was an unclaimed prize for any engineer who could work out how to fit air conditioning to the carriages. The temperature in a broken-down train in the rush hour, when passengers were packed into a stationary mass, climbed quickly past blood heat until people started passing out. No one had actually died yet, but it had to happen one day.

The driver came on the intercom. "We are being held on a red light, so there must be some sort of delay up ahead. I haven't been informed of any special problem over the radio, so I assume that we will be moving soon. I will let you know in the unlikely event that anyone tells me anything."

The driver switched off the intercom with an audible click, leaving the carriage in silence. The delay dragged on so Rhian checked the map above the seats. They must be just outside Whitechapel Station, on the way to Stepney Green. The carriage felt cold, and Rhian shivered. Someone had just trodden on her grave.

She saw a flicker of motion at the edge of her vision, but when she looked there was no one there. It happened again and she heard faint whispers, echoing like hushed voices in a cathedral. The engines under the stationary train suddenly erupted in a loud chugga-chugga-chugga that made her jump. They did that at irregular intervals, but no-one seemed to know why.

Without warning, the carriages lurched forward, banging against each other as they picked up power from the ground rails with different degrees of efficiency. The tube actually ran more smoothly when it was full. With no passengers, it tended to rattle about like an empty container ship. The whine of heavy-duty electric motors under load built up. Rhian had hopes that they were on their way when the brakes came on again, slamming the cars to a halt.

The shadow of another figure appeared in front of her. She reached for her ticket, glanced up to proffer it and her heart thumped. An old woman in a dirty brown shroud and long dress looked at her in puzzlement.

"What do you want?" asked Rhian.

The woman didn't answer. She shimmered and Rhian could see through her to the empty bench seats opposite. Rhian's mouth went dry. This had happened to her before on the tube. She found it upsetting, but the specters seemed to be tied to particular places, so they vanished as soon as the train passed on.

The train moved. Speed was difficult to estimate in the dark tunnel, but Rhian concluded that they were travelling at a slow walking pace. More images flickered on the edge of her peripheral vision but faded when she looked directly at them. The whispering started again, building up until it filled the carriage like white noise in which Rhian could almost make out odd words. She fidgeted uneasily, never experiencing such a strong haunting before on a train.

The carriage filled with specters that solidified as the train inched forward. A little girl in a threadbare coat and long skirt designed for an adult woman sidled right up to her and said something, actually spoke words.

"Mummy, Mummy, it's dark, Mummy and I don't like it. Why won't you come for me, Mummy? I'm frightened."

Rhian put her hands over her ears to shut it out, but the piping speech of the child was in her head. This had *never* happened before. The train door opened at a station, and Rhian wanted to jump out, but she could not bring herself to move through the ghostly figures.

A burly man shoved the others aside. He wore heavy workman's clothes and boots. He waved a misshapen green bottle in one hand.

"You bitch! I'll teach you to go on the game."

He threw the bottle at Rhian, who screamed and ducked, putting her arm in front of her eyes. Once she started screaming she couldn't stop. It seemed to agitate the specters until they crowded around her, cajoling, pleading, demanding, threatening.

"No, no, leave me alone, please," she said.

A door banged and someone gripped her by her right arm. She fought and tried to pull free, the wolf clamoring within her.

"It's all right, love. You're all right. There's no one here but us."

Her arm was pulled from her eyes and she found herself looking at the ticket man, who held a bulky black pistol in his right hand.

The specters had gone.

"Do you need a doctor, love? I can get you one at the next station."

"I'm okay," she said, trying to catch her breath and failing, panting with exertion.

"You're having a panic attack and hyperventilating. Breathe into this."

He spoke calmly, as if to a child. He produced a paper bag and got her to breathe into it. She wondered vaguely if paper bags for hysterical girls were standard kit for SAS men. After a few moments, her frantic panting eased and she lowered the bag. She looked at his gun pointedly and raised an eyebrow. Nobody carried guns in London, not the police and certainly not ticket inspectors.

It was his turn to blush and he put the weapon out of sight in his shoulder bag.

"I, ah, heard the screams and thought you were being attacked."

"I must have had a nightmare." She said the first thing that came into her head and cursed that it sounded so lame. "Sorry."

He grinned at her. "No harm done, love. Do you have a phone number? Just so I can check later that you are okay."

"No," she lied, suspecting that his concern wasn't entirely altruistic. In other circumstances she might have found the young man's interest flattering, but she was not looking for a new relationship. It was far too soon after James.

He pulled an old receipt and a pen out of his pocket and wrote something down, giving it to her.

"You can always give me a call if you've another panic attack and need someone to bring round a paper bag. I have a great bedside manner."

I bet, thought Rhian, but she rewarded him with a smile and put the number in her pocket so as not to appear rude.

The train finally pulled into a station and the doors slid open. Rhian grabbed her bags and fled the train in embarrassment. On the platform she organized herself, putting her rucksack on. When she was ready, she looked around to find out where she was. A tube sign announced that this was the Mile End Station.

The station was clean and modern looking, which surprised Rhian. She had always lived in the western suburbs since she had first come to London, and she had accepted western prejudices about the East End. She could wait for the next train, but the incident had shaken her. Maybe this was fate? Maybe she was meant to get off here? She could continue eastwards later, by bus if she could not bring herself to get on another tube.

Rhian struggled up the steps to the ticket hall and out onto the street, blinking in the sunlight. As usual, the clouds had vanished without disgorging water. She bought a local paper from a sales booth at the station entrance. The headline was something about another body being found. She had not bought the paper for the news, so she ignored it.

The Mile End Road opposite the station was impassable on foot, with dual carriageways separated by railings. So, being too tired to struggle along the pavement with her bags until she found a pedestrian crossing, she turned behind the station into the maze of small streets. She came to high walls with a sign indicating Tower Hamlets Cemetery. On the corner, where Hamlets Road ran into English Way, was a traditional London pub. Traditional in the sense that it was run down, with faded paint and rotten woodwork. Not traditional in the sense that it had been given a spray-on makeover by a design consultancy.

A tatty sign, which looked as it had been used as a target for spent beer bottles, admitted that the premises were called the Black Swan. A smaller, newer sign proclaimed that one Gary Hunter was the licensee. Inside the furnishings were equally worn but surprisingly hygenic. Rhian dumped her bags by a table and went to the bar. She was served a by a clean-cut man in a striped rugby shirt. He was quite old, in his thirties, but fit. Perhaps the rugby shirt was not just for decoration.

"What'll it be, love?" he asked.

"A large Coke and two packets of plain crisps, please," she said.

"One ninety-five."

She sorted the money from the change in her purse and carried her purchases back to the table, sitting on the bench seat that ran along the front wall under the windows. She sipped the Coke and ate the crisps greedily.

"You were hungry," the barman said.

"I haven't eaten since yesterday."

"You want to look after yourself or you will become all thin and anorexic. You know what happens then, don't you?" the barman asked.

"No," she said, supplying the required answer, like a straight man in a comedy duo.

"You have your picture taken wearing expensive clothes. You get on TV, marry a footballer and become seriously rich and famous, especially when you divorce him for sleeping with the entire cast of *Girls Behaving Badly*. Of course, it helps if you had an abusive childhood as well, but you can always get your PR people to invent something."

Rhian nodded and smiled at him before unfolding the newspaper and turning to the letting page. Taking out a biro from her bag, she went carefully down the list of adverts, putting rings around likely prospects. When she had finished, she slipped her mobile out of her coat pocket and dialed the first number.

"Hello, I'm ringing about the room. Oh, it's gone? Sorry to have bothered you."

The second number did not answer, so she dialed the third.

"I'm ringing about the flat share. Your advert in the paper says you are looking for a girl? Oh, you have one. Sorry to have troubled you."

And so it went on, until she was near the bottom of the page. Rooms to let went quickly in London and the paper had been published a few days ago. She dialed again without much hope.

"I understand from your advert in the paper that you need a female flatmate but I suppose it's gone? No! I could come round right away to view it. How far is Vernon Road from the tube station? Right, number three-A, I'll be there in an hour."

Rhian felt far more relaxed now. However bad the let was, she would take it until something better came along or she moved on. For a while, she had thought that she might have to find a woman's hostel for the night. She hated sleeping in hostels, as she always seemed to get the roommate who snored or worse. She remembered one who tried to get in bed with her. The next day the woman insisted that she was sleepwalking and remembered nothing of the night's activities. Rhian had moved out nonetheless.

She opened the second packet of crisps and settled down to enjoy them. The door to the gents flew open, banging against the wall. A middle-aged man lurched out, weaving unsteadily between the tables. He must have been in the toilet for the entire time that she had been in the pub. The barman stopped cleaning glasses and watched warily.

The man sat down beside her on the bench seat. His closeness made her uneasy, since he had the choice of the entire pub. She ignored him and went on with her breakfast. He leaned over, blearily looking at her newspaper, clearly finding it a challenge to focus on the print.

"Looking for somewhere to stay, girly?" he asked, obviously noting the ringed adverts. "You can come back to my place if you like."

He leered at her, guffawing at his own wit, and put his hand on her thigh.

Rhian panicked.

"Don't touch me," she screamed, pushing the drunk away.

Fear of what might happen if she lost control lent power to her voice. She could not bear to think what might happen if she lost control. Her Coke went over in the scuffle.

"I've warned you before about bothering girls in here."

The barman appeared out of nowhere. He seized the drunk by the scruff of his neck. Pushing him to the door, the barmen threw him out into the street.

"You're barred," the barman said.

He stood for a while, making sure the drunk was really gone, then returned to Rhian's table.

"You spilt your drink," the barman said to her. "Hold on and I'll get you another."

He dashed back to the bar and, leaning over it, hosed out another coke from the dispenser into a clean glass. He brought the drink back and handed it to her.

"You're trembling," he said. "Honestly, he's not dangerous, just a stupid drunken pest. Would you like a brandy?"

"No, thank you," she replied.

Alcohol could be disastrous when she was upset. The barman sat with her for a while, apologizing all the time.

"Are you still looking for staff?" she asked, partly to deflect him. She pointed to a sign on the wall above the bar.

"Yes," he replied. "It will only be temporary, I'm afraid. The brewery intends to gut the place and make it into a student theme pub. I believe that the current plan is to do it out as the bar scene from *Star Wars*."

The two of them looked at each other and shuddered simultaneously. Rhian giggled with genuine humor, something that she had not done for a while. It felt good.

"Students!" they said, together.

"I have to find somewhere to stay," Rhian said.

"I overheard you," said the barman. "My name's Gary, by the way. I'm the manager. If you want the job then come back this evening. I won't even hold being Welsh against you."

"I may take you up on that," she said. "The job, I mean."

CHAPTER 3
FRANKIE

The various editions of the *A to Z* are the Londoner's bible. The pages contain a comprehensive index and grid map to every street in the vast sprawling city. Rhian used it to find a subway under the dual carriageway and followed its guidance in the maze of streets north of the tube station. Vernon Road was a cul-de-sac, which ran off a side road that came off another side road in a sort of spiral. She followed the roads around, taking the route that a car would have to follow. She suspected that there would be a shorter footpath somewhere, but the *A to Z* did not always see fit to show those.

Vernon Road consisted of rows of four-story terraced houses that were at least a century old, Edwardian or maybe Victorian. They had been originally built for the wealthy middle classes. The front door was up a flight of steps, under which were what had been servants' quarters. Of course, over the years the properties had all been converted into small flats and blocks of bedsits. The wealthy middle classes had long since fled the city and moved out to the rural bliss of the Home Counties around Greater London.

She scanned the newspaper to remind herself of the exact address and checked off the numbers on the houses as she walked down the road. Number three was right at the end; there did not seem to be a number one. The house was behind a handkerchief-sized, but neatly cared for, front garden. Three-A was the basement flat. It had its own front door at the bottom of a small flight of steps to the side of the building.

Rhian knocked on an ornate and truly hideous brass knocker shaped like a lion's face. After a brief pause the door swung open, decisively propelled by a tall woman in a long skirt and blouse in autumn colors. They were cut in an "East European peasant style" that had been fashionable a couple of years ago. She peered at Rhian through large strong glasses that completely distorted her eyes. She looked old to Rhian, almost as old as Gary.

"You must be the girl about the room?" the woman asked in a middle-class southern English accent.

"Yes," Rhian replied.

The woman cocked her head on one side, causing light brown frizzy hair to drift across her face.

"I thought you were Welsh when I spoke to you on the phone," she said, looking at Rhian's dark hair.

Rhian sighed. She had worked hard at losing her Welsh lilt in exchange for a typical London accent, but everyone still identified her as from the valleys after only a few words.

"That's an interesting door knocker," Rhian said, for want of anything more intelligent to say.

She felt a strange aversion to the knocker that surprised her. Why an inanimate object should bother her so was a mystery. Its blank bronze eyes stared at her as if alive. She almost had a compulsion to make her excuses and walk away.

"It's a copy of the 1154 A.D. Norman sanctuary knocker from the north door of Durham Cathedral," the woman said, with the pedantic precision of a scholar.

"I see," said Rhian, who did not see at all. It was beyond her why anyone should go to the trouble of fitting such a monstrosity.

"If you rapped on this knocker to request entry and confessed your crimes, then you were absolved of sin and allowed to go free. Have you any crimes that you wish to confess?"

"I don't think so," Rhian replied, smiling politely.

"Come in anyway," said the woman.

Rhian's air of unease evaporated as if an invisible barrier had been removed, and the woman ushered her into a long corridor with high ceilings. The knocker was just an inanimate lump of metal moulded into an unattractive shape. All the rest was her over active imagination.

Like most London properties, the house was much deeper than wide, the layout allowing builders to cram in as many properties as possible along the street.

"My name's Francisca Appleyard. Everyone but my mother calls me Frankie." She held out her hand.

"I'm Rhian Jones."

Rhian took the woman's hand, consciously making herself squeeze. A supervisor had once cruelly told her that she had a handshake like a dead haddock. It was part of his petty revenge for being turned down.

"Drop your bags here and I'll show you around," Frankie said. She pushed open the first door on the left. "This is the lounge."

The room was comfortably furnished with a sofa and a red leather swivel chair. The furniture looked expensive but was showing signs of wear. Light came in through a large window, which opened onto the basement well at the front of the house. Looking up, Rhian could see the small garden and the street. Net curtains prevented people on the pavement from looking in, so the window was like a two-way mirror. A bulky TV set stood in a corner away from the window. It had been an expensive state-of-the-art device when new but was now obsolete. Rhian had the impression of declining fortunes, or maybe Frankie had bought second hand. Bookcases and cupboards lined the walls right up to the ceiling.

"You would have free access to this room," Frankie said. "I am the only other person in the house. This is my bedroom here."

She pushed open a door to a room at the rear of the house that was larger than the sitting room. A double bed took pride of place in the center. This room was lined with shelves carrying books and strange objets d'art. Rhian was struck by an ornate mask carved from polished dark wood.

"Nor'ombo chieftain's death mask," said Frankie, following Rhian's gaze. She clicked her tongue in the middle of the name. Rhian wasn't sure whether the woman was making a joke. Rhian put a polite half smile on her face, as she didn't want to appear stupid.

Frankie drew back long ceiling-to-floor drapes at the back of the bedroom to reveal French windows.

"The garden out there is mine as well, and you are welcome to use it. I am afraid that the only way in is through my bedroom, but that shouldn't be a problem during the day. I like to sit out and read in good weather, but I advise you not to sunbathe *au naturelle.* The old boy upstairs has a pair of binoculars and is a bit of a perv. The bathroom is over there," Frankie said pointing to a door on the right. "There is another door into it from the hall."

She took Rhian back out into the hall to demonstrate.

"The kitchen is in here," she opened the door on a modern kitchenette with wall-mounted storage, "and this is the guest room."

The spare bedroom door wouldn't open fully because of the bed in the way. Frankie had to slide round it, moving further in so that Rhian could follow.

"It's a bit small," Frankie said, defensively, "but it's warm and cozy, and you've the run of the rest of the flat."

The room was indeed small; the wardrobe doors couldn't be fully opened either because of the bed, but it was warm and freshly decorated in bright, friendly colors. A window at the end let in natural light and gave a pleasant view of the garden.

Something strange happened to Rhian in the little room. She saw the world in color again for the first time in ages as if someone had switched on a floodlight. No, that was not quite right because she had recognized colors, distinguishing red from green, but emotionally they had all been shades of grey. Her world had been shades of grey since James—she bit down on the emotion—since the terrible night she lost James. Something about the little room lifted her soul.

"The room is lovely," said Rhian, genuinely pleased.

"Good! Let's have a cup of tea and discuss terms," Frankie said.

Rhian sat on a stool in the kitchen and watched Frankie go through the English tea ceremony. She used a large china teapot shaped like a country cottage.

"The rent is three hundred and eighty pounds a calendar month, about ninety quid a week. Is that okay? It does include everything." Frankie said, anxiously, watching Rhian carefully.

Rhian considered. It would be tight, but the bar work would tide her through until she could find a better job. She smiled at Frankie, "That will be fine."

"I'd like one month's rent in advance as a deposit," Frankie said.

"Oh!" said Rhian.

She took out the envelope and counted the money twice. However she rearranged the notes, she could not make the deposit.

"How much have you got?" said Frankie, sipping her tea.

"Two hundred and ten pounds."

Frankie sighed. "And you will need something to live on until payday. Give me ninety quid and we'll call it quits."

Rhian handed over a ten and four twenties, and helped herself to milk. "Have you had many other tenants?" she asked, politely.

"One or two," said Frankie, evasively. "Sugar? No? Is that how you keep so slim, dear?"

Frankie shoveled two spoonfuls into her own mug. "I've been a bit unlucky with lodgers," Frankie admitted. "They tend to move on quickly."

"Have you lived here long?" Rhian asked, to fill a gap in the conversation.

"My partner and I lived here for some years," Frankie said.

"Ah," Rhian said, neutrally.

"Don't worry, dear. It's all ancient history now. He announced that he needed to find himself, so he went on a solo bus tour across North America."

"Did he find himself?" asked Rhian.

"I don't know because I haven't seen him since. According to a postcard from Nevada, he did find a nineteen-year-old blonde lap dancer called Suze 'with an e.' She thought that his English accent was cute."

Frankie said the last few words through gritted teeth. She looked at Rhian and blushed.

"Well, maybe it is not quite yet ancient history." She grinned at Rhian. "Unfortunately I had resigned from my job at about the same time to go freelance, so this household went from two reliable salaries to one slightly dodgy income. So now, Miss Jones, I have need of a tenant."

Frankie grimaced. "Sorry, what am I doing pouring out my woes to a stranger? Do you have any personal disasters that you might want to relate in retaliation?"

Rhian had a flashback. The doctors had warned her about them. She wasn't in Frankie's kitchen any more but on a building site. James lay still on the ground, head turned showing a terrible gash. His blood was black in the moonlight.

She snapped out of it. Frankie gazed at her waiting for an answer.

"No," Rhian replied quickly. She took another sip from her mug. "Would your employer not have taken you back, under the circumstances?"

"Probably, but I had already started up and I thought that I would like to give running my own business a fair try. I was not entirely happy with my late employer."

Rhian waited, but Frankie did not elaborate.

"What do you freelance in?" asked Rhian, to keep the conversation going.

"I'm a consultant," Frankie said.

Rhian entered the Black Swan at around seven that night. Three or four men leaned on the bar, and a mixed group of young people sat around a table. Gary was the only person serving. She watched him deal with the customers with polished skill, friendly with each one but moving on to the next with minimal waste of time. When he was free she walked up to the bar.

"What'll it be, love?" he said, automatically, without really looking at her.

"I've come about the job," she said.

He looked up.

"It's you, the Welsh girl who was in earlier. I wasn't sure you'd come back. You seemed a bit shook up." He looked at her, head cocked on one side. "I suppose I ought to interview you." He got out an official form and a pen. "What's your name?"

"Rhian Jones."

"Age?"

"Twenty-two."

"Address? Oh, you can fill all this in later." He put the form under the bar.

"Have you had any experience serving in pubs?"

"No, but I've worked in shops."

"Good enough, you're hired. Welcome aboard."

He shook her hand.

"We don't send temporary staff on training courses but use the mentor system. That means that you shadow another member of the staff until you get the hang of it. As I'm the only person in the place tonight, you shadow me. Take your coat off and come behind the bar."

She did as she was bid, smoothed down her blouse sleeves so they covered her arms. Gary had her watch him while he took orders and served customers.

"I only carry a limited stock, and each item has its own key on the till. Actually, it couldn't be simpler."

Rhian privately agreed. Some of the corner shops she had worked in had old-fashioned tills where you had to put in the prices yourself. She had a bit more trouble mastering the beer pumps than the till, but she persevered.

"What happens if someone wants something complicated, like a cocktail?" Rhian asked.

"A cocktail! Our customers?" said Gary, incredulously. "The people we get in here think a light and bitter is the height of sophistication. Allow me a word of advice, Rhian. If someone asks you for a Long Slow Screw Against a Wall, tell him that you're not that sort of girl. They won't be asking for a drink."

Rhian blushed, to Gary's obvious delight. She busied herself in the work. Pretty soon, he let her serve the customers while he got on with the paperwork.

One of the boys from the group around the table approached the bar. "A bitter, please."

She took a pint glass off the rack above the bar and held it under the tap. When she flipped the lever, the beer spat into the glass with a cough. She tried again with much the same result.

Gary appeared at her elbow. "The keg needs changing. I'll just pop down to the cellar."

He pulled up a wooden trapdoor in the floor that she hadn't noticed and disappeared down some steps, flipping on a light at the bottom.

"I'm a student," said the boy, engaging her in conversation.

"I guessed," said Rhian. "You're wearing a scarf."

"I could have gone to York, you know," said the boy, aggressively. "I had the grades, but I wanted to be among real working people, so I chose Whitechapel University here in the East End."

The boy's accent placed his origins from somewhere in London's rich outer suburbs in the western Home Counties—Surrey or maybe

Buckinghamshire. A series of loud clangs from the cellar indicated that Gary was coming to grips with the aluminium barrels.

"You're Welsh," said the boy.

"Yes," said Rhian. "What gave me away?"

"I expect that your father is a coal miner, sheep farmer, or something real. Mine's a merchant banker," said the boy, gloomily, as if admitting to some terrible family secret.

Offhand Rhian couldn't remember her father doing a day's work in his life, not that she had seen much of him lately, so she did not have a ready answer to that. Fortunately, Gary chose that moment to reappear.

"The new barrel's connected, but we have to draw off a few glasses to clear the pipes," Gary said.

He threw away the first two pints before trying the third. "Okay, carry on."

Rhian poured the pint and gave it to the boy in the scarf.

"One pound ninety," she said.

"Do you have a boyfriend?" asked the boy a little desperately, while handing over the exact money in silver.

"I do," said Rhian, putting a smile on her face. "He's a professional boxer at the local gym."

"Ah," said the boy, picking up his beer and going back to his friends.

A snort from the small office behind the bar indicated that Gary had overheard the conversation.

Bar work turned out to be surprisingly easy. She sold drinks and salted snacks, whose primary purpose was to make the customers thirsty. Not that East Londoners needed much encouragement to tip alcoholic drinks down their collective throat. She cleared away empty glasses and washed them up when there was no one waiting at the bar. The most difficult bit was talking to the customers. In a shop you processed people through as fast as possible, but apparently entertaining the patrons was part of a barmaid's work. Rhian normally found it difficult to talk to strangers, but it appeared that her main function was to listen. It was astonishing how many men had wives or girlfriends that did not understand them.

The evening passed quickly. Gary was soon ushering the last few diehards out at eleven fifteen. He cashed up while Rhian made them both a coffee. The pub boasted a coffee machine that made a variety of types, but the customers were not keen. She had not sold a cup all night.

"You obviously found a place to stay," Gary said.

"I've taken a room just a few hundred meters north of the station," Rhian said.

"Can I order you a taxi?" he said, as she put on her coat.

"I like to walk. It clears my head," she said, coming up with the first thing she thought of. Truth was, she could not possibly afford taxis.

"You live above the bar, then?" she asked, as he showed no sign of leaving.

"The bits that are still habitable," he said.

"Goodnight," Rhian said and turned.

"Rhian!" he called her back. "I don't want to frighten you, but there have been some killings lately. Keep to the well-lit areas."

"I will."

Morgana's brooch hung around her neck, mocking her reassurance to Gary that she would be careful. It was far too late for Rhian to be careful. She remembered finding the brooch in the mud on the building site. Something made her palm it. She should have handed it in to the archaeological dig coordinator. James had seen her and looked puzzled. Rhian was not the type to steal, or do anything daring.

You never saw the stars in London, not even on a cloudless night, what with both the murky air and light pollution. But Morgana's moon looked down on the city as it had for the last two thousand years.

The light was still on in the front room when she got home, so she knocked on the door.

"Come in, Rhian," Frankie said.

Frankie was sprawled out on the sofa watching TV with a generous glass of wine in her hand. She waved the drink vaguely at Rhian. "Help yourself, there are some glasses on the side, or have you already had enough lubricant from drinking the tips?"

"I don't think you get tips at the Black Swan, so a glass of wine would be great."

"Oh, you're working at the Dirty Duck."

Rhian poured herself some wine. She plonked herself down in the swivel chair and took her shoes off to massage her feet. A theatrical scream sounded from the TV.

"What are you watching?" Rhian asked.

"It's a late-night Hammer Horror called *Night of the Wolf*. Don't you just love those ridiculous old movies? Oh look, the witches are going to raise the devil. If only it were that easy—bloody difficult job—raising a demon—bloody dangerous as well."

Frankie raised her glass to her lips and imbibed a generous sample. The girl got the distinct impression that Frankie had already had more than a few sips of the "oh be joyful." The woman poured herself another glass and settled down in front of the idiot box.

Rhian bounded along, covering the hard-frozen ground fast. The prey's smell was overwhelming. She could scent panic and exhaustion. She rounded an ice block and had her first sight of her victim. It ran ungainly, as if its legs were too long and bent in the wrong places. It stumbled in a pool of snow and went down on one knee.

Rhian accelerated to a flat-out sprint. There was no need to conserve her wind now. This was end-game. She covered the ground fast, easily overtaking the animal. It changed direction, but all that did was enable her to cut across the corner. She timed her spring to catch its rear leg in her teeth, attempting to hamstring the beast. Unfortunately, the icy ground betrayed her and she lost traction on one rear paw. It was enough to spoil her aim, and she crashed into the flank of her victim.

Momentum rolled her over twice before her scrabbling feet got a purchase. She righted herself and took stock of the situation. The impact had knocked the prey onto its rear hindquarters. She surged forward again as her victim stood up. At the last minute the prey tried to escape by twisting away. She jumped onto its back, her heavy body pushing it to the ground. She could smell the fear oozing from its every pore. She bit deep into the back of its neck, teeth crunching through bone. She exulted at the tang of salt-flavored blood in her mouth.

She shook the beast from side-to-side ripping its body open, almost disappointed when it went limp. She dropped the corpse and stood triumphantly over it, laughing out loud. She raised her voice in a victory paean over the moonlit arctic landscape. Her howl echoed off the ice cliffs, an open challenge to anyone who might dispute ownership of her territory. At some point the wolf's howl became a very human scream.

Rhian came awake with a rush. She sat bolt upright, disorientated in the strange room. Light filtered in around the yellow curtains, lending a warm, friendly tint to everything. She sagged back on the pillow, willing her muscles to relax. She was covered in sweat, and the state of the bed suggested that she had been thrashing around in her sleep. Oh God, suppose she had really screamed, waking Frankie. She liked it here and it would be upsetting to have to move. She lay quietly listening. All she could hear was the water heater clicking on and off and the roar of the gas boiler. Maybe she hadn't yelled. Or maybe Frankie was a heavy sleeper?

She got up and crept quietly to the bathroom, closing the door carefully with a slight click. When she had finished washing, she removed the blade from her safety razor. Tongue resting on her lip in concentration, she ran the sharp edge transversely across her arm. It drew a red line across her skin. Blood welled from the wound.

James used to check her arms to make sure she had stopped self-harming. To please him, she had. But James was gone.

As usual, there was little immediate sensation, the stinging pain coming afterwards. She relished it, accepting it, welcoming the punishment. She was a bad person. She deserved to pay. Blood ran down her arm, dripping into the sink. She watched it spatter on the white porcelain. She washed the cut, wiping it dry with a length of toilet roll.

Rhian had finished breakfast when Frankie stumbled into the room in her dressing gown. Last night's wine had clearly taken its toll.

"Hello, honey," the woman said, peering at her shortsightedly through bleary eyes.

Rhian had just made herself a second mug of tea, but she handed it straight to Frankie, thinking that the woman's need was greater.

"Yuk," Frankie, said, taking a sip. "You forgot the sugar."

Rhian hastened to correct the omission.

"Have you anything planned today?" asked Frankie. "Because I thought you might like to help me. I have a commission to carry out an office job. I could do with a hand pushing the furniture around. I could knock something off the rent in payment."

Rhian's first reaction was to refuse, but she forced herself to be sociable. She was very unlikely to find a comfortable home elsewhere and she wanted to keep her landlady sweet. The rent reduction was also an attraction.

Frankie had been very vague about what she actually did, and Rhian had assumed that she was some sort of management consultant. Every second person in London seemed to work as a management consultant these days, the rest being mostly in public relations or banking.

"Yes, of course. You take commissions on Sunday?"

"Best day of the week for stinking out an office with burnt herbs," Frankie said, chewing on the piece of cold toast that was left over from Rhian's meal.

Rhian put another couple of pieces of bread onto the grill pan and triggered the gas lighter on the oven. She had heard of management consultants who ran canoeing holidays, acupuncture classes, scissor and paper games, paintball combat, yoga training, and psychometric testing. Burning herbs was a new one. Anything was possible; it was rumored that some management consultants even offered advice on management, but that was probably an urban myth.

"I am out of mint," said Frankie, waving the cold toast about for emphasis. "You should come with me to get some. You might find it interesting."

"I do need to go to the shops," said Rhian. "I could do with getting some more toothpaste."

"Shops?" Frankie laughed. "I need fresh mint, Rhian, not mint jelly for lunch. We're not going to the shops but to the cemetery. Is there any more tea?"

CHAPTER 4
WICCA WORK

"Tower Hamlets Cemetery," said Frankie, expansively, spreading her arms wide like a Lord of the Manor embracing his estate. "One of the Magnificent Seven."

All Rhian could see was a very high brick wall.

"Even the wall is a listed monument," said Frankie, meaning that it was on the list of buildings protected by preservation orders.

She waved her arm to encompass the wall, as if she was personally responsible for its all-round awesomeness and preservation.

"The Magnificent Seven?" asked Rhian.

"London's population exploded in the nineteenth century. The little village parish churchyards absorbed by the spreading city couldn't cope with the massive increase in demand. They ended up recycling the graves every couple of years."

"How do you recycle a grave?" asked Rhian, unsure whether to be intrigued or horrified.

"You dig down and smash the coffin underneath. You hammer it and any human remains flat, then you bury the new coffin on top. As well as disrespect to the dead, it was a golden recipe for spreading disease through drinking water contamination."

"That's disgusting," said Rhian.

"Yah, well, a special act of Parliament was passed to build seven giant municipal graveyards on what was the edge of London. One of them was Highgate, where all the famous people like Karl Marx are buried. Tower Hamlets was another. It was the wonder of East London; the Lord Mayor himself was on the Board of Directors. It all went wrong quite early on, of course. The East End has always been poor, and most of the burials were mass graves of up to thirty people a time, paid for using public funds. The middle classes soon shunned the cemetery because it was unfashionable. It fell into disrepair and disuse after only a few decades."

They walked through a gate into what looked like lightly wooded parkland.

"I thought it was a cemetery," said Rhian, confused.

The sun chose that moment to break through the intermittent cloud cover, warming Rhian's face and adding to the illusion that she was in the countryside. This was the traditional southern English weather, officially described as scattered cloud with sunny periods.

"There were still a few burials up to 1966 but the Anglican and free-church chapels were wrecked in the war. The Luftwaffe kept bombing the place. I don't think they ever found out what Adolf Hitler had against the graveyard."

"Hitler?" said Rhian vaguely. She was a little unsure where Adolf Hitler fitted in. She had a vague idea that he had been President of Europe or maybe the Milk Marketing Board.

"The Greater London Council bought the cemetery in the sixties and started to clear the ruins and gravestones to turn it into a park. Fortunately, they ran out of money, and the nascent Wicca community managed to bring pressure to bear. This place is magical, you see, and has been so for a long time. The location of the Magnificent Seven was not an accident, but a topographical pattern of geomancy."

"Geomancy?" asked Rhian, wondering if Geomancy was one of the new European Union States in the Balkans or Baltic or somewhere. Maybe Adolf Hitler was Prime Minister of Geomancy.

"Magic associated with spatial layouts," said Frankie, slipping into lecture mode. "All strong magic is geomantic to some degree, hence pentagrams and the like. Arabs used geomancy for divination by throwing soil thrown onto stone but in the European tradition it is associated with landscape magic."

"Like ley lines?" asked Rhian, vaguely remembering an old TV program about Stonehenge and glad to seize on an anchor point in what was an increasingly bizarre conversation.

"That's right," said Frankie. "Shakespeare made fun of geomancy in his plays, but that was the religious politics of the time. They sometimes burnt witches in those days. But everyone relied on them for medical treatment once King Henry put the monasteries out of business."

Frankie gazed around reflectively.

"The interment of a quarter of a million East Enders only added to the aura that soaks the cemetery. This place is best left to slumber in peace."

"Right," said Rhian, "but who's Adolf Hitler?"

"I see that you've enjoyed all the benefits of a modern British comprehensive state education," said Frankie, dryly. "He was dictator of Germany in World War Two."

"Oh, right," said Rhian, "World War Two. We had to write an essay at school on how it felt to be bombed. Our history teacher said that the bombing of Germany by the American and British air forces was a great crime."

"He did, did he?" said Frankie. "How politically correct of him. What did he have to say about the German bombing of London?"

"I don't think that he mentioned that," said Rhian.

"No," said Frankie. "I don't suppose he did."

Their walk brought them to the edge of the park area and into the wilderness. They followed a path delineated by salvaged gravestones, which wound into thicker clumps of sycamore trees. The way was soon hemmed in by bushes lining the path like green walls. The sun was splintered into moving shafts of light by tree branches swaying in the breeze, and the scent of flowers filled the air. The soft buzz of insects flying from bloom to bloom was soporific. Occasionally a bird sang, and, if she looked carefully, Rhian could see grey squirrels in the branches. She stopped to trace a name with a forefinger on one of the stones that was in better condition than its fellows: Isaiah Fowler, 1852.

"See the dove, ascending," said Frankie, kneeling beside her. "That symbolizes the deceased's spirit reaching for heaven. Victorian gravestones are filled with hidden meaning, if you know how to decode them."

"The next one has a dove swooping down," said Rhian, teasingly. "Does that mean that the dead person was doomed to go to hell?"

"No, silly, that's the Holy Spirit coming down from heaven to greet his soul. Come with me."

Frankie searched and found an old stone, set a little way back from the path under a sycamore. She brushed away some dirt.

"I haven't looked at this stone for ages. See the name here?" asked Frankie.

Rhian traced her finger across the letters. "E T H E L,-Ethel, but I can't see a surname."

"I don't think they put one on the stone. What do you think this is?" Frankie pointed to a symbol above the name.

"It's a tree," said Rhian.

"A yew tree, to be precise. The Church claims that yew was the symbol of everlasting life, partly because yew trees regenerate and so seem to live forever, and partly because they are evergreen. That is why you always find them in churchyards. Yews certainly do live a long time; one in Scotland is thought to be two thousand years old. The yews were often there first before the Christian churches were built. Christians often built on pagan religious centers, and yews were sacred to druids."

Rhian noticed that they were back to pagans and witchcraft again. Frankie seemed obsessed by the subject.

"Ethel was religious," said Rhian.

"In a way," said Frankie, smiling. "Do you notice anything else odd about the grave?"

Rhian considered. It was just another old grave in a tangled wilderness. An anomaly caught her eye. "All the graves are lined up the same way except this one."

"Give the girl a house point." Frankie mock-clapped her. "All the other graves are aligned east-west while Ethel's is north-south. Christian graves point west because the ancient Egyptians believed that the spirit world was in the west beyond the setting sun. The grave alignment helped the dead person's spirit on their way."

"I never noticed that before," said Rhian. "Why on earth should Christianity care about Ancient Egyptian beliefs?"

"Christianity has stolen bits from everyone. Don't get me started on what they stole off the pagans—Christmas, for a start!"

Rhian started to speak, but Frankie talked over her.

"The grave is aligned north-south so that Ethel's soul is trapped inside, preventing it from getting out and harming the living. Don't you get it, Rhian? The yew is also a symbol of Hecate, the Queen of Magic. Ethel was almost certainly a witch, something that was still illegal in the nineteenth century. The vicar who buried her must have feared her spirit haunting him so he buried her north-south on consecrated ground."

Rhian ran her hand across an old, weathered gouge in the stone.

"Shrapnel damage," said Frankie. "I told you that the Germans kept bombing the cemetery. Perhaps Hitler feared witches as well." Frankie laughed.

She pushed her glasses back on her nose, in what Rhian was coming to recognise as a characteristic gesture, and strode off, long skirt swishing around her legs. Rhian had to half run to keep up. The sycamores crowded ever closer on the path, shading it from the sun and dampening out the sounds of London.

Frankie finally stopped in a low-lying glade in the trees, a bowl filled with rich, wet soil. It was full of patches of mint plants, eight inches high with crinkly green leaves arranged in opposite pairs. Some of the plants had vertical spikes consisting of clusters of small purple flowers.

"I keep trying to grow mint but without success," said Frankie. "It must be too dry or something in my garden."

She picked a handful of stalks and placed them in her bag. Frankie carried a large earth-mother linen bag depicting flowers and fairies in pastel colors. It was just too chintzy to be true.

In the meantime, Rhian found another grave almost buried in the undergrowth. She cleared the vegetation to expose a horizontal gravestone decorated by a sculpture of a horse positioned on its stomach. Its head was bowed, like a much-loved animal waiting for a master that would never return. A century and a half of subsidence had caused the grave to tilt over. Rhian preferred not to speculate on what was responsible for the subsidence. The stone was decorated by a carved outline of a climbing plant covered in what could have been bunches of grapes.

"It's another evergreen sign, this time symbolizing that the deceased will be remembered," said Frankie, joining Rhian.

"There's no name that I can see," said Rhian. "I suppose that the people who vowed to remember are also dead and forgotten."

A large drop of water fell on the stone in front of Rhian. More began to filter through the trees, pattering gently on the leaves.

"How irritating," said Frankie, grimacing. "I packed some sandwiches and pies so that we could have a picnic."

"That's what you get for performing rain magic," Rhian said.

"What rain magic?" Frankie asked, looking confused and a little worried.

"Planning a picnic, of course. It always works as a rain spell. My pub, that is, the pub where I work, is just around the corner," said Rhian. "They don't sell food, so I'm sure that Gary wouldn't mind us eating our lunch there, provided we buy some drinks."

"I'd love to see the Dirty Duck, honey," said Frankie, with a broad smile.

"I believe Gary prefers to call it the Black Swan," Rhian said.

"Really, he can't be from round these parts, then," Frankie said, dropping into a *faux* Wild West accent.

Their labyrinthine route out terminated at a small gate in the cemetery wall on the side close by the Black Swan. Rhian had begun to have doubts about the wisdom of getting her home life mixed up with work. Still, it's only a lunch, she thought, what can go wrong?

She sat Frankie down at a table near the window. Gary materialized beside her.

"Frankie, this is Gary, my boss; Gary, this is Frankie, my landlady," said Rhian, introducing them.

"Can I get you drinks?" said Gary, eying Frankie speculatively.

"A glass of red wine, please," said Frankie, giving Gary a wide smile.

Rhian settled for a Coke.

Gary walked back to the bar to get their drinks, swinging his legs over without bothering to open the hatch. Rhian narrowed her eyes. Gary had not normally been given to athletic gestures. She noticed that Frankie watched him all the way.

"Here you go, ladies," said Gary, returning with the drinks.

Frankie handed some money over.

"You don't mind if we eat our lunch here, do you, Gary?" Rhian asked.

"Of course not, Rhian. I don't suppose that Old Fred or Willie the Dog mind either," said Gary, gesturing to the only other customers.

Two old boys sat in the corner, sharing a packet of ten Woodbines while picking winners from the greyhound racing column at the back of a paper.

"Mind if I join you?" said Gary, when he brought back the change. He sat down without waiting for an answer.

"Please do," said Frankie.

Rhian noticed to her horror that Frankie was flashing her eyes from side to side and patting her hair.

After lunch, the women tracked down the location of Frankie's commission using Rhian's *A to Z*. The office suite was in a low, rectangular, concrete-and-glass block built in the sixties. It reminded Rhian of her comprehensive school in Wales. The shower of rain had left dark grey streaks on the concrete, making the building look even more depressing than it would normally. Rust marks around cracks in the walls suggested that concrete rot would soon bring the block's miserable existence to a close.

"They put people in corporate prisons and then wonder why the sickness rate is so high," said Frankie, more to herself than Rhian.

Frankie rang a bell at the entrance, but nothing happened. After a while, she leaned on the button impatiently.

"All right, keep your hair on. I've only got one pair of hands."

A blue-black peaked cap unlocked the glass door. Under the peak, a large grey moustache, stained yellow by cigarette smoke, jutted aggressively on the face of a gaunt, elderly man. He looked at them suspiciously through ancient National Health spectacles with round wire-framed lenses.

"We're here to carry out some maintenance work on one of the office suites," said Frankie. "It's all arranged, look."

She thrust a letter on headed notepaper at the caretaker, who peered at it myopically.

"No one told me," he said. "You don't look like plumbers."

He gazed at the two women, suspiciously.

"Why don't we look like plumbers? Women can do plumbing. Women can do anything men can do," Frankie said, pugnaciously sticking out her chin.

"If you're plumbers, then where's your tools?" Peaked Cap said suspiciously, with the air of a man who had discovered the killer argument against Special Relativity.

Frankie opened her mouth, a dangerous glint in her eye.

"We don't have tools because we are not plumbers," Rhian said quickly, in an attempt to forestall further political debate.

"So why did you say you were plumbers?" he asked.

"I didn't, you did," said Frankie, her voice rising to a near shriek. "We are more in the office furnishings line. The letter instructs you to give us access to Unit Five, Ravion PLC."

"Oh, curtains and things," said Peaked Cap. "I suppose that is proper work for women."

Frankie looked as if she was about to explode.

"You'd better come in," he said, grudgingly. "It's normally plumbers in this building. Sometimes, the leaks are so bad that the water runs down the stairs."

The thought seemed to cheer him up.

The women followed him past the empty receptionist's area. A bottle of scarlet nail varnish strategically placed in the middle of the empty desk conjured up an image to Rhian of a streaky-blonde with breasts that were too large and a workload too small, who was secretly lusted after by all the middle management.

"The lifts are switched off, so you'll have to walk," said Peaked Cap with grim satisfaction.

Ravion's offices were on the top floor, but the climb was hardly onerous. There were only a couple of flights. Nevertheless, Peaked Cap made a three-course banquet of it. The company occupied the whole top floor behind a glass door. The caretaker finally unlocked it after trying several wrong keys first.

"Thank you," said Frankie, firmly. "We can manage now."

"I ought to stay and watch," said the caretaker. "I'm in charge of security."

"You have our letter of authorization," Frankie said, firmly. "We must be left on our own while working—health and safety, you know."

The caretaker allowed himself to be propelled out of the door. Frankie shut it decisively behind him. Health and safety, Rhian reflected, was the new religious mantra that allowed one to justify almost anything.

"I think that we will start by just walking around and sensing the vibes," said Frankie.

The top floor was entirely glass-walled, so Rhian could see from one end to the other. Desks with computers and headsets were laid out in rows. Frankie walked through a reception area into an open-plan office occupying most of the floor. She paraded backwards and forwards, waving her arms theatrically and touching her forehead with the tips of her fingers. Rhian managed not to laugh.

"What do they do here?" asked Rhian.

"It's a call center. I believe they give telephone advice on broadband installation or some such," said Frankie, vaguely. "I'm surprised they haven't bangalored it."

Management and interview offices lined one of the walls, like glass cells for giant honeybees. A substantial double office at the end indicated the location of the chief executive and his secretary. Rhian touched one of the computer screens. Her finger sparked before contact with the plastic. She kicked the floor, reflexively.

"I've worked in stores with cheap, hard-wearing nylon carpets like this. Sometimes the static builds up so badly that your skirt sticks to your legs," Rhian said.

The room was lit with fluorescent lights that flickered annoyingly at a rate just detectable to the human eye. One emitted an intermittent background buzz. Some of the office workers had attempted to personalize their working areas with photos or office toys but that merely emphasized the sheer inhumanity of the environment. The management had scattered potted plants around to improve the ambience, but they were doing badly. The one nearest Rhian showed every sign of being dead. The plastic in the new computers leaked organic vapours.

Rhian had only been in the office for ten minutes or so, but already her head ached. She rubbed her eyes and tried to open a window, but they were double glazed and sealed. The only fresh air came via an air conditioning system that smelled stale and metallic.

"Not feeling too well, honey? You seem very sensitive to auras," Frankie looked at her.

"What exactly have you been hired to do here?" asked Rhian, deflecting the woman.

"The chief executive apparently read an article about *feng shui* in an airline magazine, so he thought he would give it a try to cure his sick building syndrome. Eastern mysticism is currently fashionable amongst the managerial classes."

"I see. and you are an expert on *feng shui,* are you?" asked Rhian.

"I am—not," Frankie replied, with a bright grin. "I know next to nothing about it. Hardly anyone in the West does, although there are plenty of people wafting around claiming otherwise."

"Then what are we doing here?" Rhian asked, trying to keep the disapproval from her voice.

"Don't look so priggish, madam," said Frankie, laughing and wagging a finger at Rhian. "We are going to cure their sick building. You didn't think that I'd take their money and cheat them, did you?"

Rhian colored up because that was precisely what she suspected. "Of course not," she said.

"*Feng shui* has to be applied at the architectural stage of a building. The choice of location is critical, as is the exact shape of the building. Just rearranging the furniture wouldn't achieve much."

"So what are you going to do?" asked Rhian, intrigued.

"*Feng shui* translates to wind and water, and by a strange coincidence, we are going to apply the principles of wind and water. Now where did I put the herbs?"

Frankie reached into her linen bag and rummaged around, eventually hauling out a wooden container. She handed the box to Rhian, who opened it to find dried herbs mixed in with newly chopped-up leaves that smelt of mint. Frankie took out a tiny electric oven, and, after some thought, placed it on a desk by the air-conditioning outlet.

"This is where air is piped in from the sky," Frankie said, licking her finger and holding it up to detect air movements.

The little oven had an open bowl of the sort used by jewelers. Frankie plugged it in and let it stand until red hot. She took the wooden box off Rhian and sprinkled the plant material into the bowl. The chopped leaves curled up, turned brown and smoldered. White smoke drifted up towards the ceiling. It scattered as it hit the turbulent flow from the air-conditioning outlet.

Rhian used her hand to waft some of the vapor towards her and cautiously sniffed at it.

"It smells quite pleasant," Rhian said. "I suppose it works like an air freshener, but surely it won't last long."

Frankie gave Rhian what her grandmother would have called 'an old fashioned expression.' The woman took her glasses off and fiddled with them, wiping the lenses with a piece of felt. Rhian had once had a boss who had the same habit. He used it to pause the conversation while he considered how to phrase a statement he found difficult. Rhian waited patiently.

"It's a little more than an air freshener. You see, I'm a pagan," said Frankie, diffidently.

Rhian wondered what in the world the woman meant. Arsenal football team were "The Gunners," Southampton "The Seagulls," England "The Lions," but who were "The Pagans"? She had a vague idea that there was a motorcycle gang of that name, but the thought of the intellectual Frankie in a black leather jacket, perched on the back of a bike, with her arms wrapped around a hairy-arsed gang-lord stretched credulity.

Frankie rushed on, almost garbling her words in an effort to get them out.

"A pagan, Rhian. You know, a Wicca."

A stray memory popped into Rhian's head of comedienne Jo Brand on a quiz show being asked to define Wicca. "*Wicca—isn't that Old English for a mental basket case?*"

Rhian's face had a tendency to reflect her thoughts, something that had got her into trouble before. She did her best to blank her expression, but, as usual, she was not entirely successful.

"You're thinking of Jo Brand, aren't you," said Frankie, accusingly. "There's a woman who needs a good slapping. Still, what can one expect from a woman who chose to be educated at a jumped-up poly like Brunel University of Technology? It doesn't even have a History School."

Rhian deduced from this that Frankie had read history at one of England's more traditional establishments. As Rhian had never got beyond the sixth form of a Welsh comprehensive school, she tended to view graduate academic squabbles with a degree of detachment. She pointedly failed to ask Frankie the name of her old college.

Frankie mumbled something.

"What?" Rhian asked.

"I'm a witch," Frankie said. "I perform magic spells for people. I'm a consultant in white magic. I don't touch anything nasty. My previous tenants all left as soon as they found out. I thought that if you could see what I actually did, then you wouldn't be scared of me. I haven't spooked you, have I?"

Rhian stared at Frankie. This nice, silly, bespectacled, middle-class, new-age earth mother actually thought that Rhian might be frightened of her. Frightened because she made a living burning herbs and chanting spells for deluded businessmen! Rhian, frightened of a Wicca?

Her lip twitched. She tried to keep a straight face but she just couldn't. Her shoulders shook and an explosive guffaw burst from her lips.

"What?" asked Frankie, affronted. "I don't see what's so funny. One of my ex-tenants organized a candle-lit vigil of Evangelical Christians outside my door."

Rhian laughed all the harder until tears ran down her cheeks.

"There's nothing funny about a dozen loonies screaming 'burn the witch' and 'you'll rot in Hell' all night outside your flat window. You try it some time. The neighbors didn't speak to me for weeks."

Rhian clung to a desk for support.

Frankie lost the outraged expression and laughed along with the girl. "Enough," Frankie said. "So I may assume that you do not intend to flee in maidenly terror any time soon?"

Rhian shook her head. It was a few moments before she could trust herself to speak. "Sorry, Frankie, it's just that I had trouble seeing you as an emissary of Beelzebub. The, um, plant mix smells rather nice."

"I have a mix of air herbs in here—witch's broom, holy vanilla, sweetgrass, lavender, and, of course, mint. I need to activate the spell now, if you can contain yourself? " Frankie asked.

"Carry on," said Rhian. "I'll be good; I promise."

"Well, please keep quiet and don't do anything to break my concentration."

The woman closed her eyes, and, stretching up her arms into the air like a Mexican priest hailing the Sun, she began to sing.

"Great Jupiter, cleanse the air,

"Holy Indrus, give power of thought,

"Swift Mercury, send agility of intellect,

"Sylphs of the air, grant concentration."

Frankie repeated the song over and over, adding more of the herbal mix to the heater whenever the vapor flow diminished.

Scent drifted through the office. Rhian felt light-headed, and her fingers and toes tingled. She felt tired, so she sat on one of the swivel office chairs, rocking it gently. Frankie droned on, her voice retreating into the distance. Rhian closed her eyes and her head drooped. She drifted away and began to daydream.

Frankie's voice was a distant murmur and was overlaid by the sound of leaves rustling in a breeze. The wind increased in force, gusts buffeting Rhian's ears and whipping her clothes against her legs. She opened her eyes. She stood one leg each side of a great ridge that was surrounded by ice-capped mountain peaks. Splintered rock fell away precipitously each side of her for hundreds of meters, gradually disappearing into clouds.

Rhian could see as well as hear the wind. It caressed her with sub-zero icy tendrils, but she felt no pain. Faces in the gusts called to her, and she felt a compulsion to step off the ridge into empty air, to lose herself, to walk in the wind. She took a tentative step, adjusting her balance.

"Rhian." Frankie's voice sounded from a long way away. "RHIAN!"

Hands shook her shoulders and she opened her eyes.

"Snap out of it, Rhian. Air magic is very powerful in high buildings. Don't go to sleep on me, honey," Frankie said, smiling at her, "You had me worried for a moment there."

The little oven was unplugged and looked quite cold. Rhian glanced at her watch and was astonished to see that she had lost half an hour. She rubbed her eyes.

"I must have dozed off. I haven't been sleeping well lately," Rhian said, by way of explanation.

"I know, honey. I heard you," said Frankie, in a noncommittal tone of voice.

This was not a conversation that Rhian wished to pursue, so she changed the subject.

"Are we finished?"

"The air spell is finished but I still have to work water magic. Are you okay to continue?" asked Frankie.

"Sure, you go ahead," Rhian replied.

Frankie moved her apparatus to the other side of the open-plan office, near to the washrooms.

"This is where the water is piped in from the ground," Frankie said. She smiled at Rhian. "I will use water plants, coltsfoot, bulrushes, water lily, and mint for this spell," Frankie said, getting another box out of her bag.

"Mint, again?" asked Rhian.

"Mint is a connecting plant that links water to the sky," said Frankie. "It magnifies the effect of the two spells synergistically. That is why it was so important for us to get some this morning."

She placed the oven on a metal tray on the carpet and knelt in front of it. Dropping the new herbal mix into the red-hot bowl, she sang again. This time, the vapor was heavier than air, flowing across the floor like mist.

"Great Poseidon, cleanse the waters,

"Coventina, give placid flow,

"Nammu, send depth of thought,

"Undines of the water, grant concentration."

This time Rhian kept a firm grip on reality when she felt the tingling in her fingers and toes. She forced off fatigue and kept her eyes wide open, but, even so, she seemed to see two realities simultaneously. Around her was a normal office, empty except for Frankie and herself. Overlaying it, a wild grey-green sea phased in and out. Huge white-topped waves swept over her head and then dropped away beneath her. Frothy faces formed in the in the surf. Watery fingers beckoned to her, but she resolutely ignored them, concentrating on reality. She dug her fingernails into her hands until they hurt. Pain was good. Pain was a friend. Pain was absolution.

Rhian checked her watch every few moments, and the illusion of time speeding by happened again. She was beginning to suspect that Frankie added some pretty powerful dank to her herbal mix.

Frankie's voice faded into silence, and the seascape dimmed until it disappeared. Frankie hung her head as if she were exhausted. It was some time before she spoke.

"Will you rearrange the furniture, Rhian, while I rest for a bit? We must give the punters their money's worth by showing them what they expect to see."

Her voice was thick, like she had the first symptoms of a head cold.

"Sure, Frankie."

Rhian pushed and pulled various objects around into artistic curves and patterns while Frankie watched.

"You're a lot stronger than you look, aren't you?" said Frankie. "You know, that went really rather well. I thought that this might be a difficult one, but it all worked first time. Do you notice any change in the office?"

Rhian considered. "Yes, it feels airy and light, and my headache's gone."

"There is nothing better than air and water magic for sick building syndrome," said Frankie complacently.

It was Rhian's night off, as Gary had another barmaid on the shift. Frankie prepared a potato salad, then she and Rhian shared a bottle of Californian rosé in the garden, watching the play of light as the day changed imperceptibly into twilight.

"Thank you for being so welcoming, but you don't have to look after me," Rhian said. "I am used to living on my own."

"To be honest, it's rather nice to have someone around," Frankie said. "What with my work and Pete, my partner, I never really made civilian friends."

"Civilians?" Rhian asked. "Were you in the army?"

"Good Lord, no," Frankie said. "I worked for a close-knit organization, and civilians are what we called outsiders, silly really. How about you? What brought you to our fair neighborhood?"

"I just needed a fresh start." Rhian shrugged.

"Boy trouble," said Frankie, raising an eyebrow.

"There was someone, but it didn't work out, so I left." Her tone was designed to discourage further questions.

It was a moment Rhian relived over and over in her dreams. The heavy iron bar smashed James' head, with the sound like you get from crushing a beer can. His skull pulped. Blood and dark brain matter spurted from the wound. The bar swung back for a second hit, trailing a fan of red droplets that glittered in the streetlights.

Frankie took the hint. She got up and, wandering to the curtains, peered around them. "The Moon's up. Would you like to see my moon garden?"

"Moon garden?" Rhian asked.

Frankie was just full of strange surprises, as mad as a March hatter. Hang on, that wasn't right. Frankie started talking again, interrupting Rhian's thought process.

"Night flowers, Rhian. I have a witch's herb garden, and one corner is devoted to night flowers. Come on. Switch the lights off because you just have to see it in the moonlight."

Rhian was intrigued, it sounded wonderfully exotic. Outside, Frankie steered Rhian to the right area, knelt down, and pointed to some round white flowers that were about three inches across.

"This patch is the Arctic globe thistle, *Echinops.*"

Rhian knelt beside her. "They're beautiful, Frankie." She touched the petals and then smelled her fingers.

"Mind the leaves, honey, they are very prickly."

"The flowers seem to glow in the moonlight, like when you wear a white top in a club with ultraviolet lights."

"You see that, do you, Rhian? That's very interesting."

Rhian looked up sharply. How could she not see something so obvious? Something about the tone of Frankie's voice bothered her, but the woman's face was in dark shadow, making her expression unreadable.

Frankie moved to a trellis where a climbing plant grew. She teased out a bud so that she could display it in the silver moonlight.

"This is the moonflower, what botanists call *Ipomoea.* One afternoon, these buds will open and the large white flowers will bloom all night under the Moon. A heavy scent will flow out of them, a scent that only a few can smell, filling my garden and attracting moths. With the moths will come bats, Hecate's bats, and in the morning the flowers will die."

"That's a sad fate," said Rhian. "To grow all year and have just one night to bloom."

"We all have only a short time to bloom; it's only the scale that differs. Not even the gods are immortal."

"I still think it's sad," said Rhian.

"I'll harvest the flowers with the Sun, saying the right ritual so that the dried petals, when burnt, will make incense suitable for divination."

"Divination?" asked Rhian, doubtfully.

"Fortune telling, honey, I will inhale the vapor before sleeping, and in my dreams I will see the future. At least that's the theory. Sometimes all I get is heartburn," Frankie said. "You know, the spells today were almost too powerful, as if something else was pushing my magic along."

"Such as what?" asked Rhian.

"It could be any one of a number of things," Frankie replied. "For example, an artifact or haunting in the office that acted as a magical amplifier, but I think that unlikely, don't you?"

"I don't know," Rhian replied, politely. Frankie was very weird. Harmlessly weird in an eccentric English sort of way, to be sure, but definitely not quite in phase with reality.

Frankie continued as if she had not spoken. "Or it could be another witch pushing my spell along, someone who could see the moon-glow of Arctic thistles, perhaps?" Frankie looked at Rhian and raised an eyebrow.

"You think that I'm a witch?" Rhian laughed. She knew that was impolite, but she couldn't help it.

"Not consciously, honey, but you may have untrained powers. Do strange things happen to you?" Frankie asked.

"Like what?" Rhian replied, answering a question with a question, as this was tricky ground.

"Oh, it could be something quite trivial. Do you ever know who's on a ringing phone before you pick it up? Can you predict the results of random events more often than not? Does your toast always land butter side up?"

Rhian shook her head, laughing. "No, nothing like that ever happens to me. I am just an ordinary girl from the valleys."

"Do you mind if I tried a little experiment?" asked Frankie, clearly unconvinced.

"An experiment, that sounds fun," replied Rhian, tolerantly.

Frankie cupped her hands together, as if she was holding something in them. She sang softly, too quiet for Rhian to hear the words. Then she blew on her hands and opened them.

A beautiful white sphere of light hung there, making Rhian gasp. This was magic—real magic. Maybe Frankie was a witch. Six months ago Rhian did not believe in magic, but that was before the wolf.

"You can see it, can't you, Rhian?"

Rhian nodded, not trusting herself to speak.

"Put your hand into it so I can see the color of your aura. Let's find out what sort of witch you are."

Rhian tentatively reached out her finger to the ball of light and poked it. For a brief instant the ball resisted her touch, deforming and moving away. Then it exploded soundlessly into shards of white light. They writhed like streamers before fading away in hissing sparkles of silver.

"What!" said Rhian, startled. "Is it supposed to do that?"

"No," Frankie replied. "It's just a simple marker spell. If you have no talent, then it stays white. If you've talent it changes color, the shade and intensity indicating your power and skills. It's not supposed to run away. One might almost think that it was frightened of you."

CHAPTER 5
THE WOLF

Rhian scrabbled inside the darkest reaches of her wardrobe to obtain her coat. She looked it over critically. It was definitely showing signs of wear but would have to do until she had built up some savings. She slipped it on and headed for the front door.

"Bye, Frankie," she yelled at the closed lounge door.

It opened abruptly and Frankie shot out.

"Wait a moment, I have something for you," Frankie said.

She produced a twisted posy of half-dead plant material that she attached securely to Rhian's lapel with an old-fashioned hat pin.

Rhian inclined her head to study the posy.

"It's, um, very nice," she said weakly, wondering at the woman's taste in decorations.

"It's not supposed to be nice. That is a good luck charm," said Frankie.

"Like the gypsies sell?" Rhian asked.

"Sort of," Frankie replied. "I want you to promise me that you will wear it, please."

"Sure," Rhian replied, humoring her. "But I really must go now or I'll be late for work."

She gave Frankie a half smile and disappeared through the door.

She hurried, taking the short cut through the path at the end of the road. She dodged the traffic on the Mile End Road rather than going round by the subway. She arrived at the Black Swan a few minutes before opening time. She was forced to bang on the door for some time before Gary appeared and let her in.

"Sorry, I was in the cellar," he said apologetically. "The lager pump's playing up again. The brewery won't spend a penny on this place and everything is falling apart."

"Any news on when they intend to renovate?" Rhian asked.

"No," Gary replied, gloomily. "They promised me the manager's position in a swish new wine bar if I kept the old pub ticking over for just a few weeks until the builders moved in."

"How long ago was that?" asked Rhian.

"Several months," said Gary.

Rhian opened up and switched everything on. A man in a grey mackintosh came in, bought a lager, and pushed pound coins into the fruit machine in the corner. The cheep-cheep noises and flashing lights were seriously irritating. Normally, they just became part of the background, something that blended in with the general buzz. Tonight they worked under Rhian's skin, perhaps because the bar was empty. The lights built up to a crescendo and the machine gave a triumphant whoop, spilling coins out with a *chukka, chukka, chukka*. Thankfully, after the customer came over to spend his winnings, he retreated to a seat to sup his beer. The machine shut up, restricting itself to an occasional coy flutter of lights.

As the evening wore on, a handful of customers wandered in, mostly students slumming. It was getting near the end of term, and their government loans would be running low, especially for those who had squandered money on nonessentials like textbooks. The Black Swan might not be luxurious, but it did sell the cheapest pint on the Mile End Road.

The students formed a circle around one of the tables and became more boisterous as their glasses emptied, refilled, and emptied again. They spoke ever louder until Rhian could hear every word.

"I can pull that new barmaid."

"What new barmaid?"

"The cute little dark-haired Welsh totty."

"Is she new?"

"Yes, and I bet that I can pull her."

"The last thing you pulled was a calf muscle playing five-a-side."

"Very funny, laugh all you like."

"I shall."

"My technique is to amuse them. Make the girlies giggle and you can laugh them right into bed."

"A tenner says she'll blow you out."

"You're on!"

One of the students stood up and pushed back his hair, and headed for the bar.

"Pint of ordinary, love," he said.

"Coming up," Rhian said.

She took down a glass and put it under the tap that sold ordinary bitter, the cheapest drink in the pub.

"Do you know what they call a sheep tied to a lamp post in Cardiff?" asked the student.

"A leisure center," said Rhian, without lifting her head from her work.

"Oh, you've heard it," said the student, disappointed.

"From the first day I came to London," Rhian said wearily.

Rhian passed over his pint and received a five-pound note in return.

She opened the till and gave the student his change. He took it but then hovered, staring at her.

"Would you like to come out with me?" asked the student.

"A tempting offer, but I'd better refuse," replied Rhian. "My doctor says that I shouldn't go out with boys until he finds out what's causing the rash."

"Right," said the student, backing off.

"She's a lesbian," Rhian heard him tell his friend back at his table.

The friend put his hand out. "You were blown out, pay up."

"Forget it. All bets are off. You can't expect me to pull a lesbian."

"Rhian," said Gary, appearing out of his office at the back. "Would you collect up some of the empty glasses and wash them, please? I'll watch the bar."

The evening passed quickly enough; it always did when the pub was full. It was hard on the feet but Rhian preferred to be kept busy. She hated the long slow evenings when nothing happened and she had to invent work to relieve the tedium. Evenings with nothing to listen to but the cheep-cheep of the fruit machine sneering at her.

Tonight, it was eleven before she knew it. Gary ushered the last punter through the door and threw a bolt with a firm motion.

"Check the Ladies for me, Rhian, then you might as well get off. We'll finish clearing up tomorrow."

Rhian left the pub by a side door, barely noticing that Frankie's weird posy was still on her lapel.

Pools of light from irregularly spaced street lights formed isolated spots of civilization like imperial border forts strung along a barbarian frontier. Rhian pulled her coat a little tighter and walked briskly, heels clicking on the concrete paving stones.

An old hatchback pulled out of a side street and accelerated aggressively. Its small, high-revving engine screamed in bursts as the driver worked it through the gears. The youth in the front passenger seat lit a cigarette, illuminating the vehicle's interior in a brief yellow flash that froze a moment of time. The driver stared intently ahead, focussing on extracting the last possible horsepower out of the modest motor. Two girls in crop tops displaying too much skin sat in the rear, large hoop earrings swaying as they bent forward over a mobile phone. They giggled at something on the screen in the way of girls the world over.

Rhian watched, feeling envious. The car was a cozy private bubble, separate from the dark cool street. She wondered whether the couples were on their way home from a night out or maybe they were going on to a club. The car disappeared leaving her an outsider, alone in the night.

She walked on.

Something trotted out from under the bars of a gate in the wall that enclosed Tower Hamlets cemetery. At first she thought it was a small dog, but it had a long snout, pointed ears, and a full tail.

The urban fox paused and looked at her, its eyes shining green in the street lighting. That's how the hill farmers hunted foxes at night in her native Wales. They shone a spotlight across the fields and shot at green eyes hiding amongst the silver-eyed sheep and lambs.

The fox was so close that she could smell the rancid odor of its dank fur. The animal snarled, showing its teeth. Foxes had lost their fear of people since the government had introduced hunting bans. They stood their ground when confronted by a human where once they would have fled. They had even started to attack children, and Rhian, petite and slim, was little larger than a teenage girl.

She lifted her lips and growled, the deep rumble belying her small frame. The fox put its ears and tail down and slunk back into the cemetery. It vanished noiselessly into the dark.

Rhian turned into a narrow alley that curved between two buildings. Her foot slipped on something squishy on the paving, but she didn't care to speculate about the nature of the squishiness.

She rounded a last corner onto the main road, and the London night assaulted her senses in all its glory. It was like a stage musical revealed by the lifting of the theater curtain. Brightly colored light spilled from all directions. Noise surrounded her, the hum of car engines and the murmur of voices sliding over each other in layers. Burning hydrocarbons stung acidly on her throat. People spilled out of a nearby tube station from one of the last trains to run that night. Two men argued listlessly as if neither really cared about the issue. Tires squealed and horns sounded as car drivers bickered over precedence.

She could not face running the gauntlet of the drunks racing each other down the dual carriageway of the Mile End Road, so she walked on a short distance to where a ramp dropped down to a subway. The local graffiti painters had been busy spraying tags on the white-tiled walls. Council workmen occasionally made a half-hearted attempt to clean the mess off, but they were only preparing an empty canvas for the next street artist. Unfortunately, they weren't all Banksys.

The ramp was lit with white lights in strong plastic boxes placed high up on the walls. Enthusiastic stone throwers had cracked much of the Perspex. When she turned the right-angled bend down under the road, Rhian was dismayed to see that long stretches of the subway were in darkness. The few lights working seemed to be running on low voltage and, if anything, they added to the gloom.

She dithered about whether to go back up to the street and take the long walk out of her way to an above-ground pedestrian crossing. Muggers might lurk in the dark, and she was frightened of what might happen if she was attacked. Her feet ached, so she went ahead anyway.

Rhian strode quickly with the determined air of someone going to the dentist. The sound of her heels on the concrete preceded her up the tunnel, echoing off the tiled walls and ceiling. She was halfway along when she saw movement at the far end.

The street lighting behind the subway exit silhouetted two figures. Rhian paused, concealed in the dark, able to back out before the newcomers even realised she was there. The silhouettes moved slightly apart so that Rhian could see them more clearly. They were holding hands, and one had the unmistakable curves of a woman.

She relaxed and continued towards the couple. The closer she got, the more relaxed and happy she felt. A part of her mind was curious about that. Rhian was not normally a particularly relaxed and happy person.

The subway lights illuminated the tunnel in a friendly, pale light that swirled around her. She could not imagine why she had thought the tunnel dark and uninviting. She felt light-headed and warm, the night chill entirely dispelled.

Each breath slid in and out of her mouth like a strawberry-flavoured hallucinogenic drug. The air fizzed the way a carbonated drink sparkles on the tongue. Tension drained from her body and she felt truly content for the first time in, well, she couldn't remember when. The wariness that was so much a part of her character evaporated like overnight frost in the morning sun.

The scent from the twisted posy in her buttonhole smelled of a summer's herb garden. She hadn't noticed that before. Enticing snatches of different perfumes intermingled, but the aroma grew stronger and more alkaloid until it irritated her nostrils. She shook her head and pulled at the posy, but it was stuck fast. Another wave of warmth flowed over her and she forgot the minor annoyance. Her fingers and toes tingled as if she was pleasantly drunk.

The couple walked towards her. She had almost forgotten them, so distracted was she by the waves of pleasure curling gently backwards and forwards through her body, but now she could see them clearly. They glowed with vitality, tall, slim, and achingly beautiful. The man wore a dark, tailored suit set off by a striking cream shirt and pink tie. The woman was draped in a long blue gown that clung tightly to her body in all the places a gown should cling. They were more than just beautiful; they were elegant, sophisticated.

A small, still rational part of her mind wondered why a man and woman dressed for the opera or a club Up West should be walking under a road in East London, but euphoria submerged the thought.

Something stirred deep inside her, something uneasy at events, something immune to the enchantment of beauty, something indifferent to charisma, something predatory.

The woman was raven-haired with astonishing purple-tinged eyes that shone in the gloom. Her face was perfectly symmetrical, her skin flawless, her teeth as even and white as a Californian game-show hostess. Her companion was also dark with knowing grey eyes. These people were so perfect, so metropolitan, that Rhian felt unfit to share the same world. She felt cheap, dingy, and malformed in comparison. Rhian knew she was spoiled goods, shop-worn and stained.

The man beckoned her so she focused on him, drinking in his masculinity. He summoned her into his glowing presence, a prince showing kindness to the scullery maid. They understood, these beautiful people, and accepted her despite the grossness of her imperfections. She stretched out her arms walking into their embrace.

The posy in her coat lapel caught fire, burning with a fierce green intensity that flung stinging vapour into her face. She inhaled in surprise and fumes seared her lungs. Rhian turned away, coughing fiercely, unable to catch her breath. The burning sensation spread through her body like nerve toxin—and the world twisted and changed around her.

The man and woman were still beautiful, but their beauty was terrible. They no longer looked entirely human. Their bodies were too thin, too tall, like cocaine-fueled supermodels. Their arms and legs were too long, their skin impossibly white, and the woman's eyes shone with a lilac intensity that could not possibly be natural. They gazed at her hungrily, without a trace of human compassion or sympathy.

Alarmed, she backed away. The man's face twisted. He made a curious gesture with his left hand and Rhian froze like a bug in amber. Her mind disconnected from her body. In her head she struggled, but her limbs refused to obey. The couple smiled cruelly and moved ever so slowly towards her, the woman reaching out to touch.

A wolf howl rang in Rhian's head, reverberating through her mind, drowning out the world. Brutal power welled from within, freeing her. She slapped the woman's hand away and aimed a kick at her knee. The woman grimaced angrily and made a twisting motion with her hand. Something invisible, something magic, picked Rhian up, slamming her against the wall and knocking the breath from her body.

The woman laughed viciously. "This one is strong. Can you imagine how well she will taste?"

"After you, my love," the man said.

The woman leaned towards Rhian with a wide smile of anticipation. Rhian gasped for air, trying to fend her off with an outstretched arm.

There was a flash. The air in the tunnel thumped against Rhian's chest like a car tire had exploded. Rhian swallowed, trying to clear her ears. She smelt fireworks, and an irrelevant thought curled around the edge of her mind that someone had let off a Guy Fawkes' banger.

The woman looked puzzled and uncertain, like the rules had changed halfway through the game. A trickle of blood welled out of the side of her mouth and ran slowly down her chin. To Rhian, everything seemed to be happening in slow motion. There was another loud bang and the woman's body jerked.

A man in a long dark overcoat stood behind the glowing couple, right arm extended like an Olympic pistol shooter. Rhian could not work out where he had sprung from. He had materialized out of thin air. The gun in his hand fired again and again. Rhian saw flesh torn from the woman by the light of the flashes from the discharging weapon. She pushed the injured woman away, sending her spinning towards the shooter.

The gunman was so fast that Rhian barely saw him move. He caught the woman's hair and forced her head down, lowering his head over the back of her neck like a lover. Rhian caught a glimpse of canine teeth and heard bones crack. Her head lolled back, and the gunman tore at her throat with long fangs before dropping the twitching body to the floor.

The woman's companion screamed in fury. He punched towards the gunman, not even trying to touch him. Nonetheless, the gunman reeled back as if he had been hit by an invisible magical fist. His body spread-eagled against the wall tiles. His gun struck the floor with a metallic clang. The magician snarled and raised his hand while making a complex pattern with his fingers.

Rhian had no idea what was happening, but it was manifestly clear who was her enemy. She leapt on the magician's back, grabbing at his hand to spoil whatever he was doing. The man responded by flipping his other hand back towards her like he was dislodging a fly. Invisible magic punched her hard in the face. She fell backwards, the cold, unyielding concrete jarring her spine. Pressure built on her mind, the wolf awake, the wolf demanding to be set free.

The gunman scooped up his weapon and pointed it at the man. Rhian saw him press the trigger, but nothing happened. The gunman pulled desperately at the rear of the gun as the magician made a series of passes. The air flickered, images forming like shadows from decayed films. Light gushed from the magician's hands, streaming away in coils, solidifying into a fluorescent purple cable.

The magician lashed at the gunman, forcing him to roll over desperately to avoid the strike. Concrete exploded into dust and steam where the whip scoured the ground. The gunman half rose to his feet and leapt forward. He was inhumanly fast, but the magician was faster, his whip catching the gunman in mid-air.

Rhian realised with a cold clarity that left no room for doubt that the magician would kill the gunman and then her.

"All right, you bitch, do it," Rhian said, folding her arms in across her breasts, fists clenched.

The magician turned his head, giving her a curious look.

The wolf exploded from within, its triumphant howl vibrating through her body. Rhian pulled off her coat, knowing what was coming. Her muscles contracted into tetanus, twisting her back like a strung bow. Her clothes ripped and shredded, corroded by the magic flowing over her body. She dropped onto her hands, screaming with pain. Her head rotated back into her neck and an invisible hand pulled her face out by the jaw, the bones and ligaments realigning. Something terrible was happening to her legs. Her skin writhed as if covered in burning napalm. She screamed and screamed, but the sound that came out of her throat was a howl that filled the subway with throbbing sound.

Her sight failed.

When she could see, her world was monochrome and flattened. The pools of bright light surrounded by darkness were gone. Everything was at much the same level of illumination, as if she wasn't seeing with light at all.

The world was alive with smells. Human traces were everywhere in the subway but her nose told the wolf that no people were near. The things in front of her were not people. Her hearing was acute, detecting even the low rumble of the cars through the roof of the subway.

Rhian orientated the wolf on the man with the magic whip. The wolf did not intellectualize. To think was to act. She bounded forward, growling.

The magician turned to her, grey eyes widening in shock. He started to make a gesture with his free hand but the wolf sprang. She clamped her teeth on the prey's wrist, biting down hard. Her heavy body spun him around until his arm broke with a satisfying crack. Bones crunched in the wolf's jaws, and she heard the prey gasp.

The magician lashed the wolf with his whip of light, scoring the animal's fur and splashing blood from the hard-packed muscle underneath. The wolf howled in anger, pain only spurring her on. Gathering her rear legs under her body, she pounced again. She crashed into the prey's chest, knocking him over backwards. The whip lashed the subway ceiling, smashing a light cover in a spray of sparks that cascaded over the combatants like wedding confetti.

The damaged light strobed, freezing the wolf and the man in a series of stationary images like an old movie played at the wrong speed. Flashes of light freeze-framed shadows on the subway wall like echoes from another universe.

The wolf chomped down on the prey's throat. Strange, metallic-tasting blood sprayed into her mouth, matting the fur around her head. The prey struggled, but the wolf tightened her grip remorselessly, shutting off air and tearing flesh. The wolf worried and shook the throat long after the prey stopped moving, long after the last air gurgled from the bloody mess.

The wolf dropped the corpse and stalked stiffly to where the downed gunman lay on the ground. He shuffled back on his bottom and elbows until stopped by the subway wall, where he ejected the clip from his pistol. Fumbling in his coat pocket, he produced a replacement and rammed it home, pulling back the slide to ready the weapon. The wolf watched with interest, fascinated by the metallic clicks and machine-oil smell.

The gunman pointed the pistol unwaveringly at the wolf. She ignored the weapon, moving closer to him, growling deep in her belly.

"Good doggy," said the man. "Sit!"

The wolf sniffed at the man's wounds. They smelled healthy, so he would probably survive. The man held his hand out for her to scent. The wolf considered killing him, but he offered no provocation, sitting submissively like a cub being held to account by an alpha female. The wolf was bored. She licked the man's hand, tasting him.

"That's a good doggy," he said, running his hand along her muzzle to scratch the fur behind her ear.

The hand with the gun never wavered in its aim, but the wolf did not seem to understand the threat posed by the weapon. Rhian pushed upwards like a swimmer surfacing from a dive into a dark sea-pool. Changes coursed through her body, and the pain began. She screamed until merciful oblivion descended.

CHAPTER 6
FRIENDS REUNITED

Major Jameson, retired, had faced death many times in the pursuit of an illustrious career in Her Britannic Majesty's Guards. The IRA, various African militias, Serb gunmen, Afghan guerrillas and the United States Air Force had made determined attempts to kill him from time to time. During his time in The Commission, supernatural entities had tried to do things to him that made dying positively restful, but he had never been as gut-wrenchingly terrified by a daemon before.

"For pity's sake slow down, you blood-crazed lunatic," he said.

The car phone rang with an irritating beep-beep. Jameson considered ignoring it but duty won out, forcing him to trip the switch.

"Jameson, can you hear me?" asked a precise, prissy voice that was immediately identifiable.

Bloody Randolph! That was all he needed to make the day complete.

"Yes," he said.

"Oh, right . . ." said Randolph.

"Bloody Hell, watch for that lorry, you mad sucker," said Jameson.

"Letting Karla drive?" Randolph asked.

Whatever else he said was drowned out by horns. Karla forced Jameson's Jaguar across four lanes of traffic and through a red light.

"Karla, could you pull over for a moment?" asked Jameson calmly, displaying admirable control.

He hung off the seat belt. Four huge, computer-controlled disk brakes slammed the big sports car to a halt. The driver of a white transit van right behind them failed to match the maneuver. It spun into a bollard with a screech of tortured rubber and a great clang. The van's left wing lost the unequal contest with cast iron cemented into concrete.

"Okay, Randolph, I can talk now," said Jameson.

"We have a situation," said Randolph.

"Another one?" asked Jameson.

"The Wiccas are in hysterics here. All the trips have blown," said Randolph.

"You mad bitch, you could have killed me!" White van man appeared at Karla's open window.

"What's up?" asked Jameson.

"You silly cow, think you're something special because you drive a poncy Jag. I've a good mind to haul you out of there and give you a good slapping," said white van man.

Jameson glanced up from the phone. A huge, shaven-headed lout, with "*h*a*t*e*" tattooed on his knuckles, jabbed aggressively at Karla. His forefinger poked her arm.

"Really?" asked Karla, her mouth opening wide in a grin.

She threw open her door, and there was a thud as white van man absorbed the impact. Jameson winced, thinking of the delicate, multilayered paintwork that was the pride of Jaguar's body shop. He made a grab for her, but she lithely avoided him, slipping from the car.

"We picked up the trace of an active insertion zone somewhere in your area. We think that it's similar to the previous intrusions. The trace was followed by a pulse of magical radiation across the whole of East London. It's a Three."

A Code One insertion was a leak of information, and a Two involved the transfer of energy. A Three meant that something physical had penetrated the walls of the cozy little backwater of the multiverse inhabited by mankind. Something from outside. That was freakin' serious mojo.

The smack of flesh on flesh followed by a loud scream sounded outside the car.

"Do you have an analysis?" asked Jameson, pushing the phone more securely into his ear to drown out the noise.

"Yes."

"Might I have the summary?" Jameson asked.

"Just finding it."

The tap of a computer keyboard sounded over the phone.

"The source is unknown, object unknown, exact location unknown," said Randolph, succinctly.

"Great!" said Jameson. "I am glad to see that our understanding of the situation is unprejudiced by actual facts."

White van man's bullet-shaped head appeared through the open driver's window. He appeared to be crying.

"God's sake, make her stop," white van man pleaded. He disappeared abruptly, dragged away like a cork out of a bottle.

"What do you expect me to do about it?" asked Jameson.

"I don't know. Can't you round up the usual suspects, or something?" asked Randolph, coldly. "You're the field team, field something."

Another scream sounded outside.

"I've got to go. I've got a situation here, as well," said Jameson.

"I can hear," said Randolph, dryly. "Karla, I suppose. You really should keep her on a tighter lead."

"Yah, that'd work," said Jameson, clicking off the phone.

He got out of his motor to assess the damage, and cursed. Karla had white van man across the bonnet, holding him down by the throat with one hand. She was poised over him, fangs extruded. She revelled in his fear. Slowly, ever so slowly, she lowered her head towards his neck. White van man had stopped struggling. She focused on the blood running down his face. Scalp cuts bleed so ridiculously freely. It would be difficult to restrain her once she started to feed.

"Karla," Jameson said, softly, reaching towards her.

He touched her cheek and gently pulled her head round towards him. She looked at him expressionlessly, metallic green eyes glittering against white skin framed by jet black hair. He stroked her cheek, and her fangs retracted. She tilted her head sideways, rubbing against his hand. White van man took the opportunity to slide out from under her and scuttle away on his hands and knees. She was monstrous but oh, so beautiful.

"Get in the Jag's passenger seat, Karla. I'll clean up here."

She walked around the motor, moving with the elastic grace of a tigress.

Jameson took a wallet out of his inside pocket and extracted ten twenty-pound notes.

"That will fix the dent in your van," Jameson said.

"I'll have the Old Bill on you," said white van man, finding his voice.

"You won't tell the police anything," said Jameson. "In the first place, you would have to admit that you were beaten up and scared shitless by a girly half your size. In the second place, they won't believe you, and, in the third, our employer would be displeased and might send someone worse than Karla round to dissuade you."

Actually, The Commission had nothing worse than Karla on the payroll, if you excluded the daemons that made up the Human Resources Department. Jameson patted the man's cheek before climbing into the driver's side of the car. Jameson swung round a device like a sat-nav fastened under the dashboard.

"Round up the usual suspects, the man said. I suppose we could always see if any of the usual suspects have been spotted around here."

Jameson tapped out a series of instructions on the screen. Karla ignored him. When she was bored, she slipped into immobility. Not relaxed like a woman would be, but just stationary, like a machine on standby.

"Well, well, well," said Jameson. "An old friend of ours has a place nearby. I should have remembered."

He started the car, U-turning to head back the way they had come.

Rhian dreamed, dreamed of running under cold, clear skies. Her paws pounded across frozen ground. This time she was the prey, and her pursuer was gaining. Rhian pushed harder, but her paws lost traction on the ice, and she skidded. Her hunter was so close that she could smell him. He pulled alongside her, powerful muscles bunching under a thick hide. She bared her teeth at him, refusing to be intimidated.

Steam rolled off her coat, and she lolled her tongue out into the freezing air. She was tiring fast, muscles aching. She made one last attempt to increase her speed. He shoulder-charged her, bowling her over into a snow drift. She struggled to her feet to find him standing over her. He watched her intently while growling gently. She lowered her head in submission and he strutted stiff-legged to her. He gripped the loose skin at the back of her neck with his teeth. Forcing her down onto the cold, hard earth, he mounted her roughly, claiming the mating rights of an alpha male. He had proved his fitness by chasing her down. He howled his conquest to the Moon when he filled her with his seed.

Rhian struggled awake and opened her eyes. It was dark except for the flames. She coughed and gagged as smoke filled her lungs. Her eyes adjusted to the dull, red, flickering illumination. An unpaved lane was lined by low stone and wooden buildings. Some were in darkness, but others burned furiously. A roof fell in with a crash, shooting bright sparks and yellow-orange flames high into the air.

Through the crackle of the flames, she heard the screams of those too old, too weak or too stupid to get out of the burning town. Standing on the back of a chariot, she tapped the bare-torsoed driver on his shoulder. He flicked the reins across the back of the pair of horses, and the chariot started with a jerk. She gripped one of the hooped wooden rails on the vehicle's open sides. The lane opened out into a small square with a two-story building. Iron-helmeted enemy soldiers formed a defensive semicircle around the portico. They crouched behind long red shields decorated with white lightning symbols.

"*Kill them*," Rhian ordered in Welsh.

Battle chariots surged forward, warriors jumping off to strike the enemy with swords and spears. She was Morgana's instrument, the queen of water and death, the goddess of Moon and shape-shifters. She extended her right arm to the night sky, spreading her fingers so that she could see the full Moon through them. The wolf came to her like a thief in the night.

Rhian came awake with a jerk. She lay naked on her back between crisp, clean sheets in a large four-poster bed. Her shoulders were propped up on lilac-smelling pillows. The spacious bedroom was decorated with heavy cream-flock wallpaper and dark brown pelmets. Portraits and monochrome photographs of people in archaic costumes looked down from the walls. Heavy, dark drapes hung in folds under the pelmets. The room was lit by ornate bronze light-holders that were designed to look like candles weeping molten wax.

Rhian had no idea how long she had been unconscious. It always took her like that when the wolf left. She remembered every moment of the transformation into the beast, but never anything about the change back. It was as if all the energy was sucked from her body and she collapsed into unconsciousness that faded gently into sleep. Here, in this comfortable bed, she might have slept for some time.

She tried to work out whether she was truly awake or in another illusion. The bedroom was like a film set for a costume drama. She imagined Jane Austen sleeping in a room like this. But she was plain old Rhian again, not a pagan queen or a wolf, so this must be real.

She levered herself up to look for her clothes, assuming any had survived the change. Her coat should be in one piece. She recalled dropping it down her back before she morphed. There was a wardrobe near the bed, and she made the logical assumption that where there was a wardrobe, there would be things to wear. She pulled the bedclothes back and swung her bare legs over the side of the bed.

Rhian doubled up, gasping. Jagged pain thrust through her left side like a knife. She remembered the glowing whip scouring the wolf's flank and examined herself. The damage was not as bad as she had feared. The skin was an angry red but unbroken. She tried to push herself to her feet, but the pain was too much. She sank back onto the bed, concerned that she had internal damage.

"My little Snow White wakes without the traditional kiss," said a deep voice.

"What?" Rhian spun her head round.

A man leaned against the wall by a dresser. The door had not opened, so he must have been in the room all the time. How could she have not known he was there? She froze in shock. He chuckled, breaking the spell, and she pulled the sheets right up to her neck.

"A little late for modesty, wouldn't you say, Snow White?" the man said. "Who do you think cleaned the blood off and put you in your bower? I congratulate you on your healing properties. You were a real mess."

It was the gunman from the tunnel. She had only seen him briefly while human. It took a little time to join the dots and connect the wolf's impressions of the gunman to the man she saw now. He was good looking in a smooth sort of way, but he oozed an arrogant self-confidence that she disliked at first sight. Men like this frightened her, but the wolf sized him up and was not unhappy. Rhian suppressed the thought.

"You put me to bed?" she asked.

She regretted instantly the stupidity of the question. Hadn't he just told her?

"My pleasure," he said, smirking.

Rhian was close to freaking out. She clenched her fists tight, digging her nails into the skin. The pain made her feel better. Pain was control.

"How did I get here?" she asked. That was a better question.

"I carried you. I'm a philanthropist, always picking up waifs, strays, and fallen women. Like that prime minister they had some little while ago, what was his name?" The man clicked his fingers in irritation. "Gladstone, that was it. He used to tour St. James Park looking for ladies of the night to rehabilitate. Are you a lady of the night, Snow White? Do you need rehabilitating?"

"Stop calling me that," she said, losing her composure again. "My name's Rhian."

"Max." He bowed, the movement looking polished as if he had done it so often that it had become second nature. It should have looked really pseudo, really contrived and clumsy, but he made the archaic gesture seem sophisticated.

"Where am I?" She asked another good question.

"In my bedroom, and that's all you need to know."

A truly dreadful thought occurred to her. "You didn't carry me naked through the streets of London, did you?"

"Your coat survived your, ah, transformation, so I wrapped you in that. I chatted to you all the way to my car about what a lazy minx you were to want to be carried. How next time you were to wear sensible shoes. I think I was rather convincing," he said, complacently.

Smug seemed to be his default setting.

Rhian screwed her fists up. He was so annoying that she forgot to be frightened. "Where—is—my—coat?" she asked, articulating the words carefully between gritted teeth.

"It was such a tatty thing that I gave it to a tramp as bedding for his dog." He beamed at her.

Rhian was speechless. Max walked casually across the room and sat on the bed, folding his arms. Rhian shrank back as far as the sheets would permit. He grinned showing white, even, and completely normal teeth. But the wolf had seen long fangs.

"You bled all over the coat from that wound on your side," he said. "Your body underwent such impressive accelerated healing while you slept that I decided to leave you in my bed for a while. You look so decorative there, Snow White, that I may decide to keep you."

He tapped her on the end of her nose, making her blink in surprise.

"That's an interesting little trinket you have round your neck," Max said, pointing at the outline of her breasts under the sheet.

The Celtic brooch was cold against her skin. It was always cold no matter how long she wore it.

"Fascinating how it survived your transformation," he said. "One might almost think it played some role in the magic."

"No doubt you examined it carefully?" Rhian asked.

"I tried to." Max held up his hand and gave her a rueful grin. His fingers were marked by burn blisters. "It has one hell of a protection spell."

Rhian blinked. The pendant had never hurt anyone before, not directly, anyway.

"How am I to go home without clothes?" she asked, changing the subject.

"It's a puzzler," he replied.

Rhian took a deep breath. "Could you lend me some things?" she asked, politely, which took a degree of willpower.

Taking a deeper breath, she added, "Please."

If you were going to charm a man with politeness then you may as well go the whole humiliating hog. Especially when the man in question was an utter sexist pig.

He chuckled. "A cute little thing like you, Snow White, dressed in my clothes?" He spread out his arms. "Don't you think they might be a little large for you?"

Rhian ground her teeth in anger, although he had a point. He must be a good foot taller than her.

"You and I need to have a little chat, Snow White. Tell me what you know."

"About what?" asked Rhian, genuinely confused.

"The European Union's monetary policy, what do you think?

Tell me what you know about the Sith?" Max snapped at her, making her jump.

His smile had gone.

"Sith?" asked Rhian, baffled. "Aren't they the bad guys in *Star Wars*?"

"*Star Wars*?"

They looked at each other in mutual incomprehension.

"You really don't know, do you?" he said slowly.

He looked at her intently as if he was trying to see into her head. "What were you doing in that subway?" he asked, changing the subject.

"I was going home from work, if you must know; I'm a barmaid. I don't have to answer your questions," Rhian said boldly. He had bounced her into replying without thinking but she was now asserting her rights.

"You'll answer if you want to leave here alive, Snow White," he said, his voice as bleak as the Cumberland moors.

"Don't threaten me," said Rhian, meeting his eyes, wondering why the wolf was so unnaturally calm. "I'm not frightened of you."

She remembered Max's teeth tearing at the elegant woman's throat. She searched within herself and found a watchful, powerful presence. No, she really wasn't frightened, as long as the shadow of the wolf was with her.

"You're a game little thing but you must face reality, Snow White. You are all out of spells, little witch. Oh, you've some pretty party tricks—turning into a wolf was particularly good. The wolf-brooch I suppose. Your healing spell is unparalleled, but you've absolutely nothing left about your person to make more magic. I established that, personally."

Rhian blushed, eliciting that infuriating smile again.

"I might be a werewolf," said Rhian, defiantly.

"You might be but you're not. You had a professional-grade witch charm on your coat, and you don't smell anything like a shapeshifter."

He looked down and stroked her hair. "You're human through and through, my little Snow White." He let his gaze run down her body hidden under the blankets. "I checked, remember?"

"I'm not a witch and I don't know anything," Rhian said, a little desperately. "Let me go."

She was human, but was he?

He leaned back watching her, like a cat watches a mouse between its paws. He rose and moved to the dresser so fast that Rhian barely saw him cross the space in between.

"I had a look through the pockets before disposing of your coat," he said, abruptly. "You had a purse with exactly seven pounds, thirty-five pence in loose change, a door key and a mobile phone. I am afraid the mobile hit the ground too hard."

He held up shattered plastic.

Rhian bit her lip, trying not to cry. Her work clothes were destroyed. She had lost her coat, and her phone was smashed. She had only seven pounds to last until payday, and she had turned into a wolf again. She lost the unequal struggle and tears rolled down her cheeks. He walked slowly back to the bed and took her chin in his hand, lifting her head so that she could see his face clearly.

"It won't do, Snow White. Crying won't help you. Now tell me your name, who you work for, and how you turned up in that subway at just the right time armed with powerful defensive and offensive spells."

He kept talking to her, stroking her hair and gazing into her eyes. His voice came from further and further away. She was very tired and her head felt so heavy. She could hear her own voice answering him, but she was not sure what she said. Eventually, she slipped back into sleep.

Jameson drove quickly but inconspicuously, the way he had been taught by the Northern Irish Special Branch. The powerful sports car ate the miles, slicing through the heavy London traffic. Karla prodded the control of the digital music system, and the device selected a New Age instrumental. It filled the car with soft acoustic guitars that barely rose above the deep growl of the supercharged four-point-two-liter eight.

After only a few minutes, Jameson turned off into the side roads.

"Our friend retired from the service, so technically she's a civilian now."

"Retired?" asked Karla, vaguely.

"Still aren't entirely tuned into the modern world, are you, Karla?

Retiring is when someone leaves the job while still alive. Doesn't happen so often in our line of work. Of course, no one ever really retires from The Commission. They just go off the payroll."

Jameson parked the Jag and they climbed out. Karla touched the roof and the locks clicked, the anti-theft switching on with a friendly chirrup and a flash of orange lights. Jameson had never been able to work out how Karla did that. She and the car had some sort of strange affinity. Generally she was uninterested in technology.

Jameson found the right flat and rang the bell. After a few moments, a woman in a long, loose-fitting, flowery dress opened the door. Her face registered shock, and she tried to close it again. Jameson stuck his foot in the gap.

"Gods, it's you two. What do you want?" the woman asked. "And what the hell is *she* doing out in daylight?"

Jameson pushed the door fully open.

"Hello, Frankie, long time no see, can we come in?" he asked, entering before Frankie could reply.

When Karla tried to follow, the knocker glowed with a golden light that forced her back. Brass eyelids slid apart, revealing green eyes with vertical cat-like pupils.

"Daemon," the knocker hissed, opening its brass mouth to force the word out.

"Frankie," Jameson said, pleasantly.

The woman stood for a moment, indecision flitting across her face. Taking hold of Karla's wrist, she led her through the door. The knocker went back to sleep and all three walked into the lounge. Jameson made himself at home on the leather chair.

"I will reset the exclusion spell as soon as she leaves," said Frankie, taking a seat on the sofa.

Karla stood on the edge of the room. A fly circled lazily across the room. Her eyes moved to track it like a Patriot missile's search radar.

"If we really wanted to get in then I doubt you could stop us," Jameson said, gently. "You of all people know what we can do."

Frankie pushed her glasses back up her nose.

"I remember that gesture," Jameson said, smiling. "It's got to be a habit. You're looking well, Frankie."

He was not just being polite; she really did look well. In her last months at the office she had become thin and strained, fading gently away like a Victorian heiress with consumption. Since her retirement she had filled out, becoming the pleasantly plump Frankie that he recalled.

She shrugged. "I get by. Is that why you came, to see how I was?"

"No," he replied. "But seeing you again is a pleasure."

"Careful, Jameson," Frankie said, glancing at Karla. "I wouldn't want to make her jealous."

Jameson looked at Karla, really looked at her. She returned his look, parting her lips. He remembered when they had first left him alone with her in the cell. She bared her teeth and claws, terrifying him. "*I feel your fear,*" she said, backing away in confusion. "*I don't like it.*" She had curled up in a foetal ball on the floor, unable to cope with emotions foreign to her nature.

He remembered her on the roof of his building, calmly waiting for the rising Sun. She had worked out that they would kill her when the experiment terminated, so she decided to suicide. He carried her back into his flat before the ultraviolet could burn out her eyes. She was so light, no heavier than a human. That was the night he decided The Commission would have to go through him to get to her. It was not like he was happy with his life. There were worse ways to die than keeping faith with a comrade.

"She doesn't quite think like us," Jameson said. "She tends to react to actions rather than words."

"I shall resist the urge to throw myself into your arms, then," said Frankie, sarcastically.

"Probably best," said Jameson politely, not wanting to get into old history, but Frankie would not leave it alone.

Frankie said, "I've given up charity work."

"Yes, I recall Pete left you," said Jameson nastily, the jibe slipping out before he could intercept it.

Frankie tried to mask her feelings, but Jameson saw the hurt in her eyes and was ashamed. She did not deserve a crack like that. Even if she did, a gentleman would not have made it.

"I'm sorry, Frankie," Jameson said. "That remark was not cricket."

"No," Frankie said. "But it's true enough."

"Pete was a civilian. You know how rarely they can cope with our world," Jameson said.

"I suppose that I thought my love would overcome all obstacles. It's a common enough female delusion," said Frankie. "How are Mary and your kids?"

"Well enough as far as I know," Jameson replied. "I get a card at Christmas."

He shrugged. "You know how it is?"

"Yes," Frankie replied. "I know how it is. You dodged my question. Karla's a sucker. Ultraviolet breaks down her cellular structure in seconds. How is it that she's out in daylight without being fried?"

"N-acetyl-5-methoxytryptamine," Jameson replied with the air of someone who had done something clever.

"What?" Frankie asked.

"Melatonin, a photosensitive chemical controlling circadian rhythms and with powerful antioxidant properties."

"I know what melatonin is," Frankie said between gritted teeth. "But what has that got to do . . ."

She paused and looked at Karla with utter horror.

"Oh gods, sunburn tablets, you've been feeding her sunburn tablets."

"Rather clever, don't you think?" Jameson asked smugly.

"Clever, you bloody fool," Frankie replied. "You've just handed suckers the key to daylight."

"Daemons don't do technology. You know that?" Jameson said, scornfully. "And Karla is hardly likely to chat about it. Besides, melatonin doesn't give total protection to suckers any more than, well, people. She is weakened by daylight and would be ill advised to try sunbathing."

Frankie looked thoughtful. "But it shouldn't work. It's not just a matter of a photo-chemical reaction. Something else in sunlight damages daemons like Karla."

"Whatever," Jameson said, shrugging.

"Now I come to think about it, ultraviolet is the least of their problems with the Sun. Our UV guns only weaken them, not kill. It's the spiritual dimension in sunlight that really matters," Frankie said, warming to her theme.

Her brow furrowed. "Oh!"

"What?" Jameson asked. A smug, knowing smile hovered on Frankie's lips. Jameson knew that smile. It was her "I know something you don't and I'm not going to enlighten you" smile. It had always irritated the hell out of him.

"Never mind, you didn't come here to reminisce about old times, Jameson. What do you want with me? I am not coming back. I work for myself now, casting harmless spells to help people."

"You may be harmless, Frankie, but something else around here is bloody dangerous. What do you know about it?" Jameson asked.

"Nothing," Frankie replied, shrugging.

"Come off it," Jameson said, raising his voice threateningly. "People disappearing, bodies turning up without a mark on them to show how they died, not to mention bursts of magical energy. Don't tell me that you haven't noticed? I can always take you back to the office for a little chat if you won't talk to me here."

"All I know is what I read in the papers," Frankie said. "Although it's true that magic seems to be getting easier in East London."

"Like strange energy was leaking into the world?" Jameson said.

Frankie nodded.

"Some of those bodies you mentioned were drained of blood." She looked at Karla meaningfully.

The fly made the terminal mistake of wobbling past Karla in uncertain flight. She casually plucked it from the air, holding it delicately between her thumb and forefinger. The fly waggled its legs and wings.

"I remember you," Karla said to Frankie. "You were the witch who enchanted me. I can smell the magic in you."

She opened her mouth to show long fangs. She made no overtly hostile move, but Frankie looked away first. Karla lowered her head and studied the fly intently as if she had never seen one before.

"I'm sorry, Jameson," Frankie said. "I wish I had never bound her to you."

"Don't knock yourself out, Frankie. I volunteered for the experiment. It's not like anyone was the love of my life or anything. I was never much use at the relationship thing, as you may recall."

He grinned to show there were no hard feelings. Jameson had long ago retreated into a world of control, placing adamantine barriers between his inner self and the outside world. He attracted women easily and lost them just as easily when they realized that he would never let them in.

He sighed. "I did one too many tours in the army."

His mind drifted back to Iraq. The American A10 flew down the line of British Scimitars spraying thirty millimeter shells. Cavalry men bailed out, to be chopped down with shrapnel. Screams sounded from a burning tank. The sweet smell of roasting human flesh contrasted with the acrid taste of burning fuel and plastic.

"Snap out of it, Jameson," Frankie said, abruptly. "Are you still getting flashbacks about that burning pig in Belfast? I will never know why you will not take the CB treatment."

Jameson was jolted back to find Karla staring at him with uncharacteristic anxiety. She could feel his moods. A "pig" was an obsolete lightly armoured wheeled carrier that the government had insisted the army use in Northern Ireland. Heavy tracked vehicles with decent armor were deemed too aggressive and bad PR. Pigs were horribly vulnerable to fertilizer bombs.

He forced himself to smile before changing the subject. "You could not know that the love geas you placed on Karla would be reciprocal, binding me to her as much as her to me. Besides, you were just obeying orders when you cast the spell."

"Only obeying orders, now there's a phrase that echoes hollowly down the ages. I think I got tired of obeying orders," said Frankie.

She looked Jameson in the face. "I hated you at the time and I wanted you to suffer. Goddess help me, but I am not sure that did not leak into the spell."

"We'll never know, as The Commission have never repeated the experiment."

Frankie did not reply.

"Frankie?" Jameson asked.

"There were two more attempts. I did the magic both times," she said.

"I never knew that. Why was it kept so quiet?"

"Because they were bloody disasters, with the emphasis on bloody!" Frankie burst out. "That's what sent me over the edge, the cause of my breakdown. The connection between you and Karla is unique, and we have no idea why."

Karla squashed the fly.

"Snow White, wake for me, Snow White."

Something touched Rhian's lips, and she opened her eyes with a jerk. Max stood over her with that irritatingly superior smile.

"This time you got your kiss," he said.

"What happened?" she asked.

"I entranced you, Snow White, just like the Sith did in the subway, but this time you didn't have your protective herbs."

"What did I tell you when I was under?" asked Rhian, with apprehension.

"Everything, little witch, you spilled all your secrets."

She relaxed. He still thought she was a witch, so he had learnt nothing of any importance. Maybe he did not know the right questions to ask.

"Oh yeah? Give me an example of something?" she asked, defiantly.

"You've used black magic to kill, little witch, your lover, no less."

Rhian's mind froze. He thought she had killed James. Her guilt would have answered for her if he phrased the question too vaguely. He grinned at her with an expression that said "got you!" There was a long silence, then Rhian laughed. His triumphant expression slipped, which only made her laugh the more.

"I killed my lover?" Her shoulders shook helplessly.

Max looked at her thunderously. "Did I say something funny?"

"God, stop, my side hurts," she said, laughing all the harder.

The anger faded from his face to be replaced by a rueful look.

"Snow White, I am so glad I decided to keep you," he said. "You are just full of surprises."

He raised his voice slightly. "Sefrina, bring the case in."

A tall, slender woman cat-walked into the room in high heels and a pencil skirt. Blonde hair piled on top of her head in a careless style that must have taken an inordinate amount of time and money to achieve. She casually swung a large suitcase in one hand and tossed it in the direction of the bed, where it hit the floor with a heavy thump. She propped herself on Max's shoulder and studied Rhian with startling blue eyes.

"So, darling, this is your new pet. She doesn't look like much," Sefrina said in a Swiss finishing-school accent.

"I certainly don't look like an advert for a West End escort agency," said Rhian, taking an instant dislike to the woman.

She particularly disliked the way Sefrina covered Max like a measles rash. The emotion made her angry. Why should she care if Max liked some upper-class tart draped all over him? It was not as if she even liked the man, assuming he was a man. Rhian decided that the wolf must feel threatened by a rival alpha female. That would explain why she felt jealous; it was caused by emotional leakage from the wolf.

Sefrina smiled, parting blood-red lips wide to show long canine teeth.

Oh God, it's another one, Rhian thought.

"I don't think I like your new pet, Max. Maybe I should teach her some manners," Sefrina said.

She moved a step towards the bed but Max grabbed her wrist, his hand moving faster than a striking cobra.

"Leave her alone, Sefrina," said Max.

Sefrina hissed at him, showing her teeth.

Max's voice hardened and he jerked hard on the woman's wrist. "I mean it, Sefrina. She belongs to me. Or do I have to teach *you* some manners?"

Sefrina tested her strength against Max's grip. Rhian thought she intended to challenge him, but Sefrina suddenly relaxed. "Of course not, Max," she said, smiling sweetly, as if the incident had never happened.

He let go of her wrist and she stalked out, shooting one last venomous glance at Rhian. I have not, Rhian thought, made a friend there. Not that she cared overmuch.

"What's in the case?" asked Rhian.

"Clothes," Max replied, succinctly. "Clothes suitable for a small girly."

The odious man seemed to work hard at being offensive.

"I prefer the word *petite*," Rhian said.

Max laughed. "Get dressed and I'll drive you home."

Rhian didn't move, although she was relieved to hear that she was not going to have to fight her way out.

"Aren't you going to get out of bed and take a look in the case?" Max asked.

"When you leave the room," replied Rhian. "Or have you forgotten that I've nothing on?"

"How could I, Snow White?" replied Max. "It just never occurred to me that you'd still be bashful after all that has passed between us. However, if you insist."

He bowed to her, turned, and walked out.

"My name's Rhian," she said to his back. He closed the door without answering or even looking back.

She carefully levered herself out of bed. The pain her side was down to a mild ache. The wolf healed her so very quickly. The cuts she made on her arms disappeared in days without leaving scars.

Her first action was to see if she could lock the door, but the key had been removed. She hurried over to the case and lifted it. It took two attempts for her to get it up on the bed. It was heavy. That bitch Sefrina must be stronger than she looked.

Rhian unclipped the catches. They flipped open easily with sharp clicks. The tie belts were more problematical, as the case was stuffed tight. In the end, she sat on top of it to get the tension off the belts. That lousy man could have opened the case for her and spared her the embarrassment of perching naked like a monkey on a branch.

She gasped when she saw the contents. They were the sort of clothes that she had only read about in magazines. Reverently she removed a folded tan coat that was beautifully cut and lined, the tag proudly declaring it to be a product of Givenchy of Paris. She burrowed deeper into the bowels of the suitcase like a kid checking out her Christmas stocking. She unfolded a black minidress by Proenza Schouler of New York and held it against her body. She draped it over her hips. It fitted perfectly.

She pulled more clothes out of the case until she was surrounded by elite labels like a model backstage at a fashion show. She found blouses and skirts from Marni of Milan, a little black dress from Nina Ricci of Paris, shoes and boots by Jimmy Choo, and even a rather daring catsuit from the young Scottish designer Christopher Kane. At the bottom was a makeup set and Ricci perfume.

"Ready?" Max's voice carried through the door.

"No, go away," she yelled back.

After some deliberation she chose to wear Armani denim jeans with a minidress. She spent some time at the dressing table, putting a face on, dabbing some perfume on her wrists and neck as a final touch. She draped the Givenchy coat around her shoulders and examined herself in the mirror. Turning the collar up set off her short dark hair. Perfect! That bitch Sefrina wanted to play games, did she?

A heavy hand knocked on the bedroom door. "What are you doing in there?" Max asked.

She carefully closed the case and extended the handle. She stopped at the door, took a deep breath, and carefully pasted an expression on her face that she hoped indicated detached disdain. Only then did she open the door and parade out. A moment of instability on the high heels of her boots only slightly spoiled her entrance.

Sefrina lounged in a chair reading *Elle* magazine. Rhian watched the woman carefully out of the corner of her eyes. She noted Sefrina's lips tighten when she realised how well Rhian looked.

A hand clap caught Rhian's attention.

"Very nice, you chose her clothes well, Sefrina. Snow White, give us a twirl," Max said.

She had actually started to turn when she remembered that she was not going to do anything he suggested.

"You mentioned taking me home?" she asked, sticking her nose in the air.

"And so I shall. I am glad that you went to some trouble over your appearance before you came out with me. You scrub up rather well."

The arrogant so-and-so actually thought that she cared what he thought of her looks. Rhian opened her mouth to issue a denial but closed it again without speaking. He would choose to misinterpret anything she said.

"I get to keep the other clothes?" Rhian asked.

She hated giving up some of her independence but was unwilling to abandon a cornucopia of fashion that she could never have afforded.

He grinned broadly. "You may as well. They wouldn't fit Sefrina here."

"Thank you," she made herself say.

Max approached her, holding a silk scarf in both hands. "Let's get your blindfold on and we can go."

She blocked him with a hand. "Why would you want to blindfold me?" she asked.

"I can think of all sorts of interesting possibilities," he replied. "But in this case it is simply that I don't want you to know where I live. Fair enough?"

She nodded and allowed him to knot the scarf around her eyes. He gripped her firmly by the elbow and steered her out of the room. A cold wind on her face and the slamming of a door indicated that they were outside. He led her twenty paces or so then let go. She heard the electronic click of a car unlocking. He put his hand on top of her head, like the cops do on TV shows, and put her into a seat.

The car engine was quiet, but Rhian was pushed down into the seat as it accelerated away.

"May I ask you a question?"

"Why not?"

"In the subway . . ." Her voice trailed off. She was unsure how to proceed.

"Yes."

"You had fangs. You bit that woman in the neck, and Sefrina has fangs, and you both seem inhumanly strong and quick . . ." Her voice trailed off again. "You interrogated me but you've told me nothing about yourself."

"That's right," he agreed.

She waited for him to explain, but he said nothing. God, he was irritating.

"Who are you—or should that be what are you?"

He chuckled. "You really are a delightful paradox, Snow White. You turn up at a critical moment armed with high-level witchcraft and yet you seem to know nothing about the nature of the world. I shall look forward to our further meetings."

"Are you a vampire, one of the living dead?" she asked.

This time he laughed out loud.

"You've been watching too many old films," he said.

She was not sure what she felt about that and was silent for the rest of the journey.

The car stopped.

"Here we are."

She lifted off the blindfold. It was still night, but the streetlights showed her that they were outside Frankie's flat.

He put a hand on her knee and leaned across. "Do I get a goodnight kiss?"

"No," she replied, removing the hand.

"I am devastated," he said, not looking it. "I have something for you."

He handed her a phone. "A replacement for the one you lost helping me out. I've put in my number."

"Thank you," she said, nonplussed. She examined it briefly before putting it in her pocket. It had a touch screen and looked expensive.

She pulled the heavy case out and walked up the path without looking back until she heard the car drive off. She caught sight of the rear end of a large executive saloon car as it disappeared around a bend. Rhian let herself into the flat and almost bumped into Frankie, who shot out of the lounge.

"Where the hell have you been?" Frankie said, which was not quite the greeting Rhian had anticipated.

"Sorry I'm late," Rhian said.

"Late? You've been gone two days," said Frankie, snapping on the corridor light. "And where did you get a Givenchy coat?"

CHAPTER 7
FITTING IN

Rhian slept well that night; in fact, she overslept. Frankie was eating toast when she slid into the kitchen.

"I made you some tea," Frankie said.

"Thank you."

"But it went cold," Frankie said with satisfaction.

"Ah," Rhian said.

"There's another brewing in the pot."

"About last night . . ." Rhian said.

Frankie gazed at her toast reflectively.

"The marketing clowns claimed that falling sales of marmalade showed that the English had stopped eating toast for breakfast."

She scooped a generous helping of marmalade out of a stoneware pot and spread it on her toast.

"About last night . . ." Rhian tried again.

"'Course, they failed to spot that people are buying Seville oranges and making their own." Frankie said.

"About last night . . ." Rhian said, clenching her fists in frustration.

"I shouldn't have yelled at you," Frankie said. "I am not your keeper. You can come and go as you like."

"No, you were understandably worried. I'd have rung but my phone was smashed and I did not realize how much time had passed because I was unconscious or asleep most of the time." Rhian rushed it all out with one breath.

"What, you were unconscious?" Frankie asked.

She looked Rhian in the eye for the first time.

"I was mugged," Rhian explained. "I must have hit my head when I fell."

"You were attacked?" Frankie asked, mouth open.

"That was when my phone broke and my clothes were all ruined. Max bought me new clothes and a new phone," Rhian said,

"Max?" Frankie lifted an eyebrow.

"My rescuer," Rhian answered the unasked question. "He, ah, chased off the mugger and carried me back to his house to recover."

"I see," Frankie said, in a carefully neutral voice. "And he bought you the expensive wardrobe to replace your ruined clothes?"

"And a new phone," Rhian replied, thinking she might as well get it all out in the open. She fished it out of her jeans pocket and passed it over.

"Very nice," Frankie said, playing with the touch-sensitive interface. "It must have cost a bit. This Max is well off, then?"

Rhian shrugged.

"Will you be seeing him again?" Frankie asked.

"Shouldn't think so," Rhian replied. "He is older than me and we are hardly likely to meet socially."

"Ah, it must be a complete accident that he's put his number in your new phone's memory."

A smile played on Frankie's lips. She turned the phone around to show Rhian Max's name in the Contacts List. Actually, it was the only name on the list.

The rotten cow thinks I gave Max a horizontal thank you, Rhian thought. She wanted to put Frankie right but held her tongue. Better to be thought a slut than a wolf.

Frankie lost the smile. "Seriously, Rhian, if you lost consciousness you should be checked out by a doctor."

"All done," Rhian said. "I'm fine."

"Max again, I suppose." Frankie said. "He thinks of everything."

Rhian managed a weak smile.

Rhian steeled herself and went to work that night as if nothing had happened.

Gary greeted her with a smile. "Hi, Rhian, feeling better?"

"Ah, yes," Rhian replied. "Sorry about missing my shifts."

"That's okay. You can't help being ill. Frankie phoned in and said you wouldn't be able to make it so, I got Sheila to cover for you."

Sheila was a middle-aged Londoner who was the third member of their little team. Rhian rarely saw her as they inevitably worked on different days.

"Yes," Rhian said uncertainly. So Frankie had covered for her. She was the first person willing to lie for Rhian since James. She was not sure how she felt about that.

Gary fussed about behind the bar, pushing glasses onto the spinning rubber head of the cleaning machine.

"Your landlady seems a nice person." Gary said.

"Yes," Rhian replied, noncommittedly, wondering where this was going.

"Does she have a significant other?"

"Not to my knowledge," Rhian replied. "Why do you want to know?"

Gary kept his head down over the machine.

"Oh, no reason," he replied casually. "Just making conversation. Would you do a sweep for dirty glasses, please?"

Rhian buried herself in the minutiae of work. She found the undemanding tasks soothing. There was a satisfaction to doing a simple job well.

Gary tapped her on the shoulder.

"Sorry, Gary, did you say something?"

"Yes, I just asked if you were okay on your own. This is my rest night, and I wanted to catch the documentary on the BBC."

"Sure, you go ahead. What's on?" Rhian asked.

"A Horizon program on string theory."

"String theory?" Rhian asked, wondering what on earth Gary was blathering about.

"You know, modern physics, string theory, multiple dimensions and universes. CERN are setting up an experiment to test string theory using the Large Hadron Collider. Apparently quarks disappear in the plasma ball."

"Riiiight, hadrons, quarks, plasma balls," Rhian said, smiling and giving a thumbs up.

"Or I might just watch the football."

"Plasma balls versus leather balls. I can see that you're torn for choice," Rhian said.

Gary fled.

The pub's *clientèle* consisted of Old Fred and Willie the Dog reading the *Morning Star* at the bar and a small group of male students sitting around a table. Neither party was exactly splashing out. Rhian went over to collect empty glasses from the students' table in an effort to shame them into spending. They were deep in conversation.

"But Wittgenstein's duck-rabbit model clearly supports philosophical scepticism in that we can be certain of nothing," said an earnest-looking student.

"I am certain that I came to university to get laid, not to sit in a grotty pub listening to you lot going on about Ludwig bloody Wittgenstein," a second student said, gloomily.

"Can I get you more drinks, gentlemen?" Rhian asked brightly.

There was an abrupt silence. None of the students met her eye except the one who wanted to be laid. He took one look at Rhian and blushed bright red.

"I'll, uh, get a round in," the sexually frustrated student said.

A third murmured, "Bloody hell, is it Christmas or something?"

Rhian took the cash and brought the ordered drinks over. You did not normally get waitress service in a pub, but Rhian was bored. The second student examined his change carefully when Rhian plonked it in his palm. He did not give her a tip, not that she expected one. She returned behind the bar and washed the dirty glasses.

Two men came in and bought double whiskeys. Rhian noticed them because they stood out from the Black Swan's normal patrons. She guessed their age at forty or so. That was far too old to be students and far too young to be one of the old working-class codgers left behind by the deindustrialization of the East End, like flotsam abandoned by the retreating tide. The men sat at a corner table, leaning forward to converse in low murmurs. Over the next twenty minutes they were joined by two friends. The last one asked for something in a thick Glaswegian accent.

"Pardon?" Rhian said, looking at him blankly.

"A half of bitter and a large glass of Scotch," the man said, exaggeratingly enunciating each word. "Can't you speak English?"

"In the same glass?" Rhian asked, ignoring his rudeness.

"Of course not," said the Scotsman.

Rhian poured the drinks, assuming correctly that "large" was Scottish for a double. The Scotsman looked at the glass of whisky with contempt. He tossed it down in one go and held the glass out.

"Another. You English serve ridiculously short measures of Scotch."

"The measure might be English, but I'm Welsh," Rhian said, refilling his glass from the optic of Bell's behind the bar.

The Scotsman shrugged, "Same thing."

He joined the other three before Rhian could think of a suitably crushing answer.

The pub door flew open and a tall, well-built man strode in. He walked with a swagger up to the bar. His dark hair was cut neatly and brushed forward to hide a receding hairline. His pale blue tie set off a cream shirt in a blue suit tailored a little too tightly around an impressive musculature. Rhian noticed that he wore diamond-studded gold cufflinks. Everything about the man was flashy and expensive.

He stopped at the bar and gave Rhian a charming, broad smile that never quite reached his eyes. A gold tooth flashed in the light from the mirror behind the bar.

Old Fred and Willie the Dog vacated their stools and slid out of the pub. Rhian was alarmed to see that Willie did not even pause to finish his drink.

"You're new," the man said to Rhian, looking her up and down, "and a definite improvement on the usual barmaid in here."

"Do you want a drink?" Rhian asked, refusing to respond to the compliment.

She took an instant dislike to him. There was a black void behind his eyes. He was a man without a soul. Like Max, she realised, just like Max. He would be uncaring and greedy with a woman, taking his pleasure without regard to her desires or fears.

"Scotch," he said.

She picked up a glass and moved to the optic. He let her push the glass against the optic bar to release a measure before speaking.

"Not that blended crap, cutie. Get me down a bottle of malt."

He surveyed the bar.

"The Isle of Jura, I think."

That bottle was on the very top shelf. Rhian was obliged to fetch the small steps on wheels that Gary kept for this eventuality. She climbed up and reached for the bottle, feeling his eyes on her bottom. He was not really like Max, she realised. They might share the same air of menace and the same arrogance, but Max had style and manners. This man was a braggart and a bully. It did not make Max any less dangerous, but it did make him better company.

"I'll take the bottle," he said. "We'll settle up later."

The students were watching in fascination. They looked away when he turned around. He chuckled and walked to their table.

"The pub's closing for a private party," the man said to the students. "Piss off."

"I haven't finished my drink," a student looked at him defiantly.

The man picked up the student's pint and emptied it into his lap.

"You have now," the man said.

The four men in the corner stood up and the students fled. Rhian casually reached below the bar and pressed the silent alarm that alerted Gary in the flat above. He appeared within seconds and took in the situation with a glance.

"You knock off early, Rhian. I'll take over here," Gary said, quietly.

Rhian looked doubtful.

"Don't worry; I will pay you for a whole shift."

"It's not the money," Rhian said. "Will you be all right?"

"I'll be fine. I know these people," Gary said.

Rhian did not move, wondering why Gary was acting so strangely.

He sighed. "The one in the flash clothes is Charlie Parkes. He's a blagger."

"What?" Rhian asked.

"Major-time gangster," Gary translated. "The elite of the underworld. Guys who carry out the big jobs while the small fry run around organising dope sales and prostitution."

"Like the Brink's Mat raid?" Rhian asked.

"Exactly like the Brink's Mat raid," Gary said. "London has the finest blaggers in the world. Makes you glad to be British, doesn't it. Anyway, Charlie uses this pub for business meetings, so he doesn't like witnesses."

"But you must be losing money," Rhian said.

Gary shrugged, "True, but I am not troubled by the local street gangs or protection racketeers since none of them fancy taking Charlie on. He is very well connected."

"I see," Rhian said. "But couldn't you get police protection?"

Gary laughed, "This is the East End, Rhian. You clock that one in the check shirt? No, don't look too obviously."

"I see him," Rhian said.

It was the Scotsman.

"That's Detective Inspector Drudge of the Flying Squad. Charlie contributes significantly to the Metropolitan Police's unofficial pension funds. He also has a bad reputation with women, which is why I want you to shove off now. I did not know he was coming in tonight or I'd have changed your shift."

Rhian could take care of herself, but she did as Gary ordered. She was sliding into the weave of East End life, losing her anonymity as she became part of the community. The idea both pleased and disturbed her.

A few days later, Rhian sat in the kitchen drinking a cup of tea and reading one of Frankie's wicca books when the woman shot in waving her mobile phone.

"A client, a big one," Frankie said, dancing around the room. "A construction company, no less."

"You'd better have a cup of tea to steady your nerves," Rhian said, pouring one.

"Business is looking up. I shall soon be turning away commissions the way things are going," Frankie said. "Goddess knows, I need the money."

"Your fame must be spreading," Rhian said.

"Possibly," Frankie replied. Her smile slipped. "Or maybe there is just more business around." Frankie shook her head, as if to clear it. "Whatever, I've a meeting at their corporate offices. I could use someone to act as my personal assistant. Someone who has the right sort of clothes. Is there a business suit in that trunk of goodies of yours?"

"Of course," Rhian said.

"Then go and change. We have an appointment in an hour and a half," Frankie said.

Rhian managed to don her finery in less than ten minutes. She was still dragging a brush through her hair when Frankie dragged her out of the flat. Frankie set a brisk walk through the maze of terraced streets.

"Huh, the tube station is over there," Rhian said, wondering why they were going in the wrong direction.

"I know that," Frankie replied. "The client has an office in Cyprus, no tube stations in Cyprus."

"Cyprus?" Rhian yelped. "I don't have a passport."

"Cyprus, the housing estate in Beckton," Frankie said. "Not the Greek island. Do hurry up or we'll be late."

About half a mile further on, Frankie stopped in front of a row of garages and fumbled in her bag.

"The key, where's the key to the lock-up? I know I had it when we left." Frankie said, frantically searching.

Frankie's handbag was a bit of a Tardis, or perhaps a black hole would be a better comparison. It slipped out of her hand, and various contents spewed all over the pavement.

"Is this it?" Rhian asked, bending down and pointing to a key that had a brown card tag attached by a bit of string.

"Yes," Frankie said, pouncing on it. "And there's the car keys."

She shoveled the rest of the contents back into the bag. When she stood up, she pushed her glasses back up her nose from where they had slipped when she knelt down.

"You never told me you had a car," Rhian said.

"Hmmm, you never asked."

Frankie unlocked the garage door and pushed it up into the roof. Inside was the strangest motor Rhian had ever seen. It was van shaped, only with sliding windows and a rear seat. It had large wheel arches mounting round headlights. Rust-red spots marked where corrosion bubbled up through the dirty cream paint. The windscreen was small, flat, and vertical, quite unlike the molded glass on modern cars.

"How old is it? What is it? Was Postman Pat the previous owner?" Rhian asked.

"Cheeky mare, this fine example of English automotive history is a Morris Traveller. It was my mother's until I inherited it, so I suppose it is older than you. I have a log book somewhere," Frankie said, vaguely. "She's called Mildred, the car, that is, not my mother."

Rhian went to go in the lock-up, but something stopped her. Not something physical, but a sort of compulsion. She heard a howl in the distance, no doubt someone's pet dog showing off its wolf ancestry. The compulsion faded and she walked into the garage.

Frankie frowned, "You should not have been able to go in without me inviting you. I put a negative compulsion on the building to keep out guests. The protection must have decayed." She stuck her hand across the threshold. "Odd, the spell seems to be working fine."

She looked at Rhian reflectively.

Rhian shrugged and examined the car.

"The panels are held on by shaped wood."

"English craftsmanship at its best."

"Wood with green stuff growing on it."

"I haven't had time recently to sand it down and treat it with preservative stain," Frankie said, defensively. "Algae tends to get a hold on the varnish."

Rhian was familiar with the idea that cars needed servicing, but not with anti-wood-rot and anti-algae preservatives. Somehow Frankie suited the car, like an owner grown to resemble their pet. It was quite small and noticeably narrow compared to modern cars, so left plenty of room in the lock-up for Frankie to store stuff.

And store stuff, she did. A vast array of bottles, wooden containers, and strange instruments were stacked high on the shelves that lined the walls. Carved elephants and daemons decorated a large wooden trunk stood against the wall. One of the daemons had six arms holding flaming knives. Rhian assumed it was a Hindu goddess, the elephants suggesting India.

"What's this?" Rhian asked mischievously, picking up a little wooden statuette of a squatting figure supporting an enormous organ with one hand. Judging by the smile on his face, the figure was inordinately proud of said organ.

"That is a *Priapus* statuette, a Greek fertility god," Frankie replied, deftly removing it from Rhian's grip and returning it to a shelf.

"And what magic do you use that for?"

"I don't. It was a Christmas present from my Aunty Lil, albeit one to which I refuse to give house room."

Frankie fussed around collecting items and placing them in a cardboard box. Rhian considered sitting on the wing of the car but decided to stand when she considered the likely impact on her new clothes. In fact, after looking around the lock-up, she chose to wait outside. Frankie eventually unlocked the driver's door, got in, and leaned across to open the passenger door for Rhian. The car had red leather seats that were small and upright. Everything about the car was upright.

"Does it work?" Rhian asked, struggling with the seat belt.

"Of course it works. Moggies are extremely reliable," Frankie replied, sniffily.

She switched on the ignition and pressed a button on the dashboard. The engine turned over with a grinding noise, coughed, and died. Rhian said nothing.

"I don't use the car much, so the battery gets a bit flat," Frankie said, defensively. "Perhaps it needs some choke."

She pulled a knob, which slid out of the dashboard on a ratchet, and pressed the starter again. This time the engine fired.

Driving with Frankie was an interesting experience—interesting in the sense of the old Chinese curse. The car was heavy and underpowered so it built up speed only gradually after stopping. The traffic flow often stopped in London. They soon had an escort of sales reps in hatchbacks and men in white vans bunched behind them. Stopping was equally leisurely. The brakes emitted grinding noises while slowing Mildred with a stately lack of haste more suitable for an oil tanker than a London car.

Finally, there was Frankie at the wheel. It was not that she could not drive properly so much as she would not. She talked excitedly about nothing and everything, pointing out things of interest to the left and right. Less than half her attention was on the road at any one time. Frankie actually took both hands off the wheel to demonstrate the enormity of the challenge she had faced on an earlier job. Rhian gripped her seat belt and surreptitiously checked the tension by pulling on the strap. Fortunately it appeared to be bolted to a non-rusty part of the chassis.

Frankie drove down the right-hand overtaking lane of the dual carriage at some twenty miles an hour too slow, oblivious to the flashing headlights of the frustrated drivers behind. Cars in the slow lane overtook illegally on the inside. Rhian could not find it in her heart to condemn the drivers.

Rhian discovered a *Guide to the Modern East End* on her phone; Max really did think of everything. She looked up Cyprus to steady her nerves. It gave her mind something to dwell on other than wondering about the location of the nearest accident and emergency clinic.

The Cyprus Housing Estate, built in 1881 to house workers employed at the Royal Albert Docks. Named in honour of the capture of the Island of Cyprus from the Ottoman Empire in 1878.

Well, that explained one mystery. She downloaded another page.

Cyprus was extensively redeveloped in the 1980s as part of the move of the financial industry to the area. It is largely private housing, with shopping centers, some offices, and The Docklands Campus of Whitechapel University. It is served by the Docklands Light Railway.

They passed the campus. The buildings were the sort that win architectural awards but are hell to work in. Some were shaped like ships' funnels and others had strange roofs like giant sun shades on poles. Rhian was more interested in the robot light railway cars running past on the overhead railway. Patriotically painted red, white, and blue, they looked more like coaches than trains. The large windows must give a good view out over Docklands.

Frankie parked—well—more abandoned—the Morris in a shopping center car park. She struggled to fit an anti-theft device to the steering wheel. Privately Rhian thought it highly unlikely that anyone would want to steal Mildred, although a motor museum might make an offer. Frankie finally gave up, and they went to find their client's office.

Mister Ferguson, their client, turned out to be a portly man in a baggy suit. His ruddy complexion suggested a liking for alcoholic refreshment and the high possibility of an imminent stroke. His secretary was a bottle blonde of a certain age who chewed gum with total dedication.

"Your eleven o'clock is here," she said to Ferguson.

"I don't care if your bloody mother has thrown herself off the roof. I need that order now, got it?" Ferguson shouted into a mobile phone while waving Frankie and Rhian towards chairs in front of his desk.

"Sorry about that, ladies," Ferguson said, switching on a plastic smile. "Salt of the Earth, East End traders, but you have to be firm with them."

"Perhaps you could brief us on your problem?" Frankie asked, adopting a businesslike manner. Rhian crossed her legs and balanced a notebook on her knee.

"My problem is a load of superstitious bloody Poles," Ferguson said, taking his gaze off Rhian's legs with reluctance. "They've got it into their thick heads that one of our sites is haunted and have stopped working. I need you to go and pretend to exorcise the place with a bit of the old hocus pocus so that they will get on with the bloody job."

His mobile phone rang. "What? Look, I'm working on it, right? I bloody know there are penalty clauses."

He put his hand over the mobile's mouthpiece, "June will tell give you directions and a contract."

Correctly assuming that June was the secretary, Frankie and Rhian left the office, leaving Ferguson yelling into his phone. June was surprisingly efficient, if not exactly pleasant.

"Your contract, sign on the bottom," June said.

Frankie took the pen but paused to look over the document. She blinked in surprise.

"The fee is non-negotiable, so don't bother to ask," June said, manipulating her gum from one side of her mouth to the other.

Rhian sneaked a brief glance at the contract. The fee was much higher than Frankie would have requested. She glared at Frankie, hoping the silly mare was not going to blurt that out. Frankie could be so naive.

June caught the nonverbal exchange and raised her eyebrows.

"My PA is trying to get me to reject the commission," Frankie said. "She is right, of course, the fee is derisory."

June looked down at the contract. Frankie took the opportunity to stick her tongue out at Rhian, who smiled and gave a thumbs-up.

"Well, maybe I could add some expenses, for travel and lunch," June finally said. "In cash."

Cash meant that it never had to appear on the books, so no taxes had to be paid. Technically illegal, but cash was untraceable.

"That's acceptable," Frankie said, signing. "Now we are here, we may as well get on with it, Rhian."

"There's a map to the site," June said, her manner conveying that their business was concluded.

Frankie made no move to leave. "I need more information about the nature of the haunting. Mr. Ferguson was short on detail."

"Does it matter?" June asked. "You just have to put on a good show to impress the Poles."

"Humor me," Frankie said.

"It started with stuff being moved around at night when the site was closed down."

"What sort of stuff?" Frankie asked.

"Oh, tools, and pegs marking out trenches were moved into weird patterns. That sort of thing. You often get kids or drunken students messing around on building sites. The boss put some guard dogs in at night to keep out intruders."

"But that did not work?" Frankie asked.

"For a while," June replied. "But the Poles had been spooked by then, so they soon found something else to worry about."

"Such as?" Frankie asked.

June shrugged. "They claimed spirits were throwing things around. The foreman was whacked across the back of the head with a shovel. The Poles claimed it just lifted up and hit him. I reckon one of them with a grudge decked the foreman and the others covered it up with ghost stories."

"Okay," Frankie said, picking up her copy of the contact and the dosh. "We'll show ourselves out."

They walked to the door.

"And then there was the accident," June said.

Frankie turned and walked back.

"What accident?"

"A Pole fell off some scaffolding," June replied. "He died."

The map was only moderately inaccurate, so they only went wrong a few times before finding the building site. Blocks of yuppie maisonettes lay half-completed on a fenced-off wilderness. Two guard dogs paced forwards and backwards along the high wire fence.

Frankie retrieved a large cardboard box from the back of Mildred. Rhian was amused to see that the car had two cupboard-like rear doors instead of a vertically opening hatch. They walked along the fence until they found a gate by a grey prefab builder's hut resting on bricks to lift it clear of the ground. The dogs flanked them silently on the other side of the fence. Somehow that was more sinister than if they barked.

Rhian could hear a radio on in the hut tuned to a local talk station. A deep debate raged about new traffic lights. The argument had just reached the Godwin moment where the local council traffic subcommittee were likened to Nazi Stormtroopers when Frankie knocked on the hut door.

"What?" The door opened abruptly, and an elderly man with very bad breath stuck his head out. The women took one step back.

"I presume you're the watchman. We're here to exorcise the site," Frankie said. "Mr. Ferguson's secretary should have rung about us."

"The gates are unlocked," the man said, disappearing back inside and shutting the door.

Frankie knocked again.

"What?" Another wave of halitosis passed over like the wind off a marsh in high summer.

"Aren't you going to chain up the dogs?" Frankie asked.

"Not on your life," the man said. "I'm not stupid enough to go near them."

He retreated back inside his hut. Frankie banged insistently on the door, but he responded by turning up the radio.

A small group of workmen gathered in the middle distance, materializing from tatty caravans parked beyond the hut. They stood watching, arms folded.

"This is hopeless," Frankie said in exasperation. "I'll have to go home and get something to knock the animals out."

"No need," Rhian said. "I'm good with dogs. I'll deal with them."

Frankie pointedly looked at one of the dogs trying to gnaw through the wire to get at them, then back at Rhian in exaggerated astonishment.

"I'm Welsh," Rhian said. "You know Wales, lots of sheep, lots of sheepdogs. You stay there."

She pulled open the bolt on the gate and slipped inside the compound.

CHAPTER 8
INCURSION

Jameson was not happy, not happy at all. He was summoned to the seventh floor for a strategy meeting. Strategy meetings were, in Jameson's experience, largely pointless bitching sessions where the main preoccupation was the old bureaucratic game of passing the buck. He was also late. No doubt everybody else would be disgustingly punctual, allowing Randolph to bitch at him.

The lift stopped on the fifth floor. The doors opened with the grind of misaligned rollers to reveal a young man in a blue leather jacket. He jumped in, pressing the button for the ninth. Karla examined him with interest. Jameson recognised the signs. She was bored, and a bored Karla could be a cruel Karla. She was like a cat. Even when not hungry, she liked to toy with her food.

She slid across and stood far too close to the young man, who smiled at her uncertainly. She smiled back, exposing long canines. The young man twitched. He stopped the lift on the sixth and jumped out.

"I think I'll take the stairs," he said, to no one in particular. "The exercise will be good for me."

The doors slid closed.

"You promised to behave," Jameson said, accusingly.

Karla laughed, her teeth now small, neat and white.

"I just played with him a little," she said.

"Well, don't," Jameson said, exiting on the seventh floor.

The conference rooms were large soundproofed glass cubicles. Such horrors were apparently currently fashionable in corporate circles. Jameson yearned for The Commission's old headquarters in Westminster. He recalled fondly the wood-paneled walls and the faint smell of decay and death-watch beetle. The beetles had finally won and the structure had rotted around them. The bean-counters persuaded the Board that it would be more cost effective to move to a new glass tower in Docklands. It was bright, airy, and completely sterile. Jameson spent as little time there as possible.

Everyone else was already in the cubicle.

"Nice of you to join us," said Randolph when they entered.

"Heavy traffic on the A13," Jameson shrugged.

"You could always use public transport," said an elderly, shriveled woman, who gazed at Jameson and Karla with distaste.

"I could also crawl over broken glass if I was really desperate, Miss Arnoux," Jameson said, lightly.

Miss Arnoux was head of Magical Support, the group known to everyone else as The Coven.

"Some of us are busy."

"Sorry, I realize you probably have a cauldron to stir or something."

"I'll have you know—"

"If we can get on," Randolph said, interrupting. "Kendrics?"

"Ah, um, yes."

Kendrics was a geek, who would have been tall if not for his habitual stoop. Dark brown hair erupted from his scalp as if he had been recently wired to a Van der Graaf generator. He rose, revealing brown corded jeans. His jacket, slung over the back of the chair, had bulging pockets. The weight pulled the chair over with a clatter.

Randolph looked at him with studied patience.

"Sorry," Kendrics said.

Karla focused on Kendrics, snapping out of the quiescent mode she tended to adopt in meetings. Her attention did nothing for the hapless geek's inadequate coordination. He righted the chair but was flustered so failed to remove the jacket before letting go. The chair promptly rolled over again.

Karla partially extended her canines.

"Leave it." Randolph snapped, when Kendrics moved to pick up the chair once more.

Randolph glared at Karla, who smiled at him, her teeth now normal. Jameson couldn't stand Randolph, but the man had no fear, or possibly no imagination. He treated Karla with the same supercilious disdain he reserved for all Commission staff. She could kill him, but she could not frighten him. In return, she treated Randolph with casual familiarity. This was a league above the way she regarded most people.

Kendrics scuttled over to the display board and switched it on. A map of London and the Home Counties, the counties immediately around the capital, sprang into view on the lecture screen. A tap on the keyboard caused a number of stars to flash.

"Ah, as you know, there have been an unusually high number of paranormal incidents in the last few months, especially in the London region. We have been plotting them in the Library."

The Library was the Commission's research unit, [so called because it started out as Dr. John Dee's occult library housed in his mother's home in Mortlake.] The house was long since gone, being redeveloped as a brewery. It had an unsavory reputation for unfortunate incidents and bloody awful beer.

Dee's name was an Anglicization of the old Welsh word for black, and Dee had certainly left a dark reputation behind him. Lovecraft claimed that it had been Dee who translated Abdul Alhazred's *Necronomicon* into English. Magical adepts whispered that Dee had done more than merely translate and had used spells from the *Necronomicon* in the service of Queen Elizabeth I and her spymaster, Walsingham, in the secret war against Spain.

Official history certainly records that Dr. Dee worked as a code breaker for Walsingham. It also records that his library, the largest in Europe, was sacked by thieves while Dee traveled across the continent with David Kelly. That was quite untrue. Dee's library, or the more exotic volumes within, was removed by agents working for Walsingham. It became the core of the newly commissioned occult branch of the secret service, now known to a small circle of initiates as The Commission. It was rumored that the Library still had Dee's translation of the *Necronomicon* in a chamber under London heavily sealed against both physical and paranormal intruders. The Commission abounded in rumors, some true and others deliberate misinformation to hide even more horrifying secrets. And some were just rumors.

Kendrics pushed his finger across the laptop's touchpad. The view zoomed in on the most famous river shape in the world, the loop of the Thames.

"The epicenter appears to be in East London," Kendrics said. "You will also notice that incidents increase in severity around Docklands."

He tapped the keypad. The incident stars color coded from green to red through yellow and amber. The greens tended to be in the Home Counties and the reds in East London, loosely circling the Commission's new building.

"Are we under attack?" Randolph asked, rhetorically. "Is it something we are doing, or is unconnected with The Commission at all?"

Miss Arnoux carefully placed her hands on the table and addressed them softly, forcing the others to listen carefully. Jameson thought sourly that it was a cheap rhetorical trick as the old shrew could be loud enough when she wanted.

"London is always a nexus for paranormal activity because of its dense concentration of people, its size, and its long history. It has also been a hub for human activity since the rise of the western world. It is still the primary communication center, the financial center, and the air travel hub between the old and new worlds. In short, London is the center of the human world, or, at least, the bits that matter. That's why world maps always show it in the middle. All that human energy and emotion channeled through one place inevitably attracts attention in the Otherworld."

"I believe Australians print maps with the south uppermost and Australia in the middle," Kendrics said.

"Ah, well, the colonies . . ." said Miss Arnoux.

"Quite," Randolph interrupted, apparently not at all interested in Miss Arnoux's opinion of the colonies.

"The East End is the most magical place in London because it has been a sinkhole of poverty, misery, and human degradation. The emotional energy released attracts paranormal entities and human sensitives, reinforcing a positive feedback loop. The plague pits for London are here, John Wesley preached his first sermon outside the Blind Beggar Pub here, the liberty bell was made here, and Jack the Ripper sacrificed here."

Randolph winced. "Shutting him down was possibly the most

expensive operation in The Commission's long history. We lost almost half our strength. Fortunately, it was easier to suppress information in those days."

"The point is that in East London the barrier between the material world and the Otherworld is weak and easily penetrated," said Miss Arnoux.

"Or, leaving aside the mumbo jumbo, the walls in the multiverse are porous because of so much human information reducing entropic impedance," Kendrics said.

Miss Arnoux looked at him in distaste. The Witches and the Library both saw themselves as the keepers of the true spirit of The Commission. Whereas the Wiccans perceived the paranormal through a spiritual lens, the Library was bang up to date with the worldview of modern physics. Jameson sometimes wondered whether The Commission actively encouraged its various departments to be deeply suspicious of each other as a safety system, divide and rule and all that.

"Okay, we get the point. Cause and effect are difficult to separate. From a field agent's point of view it hardly matters anyway. We just want to shut down whatever's happening before it gets worse," Jameson said, heading off another departmental turf war.

"Bloody elves and dwarves," Jameson said, as an aside to Karla, who smirked.

Elves and dwarves were one of those literary tropes that repeatedly surfaced in real life. Elves were poetic, spiritual, and mystical and dwarves were rational, horny-handed sons of toil who beat metal and built things. Wells used an extreme version of the trope for Eloi and Morlocks in his novel *The Time Machine*. Jameson found it easier to interact with the dwarves but had a horrible suspicion that the elves had the more accurate perspective on what passed for reality.

Randolph shot Jameson a "shut-up" look, but just for a moment the corner of his mouth lifted as if in amusement. Jameson decided he must be seeing things. Randolph famously had no sense of humor.

"And it is getting worse," Kendrics said, unexpectedly. "The incidents are becoming more serious with time. Look at the pattern."

Under Kendrics' control the stars were removed and replaced on the screen in a time sequence. The early ones tended to be green, but red dominated by the end.

At that point, Randolph's phone chimed. "What? Yes. I see."

"There has been another incident, a bad one in broad daylight. The Gamekeepers have been dispatched. The details are being downloaded to your mobile phone."

"We're on our way," said Jameson.

The Jaguar's GPS guided them to a location just off Docklands. It was by a complex of luxury low-rise apartment blocks around Limehouse Basin. The Basin was formerly known as Regent's Canal Dock because it was where ocean-going ships in the Nineteenth Century unloaded into canal boats. The canal gave access from the Thames to the whole British waterway network. Now it was an exclusive waterside development used by pleasure boats coming down from Little Venice.

The brief on Jameson's mobile was singularly unhelpful, noting only that a body had been found and magical incursion was suspected. A police cordon marked off the incident zone. When Jameson drove up, two uniformed policemen moved to intercept him.

"You can't stop there," an officer ordered.

Jameson got out his wallet and selected an ID card which identified him as a Special Branch Commander, the police department responsible for anti-terrorism.

"Let Commander Jameson through, Perkins. Special Branch are a law unto themselves, their mysteries to perform."

The speaker was a middle-aged man in a raincoat and tartan neck scarf. Civilian clothes did nothing to hide the fact that he was police. Inspector Fowler was an old-style Metropolitan copper risen through the ranks by dint of hard graft. He resented everything about Jameson, his car, his accent, his clothes, and his Special Branch Warrant Card. To Fowler, graduate entrants like Jameson lording it over honest coppers were an example of all that was wrong with the modern police force. Of course, Jameson was not a policeman at all but Fowler did not know that. Jameson rather liked the man.

"I wondered when you would show," Fowler said to Jameson.

"Brief me, if you please, who found the corpse?" Jameson asked.

"Not sure if corpse is the right word. Hell of a mess, body bits everywhere," Fowler said. "The victim was ripped to pieces."

"Who found the mess, then?"

"There was a witness, a young woman. She's being interviewed by your people. We did not get much sense out of her. She's bloody hysterical," Fowler said.

Blood splatter marked the scene of the incident in a short alley between two of the developments. A man's black lace-up shoe lay on the paving. Jameson thought that they had already moved the body until he realized the shoe still contained a foot. There was nothing left of the victim bigger than a shoulder of lamb. His entrails were wound around the bollard that blocked the alley to cars.

Karla folded her hands into fists, covering the nails. She inhaled deeply and looked at Jameson, her eyes glittering metallic green in the sunlight. He knew that if she opened her mouth, it would reveal long canines. She was a monster, no less a monster than whatever had torn a man to pieces, but she was his monster. Jameson turned away and examined the bollard. Amongst the gore glittered silver rakes in the iron where the paint had been gouged down to the metal.

"We think the attacker must have used a heavy gardening tool like a scythe or maybe a chainsaw," Fowler said.

"Quite likely," Jameson replied, lying. "Have you identified the victim?"

"We got his name from his car number." Fowler nodded at a silver BMW ZX sports car parked across from the alley. "He was a merchant banker called Henry Fethers, a partner in a small outfit specializing in commodity trading. He was married, two children at public schools, lived in Surrey but has a pied-a-terre in an apartment complex in the Basin. No previous under that name, but we'll have to do a DNA check to be sure."

"Thank you, Inspector, I think that will be all. My people will clear up here. If you'd like to return to your men and maintain the cordon. Keep everyone indoors."

"The SOCOs have not yet examined the evidence," Fowler said, holding his ground.

"My people will carry out such scene-of crime operations as are necessary," Jameson replied.

"Right," Fowler said, between gritted teeth. "Another Goulston Street job."

Fowler was more right than he knew. A piece of bloodied cloth from Catherine Eddowes's apron had been found in Goulston Street on the thirtieth of September, 1888, the night the Ripper killed Elizabeth

Stride as well as Catherine. The official report noted that chalked on the wall above was a line of graffiti that read something like "*The Juwes are the men that will not be blamed for nothing.*"

A number of versions were reported by different witnesses, but all agreed on the basic meaning. All the witnesses lied or were misled. No one will ever prove that as the graffiti was immediately destroyed by Police Superintendent Arnold. Commissioner Warren gave the order, ostensibly to avoid an anti-Semitic race riot. The Library knows what the graffiti really said, but they aren't talking.

"This is clearly a terrorist attack and as such is subject to a DA-Notice," Jameson said.

Fowler nodded and stalked off with the air of a man washing his hands of the business. DA-Notices were such useful things, putting a blanket of secrecy across anything. The threat of decades locked up in one of Her Majesty's less salubrious holiday resorts hung over potential leakers. They were introduced as a temporary measure during the Cold War to protect national security, maintained during the IRA bombing campaigns, and given a new lease on life by Islamic suicide bombers. They were so useful that a reason would always have to be found for keeping them. Fortunately, the tabloid press were easily wound into hysterics by some fashionable menace to use as justification.

"Let's find the Gamekeepers," Jameson said.

Gaston and his team had parked their van behind the victim's Beemer. The van was a large six-wheeled vehicle painted as an ambulance. Jameson knocked on the door and Gaston appeared dressed as a paramedic. Gaston was a black working-class Londoner of West Indian descent, which meant that his only connection with the Dark Continent was an inherited skin color. He had been recruited by The Commission from the Parachute Regiment, whereas Jameson had been a major in the Guards. That meant they understood each other very well, and not necessarily in a good way.

"I wondered when you'd show," Gaston said, making Jameson feel he was listening to an echo. "'Course the Guards were always a bit slow getting in to action despite their Swiss watches."

Gaston was on form today getting in two digs at the Guards in the first few seconds. The first was that the Guards had failed to relieve the Paras at Arnheim, notoriously halting for tea breaks. The second was that the Paras considered the Guards a bunch of rich, incompetent, toffee-nosed, chinless, aristocratic inbreds incapable of reading the time despite owning expensive foreign timepieces.

In return, the Guards took the view that the Parachute Regiment dragged their knuckles on the ground when they walked– and that was only the officer's mess. Of course, both considered the Light Infantry to be farmers with guns who still had straw sticking out of their hair and the Royal Tank Regiment to be sweaty spanner-heads with oily hands. Sometimes Jameson found it surprising that the British Army managed to find any time at all to engage the Queen's enemies.

"The Guards add tone to what would otherwise be a vulgar brawl," Jameson said, loftily.

"Hello Karla," Gaston said, ignoring him.

The two grinned at each other without humor like two rival Mafia Capos at a mob "sit down." Gaston and Karla went back a very long way. Gaston led the Gamekeeper team that captured Karla. He lost a trooper that day. The trooper was not just a colleague but also his girlfriend.

"Where's the witness?" Jameson asked.

"Jane Littlewick, in there," Gaston pointed to the van.

The witness was a petite blonde girl in her early twenties, perched on the edge of a fold-down chair like a bedraggled sparrow on a TV aerial. She was dressed in a smart business suit that showed her legs off to advantage. Unfortunately her tights were splashed in blood, rather spoiling the erotic effect unless you had somewhat unusual tastes. Jameson went through the motions of showing her his Special Branch Warrant Card, but she was white with shock and hardly looked at it.

"What did you see?" Jameson asked, softly.

"Ripped to pieces, he was ripped to pieces," her voice was monotonous, like she had withdrawn her emotions into a ball. She did not react to Karla at all, which was unusual. Karla was normally the first thing people noticed, one way or another. The paramedic with the Gamekeeper team had probably given her a light sedative.

"Start at the beginning, Jane," Jameson said, encouragingly.

"Mister Fethers parked the car and we got out and walked into the alley."

Mister, so she was not his daughter or niece, probably a secretary or personal assistant then.

"You worked for Mister Fethers?" Jameson asked.

"No, I'm a student. He's a client—was a client," she replied after a pause.

Jameson looked at her blankly before the penny dropped. She was an escort girl, a student paying her college fees by upmarket whoring. The hours were short and the pay was good, three hundred pounds an hour and plenty of time to study. That explained the business suit. The girls wore them so as not to attract attention in the expensive hotels where they serviced their clients. Jameson felt in no position to judge her. You all did what you had to and he wished he could forget half of what he had done. Whoring, by comparison, was an honest, victimless trade. That led him to another question.

"Why were you going to his apartment?" Jameson asked. "What made you take the risk? He could have been a psycho."

Hotels were safe because the clients had to book a room with their credit cards.

"He was a regular," she said. "The escort agency knew him."

"I see, go on," Jameson said, encouragingly.

"There was a crash and a clang like a girder hit with a hammer. I jumped and looked around, but there was nothing there. Something had hit the bollard. Paint was gouged off, but there was nothing there," she said dully. "A sudden gust of wind blew dirt in my eyes, so I covered my face with my hands."

She paused.

"Go on," Jameson said.

"Screams, terrible screams, and when I looked his face had gone, ripped off, blood everywhere. He tried to run but it slashed him to pieces. Bit by bit, like they strip meat off a kebab spit. I covered my eyes again for a long time, and when I opened them it was gone, so I phoned the police."

"You keep saying 'it.' What did *it* look like?"

"I told you, there was nothing there. It ripped him to pieces but there was nothing there." Her voice rose to a scream and she stood up, hitting Jameson ineffectually on the chest. A Gamekeeper shoved a needle into her arm and Jameson caught her as she collapsed, lowering her gently to the floor.

"Ripped to pieces by an invisible daemon, just like Abdul Alhazred," Jameson said softly.

"Whatever it was, it's gone," Gaston said.

"Not very far," Karla said, speaking for the first time.

"What?" Jameson asked.

"I can feel it waiting, just outside," she replied. "It's satiated for the moment, but now it knows where there is an open door to food."

"What is it?" Gaston asked.

Karla looked at him and cocked her head.

"A hunter," she said, as if that were obvious.

Karla tended to divide the world into hunters and the hunted, so her reply was not especially informative.

"Gaston, get a combat team ready," Jameson said.

"Yes, Major," Gaston replied.

Jameson fished out his mobile and pressed a key while the Gamekeepers changed into combat uniforms and body armour. It rang twice and then a handshake logo flashed as the phone accepted the encryption code from the exchange in The Commission building.

"Yes," Randolph answered.

"It's a bad one. I need a clean-up team with Coven support. There was an incursion, and there is still a hole, so I'm putting the Gamekeepers on it."

"Understood," Randolph rang off.

The Gamekeepers checked their bolt guns, wide-bore magnetic rail-gun carbines that fired wooden bolts reinforced with steel strips. Jameson fished a similarly shaped pistol out from a holster and examined the power level and ammunition load. They returned to the bollard, trying not to step on body parts. The Gamekeepers took up firing positions.

"One thing puzzled me," Gaston said. "Why did the daemon focus entirely on the man and leave the totty alone?"

Karla stared intently at nothing and gave a soft laugh.

"What?" Jameson asked, deflected from Gaston's observation.

"It knows we're here," she replied.

The air above the bollard shimmered, and mist coalesced. The wind pulled it into white tendrils. Jameson felt a sudden chill. Something sucked entropy out of the alley. He slipped the safety off his gun. There was a whine of charging capacitors, and a green light came on indicating it was live.

Karla smiled at Jameson, showing long fangs. "It's coming," she said, happily.

"Sarn't?" Jameson asked.

"Sir!"

"Stay here with your men and shoot anything unusual that comes into the alley. See if you can illuminate it with ultraviolet torches."

"Unusual, right," Gaston said. "An invisible unusual."

"After you, Karla," Jameson said.

"You're not going in after it?" Gaston asked.

Karla looked puzzled. "Of course, how else do we hunt it down?"

"Is this a good idea, major?" Gaston asked.

"Probably not, but it may be visible in the Otherworld," Jameson said.

He was rationalizing. Karla would hunt the daemon, and he would support her. What else could he do? On her own, she could get hurt and that would be intolerable. If he went with her the worst that could happen was that they both died, and who would miss him? Hell, he wouldn't even miss himself.

CHAPTER 9
THE POLTERGEIST

Frankie yelped and made a grab for her, but Rhian was too quick. The dogs stood nonplussed. Their body language said this could not be really happening. You threatened humans and they ran, or screamed, or both.

Rhian focused on the wolf within and began to growl softly in her throat. The dogs responded by moving to surround her, showing their teeth and snarling. Rhian felt the wolf's amusement at the challenge. It surged within her, the growl in her throat deepening into a rumble. The dogs dropped their tails and cringed, ears back. Rhian took a step towards them and they broke, scuttling off to hide in a far corner of the compound.

Rhian laughed, but it sounded almost like a howl of victory. She pushed the wolf down, soothing it back to sleep. There was a collected sigh from the watching workers.

"You can come in now," Rhian said.

Frankie shut the gate carefully behind her, bolting it with a sharp clang.

"You are full of surprises, honey, aren't you?"

"I said I was good with dogs," Rhian said, grinning and lifting her hands palm up.

"How are you with boxes?" Frankie dropped the cardboard box onto Rhian's hands.

Frankie strode around the building site, her long loose skirt whipping around her legs. She stopped every so often, now stretching her arms out like a sleepwalker in a silent movie, now putting both palms flat on her head like a TV psychic. Rhian sighed and followed. She was prepared to believe Frankie did have magical powers, but was it really necessary to ham it up like this? Sometimes the woman could be so embarrassing.

It was hot on the site, and the air smelt dry. The box became heavier in Rhian's arms. Haphazard breaths of wind swirled cement dust around her feet, occasionally lifting it into her face. She fancied she could taste the quicklime and wished she had thought to bring a bottle of lemonade with her. They walked up and down between half-built brick houses supported by scaffolding.

A sharp noise made Rhian jump. A blue plastic cement bag hooked over the top of a steel rod whipped in the wind, slapping against a concrete pylon with repetitive cracks. Frankie picked up some dust and threw it into the air, watching it sparkle in the sunlight.

"The place is haunted," Frankie said. "There are magical traces all over."

"So we are talking ghost?" Rhian asked.

"Don't sound so skeptical," Frankie said. "We are talking poltergeist; although the word literally means noisy ghost."

"But definitely things that go bump in the night?" Rhian asked.

"Or day," Frankie replied. "Most poltergeists are faked by attention-seeking adolescents. Sometimes they can be the result of raw psychokinetic energy from troubled people. In this case, I think we have something more serious. I suspect there is a leakage of power from the Otherworld. The barrier here has become thin and porous. I suppose you could call it a ghost."

"Oh, a hole!" Rhian said. "That sounds worrying. What causes that?"

"A natural event that releases a storm of violent emotion, like a murder. Of course, holes can be deliberately opened by the right magic."

She flashed Rhian a quick smile. "Don't look so anxious honey. It's easily fixed."

She took the box from Rhian and knelt down to set up her equipment, which included a small gas camping stove. She lit it with a battery-powered electric spark and placed a small metal bowl on top. Frankie waited until it glowed red hot.

"The trick is to seal the holes," Frankie said. She chanted and sprinkled herbs into the bowl. They crinkled and browned, releasing acrid fumes into the air.

Rhian noticed that the wind had dropped. The cement bag drooped silently from the scaffolding. The air hung hot and still like the prelude to a massive electrical storm. A trickle of sweat ran down Rhian's face. Nothing moved except Frankie, and her voice seemed to recede, muffled as if far away. A tiny dust devil barely a meter high danced across the ground, picking up cement dust. It spun into the shade of a wall and collapsed in a puff of smoke like something from a stage magician's act.

It was not the first dust devil Rhian had seen since coming to London, but she still found them fascinating. She had never encountered one in Wales. It was too windy there, but conditions were favourable in the low, flat Thames basin. Another dust devil appeared, then a third. More sprang up until she was surrounded by them.

Frankie's voice strengthened as if a veil had lifted. The brick walls of the half-finished buildings shimmered and faded, collapsing into themselves. They reformed into mudbanks and reeds. Frankie clicked into sharp focus, kneeling in long grass. The sky was so large. Rhian could see to the horizon in each direction. Pools and streams were everywhere, scattered between grassy hillocks and reeds beds. Frankie chanted and burnt her herbal mix, seemingly oblivious to the transformation.

"Frankie?" Rhian asked. "Is this supposed to happen?"

She got no answer. Frankie did not even seem to have heard the question.

Dust devils danced across the flat landscape. They were bigger than on the building site, many two or three meters high. One strayed over a pool, sucking up cold water and collapsing in a localized shower of rain. The whirlwinds danced around Rhian and Frankie, colliding and merging. The resulting amalgamations spun with greater energy and were darker and more solid. Eventually, there was only one. It curved slowly in towards the women.

"Frankie," Rhian said again, shaking the woman's shoulder without response.

Rhian watched the dust devil suspiciously. She fancied she could see a face in the wind, an old woman, a hag. She heard the whirlwind, heard mad laughter and a creaking voice.

"At last, at last, a sister, a vessel!"

Rhian stood on four legs and the world was monochrome.

Rhian was the wolf, morphing instantly without pain, Rhian one moment and the wolf the next. She did not have time to consider the simplicity of the transformation. The dust devil sucked mud from the ground, spraying it into the air. It stuck together, becoming first a pillar, then a dirt-encrusted figure. The dust devil collapsed but the figure remained.

It moved. Mud flaked off with every step to expose a walking corpse. Rhian had seen bodies in the British Museum that were natural mummies, desiccated and blackened by the dry Egyptian desert. This thing looked like them. Strands of hair that still showed a definite ginger hue trailed from its emaciated skull. Not just a walking corpse but a walking ginga corpse.

Frankie knelt transfixed, so the wolf gave her a heavy nudge with her snout. It seemed to wake Frankie up and she looked in horror at the wolf and gave a little cry. The wolf licked her face, startling Frankie even more. From her expression, she could not have been more astonished if the wolf had given an impromptu performance of "Singing in the Rain" with a brolly clutched between her jaws.

"Rhian?" Frankie glanced around, but, apart from her, there was only the advancing corpse and the wolf.

The wolf made a small, whining croon, like a wolf mother to a cub, and licked Frankie's face again. Frankie pushed her off. "Yuk!"

"Rhian, is that you?" Frankie asked the wolf.

Rhian wondered if she expected an answer. The wolf looked meaningfully at the corpse and growled. The mummy sped up, its gait smoothing as if it was relearning how to walk.

"I guess you are the wolf," Frankie said, "but what is that?"

She adjusted her glasses and examined the corpse, which had broken into a shambling jog-trot.

"Oh Goddess, it's *that* sort of poltergeist," Frankie said in alarm.

She held both hands out and began to chant. Blue light flickered around her fingers, thickening and spreading as she sang. She pushed at the light and it drifted forward, forming a transparent shield between them and the corpse. A withered claw touched the light and recoiled as if it was electrified. The mummified thing laughed, a dry, cackling, wheezy sort of sound.

"Is that the best you can do, sister?" it asked, voice like a creaking door.

It raised a withered hand and ran a finger like a claw down the blue light, splitting it in two. The halves fell away, dissolving into the swamp. The water flickered and fizzed with blue froth.

"Bugger," Frankie said. "It wants me, not you, Rhian, so save yourself and run. Tell The Commission, tell Jameson."

Frankie kept her eyes on the corpse.

The Rhian part of the wolf wondered where the hell she would run to and what The Commission was. Frankie had clearly enunciated capital letters. She was reluctant to leave her friend and the wolf agreed. You did not leave a pack mate to a predator; even, especially, a weedy pack mate like Frankie. The wolf defended what was hers. To flee was foreign to her nature.

The wolf covered the distance to the corpse in a single bound. The monster reacted with astonishing speed for a dead, mummified thing. It slapped the wolf around the head, rolling her over. The corpse promptly ignored the wolf, reorienting on Frankie. Such monomania was not only rude but bloody stupid. The wolf bounced to its feet and charged, knocking the corpse head first into a pond. The wolf seized its shoulder. It was like biting into a tire except that the flesh tasted leathery.

The corpse twisted and lashed out with its free arm, hitting the wolf in the shoulder with a punch like a pile driver. Something cracked and the wolf snarled. Her left front leg hurt when she put her weight on it. The corpse cackled in delight, regained its feet, and reached out.

The wolf feinted a leap but slid under the grasping arms so that the corpse was left hugging itself like a disappointed child. Rhian had an urge to giggle, but it came out as a snarl.

While the corpse looked stupidly at its empty embrace, the wolf pivoted on her hind legs. Rearing up to place her good front paw in the small of the monster's back, she pushed with her whole body weight. She forced the corpse back down into the mud. Then she jumped on it.

The wolf bit deep into the hole in the corpse's shoulder until her teeth scraped bone. She clamped her jaws shut and shook her head. Her powerful neck muscles ripped out the corpse's shoulder joint. The monster hissed and swung its good arm. This time the wolf anticipated the blow, jumping clear.

The corpse's left arm dangled uselessly on strips of dried muscle. The wolf sprang and took the corpse by the throat as it tried to get up. They tumbled over together and the wolf mauled and tore until the corpse's head came off.

The monster lay in three pieces. The clawed fist on the torn-off arm opened and shut convulsively. The detached head glowered helplessly at the wolf. The body pushed itself up to its knees, using its remaining arm. Steam hissed from its wounds. It thickened to grey vapor that rolled off the corpse in clouds like the smoke from a bonfire of wet leaves. It covered the wolf causing sensory deprivation. Rhian's personality dissolved in the swirling vapor like sugar in hot tea.

Cold rain lashed Rhian's face, falling from a dark and overcast sky. She was human again, but she was dressed. Her clothes were wet but otherwise unharmed. There was no pain, no real pain, that is. Her left arm hurt but that was nothing compared to the usual agony of transformation.

Rhian looked around in bewilderment. Lightning lit up her surroundings, and she saw she was back on the building site. Thunder crashed immediately after the flash, and she smelt ozone. The storm must be right overhead. The air was alive with static charge, causing fine hairs on her arms to ripple.

"Come on," Frankie said.

Rhian jumped. The woman was right behind her, clutching the cardboard box, which was already bedraggled and starting to collapse.

"Come on."

Frankie grabbed Rhian's arm, the wrong one. Rhian gave a little cry.

"So the wolf was actually you and not an avatar," Frankie. "We need to talk, but not here."

They raced back to the car, Frankie tossing her box into the back.

She was intercepted by one of the workers as she slid behind the old-fashioned oversized steering wheel.

"Wise-lady, it's fixed? The *duch* is gone?"

"It will be," Frankie replied. "Tomorrow, the ghost will be gone tomorrow."

The Pole nodded, crossing himself in the Catholic tradition.

Frankie's ancient car mercifully started first time. They drove in silence for some time until Rhian spoke.

"Where were we exactly and how did we get there?"

"That was the Otherworld. As to how we got there, I suspect it was my fault. I accidentally triggered a gate, but I don't understand why it took that form. If I'm right about the source, then the Otherworld should have looked like some version of nineteenth-century London. Do you have an explanation?" Frankie asked.

She darted a quick look at Rhian.

"I've seen it before," Rhian admitted, "in my dreams of Roman and Celtic warriors."

"I see. I suppose that was the Otherworld shadow of the Thames Estuary in Roman Britain. Celtic warriors suggest the time of the conquest in the first century AD," Frankie said. "And are you a wolf in your dreams, Rhian?"

"Sometimes," Rhian said. "And sometimes a Celtic Queen who turns into a wolf."

"How do you know she's Celtic?" Frankie asked.

"Because she speaks Welsh," Rhian said, simply.

"Of course," Frankie said, softly to herself. "The Queen is Celtic and speaks Welsh, just like you, Rhian."

"English is my first language," Rhian said, defensively. "We spoke Welsh at school."

"And have you turned into a wolf before?" Frankie asked.

Rhian had been expecting, and dreading, the question. She decided to tell the truth, or so much of it that was relevant. She was so tired of running and hiding, and surely Frankie would understand. The woman was a bloody witch, after all.

"Yes," Rhian said, tightly.

"In the real world?"

"Yes."

There was a long silence.

"Why did the monster call you sister?" Rhian asked, more to fill the gap in the conversation than because she cared about the answer.

"Witches often call each other sister," Frankie replied. "The monster was a poltergeist, but a rather special one. Did you know some poltergeists can take over human beings?"

"Really?" Rhian replied.

"Really!" Frankie said. "There is a rather nasty type called a *litesch*. A witch can extend her life way beyond the normal span by stealing bodies. The magic suppresses the victim's spirit and overlays it with the witch's. It's like reprograming the chip on a credit card with a new identity, so I'm told."

"That's . . ." Rhian said.

"Bloody wicked, yes, but all professions have their black sheep."

The Morris car jerked. Frankie let the revs fall too low while climbing a ramp onto a flyover. She changed down into third far too late and lost more speed until that gear was also too high. She finally got it into second with a grinding screech of protest from the gearbox. A crash of metal from behind added to the cacophony. Rhian twisted her head to see. A white van was welded to the back of a hatchback that must have braked sharply on the wet road to avoid hitting the Morris. Frankie drove on, oblivious of the carnage.

"Of course the new body also dies, and the witch has to take over another. Each time, it gets a little more difficult as the witch's spirit weakens with each transfer. It's a bit like making photocopies of photocopies with the quality decaying every time."

"So spirits are analog, not digital," Rhian said.

"What?" Frankie asked, turning around to look at Rhian. Mildred drifted towards the crash barrier.

"Nothing," Rhian replied, gripping her seat belt.

Frankie turned back in time to correct the drift before they hit.

"Eventually the transfer fails and the witch is trapped in a decaying corpse."

"There was nothing weak about that lightswitch," Rhian said, struggling over the unfamiliar word.

"*Litesch*," Frankie said. "But you're right. Something is very wrong in East London. Magic is getting stronger and the Otherworld is intruding."

The women sat in silence.

"How long have you been able to turn into a wolf?" Frankie asked.

"Not long," Rhian replied.

"Could you do it before you came to East London?"

"Yes," Rhian replied.

"That scotches one theory. Your—issues—can't be connected to current events," Frankie said, carefully choosing her words. "Come on, honey, open up. I don't know what questions to ask. You are not a witch and you would have set off all sorts of alarms at my flat if you were a werewolf. Why don't you just tell me your story?"

Rhian's head was awhirl. Where to start? The brooch was the start. She pulled out her pendant.

"You see this?"

Frankie took one hand off the thin spoked steering wheel of the Morris and leaned over to look. The car drifted towards the right hand side of the road until a blare of horn from an oncoming car alerted Frankie and she swerved back into the correct lane.

"That looks like a Celtic brooch. Is it real?" Frankie asked.

"Yes."

"You got it in Wales?"

Rhian shook her head.

"West London. I found it on an archaeological site near the Thames. Something made me conceal it. I suppose you could say that I stole it. James put it on a chain for me to wear as a pendant."

"James is the boyfriend who left you."

"Yes," Rhian said.

There was a long pause.

"Sorry, honey, I started asking questions again, and you don't like questions. Why don't you just tell me in your own words?"

"James left me because he's dead and I was responsible for his death." Tears welled up.

"There's a box of tissues in the glove compartment," Frankie said, gently.

Rhian dried her eyes and blew her nose.

"A speculator wanted to build on the location. He bribed the archaeologist in charge of the preconstruction check to downplay evidence of ancient artifacts. James and I were part of a protest group occupying the site. We did the night shift on our own, and the speculator sent in a gang of thugs to burn us out. James would have run if I hadn't been there, but I was, and he tried to protect me. After they killed him, they hit me. My blood splashed on the brooch. I remember it glittering in the moonlight."

Rhian stopped.

"I begin to see," Frankie said. "Is the brooch dedicated to Morgana?"

Rhian nodded.

"The Celtic goddess of the Moon and of shapeshifters," Frankie said, mostly to herself. "Your blood, your Welsh Celtic blood, and moonlight together on the brooch. And you were in a state of high emotion. You transformed into a wolf, right?"

Rhian nodded again.

"And the wolf attacked the thugs?" Frankie asked.

"Ripped them to pieces. The police thought they had been attacked by a pack of feral dogs," Rhian said, unemotionally. "I had the power to protect James but all I did was stand there and watch him die."

"Not your fault, Rhian. How were you to know? And it would have created complications for you if you had deliberately used the wolf—magic—as a weapon to kill. But it was all an accident, and intent is everything in magic."

There was a pause.

"What aren't you telling me, honey?" Frankie finally asked.

"The property speculator," Rhian replied. "He, um, died."

"I see," Frankie said, quietly. "You used the wolf."

Rhian remembered. She stood naked in the car park in the moonlight. The speculator called her a mad bitch. She cut herself and let the blood drip on Morgana's brooch. He ran for his car, but who can outrun a wolf? She pushed down the thought.

"So my soul is stained, I suppose," Rhian said.

"Something like that," Frankie said, vaguely.

"Eight words the Wiccan Rede fulfil, an ye harm none do what ye will," Rhian said.

"I see you've been reading my books," Frankie said. "Doreen Valiente, I suppose?"

"Yes," Rhian said.

"Don't worry about it, Rhian. The Wiccan Rede is less a rule than a set of guidelines."

"And you've been watching Johnny Depp," Rhian accused.

"He is rather cute," Frankie cooed.

Rhian opened her mouth but Frankie talked over her.

"It does make it more difficult to cure your problem," Frankie said. "You bonded with the wolf spirit with that killing. I would guess that you do not need blood or moonlight, or even the pendant to transform now."

"No, I wear the pendant to remember James, but the wolf is always with me."

"I am amazed that you weren't ripped apart, or stuck as a wolf. Body transformation in the real world is tricky, especially if you've no control over the magic."

"It hurts like hell," Rhian admitted.

"Does that Celtic warrior queen you dream about have a name?" Frankie asked.

"Her warriors call her *Buddug*," Rhian replied.

It was dark by the time they reached Tower Hamlets Cemetery because they had to go via Frankie's lockup to pick up some things. She was being mysterious and refused to answer Rhian's questions. She parked Mildred illegally on a double yellow line.

"You'll get clamped," Rhian said.

"No, I won't," Frankie said.

She pulled a card out of the door pocket on the driver's side and put it on the dashboard.

"Some sort of magic device?" Rhian asked.

"Of the most powerful type," Frankie replied. "It's a Disabled Driver Parking Permit, letting me park anywhere. I sort of forgot to return it when I left The Commission."

"Your employer forged disabled parking permits?" Rhian asked, feeling a little shocked.

"That was the least of their sins," Frankie replied with a snort.

Frankie walked swiftly into the cemetery. She flicked an electric torch from tree to tree until she found one that suited. Taking a knife shaped like a small dagger, she cut down the end of a branch.

"Yew, the witching tree," Frankie said, answering Rhian's unspoken question.

She brushed aside all further questions from Rhian, saying nothing until she stopped at a gravestone. Rhian noticed it was aligned at right angles to the other graves. Frankie indicated that Rhian should keep back.

"So, sister, the vicar who buried you had good reason to fear you leaving your grave," Frankie said, pulling boxes and her little paraffin stove out of a rucksack.

She placed the stove on the grave and lit it. Rhian noticed that she was careful not to touch the grave itself.

"I probably woke you when I touched your gravestone. I created a link between us that you could use. I wonder what happened on that building site to make that the contact point. Was that where you took your last body before the transfer failed? I don't suppose you will satisfy my curiosity, and it probably doesn't matter. Maybe it was simply that the wall was thin there."

"The corpse thing was Ethel the witch?" Rhian asked.

"Oh yes," Frankie replied. "Who else could it be?"

"But she's dead now, surely? The wolf killed her."

"The wolf—you—stopped her taking over my body, but you can't kill a spirit. You can, however, banish her from the world."

Rhian shut up and let Frankie get on with it. Her understanding of reality was undergoing another transformation. Witches, spirits, spells, the Otherworld, all seemed utterly unreal but she had seen them all. And she was possessed, never forget the wolf.

"It must have been a shock when the transfer failed and you found yourself in a rotting corpse, Ethel," Frankie said, conversationally, as she worked. "Must have driven you quite out of your mind. Not that a *litesch* is exactly sane in the first place. It was always going to happen eventually. You must have known that?"

Frankie sprinkled herbal mixes into the stove. They burnt with a hiss, sparking and popping with sharp cracks. Vapor rolled off, not like smoke but more like a mist, spilling and pooling around the grave.

"The magic flowing around London brought you back and I woke you. That makes you my responsibility, my problem. There are enough black marks on my soul without adding to them by leaving you awake."

Frankie raised her arms and chanted in a language Rhian did not recognise. She added more herbs to the stove, all the time talking to the grave.

"You found a hole and tried to possess the Polish worker's body. Still didn't work, did it? He was able to kill himself, just to keep you out.

You must have despaired, but then I arrived. You already had a link to me, and I started an exorcism spell that let you yank me right into the Otherworld. There you could draw on unlimited power to make the transition into my body. You did not expect Rhian, though, did you, sister? Got more than you bargained for, hmmm?"

Frankie began to chant again. Her face looked daemonic, red light from the stove under her casting shadows in all the wrong places. The air was still with the static charge that Rhian was beginning to associate with magic. The mist swirled around the grave, illuminated by the flickering red flames. It spun faster and faster and began to rise into the air in a column not unlike a twister.

"So there you are, sister," Frankie said. "Nice of you to join us."

Rhian had expected the acrid wet-bonfire smell of burning herbs, but the vapor smelt more like a decaying corpse. The stench thickened until Rhian had to fight down the urge to gag. Frankie gripped the yew branch.

"*Combustio frigus,*" she shouted.

The yew branch caught fire, burning with strong green flames. Frankie thrust it into the column of mist. The grave writhed.

"*Abire,*" Frankie shouted, "*abire.*"

The branch fizzed and crackled, lighting the mist in green. There was a hollow scream that faded up into the night sky, and the column collapsed. A cloud occluded the Moon and the green flames died. The gravestone shattered in a sharp explosion, into shards that exploded in their turn. And so on until there was nothing but gravel and dust. Rhian held her hands in front of her face to protect her eyes.

Gravestones split and fell around them in a ripple that spread out in a circle from the grave. Deep in the bushes, a mausoleum collapsed in on itself.

Eventually there was silence.

"Whoops," Frankie said.

The next morning Rhian took a bus ride up to the Tesco Express to get in the shopping. They were out of bread, milk, and almost everything required for a civilized life. Frankie would be in a foul mood all day if she missed breakfast. The woman had been still asleep when Rhian let herself quietly out of their flat.

The spells had exhausted Frankie, so the trip home from the

cemetery in Mildred had been even scarier than usual. Magic seemed to drain the woman of something vital, and yesterday she had cast some amazing spells. Rhian smiled to herself. It took something very special these days for her to class it as amazing.

She walked around the supermarket, selecting items. It was surreal but calming to be occupied in so ordinary a task in a mundane world. She bypassed the queues for the tills by going to the autocheckouts. Putting her basket on the balance, she tapped the touch-sensitive screen to activate the barcode reader.

The first item worked all right, and she dropped it in the plastic carrier bag that measured the weight transfer. The computerized till beeped to itself in a self-satisfied sort of way as it ran up the sale. However, the second item took a few goes before the reader acknowledged its existence, despite Rhian turning her purchase at different angles. When she tried to put the third item through, the machine went into a sulk. A sales assistant responded to the computer's frantic complaints by putting her security key in the slot to shut it up.

"I need to verify your age if you want to buy alcohol," said the assistant.

"I am trying to buy milk," Rhian said, showing the assistant the plastic container.

"It says alcohol here," the assistant said, pointing to the screen.

"It's milk," Rhian said firmly.

The assistant peered at it and in her carrier bag, reluctant to believe that the holy of holies, the computer, could be in error. She punched a few keys on the touch-sensitive screen to reset the system and passed the milk through herself. It registered perfectly.

"You must have done something wrong," the assistant said, accusingly. "I will watch while you put the next item through."

Rhian gritted her teeth and put the next item over the barcode reader. It beeped, paused, and all hell broke out. The screen flickered, flashing through menu options faster and faster while emitting a string of noises like a toy robot. Rhian stepped back in alarm when she saw a thin trickle of smoke curl out of the back. There was a loud bang and all the automatic tills shut down, followed by the manned checkouts and lights.

Then the water sprinklers went off.

◑

It was lunchtime when Rhian got home, clutching her modest bag of groceries. A new edition of the local free paper was jammed in the letter box. The lead story was about vandalism in the Tower Hamlets Cemetery. Frankie was up but still in her dressing gown. She was absorbed in one of her ancient books, a mug of milkless tea cooling beside her.

"You're wet. Is it raining?" Frankie asked, vaguely.

"No," Rhian replied, curtly.

"You've bought some milk?" Frankie asked. "Wonderful, and some bread, you lifesaver."

"Sorry I was so long," Rhian said, flopping down in her chair. "The entire electrical system in Tesco's went haywire and I had to use a Waitrose. Cost a bit more, I'm afraid."

"Ah," Frankie said, in a tone that was a bit too carefully neutral.

Rhian looked at her suspiciously. "You know something?"

"Um, maybe. You didn't touch one of their computers, did you?" Frankie asked.

"No," Rhian replied, then thought about it. "Well, only their self-service till."

"Which is a computer, connected to all their other computers," Frankie said. "You have been in the Otherworld and so will be soaked in magic. It tends to bugger up digital systems. Apparently it's something to do with quantum mechanics and the Heisenberg Uncertainty Principle, whatever that is. Sorry, I should have warned you."

Now she thought about it, Rhian realised that Frankie did not own a computer, or anything electronic more complicated than a basic phone.

"I work as a barmaid, Frankie. Pubs have electronic tills," Rhian said.

"The effect will quickly wear off," Frankie said with a smile. "It's not as if *you* are a witch."

She poured some milk in her tea and took a satisfying sip.

"I've been doing a little digging," Frankie said, gesturing at the book. "This warrior queen you dream about, are you sure she was called *Buddug*?"

Rhian nodded.

"Do you know who Buddug was?" Frankie asked, mysteriously.

Rhian shook her head. "It sounds a bit like the Welsh word for victory. I suppose you could call her Victoria in English."

"Possibly," Frankie said, "but Tacitus called her Boudicca and the Victorian English Boadicea. I think scholars currently call her Boudica."

"I know about her," Rhian said excitedly. "She was the Queen of the Iceni who fought the Romans in the days when the Welsh ruled Britain."

"She did more than fight them," Frankie said. "She nearly drove them out of Britain altogether. She annihilated the Ninth Legion, the *Hispana*. Only the general and his cavalry escort survived by legging it. She burnt Colchester, St Albans, and London to the ground, slaughtering eighty thousand Romans and British Quislings. The Roman procurator in London was so shit-scared he did not stop running until he reached France. It was touch and go whether the Romans could hold the province. The Roman general Suetonius Paulinus kept his nerve and blocked the crossroads where the Fosse Way met Watling Street with two legions. He won a famous victory, which is why we are having this conversation in English rather than Welsh."

Frankie grinned at Rhian, who ignored her. The bloody English only got more arrogant if you encouraged them.

"It has always been a bit of a mystery how Boudica possessed so much influence over the British that she could recruit an army of thirty or forty thousand warriors. The Celts were not exactly hot on feminism. Now we know the answer. If she could turn into a wolf, they would consider her Morgana's instrument and beloved of the Gods. It would explain why the commander of the Ninth ran away. Roman generals weren't noted for fleeing, but you can't fight the Gods."

Frankie paused to partake of more tea and picked up a book.

"Dio has a description of Boudica, who he describes as more intelligent than is usual with women. Cheeky sod, typical male sexist pig, it's amazing how nothing changes. I was in the bank last month and . . ."

"Dio?" Rhian asked. Frankie was quite capable of holding forth for some time on the subject of male failings. Her abandonment by her partner, Pete, had cut deep.

"The Roman historian Dio described Boudica as tall, having long red hair, with a piercing gaze and harsh voice."

"She sounds a charmer," Rhian said. "Very few modern Welsh are gingas. We are normally brunette."

"The Iceni were Belgae, or Southern English, as we now call them. Modern Welsh are descended from tribes like the Silures, who were dark-haired even in Roman times. But her hair color doesn't matter. It's her clothes that are interesting. Dio said she wore a thick outdoor cloak over a many-colored tunic. The cloak was attached by a Celtic brooch dedicated to Morgana and depicting a wolf's head. Could I see your pendant, Rhian?"

Rhian passed it over.

Frankie held it in one hand and rubbed the other across its surface, tracing out the letters and design. Rhian felt uneasy watching someone else touch Morgana's brooch, James' pendant. It seemed wrong somehow.

"I never thought I would hold Boudica's brooch," Frankie said, wonder in her voice.

She became more businesslike. "It currently feels magically inert. I thought it would be, or the wards guarding my flat would go off every time you came in."

"It isn't always inert. It has burnt people who try to touch it uninvited."

"People?" Frankie asked. "I can't be certain without carrying out destructive testing but I think this is a shiffoth."

Rhian must have looked as blank as she felt because Frankie hurried to explain.

"A shiffoth is a powerful magical device connecting the wearer to the Otherworld for a variety of possible purposes. In this case it attracts a wolf spirit that allows the wearer to become a wolf daemon. The idea is that the spirit flows back to the Otherworld through the shiffoth when the user has finished with it. It's like a radio, a transmitter and receiver for spiritual energy. The problem is that you triggered it accidentally. You had none of the warding talismans that the original owner would have used. The wolf did not return to the Otherworld and so is within you all the time. I'm amazed you survived the transformation and that you are not permanently a wolf."

"The shapeshift was not pleasant," Rhian said. "It still isn't."

Frankie examined the pendant. "I'd guess your Welsh heritage offered some protection. This is a Celtic artifact that would have incorporated Druidic blood magic. Ever wondered why the Romans took so long to invade Britain or why they had such difficulty holding it down when Julius Caesar conquered Gaul so easily?"

"I never gave it much thought," Rhian replied. A nice lady, Frankie, but inclined to lecture. It was best to let her get to the point in her own way.

"The Druids were taken by surprise in Gaul by the sheer speed and power of the Roman Army. They were destroyed before they could react in France, but they had time to organize a defence in Britain. It is hardly a coincidence that both of Caesar's invasions in 54 and 55 BC were stopped by storms smashing up his fleets. The Emperor Caligula's invasion was aborted when he went off his head at Boulogne and ordered his soldiers to collect seashells. Even Claudius' troops initially mutinied when massed for the invasion. None of this happened by chance but by powerful magics. The Romans hated and feared the Druids for their human sacrifices, and quite right too. Blood magic is always nasty. Some of the things The Commission found buried in Anglesey . . ."

Frankie shook her head like a wet dog shaking water off its fur. The horror in her eyes suggested that she was trying to shake off memories. Rhian knew it wouldn't work. Memories could not be disposed of so easily.

"The Isle of Anglesey, in Wales?" Rhian asked.

"Yah," Frankie replied. "Druidism was the only religion that the Romans utterly destroyed. They were a pragmatic people mostly about their subjects' religions but Druidic magic was something else. Have you never wondered why the Roman Republic collapsed after subjugating Gaul, and all the early rulers of the subsequent Empire went mad?"

"Can't say I have," Rhian replied, suppressing a smile.

"Watch *I Claudius*," Frankie said. "Anyway, the center of Druidism was at Mona, the Isle of Anglesey."

"But how does this relate to my pendant?" Rhian asked, wishing Frankie would get to the point.

"I am coming to that." Frankie said. "The Romans invaded Britain in 43 to destroy the Druids. By AD 60, General Suetonius Paulinus was in a position for the final strike on Mona. The Roman historian Tacitus described the invasion. Listen to this."

Frankie pushed her glasses back on her nose and began to read out loud.

"On the shore stood the opposing army with its phalanx of armed warriors, while between the ranks dashed women, in black attire like the Furies, with hair disheveled, waving brands. All around, the Druids, lifting up their hands to heaven, and pouring forth dreadful curses, scared our soldiers by the unfamiliar sight, so that, as if their limbs were paralyzed, they stood motionless, and exposed to wounds. Then urged by their general's appeals and mutual encouragements not to quail before a troop of frenzied women, they bore the standards onwards, striking down all resistance, and wrapped the foe in the flames of his own brands. A force was next set over the conquered, and their groves, devoted to inhuman superstitions, were destroyed. They deemed it indeed a duty to cover their altars with the blood of captives and to consult their deities through human entrails."

"Yuk!" Rhian said.

"Quite," Frankie replied, primly. "And this is where Boudica comes in. She led the massive revolt against the Romans in 60 AD. It was supposed to be timed to protect Mona by drawing off the Roman Army, but she was too late. Suetonius Paulinus was just too quick. The Druids always underestimated the speed of a Roman advance because they were not used to dealing with professional armies. Mona was destroyed and Boudica's rebellion doomed to fail, but it was a close-run thing. That brooch of yours was made by the Druids as a weapon for Boudica."

"This history lesson is all jolly interesting, but how does it help me?" Rhian asked, trying not to be curt with Frankie but getting increasing impatient with her academic flow.

"Don't you see, Rhian? Now I understand how the brooch was made, I can modify it to ease the transformation process so it is less painful," Frankie said.

"Oh," Rhian replied, feeling a little foolish.

"I bet the transformation was much easier in the Otherworld," Frankie said.

Rhian nodded. "And I got to keep my clothes."

"Yesss," Frankie said, pursing her lips as she drew out the word.

Rhian knew Frankie was thinking of Max and felt her cheeks burning, which was ridiculous. She hadn't done anything with him.

Frankie smiled. "That is just a question of including them in the transformation. I can tweak the spell."

Rhian took a deep breath and when she spoke it took a special effort to keep her voice calm and even. "Is there no way to transfer the wolf back into the pendant permanently?"

"You created a strong bond between the wolf spirit and your soul when you deliberately used the shiffoth to kill," Frankie said gently.

Guilt washed over Rhian. Not a new feeling, but not one that got any better either.

"I hadn't used any magic," Rhian protested. "It just happened when my blood covered the brooch in the moonlight."

"Yes, the power of human blood. Boudica's brooch was created by Celtic blood magic, so it was triggered by your blood, as you intended," Frankie said. "The wolf spirit is locked deep within you. You appear entirely human, but it's there."

"So the magic can't be reversed," Rhian said, blinking back tears.

"Not easily. I can't banish the wolf," Frankie said. "The Commission witches could; in fact The Commission would insist upon it if they discovered you. That's their job, you see, plugging holes in reality."

"Then I can escape the wolf?" Rhian asked.

"Oh, yes," Frankie replied. "But there is a catch."

"Like what?" Rhian asked.

"The spell will kill you."

CHAPTER 10
THE HUNTER

It was always different. Sometimes the transition into the Otherworld was so gradual that one was hard pressed to define where the change occurred. Other times it was like stepping through a door from one universe to another. This was one of the latter times.

Jameson walked through a gloomy forest of dead, rotting trees. The stink of decay thickened the air to the point where he could taste the rot. The boggy ground squelched with every step. He held the bulky bolt pistol double-handed, close to his chest. This was the ready stance developed by Churchill's Special Operations Executive in World War II. He rotated through three-hundred-sixty degrees, gun ready, but nothing moved. Where the hell was Karla?

She tapped him on the shoulder with a clawed hand, laughing at his alarm.

"Don't do that," Jameson said. "I could have shot you."

Karla laughed again, eyes flashing emerald with delight. She was a hunter; she lived for the chase, for the kill. Jameson found himself smiling back. He was a hunter too.

"Where the hell are we?" Jameson asked.

Karla shrugged. "The Otherworld, does it matter?"

"No, I suppose not," Jameson said.

The trees were splintered as if they had been smashed by giant hammers. The land was a waterlogged swamp. Streamlets overflowed from one pool to another, meandering gently between tussocks of grass. Slimy red-brown algae ringed open water so that ponds lacked defined edges. Thick-stalked plants rose from the water to a height of two or three feet. Leafless, they were topped by bright yellow flowers with overlapping petals, likc tulips.

What struck Jameson was the stillness of the air and the silence. Londoners were enclosed by the constant bubble of the city. The buzz of cars, planes, trains, and the sound of seven million people living their lives. Here there was nothing, no movement, no sound, not even a whine of insects.

A ripple in the pond crashed over the silence like breaking surf. Jameson whirled, extending his pistol. A green, flat snout parted the algae in a nearby pool, and an oversized frog climbed out. It squatted in the slime, observing Jameson stolidly. Orange warts decorating its olive-green skin lent a surreal effect. Jameson kept his pistol leveled but the frog made no move, hostile or otherwise.

"I guess that isn't our quarry?" Jameson asked, rhetorically. Karla did not bother to answer.

The swamp came slowly to life as if the frog had broken a spell. A cacophony of rustles, clicks, and chirrups started, like an orchestra tuning up before a performance. Jameson's attention was drawn to grass moving in rhythmic patterns about twenty meters away. A reptilian head on a long neck as thick as Jameson's forearm lifted into view. It was eyeless but a thin tongue flickered from a slit mouth tasting the air. The yellow head waved from side to side like a radar scanner before centering on Jameson. It dropped down into the grass and was hidden from sight.

The waving grass pattern headed for him, resolving when closer into a yellow snake body pushing against grass tussocks to glide through the mud. A black saw-tooth pattern ran down the spine like the markings on a British adder.

Karla watched the snake intently. It ignored her, its tiny snake mind focused entirely on Jameson. Perhaps she did not register as food so was no more important to the snake than a dead tree trunk.

She moved to intercept and the snake stopped, its head flicking towards her uncertainly. Karla froze, still as a granite boulder. Jameson flicked the safety catch of his gun with a click and deliberately stamped his foot. The snake refocused its attention on him.

Karla moved so fast she was a blur. The snake swung back towards her, opening its mouth wide. Hinged fangs swung out but it was too slow, way, way, too slow. She grasped its neck with both hands, talons digging in, so it couldn't get its head around to bite her. It spat something into the air and Jameson jumped back. Grass blackened where the venom splashed.

Karla twisted her hands in opposite directions, trying to wring the snake's neck. Its muscles knotted and its eyes bulged, but the neck wouldn't break. Her hands slipped, talons tearing through scales and flesh. The snake thrashed against her legs with its coils, and she lost her footing on the mud. She fell backwards, hitting the soggy ground with a slap of displaced fluid.

She kept a tight grip on the animal, struggling to keep its head pointed away from her face as it thrashed and twisted. Jameson couldn't get a clear shot, so he jumped in close and smacked the snake with the heavy pistol. The blow slapped its head away. Karla took the opportunity to sink her fangs deep into its neck. Its spinal column snapped with a crack and the snake whipped in death agony. Karla threw it into a pond, where it coiled and writhed aimlessly, churning the water into brown-green foam.

Jameson held out his hand to help her up.

"I hate the taste of snake," she said.

"If you think I'm kissing you before you clean your teeth after that . . ." Jameson said.

"Ohhh," Karla said, pouting. She walked right up to him until her breasts touched his chest and tilted her head up.

Oh, sod it, Jameson thought, kissing her anyway.

"You'd get mud all over your clothes if we do that," Jameson said, pushing her away.

"I've already got mud on them," she said.

He was tempted, oh, so tempted, but they were hunting a monster in an Otherworld swamp, for freaking sake. Just because she got off on danger. Actually, so did he, but a healthy dose of terror-induced rationality overcame his hormones. Karla didn't do terror or rationality. She did what she desired, living for the moment. That was her nature.

She slipped into a semi-quiescent state when unstimulated by events. In this condition she was taciturn and remote, almost machinelike. But danger and the hunt brought her alive. When Karla was up, she burned with an emotional intensity greater than any human being. Jameson was one of the few people ever to see her in this state—and live.

Suckers were only immortal by human standards of time. Over centuries, they became increasingly powerful, but their minds decayed until they were little more than vicious monsters motivated by only hunger. Commission operatives called ancient suckers Grendels, after the mythical monster slain by the hero Beowulf. Mythical? Perhaps? Except that Grendel has a very good description of a degenerate sucker, something humanoid but not human, something terrible that feeds on men, something of the dark.

The Commission never used the word vampire. Vampires were creatures from mythology, but suckers were all too real. The vampires of myth shared some of their characteristics but not all. Crosses held no fear for Karla, and people she fed on did not turn into vampires.

In truth, the Commission had never really established what a sucker was. They didn't reproduce, but new ones turned up from time to time. The Library favoured the explanation that they were some form of alien information pattern from outside our universe imprinted over a human mind. The Coven agreed more or less but employed words like possession and evil spirit.

It was possible that they were physical manifestations from outside, but suckers seemed to be too much part of our world to be wholly alien. It was no use interrogating them about their origins as they either wouldn't or couldn't answer.

Karla was old when they captured her; she didn't know how old, and they couldn't tell. She had forgotten many things as her mind decayed and had lost context to much of what she retained, but she was still semi-rational.

That was the combination the Commission needed: Karla was an old, powerful sucker who could still respond to verbal commands. She would be a very useful weapon—if she could be controlled.

The method they chose to bind her was a love geas. It had to be attached to a person; suckers have no ideology and have trouble comprehending loyalty to anything, let alone abstracts such as The Commission or the human race. Jameson volunteered to be that person.

Up to a point the experiment was a roaring success, until Karla started recovering her mind and personality. That was the first sign that the geas had unexpected side effects. The most important of which was that it did not just bind Karla to Jameson but was reciprocal, binding him to her. That created problems when the experiment ended and the time came to terminate Karla. Jameson gave the Commission a choice, back off or kill him as well. It was uncertain which option they would select, but Jameson was past caring. Either choice worked for him, albeit in different ways. In the event, Randolph opted to continue the experiment.

Jameson knew that the problem had only been kicked down the road a bit, a stay of execution rather than a reprieve. One day Jameson would die and then what would Karla do? Stay loyal to The Commission or revert to type? But that was a problem for another day as Jameson had no immediate interest in dying.

Karla claimed to have been Shakespeare's lover, not an impossible scenario. She had lived in London a long time. At least Karla seemed to remember The Bard, and she recalled a lover who was a poet, but it was all jumbled in her head. Jameson read English Lit. at Cambridge, and some lines in the Dark Lady Sonnet haunted him because they described Karla so well.

"*Then will I swear beauty herself is black, and all they foul that thy complexion lack.*"

"*So shalt thou feed on death, that feeds on men, and death once dead, there's no more dying then.*"

"*For I have sworn thee fair and thought thee bright, who art as black as hell, as dark as night.*"

Jameson would never know for sure but he always thought of Karla as the Dark Lady.

"Come on," he said, "business first, pleasure later."

She sighed theatrically, "I might not be in the mood later."

Sometimes she behaved just like a woman.

Karla and Jameson picked their way across the swamp, heading for drier land. Karla led the way, tracking the daemon by smell. It had entered the real world, so it left a whiff of reality behind. Reality was a stain that stood out in the Otherworld. Dry going did not make the journey any easier. The jumble of smashed trees was denser, and they often had to detour around barricades. Eventually there was no way round and they had to climb.

A hiss made Jameson jump, and he looked anxiously round for a snake. A flat piece of wood moved and two antennae waved. The "wood" was a camouflaged insectoid about a foot long and shaped like a cockroach. It compressed its thorax, making the hissing noise again. Jameson bunged a piece of bark in its direction and it scuttled off, slipping between two tree trunks. Karla scrambled to the top of the jumbled pile of wood and reached down to pull Jameson up.

That was when it hit Karla from behind.

Jameson had a glimpse of grey, batlike wings which lifted her off the ground with powerful downbeats. He drew his gun and sighted on the creature. It rocked from side to side, clearly having trouble supporting Karla's weight despite its four-meter wingspan. Long, scaly legs ended in impressive claws that dug cruelly into her shoulders. It swung a vulturelike neck and head from side to side, cawing like a giant crow. The rear of the wings joined the body at the hips, an anatomy more like a bird than a bat.

Karla reached up and grabbed its legs, tearing her body free from its claws. She swung up like an athlete on the parallel bars and kicked it in the chest. The monster screamed like shearing metal. It opened its beak to reveal rows of pointed teeth. Karla let go, falling several meters to the ground.

It wheeled in the sky, wings beating to gain height as it maneuvered to attack her again. Jameson yelled and waved his arms to attract its attention. The thing turned its head, yellow eyes locking on his. It half folded its wings and zoomed down towards him. He held his pistol outstretched at head height. At the last moment the monster spread its wings, checking its forward motion with a crack like the opening of a parachute. Two sets of triple claws reached for him.

Jameson fired a double tap at the center of the beast, using the SOE's technique. The heavy bolt projectiles imparted a powerful recoil on the gun, lifting the barrel. He dragged it down and gave the monster another double tap, exhausting the four-round clip.

Blue light flickered around the rail gun's nozzle, and the sharp tang of ionized air drove the swamp stink from his nostrils. The monster shrieked and flapped, a wing knocking Jameson over. He fell awkwardly. He managed to keep a firm grip on his pistol, although the impact drove the breath from his body. He groped in a pocket for a new clip of bolts and reloaded while still lying on his back gasping for breath. Gun extended, he searched the sky, but it was empty.

Karla was sitting on a branch when he found her, shoulders so badly ripped that he could see bone through the bloody wounds. It must have hurt like hell, but she waited stoically. Karla healed quickly, but this was bad. Fortunately he had the means to speed up the process. He took off his jacket and rolled up his sleeve. Her fangs extruded and she lowered her head like a lover. It did not hurt at all when she bit into his wrist.

Suckers needed human blood to survive the way people need water. No one knew quite how it worked. Calories were not the issue. Blood was a powerful catalyst to power magic, human blood the most powerful of all. Daemons like Karla fed on that energy.

The ancients used blood-powered necromantic spells to open gates to the Otherworld. The Odyssey describes Odysseus entering Hades, the underworld, using a spell powered by the blood of a sacrificial ram. Homer sanitized the story for the benefit of a civilized Classical Greek audience. The Bronze Age necromancers of Mycenae would have used human blood. In the Greek myths, Agamemnon sacrifices his daughter Iphigenia for a magical wind to carry the Achaean fleet to Troy. All successful religions and societies ban blood magic, especially human sacrifice. It is too powerful, too uncontrollable, just too damned evil.

Jameson's blood had an especially powerful effect of Karla because on their connection. Her flesh writhed and healed as she drank. New tissue flowed over exposed bones and ligaments. She reluctantly lifted her head from his wrist. Her body shuddered. Her eyes gleamed like chips of burning barium.

He gazed at her affectionately. It took tremendous willpower for her to stop feeding while blood was still available. Doubly so if the blood was his, because it was core to the magic that connected them. Something else the Coven had failed to grasp when they bound a daemon to a human being. She watched him with total concentration, green eyes lighting up the gloom.

Gloom? Jameson looked around to find the swamp gone. He still sat on a fallen tree trunk but was surrounded by tall pines that were definitely not there when he last looked. The air carried a distinct chill, and he couldn't see the Sun for dark clouds that tumbled quickly across the sky.

"What the hell?" Jameson asked.

"The hunter carried us with it when it fled. You must have given it one almighty scare my love." She gazed at him fondly, like a woman who knew her man would be a success if given the right guidance.

"The bastard gave me one almighty scare," Jameson said, ruefully.

He checked the safety on his pistol and put it away. He had a special holster cut into the inside of his jacket. The bulky rail gun was difficult to conceal, but its wood-and-iron bolts had a devastating impact on magical beings. A single bolt to the head or chest could kill daemons who shrugged off lead bullets like flea bites. Alternative weapons of similar effectiveness, such as crossbows or longbows, were even more difficult to carry inconspicuously. Better to be confused with armed police or even a gangster than be thought a nutter with a William Tell fixation.

"Can you still smell the bastard?" Jameson asked.

"He's nearby," she said happily. "This is his home."

"Then let's get him," Jameson said.

They moved through the pine forest, Karla leading once again. They followed a stream flowing sluggishly, waters dark and viscous. The clouds parted and sunlight sparkled down, illuminating the forest and causing Jameson to look up at a surprisingly bright blue sky. The Moon was visible. It was way too big, hanging in the sky like a hot-air balloon. Even more curiously, a small second Moon trailed behind.

Jameson had a vague memory of an article in the *Times* claiming that Earth had once had two moons. He couldn't remember when they were supposed to have collided, other than it was a long time ago. He looked around suspiciously for the next surprise, expecting bloody dinosaurs. The pines looked modern, but when did pine trees evolve? Were they contemporary with dinosaurs? He was a bloody literature graduate, for God's sake, and Cambridge unaccountably failed to include basic palaeontology in its literary degrees.

The clouds boiled and recovered the sky, plunging the forest back into gloom. The disappearance of the moons made it easier to put the whole thing out of his mind. That was good, he told himself. Concentrate on the daemon. That was real. Do not get distracted by vague fears of the unknown. He took out his pistol and checked the power level again. Karla looked at him quizzically but said nothing.

They went downhill to the edge of a natural bowl in the forest. Heavy, ruined walls filled it. So much for dinosaurs, Jameson thought. The ruins reminded him of one of the great monastery complexes after Henry the Eighth had done his worst. The roofs had gone and the wooden floors rotted from the multi-story buildings, leaving only stone stairs and galleries. The site was overgrown and partly hidden by deciduous trees, bushes, and climbing plants.

Karla sniffed the air like a hunting dog.

"It's down there," she said.

He drew his pistol.

The going was much more difficult than in the pine forest. Brambles formed entanglements like barbed wire on the Western Front. Yew trees, witching trees, were everywhere among the oaks and sycamores. They followed the path cut by the stream to where it emptied into a large dark pool. The edges were suspiciously regular for a natural structure.

"The black gowns liked to eat fish," Karla said. "A tribute to their risen dead god. I never understand your religions."

"A medieval eel pond," Jameson said. He looked up at the ruined walls. "So it *is* a monastery. It should be surrounded by fields, or at least their overgrown remains."

"The black gowns left a long time ago," Karla said.

"I suppose so," Jameson said.

The ruins were depressing, a reminder of the futility of human endeavor. They were silent witness that in the long run we are all dead and all is ruin.

"Look on my works, ye Mighty, and despair," Jameson said.

"What?" Karla asked.

"Nothing," Jameson replied. "Just a poem."

"I like poets," Karla said.

"Yes, I know," Jameson replied, hiding a sharp pang of jealously.

Karla smiled, sensitive to his moods. He examined the nearest wall. It was made of some hard grey stone and still stood four meters high.

"This probably encloses the whole compound for defense," Jameson said. "But there will be a gate. Come on."

He followed the wall around, but progress was depressingly slow. Eventually they came to a high Gothic archway with a stone gargoyle perched on top. It had claws on folded bat-like wings. Jameson observed it suspiciously, not liking its resemblance to the daemon, but it was just a statue.

The wooden gates had long gone. Not that it helped, because the gateway was choked with brambles.

"We would need a bloody flame-thrower to get through that lot," Jameson said. He turned to Karla. "You're sure it's in there?"

Karla nodded. "I'm sure."

Jameson thought hard. It could take hours to circumnavigate the walls, and there was no certainty of finding an entry anywhere, as the damned monster could fly in and out. Then it occurred to him that monasteries were forts by another name. The monks stored food, but what about water? They might have a well inside the cloister, the courtyard, but they might have obtained drinking water from the stream.

He retraced his steps back to the pool and found where the stream flowed out. They followed it to where it ran close to the wall. Jameson searched in the tangled vegetation but found nothing.

"What are you looking for?" Karla asked.

"I hoped there was a door, so the monks could fetch water." Jameson shrugged.

"I see."

Karla walked along the stream and poked around a jumble of boulders where a large tree grew. She flashed Jameson a smile, braced her back against the tree and pushed at one of the boulders with her legs. The tree swayed but the boulder pivoted sideways. Karla wriggled inside the resulting hole.

"Hey, wait for me!" Jameson followed.

He struggled to slip through the gap between the stone and the tree. Karla was noticeably slimmer than him, ridiculously petite for something that could out-wrestle a polar bear. Fortunately, it opened out inside and he could almost stand upright. Light filtered in from somewhere, confirming that the cave was artificial. The roof was a corbelled structure of rough stone, each block overlapping the lower to form an arch.

"It's a sally port," Karla said, proudly.

"I thought they were just small doors in castle walls for making quick sorties," Jameson said.

"Much better to have a tunnel with a hidden exit," Karla said.

"Yes, I see that," Jameson replied. "How do you know about sally ports?"

Karla shrugged, either unable or unwilling to tell him. She had probably seen one used at some point in her long life.

The tunnel made a sharp right-hand turn—to hinder a right-handed man with a sword trying to force the passage, and opened into the cloister. Rust flakes and corroded iron rods from what had been a gate were scattered around the exit.

A loud caw and the beat of wings echoed around the walls. Jameson tracked his gun around the ruins, but nothing moved. The cloister was rectangular, the short walls to their right and left lined with the low, broken walls of one-story buildings.

In front of them an impressive ruin reached up three stories. On the end was a massive stone keep. Parts of it had fallen, littering the ground with rubble. A headless torso of a broken statue was half buried amongst the broken shards. The remainder was a confusing mass of masonry and shadows. Jameson approached it with his pistol ready and Karla flanking.

The building was lined with giant Gothic archway windows that reached right down to the ground. Some still joined at the top, forming the classic Gothic point, but many were broken. Up close, they could see that the building was an empty shell, so they turned their attention to the keep. A stone ramp, largely intact, gave access to the first floor. A wooden drawbridge must once have spanned the two-meter gap from the top of the ramp to the entrance to the keep but it had long since rotted away.

Karla went first, jumping easily across from a standing start. She disappeared inside for a few moments before reappearing and signaling for Jameson to follow. Two meters is not a great distance to jump. Athletes confidently expect to achieve at least four times as much, but they are not fully dressed, carrying a bolt pistol, and three meters up. Then there was the matter of the blood-crazed monster. So Jameson felt comfortable about his decision to take a decent run up. In the event, he cleared the gap easily. He would have pitched head first into the keep had Karla not caught him.

Inside was a small, empty stone room remarkable only for the purple-veined ivy that climbed the walls. The only way out was a spiral stone staircase that wound through the room. Jameson signaled to Karla that she should descend while he would go up. Her night vision was considerably better than his.

He climbed the clockwise spiral with his pistol in his left hand. That way he could get a quick shot off around the curve of the staircase in the event of meeting something unpleasant. This was not natural for a right hander, but needs must when you're expecting to meet a devil. He reached a landing, where a corridor branched off the stair deeper into the building. Jameson tossed a mental coin and went into the corridor, holding his pistol in a more comfortable two-handed grip. He rounded a corner and found himself standing on the lip of a sheer drop.

Jameson did not like heights. He was not acrophobic or anything, but equally he would not volunteer to abseil down cliffs if given any choice in the matter. He steadied himself with his left hand, and leaned over. The whole center of the building was hollow down to the sub-sub-basement. It had once had wooden floors. The socket holes for the supporting beams were still visible. On the opposite wall was a rounded stone chamber with a flat floor. Upwards, the building was open to the dark grey sky.

The bat-thing erupted into the hollow center of the building at a lower level. Karla's clawed hand was not far behind, but she missed her strike. Jameson held his pistol extended in his right hand and sighted down the barrel, adopting a target-shooting stance.

The monster was having trouble flying. Something was wrong with its left wing. It fluttered like a moth, which unfortunately made it a difficult target. It gained height with difficulty and just managed a landing on the floor of the stone chamber opposite Jameson. He fired, the clang of bolt on rock indicating a miss. The monster scrabbled up into the chamber and disappeared.

"What the hell?" Jameson said, gaping.

Then he realised what he had seen. "Oh Christ, the chamber's one huge fireplace."

He leaned over and shouted down to Karla, "It's climbing up the chimney."

She gave him a fanged grin in reply. He was glad somebody was having fun.

Jameson ran back down the corridor to the landing. He took the stairs upwards two at a time. The spiral staircase terminated in a little turret with a window that gave a great view of the surrounding wilderness. Unfortunately, Jameson had no time for sightseeing. He emerged onto the corner of a platform that must originally have supported the roof timbers. It formed a stone walkway just a couple of feet wide around the perimeter. A low wall ran around the outside, but there, nothing but a sheer drop down on the inside edge. This was not something that helped his equability of mind.

The bat-thing clung to the stone chimney opposite, using hooked claws that emerged halfway down the leading edge of its wings. It twisted its head around and cawed at Jameson. He tried to aim his pistol but his hand shook. Jameson cursed; trying to fire while panting from his climb was a beginner's mistake. Nobody could shoot accurately after running. He had only three bolts left and might need all of them. He had no margin for error.

The monster descended the chimney, partly opening its wings as it swung from claw to claw. Jameson noted with some satisfaction wing tears where he had scored hits. It couldn't fly properly, so it was vulnerable.

He needed to get close to guarantee a killing strike, so he walked slowly around the perimeter towards the chimney, letting his breathing steady. He wondered where Karla had got to but decided he couldn't wait for her. The thing twisted its long neck to look down at the ground, trying to decide whether it could make it down. The tears in its wings would lengthen with every beat, but it was a short fall.

"Hey, beasty, remember me," Jameson yelled and waved his arms. "I'm the one who hurt you."

Yellow eyes glared at him vindictively. Mind made up, the monster dropped onto the parapet. It stalked towards Jameson on its hind legs, claws clicking on the stone. It dropped onto all fours to round the corner, using its front claws as feet. This posture tilted its wing tips up like a naval plane being stored on an aircraft carrier. It took Jameson a moment to place the vaguely familiar outline. The damn thing was like a model he had seen of a pterodactyl.

So it was dinosaurs after all, he thought, chuckling at the absurdity of it all. Here he was, stalking a pterodactyl on the top of a ruined monastery under two moons like John bloody Carter. Join the

Commission and experience all life has to offer and then some. The monster cawed, bringing him back to what passed for reality in his world.

It reared up onto its hind legs just a couple of meters away. Jameson gripped his gun in both hands. He might only get one shot off so it had to count. He raised the pistol and took careful aim, squeezing the trigger.

The monster gave a piercing steam-whistle scream, causing Jameson to jerk involuntarily as he fired. The bolt flew wide. The monster half jumped, half flew at him. That was its hunting technique. Scream to paralyze the prey with fear and then pounce, but Jameson wasn't easy to intimidate.

He fired again at point-blank range. The bolt flew true and smashed into the monster's chest. Dark ichor spurted, boiling into green fumes. The heavy body slammed into him. Not again, Jameson had time to think, before his hip hit the perimeter wall with a jolt so hard it numbed his whole leg. He grabbed at the wall, fingers catching the edge, but the monster's weight pushed him over.

"Oh shit," Jameson said.

CHAPTER 11
MAX

Rhian sat in a white circle that Frankie had sprayed on the ground with a can of aerosol paint. She huddled inside her jacket, collar up to keep out the cold.

"Do we have to do this at night in the cemetery?" she asked.

"It is traditional," Frankie replied, with a smile. "The cemetery is like a big battery of power just waiting to be tapped. Actually, there is so much magic sloshing around East London at the moment that I could probably do this in my back garden, but there are other considerations."

"Such as?" Rhian asked.

"Such as the spell is powered by human blood, your blood, to be exact."

Rhian opened her mouth, but Frankie talked over her.

"I know, blood magic is bloody dangerous."

Frankie was clearly not trying to be funny.

"But it is the only way. Celtic magic is blood-driven."

"I was only going to say that explains the knife," Rhian held up the dagger Frankie had given her.

"It's not a knife, it's an athame," Frankie said.

"Whatever," Rhian said. "This blood magic?"

"Yes?"

"Won't that put you in danger, or your soul, or something?" Rhian asked.

"Not if I'm careful," Frankie replied. "My soul has taken such a beating over the years that one more stain won't show. The real danger is that blood magic is forbidden by The Commission, except when *they* use it of course or they choose to turn a blind eye for some other reason. The cemetery is the nearest convenient place where we can be unobserved and where nothing can be traced back to me."

Frankie sprayed a second circle around herself, making sure that the ends joined cleanly and there were no gaps. She set up her little stove and sprinkled herbs into the bowl, chanting softly. Rhian strained to hear. Some of the words sounded Welsh. The ceremony went on and Rhian's mind drifted away. She daydreamed about her times with James.

A charge of static built up around Rhian, causing the fine hair on her arms to lift. Something similar seemed to be happening to Frankie. Her hair frizzled and stuck out. Rhian giggled. Frankie was not the best-groomed person in England at any time, but she was not usually quite so disheveled.

Frankie sat in a glowing column of air that cut off abruptly at the edge of the circle. Rhian was surrounded by a similar chamber. Her body felt light, as if it was becoming transparent to gravity.

"Nick your thumb with the athame and squeeze blood on the brooch," Frankie said.

Except that she did not say it so much as the voice seemed to be in Rhian's head. She lifted the chain that James had threaded through the brooch off her neck and placed it in her lap. She drew the athame across the tip of her thumb, cutting herself like she had done a million times before. Unusually, it didn't hurt. Blood welled up along the line, and she rubbed it onto the brooch.

The pain hit her like a blast of fire, twisting her body until every muscle contracted simultaneously. She tried to scream but her jaw locked. Then it was gone. Rhian sagged and moaned, her sight contracting into a monochrome circle. It was like looking out of a drainpipe into the night.

"Rhian, Rhian, call the wolf Rhian."

Frankie's voice sounded in Rhian's head and she wished the woman would go away.

·"Call the wolf."

It wasn't difficult. The wolf was thoroughly alarmed. It already lurked on the edge of Rhian's mind. All she had to do was let it in. The wolf enveloped her and she stood on four legs, instantaneously, like magic. Rhian laughed to herself. Like magic, it was magic. That was the whole point.

The wolf examined Frankie with suspicion. It moved towards her but bounced off the edge of the circle. It reared up, forelegs scrabbling, but the circle extended too high. It was trapped, not an agreeable experience for such a wild spirit. I can get us out, Rhian thought, if you let me. The wolf must have agreed because Rhian became Rhian again, on two legs, not four.

Frankie cut the circle around her with an athame, and the column of light vanished. The white circle was just spray paint again. She cut open Rhian's circle to free her, and the wolf went back to sleep.

"I think that went rather well," Frankie said, as they walked back though the cemetery.

"Well! It hurt worse than anything I've ever known," Rhian replied. "After this, childbirth will be a doddle."

"Hmm, yes, I thought it might be a little uncomfortable," Frankie said, like a dentist whose patient has just complained.

"It definitely hurt me more than you," Rhian said.

"I know, but the wolf had to be tamed," Frankie said. "*He's mad that trusts in the tameness of a wolf*, as the Bard put it."

"What bard?" Rhian asked.

"The Bard of Avon," Frankie replied, theatrically.

Rhian gave her a sideways look that she hoped conveyed her heartfelt desire that Frankie would speak bloody English for once.

"Um, Shakespeare," Frankie said. "From his *King Lear*."

"Oh, Shakespeare," said Rhian, "Didn't he play in defense for Newport Pagnel?"

It was Frankie's turn to give a sideways glance.

"No, um, Shakespeare was a playwright . . ."

"I know who bloody Shakespeare was," Rhian snarled. "Even if I never made university."

Frankie changed the subject, reminding Rhian who was doing whom the favor. "The situation was unstable. One day the transformation would have been fatal or you might have been unable to revert back to human. Besides, do you really want to keep being found unconscious and naked all over London? Hmmm?"

Rhian had no answer to that, so she said nothing.

"You seem to have been fortunate with this Max character. Next time you may not be so lucky."

Frankie clearly equated Max with "harmless sugar daddy." Whatever Max was, neither sugar nor daddy aptly described him, but Rhian did not want to get into a conversation about Max. She changed the subject.

"Why are you still on your own, Frankie?" Rhian asked, slightly cattily. "You are not that old, and still attractive to men." Gary, for one, Rhian thought, but the idea of her boss getting off with her landlady was just too yucky to contemplate.

"I realize that anyone over the age of twenty-five must seem decrepit to you, but I still mostly have my own teeth," Frankie replied. "I might ask you the same question, why no boyfriends?"

"You don't think the wolf thing might be a bit off-putting?" Rhian replied. She lowered her voice to simulate a husky male. "Hi, this is my girlfriend but better not annoy her because she's a werewolf."

"You are not a real werewolf," Frankie said pedantically. "Anyway that's just an excuse." Frankie softened her voice. "You have to let go sometime, Rhian. You think your dead boyfriend would want you to sacrifice your life to his memory. He died so that you could live—so live."

Rhian's eyes prickled with tears. She felt sorrow, shame, and not a little anger. James, you bastard, she thought, why did you have to leave me? But most of all, she felt the grinding guilt that she was alive and James was dead.

"I didn't mean to make you cry, honey," Frankie said. "It's not your fault James is dead."

"What would you know about it, Frankie?" Rhian asked, annoyed at the intrusion into her private life.

"Oh, I know," Frankie replied. "I was pregnant when Pete left me, perhaps that was why he left me. I did not just walk out of The Commission on a whim. Truth is, I came apart and was retired. I tried to kill myself but I survived. Unfortunately, my baby didn't."

Rhian thought of her room at Frankie's flat, all painted in bright, friendly colors. A room that was rather too small for an adult bed but just right for a cot.

"Trust me, I know all about guilt," Frankie said.

✳◗✳

A hand grabbed Jameson's wrist with a grip like a great white's bite. He swung like a pendulum until he crashed back against the wall. Karla hauled him up effortlessly and stood him on the roof. He swayed and would have gone back over if she had not retained her hold.

"You cut it fine," Jameson said, trying for a Bondlike insouciance and failing badly.

"Are you all right?" Karla asked.

"Oh, I'm just bloody marvelous," Jameson replied. "My body feels like Mike Tyson's punch bag." He looked around. "Where's the daemon?"

Karla pointed over the wall, so he leaned carefully out to look. A black burn mark stained the grass in the courtyard. If he screwed his eyes up he could imagine it was in the shape of the monster. Green vapor drifted lazily away.

"You killed it, my love, hunted it down and killed it," Karla said, eyes shining emerald green.

She gazed at him with something resembling adoration and pride, the way a woman should look at her man. Could she really love him? The Commission witches would have laughed at the idea that a sucker could feel such an emotion, but Jameson was not so sure.

"Yeah, well," Jameson said, feeling embarrassed. "We got it."

He held up a hand to forestall further arguments.

"Let's go home, which way to the gate?"

"It's gone," Karla replied.

Jameson took a deep breath before replying. "Gone?"

"Gone, the daemon created it, so when the daemon died . . ."

"Right," Jameson said. "I get the picture. Tell me, you can find another?"

"Sure," Karla replied.

There was a pause.

"You want me to find another route?"

Jameson nodded. Karla could be so very literal.

They went down the stairs and out into the courtyard. Karla wandered around, sniffing the air like a hound dog. She selected a place and dug into the ground with her claws, cocking her head and listening before digging slightly to one side. Carefully she extracted a skull stained brown with dirt and minerals. She held it up and gazed intently into its eye sockets.

Jameson wondered what the hell she was up to. He did not recall her getting a bang on the head. Of course, he had taken a few, so maybe it was him not her that was ga-ga.

She shook the skull until something with multiple legs fell out and scuttled away. Her boot squashed the wriggler before it got more than a few centimeters. She gazed at the skull again, nodding as if she was in a conversation.

"Getting somewhere?" Jameson asked, tentatively.

"Sure," Karla replied.

She crushed the skull between her hands and dropped the splintered bone fragments.

"This way," she said, walking back across the cloister.

Jameson followed her into the tunnel. It turned out to be longer than he remembered. He touched the roof and discovered that it was concrete rather than stone corbelling. They were on their way through the Otherworld to a different place, maybe a different universe. They emerged into daylight from between two shattered concrete blocks. He had to duck under rusted iron strands hanging from ruined ferro-concrete.

The sky was still grey and cloud covered. They climbed through twisted rubble that resembled a bunker complex that had been comprehensively smart bombed. Shattered remains of modern buildings hemmed them in. Bushes sprang up wherever enough earth lodged in hollows to sustain their roots. Creepers climbed the shattered concrete columns. Whatever happened here was years old judging by the plant growth, maybe decades old.

Water trickled from under a fallen wall, running down to join a brook that flowed in a straight line alongside a zone that was largely clear. Wreckage lined each side like—like a shattered street, except that the surface consisted of grass. Jameson scraped some away with his foot to reveal the remains of tarmac.

They walked along what was left of the road. Gradually the damage lessened until the buildings were substantially intact. Most had lost their roofs, but the deterioration seemed to be from decades of neglect rather than violent destruction. Ivy climbed the walls, turning structures into romantic ruins like the follies Victorian gentlemen built on their estates. A sycamore grew out of what had once been a showroom window.

They arrived at a crossroads and Karla stopped.

"Where now?" Jameson asked.

Karla did not answer, occupied by gazing thoughtfully down one of the side streets.

"What the hell is this place?" Jameson said. "The Otherworld shadows the real world, right?"

"The parts we can access do," Karla replied.

"So where are we?" Jameson asked again.

"London, or an echo of a London," Karla replied. "It may never have existed. You people are so confused in your thoughts, but you have such powerful ideas, such vivid imaginations. You project images of your dreams and nightmares into the Otherworld, shaping its form and substance."

"Hmm," Jameson said. He had heard that explanation before, but this place spooked him.

Karla turned left at the crossroads, leaving the stream that tumbled on along the middle of the main road. Jameson followed but found he missed the comfort of the stream, the only friendly, living feature of the landscape. The clouds were thinning, allowing sunlight to illuminate the ruins. This did not improve Jameson's mood because it made the city look more abandoned and sad.

A clink of stone in a ruined building jolted him out of his ennui. He whirled, gun in hand. A scruffy mongrel with mottled yellow ochre-and-brown fur emerged from behind a wall. It was not particularly large or heavily built, and showed no sign of aggression, so Jameson relaxed.

He pursed his lips and whistled. "Here, boy."

He was pleased to see the dog. It was the first animal they had come across in the dead, silent city.

The dog watched him, sniffing the air. More crept out of the rubble, spreading out to encircle him and Karla. They were near identical in size and color so they could not be mongrels, but equally they were no breed he recognized. They made no sound, no canine whines of welcome or even threatening barks. Jameson felt cold. They behaved like a pack of African hunting dogs. They might be descended from family pets but they were now completely feral.

Karla laughed delightedly.

"Here, little hunters," she said mockingly, stepping towards them and beckoning with her hand.

Two attacked without warning, no growls, no threat displays, just naked aggression. They split like a well-trained combat team to hit her simultaneously from both flanks. Compared to Karla they were as slow as engine oil flowing down a dipstick. She ran at the one on the left and kicked it like Beckham faced with an open German goal. The dog bounced over the ground, head flopping on a neck bent at an impossible angle.

Momentum swung Karla round and the second dog took the opportunity to leap for her throat. Jameson started forward but he moved in slow motion, even slower than the dog. Karla was quicksilver in comparison. She caught the dog by the neck, talons sinking through the fur. It wriggled and snarled, the first sound it made—and the last. She squeezed and crushed its windpipe until its tongue lolled and its eyes streamed blood.

The rest of the pack watched silently. One dog advanced a few steps and looked around at its pack-mates, as if seeking support. Karla hurled the corpse at the animal. It turned and fled back into cover, breaking the spell. The rest of the dogs followed. The only sign that the pack had ever been there were the two bodies.

Karla laughed delightedly.

"I do wish you would not provoke trouble," Jameson said. "One day you are going to give me a heart attack."

"They would have followed us and attacked sooner or later," Karla said. "Better it be on our terms rather than theirs. Now the little hunters know."

"Know what?" Jameson asked.

"That we are death, not food," she said with her usual succinctness.

"We need to get on," Jameson said. "The Sun is going down and I don't fancy being here after dark."

They walked on until they came to a strange structure in the road. It was a skeleton of thin strips of wood. Two large box shapes were connected by a central spar on which was attached a plywood egg. Thin strips of tattered canvas hung from the frame, presumably the remains of a cloth skin.

Jameson walked around the whatever-it-was. A trail of wreckage suggested that there had been more canvas-covered boxes behind.

"What on Earth have we here, some sort of water storage?" Jameson asked, not expecting an answer.

Karla had little curiosity about such matters, but he should not complain. Her monofocus had advantages, as, unlike him, she was unlikely to be distracted from what mattered.

He stood on tiptoe to peer into the egg. It was open at the top and had a thin seat inside surrounded by levers. Pulleys suggested that they had once operated cables long since rusted away. His imagination conjured up some sort of signaling device, but communicating what to whom? And what was it doing lying there in the middle of a London street? It had no wheels or any sign that it had been attached to anything that might have lifted it up. It just seemed to have dropped from the sky.

"Of course," Jameson said. "The light build is a clue. It's a primitive airplane—as it has no engine, a glider."

He grinned in delight at Karla, pleased with his own cleverness. She smiled back, happy that he was pleased.

"It must have looked like two box kites with some sort of tail," Jameson said. "What a strange contraption. Hell to fly in something so unstable in anything but perfect conditions."

His smile faded as a thought occurred. "I know where we are."

Karla looked at him gravely, picking up on his swift change of mood.

"This is a *drachenflieger*, kite-like gliders carried by German airships in Wells' *War in the Air*. They attacked enemy airships, like planes operating off carriers. I suppose this is what the German airships did to London."

He spread his arms out to indicate the city.

"That's why there are no cars," he said. "It was 1900 or something. But there should be human and horse bones from the purple plague that depopulated the city before its destruction."

He frowned, recalling the feral packs of dogs. Chewed bones would be scattered in amongst the ruins.

"Wells predicted the destructiveness of air warfare. He saw the airships as unstoppable, so the war went on until civilization collapsed. Of course, the German airships turned out to be easy meat for the new fighter planes when real Zeppelins attacked London."

No wonder this city looked so sad. It was a cenotaph to a lost empire, a dead civilization. The Otherworld was full of the relics of human disasters, both real and fictional.

"What a bloody depressing place," Jameson said.

"Do you think so?" Karla asked in surprise. "I rather like it."

That didn't surprise him. Karla's concept of pleasant surroundings bore as little relation to human preferences as her other likes and dislikes.

"Is the gate near?" he asked.

"Yes," Karla replied.

She hesitated and Jameson raised an eyebrow.

"This air war story?" Karla asked.

"Yes."

"Is it very popular?"

"No doubt at one time but almost forgotten now, I should think," Jameson replied. "Wells may have been prescient, but the novel wasn't very good. It had too much political preaching, too little story, and was overtaken by real events. People didn't need air attack on London fantasies after the World Wars. They had a bellyful of the real thing."

"So if the book is forgotten, what fixes this reality?" Karla asked.

That, Jameson thought, was a good question. The imaginations of masses of people created the shadow realms of The Otherworld, so this city should have faded away when people forgot Wells' story. Someone must have a contemporary use for this place, and the fact that it appealed to Karla rather than Jameson suggested that the someone was not human.

"The way here was too easy," Karla said. "Like we were invited in."

"Come into my parlor said the spider to the fly," Jameson said.

Karla nodded.

He checked his pistol again as you never knew in the Otherworld. The bolts might have been breeding. Unfortunately, he still only had one round. When he looked up, Karla was disappearing between two ruined buildings. He hurried after her, and they pressed on to a forest of tangled bushes and trees. A rhododendron bush was in full flower, covered in hemispherical purple flowers like the decorations on a Christmas tree. It looked cheerfully out of place in the abandoned city.

It was the sound that he first noticed, a rhythmic squeak like the slow turn of a rusting wheel. They found the children's playground in amongst the bushes. The top of a slide projected out of a bramble patch and a wooden play-wheel rotated slowly, making a grating noise as it spun. It had once been brightly painted in blue and yellow, but the colors had faded. It slowed, stopping completely after three or four more revolutions. Jameson wondered who or what had started it spinning in the first place. He could still hear the squeak.

"I'm over here," a woman's voice said.

Jameson moved sideways to see around a holly bush without getting too close. He did not want to come face to face with the owner of the voice unexpectedly.

A tall woman in a long yellow-and-white floaty summer dress sat on a child's swing, her blond hair permed into waves in a style that reminded him of the 1930s. She rocked backwards and forwards, and the swing's chains squeaked where they passed through metal hoops on the supporting frame. Jameson kept his gun trained on her. She looked harmless, which proved exactly nothing.

"Go on, give me a push," the blond said.

"Sefrina!" Karla said from behind Jameson.

Jameson kept his pistol centerd on the woman. If Karla recognized her, there was no doubt in Jameson's mind of what she was, how bloody dangerous she was.

"Spoilsport," Sefrina said, pouting. "I heard your latest pet was quite hunky, but the gossip didn't do him justice, Karla. I don't know how you pull them at your age and with your dress sense."

She looked Karla up and down with a sneer. Karla's leather jacket and trousers had seen better days.

"I think you look damn sexy," Jameson said loyally to his partner.

Karla shot him a smile.

"What do you want, Sefrina?" Karla asked, moving in front of Jameson but careful not to block his line of fire.

"It's not what she wants but what I want," said a male voice.

A man in precisely pressed fawn chinos topped by a navy blue polo shirt emerged from the shadows under the trees. He looked like a politician dressed in smart casual for a photo-op on his holiday. Of course, politicians didn't usually hold an automatic pistol.

"Still playing with guns, Max," Karla said. "You surely don't imagine that toy would stop me."

"Not you, Karla, I wouldn't use anything less than a cannon to stop you," Max said. "But it will make a nasty mess of your little pet there. I am willing to bet you aren't ready to lose him."

"And my bolt pistol will make a nasty mess of your girlfriend," Jameson said, getting a little fed up with being treated as a passive part of the background.

"I doubt Max cares," Karla said to Jameson.

"Not quite true," Max said. "Sefrina has her uses. It would be annoying to have to find a replacement."

If Sefrina was upset by his callousness then she bravely managed to conceal the fact.

He put the gun in his pocket and walked slowly towards them. Karla tensed.

"But there is no need for any unpleasantness. I only want to talk."

"So talk," Karla said, folding her arms.

Max bowed mockingly.

"This little pet of yours is a Commission enforcer, is he not?" Max said. "Karla and Jameson, the invincible kill team, the toast of Old London Town."

"So?" Karla asked.

"You always had a way with humans," Max replied, "but this time you've surpassed yourself. Subverting the entire Commission is truly impressive, my darling."

It was an insight of how Jameson's relationship with Karla must look to other daemons. They could not conceive of how she had been bound to him, so they would assume that it must be all Karla's doing. They thought she must be running some complicated plot. The fact that they could not work out what she was up to merely proved how subtle and cunning she was.

Karla looked bored. "And you've always been a windbag. Any chance of you coming to the point?"

Max sighed. "You are a bit of a mystery, Karla. I heard you had sunk into the madness of the blood fugue. No one comes back from that, but you did. How is that?"

Karla grinned humourlessly. "You are nearly as old as me. Why haven't you succumbed to the madness?"

"Good question. I've always thought that it was because I have a purpose. I am the last of the Protectors," Max said.

Karla laughed. "A purpose with no purpose."

"What's a Protector?" Jameson asked.

"They were a pact of my kind that expelled one of the ancient daemon lineages from the world," Karla replied.

"What did you fight over?" Jameson asked.

"Humans," Karla replied. "They fed on humans and would have used you all up. We could not permit that."

Of course not, Jameson thought, stupid question. Why do shepherds protect sheep from wolves? The idea that suckers could have pacts was worrying. He had not thought them capable of such organizational skills.

"Quite right," Max said. "What a boring world it would be without humans, boring and hungry."

"Don't worry about it, Maxy. It's you that's the endangered species, not us," Jameson said, with a sneer.

Max snarled, displaying long canine teeth. "Keep your pet under control, Karla, or I will have to discipline him myself."

"You can try." Jameson moved his gun hand slightly to draw attention to his bolt pistol.

"You wanted to talk, Max," Karla reminded him.

"So I did." The easy smile was back on Max's face. "Your pet is not entirely wrong. We are an endangered species, but then, so are humans. The Sith are back."

Karla sucked in her breath. "Impossible. The Protectors hunted down every last one and sealed in the survivors. They can't get back. Unless . . ."

"Unless some idiot on this side of the barrier opens a hole," Max finished for her.

"What the fuck are the Sith?" Jameson said. "And I will shoot the first sucker that mentions *Star Wars*."

"What is this *Star Wars*?" Max asked. "Snow White mentioned them."

"Snow White? As in Grimms' Fairy Tales?" Jameson asked, utterly confused by the direction the conversation was taking.

"You'd know her as Rhian," Max replied.

Jameson looked blank, unenlightened by the explanation.

"How interesting, I assumed she was one of yours," Max said.

Jameson quickly smiled as it was a firm rule that you never gave anything away to a daemon. They had no concept of idle curiosity. Everything they said or did was directed to their personal goals.

"I find it difficult to believe that you've never heard of *Star Wars*," Jameson said skeptically. "Where have you been for the last four decades?"

"I was—resting," Max said. "Until the Sith, that is."

"What are the damned Sith?" Jameson asked, again.

"The Daoine Sith, Elves, Fairies, the fair folk, the Lords and Ladies," Karla replied. "You people have lots of names for them."

"But fairies are just a myth," Jameson said.

"So are vampires," Max replied, showing his teeth.

"Okay, point taken, myths can have cores of truth, but fairies and elves are harmless," Jameson said.

The three suckers laughed at him, like adults amused at the naive credulity of a small child. Jameson felt a pang of jealousy that Karla was siding with her kind against him. Karla picked up the emotion immediately and turned to him.

"Humans have erased the real memory of the Sith from their collective memory. They were too awful, so you sanitized them with fairy tales." Karla said. "They fed on your pain and terror. Look up some of the old Irish myths about the Sidhe or the *Svartálfar* in the Scandinavian Edda and you will find echoes of the true nature of the Sith."

"Never mind the history lesson," Max said. "The Sith are back because someone in London is opening holes in the barrier for them."

"We noticed the holes," Jameson said.

"At the moment the gates are unstable and soon shut, but the problem is getting worse. If they get a permanent gate it will take a major war to expel them, like the one that brought down the human empire."

"Rome," Karla said in answer to Jameson's unspoken query.

"So what you are saying is that we are in deep shit," said Jameson, summing up.

"As deep as the ocean, little man. I need the help of the Commission to seal off the Sith. I need human magic."

"Yah, suckers don't do magic," Jameson said, thoughtfully.

"Sith do," Max said.

"I can't quite remember, it's been too long, but wasn't it a human who created the barrier?" Karla asked.

"The sorcerer Merlin," Max said. "He was a Sith-human hybrid."

"Sith breed with humans?" Jameson asked incredulously. Sex between humans and daemons was hardly unknown, he was living proof of that, but hybrid issue was something else.

"They can," Max replied. "It helps them consolidate their position. Full Sith can only tolerate the world for short periods, but hybrids are immune."

He took a deep breath as if what he was about to say next would be physically painful.

"So, I want a blood pact with you, Karla. I need the magic of your Commission witches."

"I'll think about it," Karla said.

Max nodded, as if he had not expected an immediate decision.

"Talking about immunity, I'd be curious to know how you protect yourself from the Sun. Word is that you've been seen out in the real world in daylight," Max said.

"Really," Karla replied.

"Really, and don't give me any rubbish about suntan cream or pills. Like that hasn't been tried and failed. It's something unique, something new, something to do with him?" Max gestured at Jameson.

"You are boring me now, Max," Karla said. "How do we get home from here?"

"You go that way," Max said, pointing to a path through the trees.

Rhian felt as if she were living in two overlapping worlds. Here she was, walking to work along the same old mundane London streets, filled with the same old mundane London people. A Rastafarian, dreadlocks held up in a red, gold, and green woollen cap, walked past with a rhythmic gait. He nodded and clicked his fingers to a beat only he perceived. The whiff of holy ganja trailed him. A lycra-covered cyclist shot past, moving faster than the cars. Across the street two heavily made up women in sensible business suits tapped their feet and checked their watches. A sign in the small front garden of the terraced house behind announced that it was for sale, so they were estate agents waiting for a client. Given the state of the economy, it was a buyers' market. He would be as late as he wished or he might not turn up at all.

The Sun had set earlier. The streets were still lit by the long northern twilight, but darkness pooled around walls and cars. The evening street was symbolic of the second shadow London that had enveloped Rhian since she found Morgana's brooch. A London of wolves, vampires, and witches who made real magic. A place where one false move could drop you into an Otherworld. A city where reality was a thin skin on a viscous pool of potential dangers.

Sometimes, she thought that she had never come round from the attack that had killed James. That she was really lying in a hospital bed full of tubes and wires like a character from *Life on Mars*. Maybe this was all a dream. Would she vanish when the doctors finally gave up on her and pulled the plug, or would her soul move on? To Heaven or Hell? Maybe she was already in Hell; it hurt too damn much to be Heaven.

She arrived early for her shift at the pub, as she needed to fill in her time sheet. Old Fred and Willie the Dog sat on barstools in their usual corner. They sipped interminable half pints of bitter. Sheila manned the bar—or should that be womanned? Rhian never could remember which bits of political correctness were currently in vogue. Her life flew below the radar of middle-class fads and fashions.

Sheila nodded to her when she swung up the countertop to enter the bar, but carried on cleaning glasses. It was considered a point of honor to clean up before one left, and Sheila's shift was nearly over. Rhian went into the small back office and rummaged.

"Sheila, where are the time sheets?" she asked.

"No idea," Sheila replied. "You had better ask Gary. He's upstairs in his flat."

Rhian mounted the stairs two at a time. They were narrow and steep, like you find in old buildings. At the top, she knocked on the door separating Gary's flat from the public areas. After a short interval, he appeared, and she explained why she was there.

"Oh right, time sheets, I think I have some more somewhere," Gary said vaguely.

She followed him up onto a landing where he opened the door to a small room and snapped on a light. The bulb hung naked on an old-fashioned cloth-covered electric cable. Stacks of cardboard boxes sat on unpainted wooden floorboards. The wall plaster had fallen away completely in places, exposing wooden batons. The latch on the wooden window was broken, the rope sash hanging down. The window had been nailed permanently shut. Rhian doubted if it could be lifted, even without the nails, as it was thickly painted over.

"This is one of the unliveable rooms," Gary said, somewhat defensively. "But it is dry, so I store stuff in it."

The room did smell a bit musty, but not damp. He carried on searching, shuffling boxes around. While waiting, Rhian was aware of a strange swishing noise coming from another room. It stopped abruptly with a crash.

"Oh no," Gary said, and dashed out.

Rhian followed him into the next room, wondering why he was so alarmed. A large table on trestles filled the space. Models covered it, creating a miniature English scene: a village pub and a church, a canal, a small town, trees, and rolling green hills. There was even a small grass airfield with a little yellow biplane. She walked, fascinated, around the complicated model railway.

The little people had old-fashioned clothes, and the policeman had a bicycle. The cars were black boxes on spindly wheels or open sports cars, like an Agatha Christie story in miniature. That old duck in her garden must be Miss Marple and the rotund man on the platform must be Poirot—or possibly the Fat Controller. Though she could not see Thomas the Tank Engine anywhere. Even Frankie's Mildred would be too modern for this diorama.

Rhian giggled, unable to help herself.

Gary appeared from behind the table holding a steam train and carriages like a mother holds her new baby.

"It's okay, I think," Gary said. "I set the speed too high and it came off the table, but it is the Flying Scotsman. I suppose I shouldn't have left her running unattended."

"Do you have a whistle and a peaked cap?" Rhian asked solemnly.

Gary colored.

"I suppose this does look like a strange hobby for a grown man," he said.

"No stranger than other grown men's hobbies," Rhian said soothingly. "I knew a man who fought battles between miniature elves and dwarves."

"Now that's just silly," Gary said with a grin.

"Then there's stamp collecting, angling, flying toy planes, train spotting, slot cars, coin collecting, football, ferret racing, sword collecting, darts, ham radio, gun collecting, ufology, putting ships in bottles, paintball, metal detecting, beer mat collecting . . ."

"Okay, I get the picture," said Gary, with a lopsided grin. "Men are weird, childish, and collect strange things."

"Model railways are pretty tame stuff compared to extreme ironing," Rhian said. "I think it's the male competitive instinct. Ask a man to iron a shirt and you get nothing but foot dragging, but tell him its extreme ironing and challenge him to do it hanging upside down from Tower Bridge, and the poor sap can't wait."

"And the difference between men and boys is the cost of the toys," Gary said.

They both laughed.

"I think model railways are cute, and it's not likely to hurt anybody," Rhian said in a conciliatory sort of way, remembering that Gary was her boss.

"I'm not so sure about that. This place has 1930s wiring, so one wrong move and *phut*," Gary said, drawing a finger across his throat. "Have you noticed that the light switches are made of Bakelite?"

"What's Bakelite?" Rhian asked, examining a switch. It was dark brown and bulky but otherwise unremarkable.

"Never mind, they stopped making it before you were born, Hell, before I was born."

"That must have been a long time ago, then," Rhian said, straight faced.

Gary looked at her suspiciously but forewent further comment.

Rhian took over from the taciturn Sheila and dropped back into the reassuringly unexciting business of barmaiding. After some debate, and a rigorous and extensive search through their pockets, Willie the Dog and Old Fred stumped up the readies for two more halves of ordinary bitter. A trickle of students passed in and out of the pub on their way between the college and digs.

"Would you like to come out with me?" a student asked, pocketing his change.

Rhian lifted her eyes from the till and looked at him. Actually, he wasn't unhandsome if you disregarded the acne. It was nice to get a direct approach rather than a stupid chat-up line. She cocked her head one side and considered his request, thinking about Frankie's advice. Maybe she should take him up on his offer? It was just an invitation for a drink, not a marriage proposal, but she couldn't see where the relationship could go. Sooner or later he would meet the wolf.

"Thanks, but I am not quite ready for a relationship. I only split from my last boyfriend recently."

The student grinned at her.

"Well, that's a better response than everyone else has got," he said.

"Everyone else?" Rhian asked.

"At uni, we've opened a sweepstake, and the first one to take you out wins."

He winked and went off with his drink, leaving Rhian speechless. They'd opened a bloody sweepstake on her favours?

She was still fuming when the door opened to admit two large bald men with no necks and expensive suits that didn't quite fit. One of them causally beckoned to her.

"Come on, Mister Parkes has decided to take you clubbing Up West and has sent us to fetch you," the goon said.

"Up West" meant the West End of Central London, where the theatres, expensive restaurants and nightclubs were to be found.

"I don't think so. I don't know any Mister Parkes."

"Everyone knows Charlie Parkes," the goon said, "and I was telling you, not asking. Hurry up, Mister Parkes don't like to be kept waiting."

Rhian got it then—Charlie Parkes, the blagger who hung out with bent coppers.

"Tell Mister Parkes that I can't spare her," Gary said, politely, putting a hand on Rhian's shoulder.

Rhian had not heard him come down.

The two goons walked up to the bar.

"I haven't got time for this, Hunter," a goon said, putting thick, heavy hands flat on the bar. "Would you prefer to spare her or your fucking kneecaps? She's going with us anyway, whatever condition we leave you in."

"It's okay, Gary," Rhian said, a smile covering her burning fury at being treated like a whore. "I don't mind going for a little ride with these nice gentlemen. I might find it quite interesting. So might they."

The snarl she felt in the core of her being was the closest the wolf got to a laugh. It was amused, so things could get very, very interesting once they were outside.

"No, it's really not all right," Gary said.

Rhian saw his hand sliding towards a baseball bat he kept out of sight under the bar. She tensed, the wolf stirred. Things were about to kick off. She had hoped to do this outside on the dark street, where there were no witnesses.

Two hands casually moved the goons aside as if they were made of *papier-mâché,* revealing a tall, slim man in an ankle-length black leather coat. It should have looked ridiculously pretentious, but on him it was perfect.

"What do you want?" Rhian asked, wearily.

"Snow White, is that any way to greet an old friend and confidante?"

"Hello, Max," Rhian said with resignation.

CHAPTER 12
REVELATIONS

Jameson knew he was close to home when the air stank of sulfur oxides and sewage, and the smog was so thick as to cause perpetual gloom. He coughed, and spat into the cobbled street to get the acrid taste out of his mouth. The alley was barely a couple of meters wide, and wooden houses overhung on both sides. Figures loomed as shadows out of the gloom and disappeared as quickly. The smog did not just smother the senses of taste and sight but also seemed to dampen sound like a thick duvet. He could just hear the clop of iron horseshoes on stone in the distance, but had no sense of the direction of the sound.

This was one of the most powerful Jungian psychoanals of the London Otherworld. The Dickensian rookery was an archetype not just of Dickens and other classical writers but a thousand modern books and films. Here stalked Sherlock Holmes, The Ripper, Doctor Jekyll and Mister Hyde, and a vast supporting cast of blowers and broadsmen, chivs and chavs, dippers and dragsmen, jacks and judies, lags and lurkers, macers and mugs, palmers and pigs.

A woman in a bonnet and long ragged clothes sprang out of a doorway at Jameson. She had a straw basket in her left hand and something purple in her right.

"Buy some lucky heather, darling. A square-rigged toff like you needs his toll of luck in this manor."

Her remaining teeth were blackened, and between them oozed breath that stank so badly as to overpower the general miasma. Jameson pushed past the woman without speaking and hurried after Karla. It was best not to interact too closely with the shadows of the Otherworld or you could be sucked into their reality.

Karla opened the wooden door of a lean-to in a small square and went in. Jameson followed. It was pitch dark inside until Karla opened an internal door and flooded a walk-in larder with yellow electric light. The next room was a kitchen with an old-fashioned gas stove, brightly colored blue Formica-topped storage units, and a floor covered with yellow tiles. Jameson had a shrewd idea where they were even before he opened the kitchen door.

He preceded Karla into an old-fashioned London pub dominated by a long mahogany bar. Pint mugs hung from the wooden screen over the bar, behind which was a mirror advertising Gordon's gin. In its way, the Victorian-styled pub resembled a secular church. The screen separated the holy of holies where the priest officiated, from the seated punters beyond. Of course the priest was a barman and they worshipped other gods than the Biblical, but alcohol and nibbles still featured in the service.

"On the seventh day God rested and popped down the Blind Beggar for a swift half," Jameson said to himself, as if chanting a litany.

"Can't you come through the front door like anyone else, Jameson?" the barman asked, spoiling the analogy.

"Depends where I'm coming from, Henry," Jameson replied.

Henry gazed at him sightlessly, eyes concealed behind a sepia-stained cloth tied around his head. The Blind Beggar pub in Whitechapel was ancient. How old, no one knew, but it probably started as a Roman fast-food bar on the London-to-Colchester road. By Medieval times it was a coaching inn, although the current building was Victorian.

The pub was named after Henry de Montfort, who had his eyes put out by the victorious Royalists after their victory in 1265. According to legend, Henry gravitated to Whitechapel and begged at a crossroads on the old Roman Road. He found fame as the Blind Beggar of Bethnal Green. The story goes that a duchess nursed him back to health and bore him a daughter, Bessie, remembered in the name of a nearby road.

It was probably all bollocks. Just another London tale invented to entertain tourists in exchange for free drinks, but the barman was blind and he was called Henry. Which came first, the barman or the legend? Was Henry the Blind Barman an avatar of Henry the Blind Beggar? Who knows? In London, myth and history swirled together like a raspberry ripple.

Henry was not entirely human, but he never left the Beggar, so The Commission had no particular interest in him. Besides, the Beggar was useful. The walls between reality and the Otherworld stretched and distorted to the point of insubstantiality in this place. That was true all over Whitechapel, but the Beggar was a semi-stable halfway house between the worlds. That made it a useful place for meeting on neutral ground. Every so often the pub was raided by The Commission, often with interesting results.

It was no accident William Booth chose the street outside the Beggar to give the seminal sermon that kicked off the Salvation Army. Evil oozed out of the place like lava from the mouth of a volcano. By opening his preaching in such a place, Booth laid down a challenge to the forces of darkness. He made a declaration of total war. It was a bit like striding up to the castle of a robber baron and pissing on his portcullis, or attacking motherhood on Mumsnet.

Jameson was horrified to find himself sporting a collarless grey suit, zip-up ankle boots, and an original Beatles haircut. He felt bloody ridiculous. Karla looked rather fetching in a white hairband, silver babydoll mini-dress, and light purple boots.

He sighed, "The bloody swinging Sixties again."

Through the window, Jameson could see an Austin Mini Cooper, gaudily painted lemon yellow. The blue, red, and white stripes of a Union Jack motif decorated its roof. The Beggar had a tendency to revert to the Sixties when in resting mode. That was when East End Ganglord Ronnie Kray topped George Cornell with a nine-millimeter Mauser in the bar. Cornell was an enforcer for the South London Richardson Brothers' Torture Gang.

This seemingly trivial East End incident triggered events that brought down both gangs, ruined a number of political careers, and led to the biggest clear-out of bent coppers from the Met for a generation. Even the Head of the Sweeney, the Commander of the elite Flying Squad, was implicated. "Sweeney Todd" meant Flying Squad, in

London rhyming slang. It is no exaggeration to say that events that night in the Beggar changed the lives of thousands of Londoners, creating a psychic shock that was imprinted on the brickwork.

"Be seeing you," Jameson said to Henry.

"Don't be in any hurry to come back," Henry replied.

Karla and Jameson walked out of the Beggar into modern London. The Mini Cooper was still there, still lemon colored, but was a BMW mini with the Red Cross of Saint George and England painted on its roof. Tropes evolve, like everything else.

Jameson checked his mobile phone and waited while it locked on to a network. He touched an icon, which changed when it acquired a secure line.

"Randolph," said a voice.

"Re our little problem, find out all you can about the Sith," Jameson said.

"I wondered where you had got to," Randolph said. "What are Sith?"

"Try looking under Irish elves," Jameson suggested. "And find out what information we have about an organization of suckers called Protectors. Supposedly they defeated and banished the Sith."

"Protectors and Irish elves." Randolph sighed. "I suppose it's better than leprechauns."

"I'm going home for a shower and a sleep. I'll come in later."

"Decent of you to grace us with your presence," Randolph said, ringing off before Jameson could come up with a suitably crushing reply.

"I have a proposition for you, Snow White, so why don't we have a little chat?" Max asked.

"My name's Rhian. Snow White's a character in a fairy tale."

"Aren't we all in a fairy tale?" Max asked, rhetorically.

"What's your game?"

A heavy materialised at Max's side. He looked more bewildered than angry, as if he could not quite believe what had happened. Max looked him up and down. The heavy obviously failed to impress Max, who turned back to Rhian.

"I'm talking to you," the heavy laid a hand on Max's arm.

This proved to be a bad decision. Max's reaction was

breathtakingly fast. He wrenched his arm free and backhanded the heavy across the face. Max did not appear to exert himself unduly, but the gangster flew across the room, only stopping when he demolished a table. Beer, glass, and wood exploded, an unfortunate customer going backwards over his chair, still clutching his newspaper.

The second heavy was clearly having problems dealing with the intellectual challenge posed by such an unprecedented situation. His face contorted with concentration as great as Einstein's must have been when postulating Special Relativity, Darwin's when struggling with evolution, or Harry Fox's when he devised the Foxtrot.

However, the goon brightened at the onset of a fight. This, his expression seemed to say, was his metier, his *raison d'être*, the purpose for which he had been put on Earth. It was a shame that it all went wrong so quickly.

The heavy charged, arms flailing. Max took a step back at the critical moment, and the heavy went past like a buffalo heading for the water hole. He covered the ground with impressive speed for such a large man until he made intimate contact with the fruit machine. It made an angry chucka-chucka noise at the heavy's impudence, vindictively spraying the gangster with coins while flashing colored lights like a Japanese car console.

"Friends of yours?" Max asked Rhian.

"Do they look the sort of people who would be friends of mine?" Rhian asked witheringly.

The fruit machine shorted out with a loud bang.

"I am sure your employer can spare you for the rest of the evening," Max said smoothly.

"I have to earn a living," Rhian said.

"Indeed, and that is what I wish to discuss with you, in private," Max said, pointedly.

"Do you know this man?" Gary asked, meaningfully cradling the baseball bat.

"Yes, he's a pain in the neck but not dangerous," Rhian replied, mentally crossing her fingers.

Gary laughed humourlessly, looking around at the wreckage of his bar. "Tell that to Charlie Parkes' enforcers—and my slot machine."

Max took out his wallet and laid an impressive wad of twenties on the bar. "That should cover breakages."

"Perhaps it would be best if I find out what Max wanted, if that's okay?" Rhian asked Gary, diplomatically.

"Why not? I don't seem to have many customers left," Gary said gloomily, securing the notes.

The pub had emptied except for the heavies, who had lost interest in the proceedings.

"Excellent," Max said.

"I'll get my coat."

Ever the gentleman, Max held the door open for Rhian. Once outside, he lit a cigarette with an old lighter that smelled of petrol.

"Those things are dangerous," Rhian said disapprovingly.

Max took a deep lungful and exhaled. The smoke curled up, briefly illuminated by the dim street lights before vanishing into the dark.

"The lighter or the fag?"

"Both."

"I've a strong constitution," Max said.

Rhian could not see his face, but she just knew he would have a smug smile plastered all over it. Max offered his arm and Rhian found herself resting her hand on it as they walked, like some Edwardian gentle-lady out with her beau. It was all rather old fashioned but somehow right. Refusal would have been churlish and demeaning to her, rather than him. Good manners, she reflected, could be very disarming.

"You said you had a proposition." Rhian said. "A *business* proposition, I trust."

"Of course," Max replied. "You continue to intrigue me, Snow White."

Rhian opened her mouth to correct the use of her name but shut it again. The bastard was only trying to get a rise out of her.

"So I've done a little digging into your past."

"Really?" Rhian asked.

"Really," Max replied. "And guess what I found?"

"No idea," Rhian replied.

"Nothing," Max said. "You are a high-level witch that no one has ever heard of. I assumed you were a Commission protégée, as you work in partnership with an ex-Commission witch, but they don't seem to know that you exist."

Max did not seem to be taking her anywhere in particular, just looping through the side streets of terraced houses around the pub.

"I need magical support to deal with the Sith. I tried The Commission, but Karla was unhelpful, so I'd like to put you and your partner on a retainer. Shall we say . . . fifty a day plus expenses, with negotiated bonuses for specific tasks?"

"Each?" Rhian asked, wondering who Karla was.

"Okay, each, you drive a hard bargain, Snow White."

Rhian had the impression that money was meaningless to Max. She wished she had asked for more but a deal was a deal.

"These Sith must be important?" Rhian asked.

"They are bloody dangerous," Max replied, "But you know that, Snow White, because you've met some."

Rhian thought of the glamorous couple in the subway and shuddered.

"Quite," Max said.

She and Max ambled along beside storage units built right onto the pavement. The street was narrow here and used by heavy trucks, so it was double-yellow-lined to keep it clear of parked vehicles. Cars passed at regular intervals, part of the London ambience. She took no particular notice when headlights approached on the other side of the road.

Twenty meters off, the car accelerated suddenly and swung across towards them. Max reacted instantly, picking Rhian up. He ran towards the car before holding her tight against the wall, covering her with his body. The headlights bounced as the car mounted the pavement with its offside front wheel. The driver couldn't turn in quite fast enough. It missed Max by millimeters, glancing off the brick wall less than a meter beyond them with a rasp of tearing metal. Rhian had the impression of a large German saloon car, a BMW or a Mercedes.

Flashes lit up the car's rear window as it drove away, and there was a series of loud cracks. It took Rhian a moment before she realized someone was firing at them. People didn't fire guns in London. It just never happened.

Still holding Rhian with one hand, Max returned fire on the back of the car with his pistol. Rhian was astonished. He must walk around the streets permanently armed, so how did he avoid getting picked up by the police? There was a tinkle of glass, and all the car's lights winked out. It vanished around a corner and did not return.

"Are you all right?" Max asked, putting Rhian down.

She leaned against the wall in shock, feeling faint. She grabbed Max for support, and he winced. One of her hands came away from his side covered in something dark and sticky.

"You're hurt," she said. "I'll call an ambulance."

"No thanks," Max said. "I'll heal quickly, Snow White. It was only a bullet."

"It could have been me," she said, realizing he had protected her at some cost to himself. Max wasn't human and bullets probably couldn't kill him, but it obviously hurt.

He still held her against the wall, moving his leg between hers until she gripped him with her thighs. He kissed her long and hard and she closed her eyes, surrendering to his passion.

"I've another proposition for you," he said, his voice thick.

"I'm not scared of you. I could rip your throat out if I wanted," she said, opening her eyes.

"I know you believe that, and maybe it's true," he said, shaking his head with a smile. "A human who doesn't fear me, I suppose that's what makes you so bloody exciting."

He nuzzled her neck with his teeth. She tilted her head back, allowing him access.

The trouble with academics, Jameson often thought, was that their brains were so stuffed with information that they could never describe a wood without arguing about the definition of a bloody tree.

"It's difficult to draw any conclusions. The ancients used terms like elf, goblin, fairy, troll, and dwarf interchangeably," Kendrics said. He winced as if the idea of such inaccuracy caused him physical pain.

"But the name Daoine Sith does appear in Irish folk tales in the context of intelligences from outside our universe." He shrugged.

Miss Arnoux opened her mouth. From the light of battle in her eyes, she intended to challenge the multiverse model with her view of the Otherworld. However, she shut up after a frown from Randolph promised pain worse than eternal fire on anyone wasting his time.

"Anything in the library about sucker Protectors guarding the human race from the Sith?" Jameson asked.

Kendrics shook his head. Miss Arnoux polished her spectacles.

"An organization of suckers sounds as unlikely as a conclave of cats," she said.

Jameson tended to agree with her.

"The word Protector was found on an inscribed stone at Castell Dwywran in Wales and is also recorded in the writings of the British monk Gildas the Wise. It is the title of the sixth-century Irish King Voteporix, who ruled Pembrokeshire. One assumes it is a bastardization of the Latin *protectores*, the word for a staff officer in the late Roman army. It could just mean bodyguard."

Kendrics glanced around. Unnerved by the blank stares of his fellows, he started to babble. "The exact word on the stone is *protictoris*, but that's probably a spelling error because the scribe lacked a classical education."

Randolph gave him a look that could split granite.

"Voteporix was one of the petty tyrants running a successor barbarian state after the collapse of Roman authority," Kendrics added frantically, before winding down like the toy rabbit powered by just the ordinary battery in the television advert.

"And this is relevant?" Jameson asked.

"Probably not," Kendrics replied.

"So there is no information in the entire Library records that are of the slightest value?" Randolph asked.

Kendrics winced and Miss Arnoux smiled grimly. The annual budget assessment was only nine weeks away. No doubt she had plans to use this as ammunition in another bid to grab some of the Library's money. One had to keep an eye on what mattered. Saving the world was desirable, all things being equal, but the annual budget assignment was important.

"There are hints and speculations . . ." Kendrics' voice died away.

"So speculate," Randolph said.

Kendrics cleared his throat. "The Sith come from the Gaelic Otherworld. They enter and leave the world at specific magical places, such as fairy rings or barrows, where the barrier between the worlds is thin."

He glanced around the meeting room to see how his words were going down. Randolph flicked a finger, indicating that he should continue, so Kendrics cleared his throat again.

"The barriers are considered thinnest at sunrise and sunset."

"They enter the world at sunset and leave before the dawn, before the Sun burns them," Miss Arnoux said.

"Um, quite," Kendrics said. "There are suggestions in the Irish *Book of Invasions* of a war between the Sith and Milesians. The Milesians win and drive the Sith back into the Otherworld. According to the myths, the Irish are descended from or owe their existence to these Milesians. The name is probably from the same root as *miles*, Latin for a soldier, from which we get words like military or militia. So a Milesian is probably a warrior or soldier . . ."

"Or Protector?" Jameson asked.

"In the sense of soldier or bodyguard, yes," Kendrics replied.

"So, to sum up," Randolph said, "some unknown powerful magicians are opening gates for paranormal monsters to enter the world, including some particularly unpleasant Elves that threaten the existence of the human race. But not to worry, because an organization of home-grown supernatural killers intend to fight them to a standstill with London and its seven million inhabitants as the chosen battleground."

"Put like that . . ." Kendrics began.

"We're fucked," Jameson finished for him.

"I hesitate to ask this, but does anyone have any additional good news for me?" Randolph asked.

Jameson raised a hand.

"It would be you," Randolph said. "Do tell, is the Sun about to go nova, the seas boil, or is a plague of frogs due in St. James Park?"

"It may be of no great import, but this Max character suggested the Sith mated with human beings."

Miss Arnoux sniffed. "It is not unknown for people of low morals to have sex with daemons," she said, looking pointedly at Jameson.

"Not just sex, but viable reproduction leading to hybrids, which I did not think possible. I realise sex and reproduction are outside your frame of experience . . ." Jameson said to Miss Arnoux.

He stopped when Miss Arnoux looked sick and Kendrics had turned white.

"What?" Jameson asked.

"The Children of the Gods, the Heroes," Kendrics muttered.

Miss Arnoux, who was made of sterner stuff than Kendrics, quickly regained her composure.

"There are many stories in Classical times about hybrid children descended from a god or other mystical being and a human woman."

"Zeus appearing as a shower of gold or a swan to have his wicked way with a human maiden," Jameson said with a grin.

"Yes, and the children would be powerful beyond human imagining, and they could have grandchildren."

"The sons of Hercules," Kendrics said.

"Quite." Miss Arnoux paused to choose her words before continuing. "It's why the conceptual barrier between the divine and the mundane was less distinct in the Ancient World. The emperors could project themselves as gods to their peoples without inspiring ridicule."

"Even if true, this is surely ancient history," Randolph said. "All very interesting, I suppose,"—his tone suggested otherwise—"but of minimal relevance to our current predicament."

"Not that ancient," Kendrics said. "Take Morgan La Fay, for instance."

"The nightclub off Regent Street, with the gay sex dungeon?" Randolph asked.

Everyone looked at him in silence.

"Are you sniggering, Kendrics?" Randolph asked.

"No, sir," Kendrics sat up straight. "Morgan La Fey as in the, ah, mythological sorceress and enemy of King Arthur," Kendrics said. "Named after the Celtic Goddess Morgana. 'La Fay' literally means The Fairy, meaning that she was partly descended from a supernatural being, not that, ah, um, her sexual orientation was . . ."

Randolph said. "So what?"

"Don't you see?" Miss Arnoux asked rhetorically. "Suckers kill individual people, but they need them: no people, no food. These Sith things interbreed to produce viable offspring, powerful magicians that can walk under the Sun. How long before we ceased to be human at all?"

"It may be worth noting that the putative Milesian-Sith war coincided with the Dark Ages. Roman culture in the British Isles was completely annihilated. When English settlers arrived, the cities and villas of the Roman lowlands were ruins and the land was empty. Only the Celts hidden in the mountains and the offshore islands survived to become the Welsh and Irish," Kendrics said.

"Terrific," Randolph said. "So how do we stop this happening again?"

There was dead silence.

"Any ideas, anyone? Don't all talk at once." Randolph asked.

Karla was gazing up at the ceiling with an expression of mild boredom.

"You stop the enemy before they get in," she said. "Find out who is opening the gates for the Sith and kill them."

She lowered her head and smiled at Randolph, showing long fangs. He smiled back. No fangs, but he had an expression just as predatory. They looked like two cats discussing what to do about mice.

"A plan with the merit of simplicity," Randolph said. "It could even work."

"And if it doesn't?" Miss Arnoux asked.

She didn't like Karla at all. Every so often she tried to persuade Randolph to "terminate the experiment," as she put it.

"Then your worries are over," Karla said.

Kendrics cleared his throat.

"You have a contribution?" Randolph asked.

"It occurs to me that the daemonic intrusion at Limehouse Basin was somewhat atypical," Kendrics replied.

"In what way?"

"It takes a considerable effort to open a matter transport gate to let in mass rather than just information or energy."

Jameson translated that in his head as to let in a daemon rather than a spirit.

"And yet the daemon immediately targeted a single individual, ignoring a bystander, and just left. Why didn't it go on a killing spree?"

"Yes, Gaston noted that at the time," Jameson said. "You think it was assassination by summoned daemon."

"It wouldn't be the first time," Randolph said. "What do we know about the victim?"

Kendrics opened a file on his laptop.

"Name of Fethers, owned a small bank specializing in commodity trading. No previous criminal convictions, no membership of strange cults or religions, just your ordinary City shark. Of course, I don't have the capability of going through his business dealings."

"No, but I know a man who does," Jameson said, getting to his feet.

Frankie was still up when Rhian arrived back at the flat.

"Gary rang to say you had left work early—with this Max character," Frankie said neutrally.

Rhian gave her a sharp look. This was like having an elder brother and sister who could not keep their noses out of her business.

"I didn't know Gary had your number?"

"I must have given it to him sometime," Frankie said casually. "Gary said there had been some trouble at the pub."

Rhian shrugged. "Some local hoodlum sent a couple of heavies to fetch me for a date. Max wanted to talk business, so he tossed them out."

Frankie's eyebrows shot up faster than a nun's knickers. She was clearly reevaluating her opinion of Rhian's admirer.

"What business could Max have with you?" Frankie asked neutrally.

"With you, actually. Max needs to call on witchcraft and has offered you a contract," Rhian said.

"Indeed," Frankie said.

"He is offering a retainer of fifty quid a day with bonuses for actual jobs," Rhian said, slightly defiantly. She handed Frankie a check. "That's three months' installment on the retainer."

Frankie's eyebrows travelled so far north that they were in danger of disappearing into her hairline. She resembled a geriatric film star with too harsh a facelift, the sort of plastic surgery that relocates your navel to under your chin.

"That is a considerable sum of money," Frankie said, slowly. "What would one have to do to earn it?"

"I didn't ask that," Rhian admitted.

"Tell me about Max." Frankie said. "I know you don't like talking about your private life, honey, but this is important. I want every detail, no holding back."

Rhian told her everything, well, almost everything. Frankie was a good listener and interrupted only to tease some detail out of Rhian's memory.

"You know what Max is?" Frankie asked when Rhian had finished.

"A vampire," Rhian replied.

"We prefer to call them daemons, EDEs, or just suckers. Vampires are mythical monsters," Frankie said primly.

"EDEs?"

"Extra-dimensional entities."

"And 'we' are?" Rhian asked.

"The Commission, my ex-employers, I suppose I should call them 'they' now I've left, but old habits, and all that. Suckers are, well, daemons but not vampires." She sighed. "But I agree that it's a distinction without much difference. So our potential new rich client is a sucker, which explains why he needs to hire witches. Suckers are daemonic monsters, but they don't usually do magic. They sort of *are* magic, if you see what I mean."

Rhian didn't, but she didn't suppose it mattered much.

Frankie stood up and looked at Rhian, head cocked to one side.

"Max turned up very conveniently to dispose of the gangsters," Frankie said. "How did he know where you worked?"

"I don't know," Rhian replied. "I didn't tell him."

"You got your phone from him, so he knows the number. I suppose he might have pinged it to get your location. Journalists do that to track down celebrities to their drinking holes and mistresses' flats."

"How do you ping a mobile?" Rhian asked.

"You bribe a policeman. The Met has the technology, but suckers don't normally turn to technology or officialdom. Unfortunately, there is another possibility."

Frankie went into her bedroom. Rhian could hear her searching through a cupboard for something. She reappeared with a white plastic desktop lamp. Its fashionable square head looked quite out of keeping with the rest of Frankie's rather old-fashioned furniture.

"A sun-ray lamp," Frankie said, answering Rhian's unasked question.

Rhian could not imagine why on Earth the pale-skinned Frankie required a tanning lamp. The woman pulled a chair to the wall where the electrical sockets were fixed. Old London houses never had enough electrical outlets for modern demands, so Frankie had a dangerous array of multiple adaptors plugged into the only two in the room.

"Sit here," Frankie said.

Rhian did as she was told. Frankie pushed her head back and played the ultraviolet-rich light on her neck.

"You've met Max twice, right?"

"Yes," Rhian replied.

"You've evidence of two bites on your neck. One is old, the other recent, very recent. Max doesn't need a phone to track you down. He has taken a little of your blood, your life force. He knows where you are and how you are feeling about it. The connection will fade with time, provided it isn't reinforced by other intimacies."

Rhian felt her cheeks burning.

"Oh, I see," Frankie said.

CHAPTER 13
FINANCIAL INCENTIVES

Jameson gave Inspector Fowler a week to investigate Fethers activities before arranging a meeting. The Inspector suggested a pub in Southwark called The King's Men, which somewhat surprised Jameson. It did not surprise him that Fowler chose a pub. Policemen always wanted to meet in pubs as homage to some tradition of the Ancient Guild of Plod. What was unexpected was the location of the hostelry.

Southwark, on the south side of London Bridge, meant The South Bank, Shakespeare's Globe Theatre, The Tate Modern, and all things arty. The King's Men presumably referred to the acting company to which Shakespeare belonged in his early days. It occurred to Jameson that Fethers was having a little joke at his expense, a dig at his Cambridge literary degree. He would not have credited the inspector with that much comedic subtlety.

He looked up the exact location of the pub up on his phone. It wasn't on the South Bank of the Thames at all but down in the heart of Southwark Town where Watling Street, the old Roman Road to the Channel Coast, terminated.

Jameson parked the Jaguar just off Watling Street by Tabard Gardens, cheerfully ignoring the parking restrictions. He put the Police Special Branch car ID on the dashboard to frighten off traffic wardens.

A plaque on the redbrick office block that came hard up to the pavement announced it was the site of a Roman temple dedicated to a Celtic god from Rheims. He recalled that archaeologists had come across impressive remains of Roman Southwark when putting in the new Jubilee Tube Line. They had found the burial of a gladiatrix, a lady gladiator. This news was far more interesting to the press as the burial artefacts included her leather bikini bottom. Some things never change.

The construction work had uncovered a black layer indicating that Boudica's warriors had burned Southwark when they sacked London. Modern strategic analysis had suggested that Boudica's real target was London Bridge. By burning the bridge she isolated her chosen battleground of central England from the south. Rome had allied tribes in the south, and the main Roman field army under Governor Suetonius Paulinus drew supplies over London Bridge from its depot at Richborough in Kent.

Jameson thought that was a load of bollocks dreamed up by military planners who didn't understand the difference between a Celtic warband and NATO. Boudica attacked London because it was undefended, because it was a port depot and full of loot, because a cheap victory would embolden her warriors to take on the Roman army, and because it would provide numerous prisoners for blood sacrifice and blood magic. Mostly, she attacked London because it was there.

A short walk north towards the river took Karla and Jameson to the junction, and they found The King's Men a few meters down Long Lane. He laughed when he saw the pub sign. It had nothing to do with Shakespeare. It showed a couple of redcoats imbibing deeply from a cask of ale. He was pleased that he had not misinterpreted the Inspector's character. It was unnerving when one's judgment was so far off. It made one wonder what else one was missing. What you didn't know could get you killed in Jameson's line of work.

Fowler stood at the bar in the crowded pub, sipping a pint of bitter. A no-go area clear of other drinkers around the Inspector showed that he was known to the other clientèle. Jameson joined Fowler and ordered himself a scotch. Karla leaned back against the bar and observed the customers. The no-go area around them suddenly increased in diameter, a ripple of movement following her eyes.

"Can I get you something, Inspector?" Jameson asked.

"Why not? I think I'll have a double of what you're having," Fowler replied.

"You sure you wouldn't prefer another half pint?"

"No, thanks."

Jameson and Fowler knew each other well enough that they did not have to go through the pantomime of the policeman refusing a drink "because he was on duty" and being reluctantly persuaded.

"Anything you fancy to drink, Karla?"

She turned her head and gave him an amused smile.

"They don't serve that," Jameson said.

Fowler was oblivious to the exchange, busy sinking what was left of his beer in a single gulp. Jameson gave his order to the barman and paid.

"What have you got for me?" Jameson asked.

Fowler tasted his Scotch, with every sign of appreciation before reaching into the inside pocket of his mac to pull out a brown manila envelope. He handed it to Jameson.

"It's all in there."

Jameson carefully folded it and stowed it away in his jacket.

"You know, you spooks in Special Branch really piss me off," Fowler said.

His irritation with Jameson did not seem to spoil his enjoyment of the whisky.

"Really," Jameson replied, in the tone of one who did not give a damn.

"Most of the time, we operate on thin air, but you snap your fingers and I get unlimited staff, unlimited computer time, and unlimited overtime. I think I spent more on this case in a week than the last three murder investigations added together."

"National security and all that," Jameson replied, vaguely.

Fowler snorted and took a gulp of the scotch, to show what he thought of national security.

"Why's it so important anyway? Terrorist blows up banker, so what? Half the public would vote to give the hit man a medal."

"I could tell you but . . ."

"I'd have to kill you," Fowler finished the line of the old joke.

"Well, not kill you, but maybe arrange a posting to the Falkland

Islands to guard the penguin colonies or something," Jameson said with a grin.

"Why do I think you're not joking?" Fowler asked, sourly.

Jameson sipped his whisky cautiously. It was a cheap blended but did not actually seem to be adulterated or, worse still, Korean. Fowler was a pain in the arse but he was a good investigator, unpolitical and honest. Good reasons why he would never rise higher in the Metropolitan Police Service. That was not entirely fair. The upper echelons at Scotland Yard had nothing against being a good investigator, but they did not value it highly enough to offset Fowler's other disadvantages, such as integrity.

His qualities were highly valued by The Commission. Fowler had that indefinable copper's nose for something that just did not smell right and a bloodhound's instinct for following a trail to source. Having The Commission on his side gave Fowler a wall of protection when the Met put him in the frame for downsizing.

"You've been through the file yourself?" Jameson asked.

"Of course," Fowler replied.

"Anything strike you as suspicious?"

"Not really; Fethers was your usual merchant."

Merchant, as in merchant banker, was London rhyming slang for wanker. It was not clear which meaning Fowler meant. Probably both, as they were hardly mutually exclusive.

"Pillar of society in Surrey, wife, kids, member of the Rotarians, Mason, and Friends of The Old Puffer."

Jameson looked at him. "Puffer?"

"A steam train restoration society," Fowler explained. "He was a bit of a lad in London. He liked cute young escort girls, did a bit of coke, and played in the casinos but lost no more than he could afford. He sailed a bit close to the wind at times but did nothing that would cause the Serious Farce boys to come out of their communal coma."

Fowler did not just despise the Special Branch. He spread his contempt evenhandedly, loathing most of the specialist police units with the possible exception of the Dog Handlers. Mind you, he had something of a point with the Serious Fraud Squad, universally acknowledged to be useless. To be fair, they were not encouraged to be dynamic by their political masters. London was the world's largest finance center. The industry made vast sums of money for the British Exchequer, as well as giving generous financial donations to political parties. It was in nobody's interests to probe too deeply into the entrails of the Golden Goose. One might find something rotten that would force the Government to garrotte the bird. Nobody wanted that, least of all the politicians.

There was a long silence while they both drank their whisky. It was eventually broken by the Inspector.

"There was one thing," Fowler said. "Fethers' death was conveniently timed."

"For whom?"

"For Greyfriars Venture Capital."

"Oh?"

"Hmm, you know the teenage high-street fashion chain, Go-Girls?" Fowler asked.

"No, I don't have much contact with teenage girls," Jameson said.

"Lucky you," said Fowler, who had three daughters. "Go-Girls are in trouble, and Fethers was organising a recapitalization. Of course, that collapsed with his death, and Greyfriars were able to pick the chain up for a song."

"Who owns Greyfriars?" Jameson asked. "Who pulls the strings?"

"The usual crew of hidden offshore trusts own the company," Fowler replied. "I suppose the SFA could track them back if you gave them a couple of years, but a man called Fyodorovich von Ungern-Shternberg is the real owner."

Fowler looked meaningfully at his empty glass, so Jameson ordered a refill.

"Have you run a background check?" Jameson asked, playing the game.

"Of course," Fowler pulled out another brown paper envelope with the air of a stage magician producing a rabbit from a hat.

"Shternberg is part of the flotsam that floated west when the Iron Curtain burst. He arrived in London via Milan with mucho capital so was welcomed in with open arms as a non-dom, no embarrassing questions asked."

"What's his official nationality?" Jameson asked.

"British now, his company contributes generously to party funds," Fowler replied cynically.

"Which party?" Jameson asked. The answer might give an insight into Shternberg's attitudes.

"Whichever one is currently in power," Fowler said, which was informative in its way.

There was a burst of laughter from the corner of the pub. Jameson realized that he had lost track of Karla. She stood in front of the dartboard, having thrown a clean one hundred and forty. Her opponent could not get out the dart sunk in the double top.

"Thank you, Inspector; we will no doubt be in touch," Jameson said, hurriedly.

He went to retrieve his beloved before someone got hurt.

Sheila was on duty behind the bar when Rhian put her head around the door of the pub.

"I thought Gary would be working this lunchtime?" she asked.

"He's had an accident so I'm doing extra shifts," Sheila replied.

"Where is he?" Rhian asked.

Sheila jerked her head upwards. Gary was either in his flat or heaven. Rhian assumed it was the former so went through behind the bar, up the stairs and knocked on the door at the top.

"It's open," Gary called from inside.

She let herself in and followed the sound of a television to the flat lounge. Gary was slumped in a chair in a bathrobe. He tried to rise but sank back with a wince.

"What have you done to yourself?" Rhian asked.

"I fell down the stairs and bruised a rib—silly really," Gary said.

"Have you seen anyone?" Rhian asked.

"Oh, sure, I got a taxi down to the health center for a check-up. Nothing to be done about it but to rest and take it easy for a bit."

Rhian pushed aside his robe. Gary started to protest but subsided after she gave him a sharp look. He had a fine collection of blue and purple bruises on his chest.

"Where's your kitchen?" she asked.

"Next left," he replied.

The kitchen was a tiny corridor of a room with a cabinet down one side and a sink at the end. She filled the small electric kettle and hunted through the wall cupboards for tea bags and a couple of reasonably clean mugs. Another search revealed a packet of digestive biscuits. The top one or two were soft and stale when she prodded them, but those underneath were not too bad.

The kettle came to the boil and turned itself off with a loud click. She filled the mugs. She sniffed suspiciously at the carton of milk in the fridge, but it seemed okay. Rhian stirred and prodded the tea bags with a fork to speed up the brewing process. After three or four minutes she judged the color to be adequate and removed the bags. She put two sugar cubes in Gary's, whether he wanted them or not, and carried the tea and biscuits into the lounge. Gary turned off his television with a remote and Rhian handed him a biscuit.

"I'm not hungry," Gary said.

"Eat it and drink your tea," Rhian said in a voice that brooked no argument.

"Right," Gary said, doing as he was told.

"What did you have for lunch?" Rhian asked. "I didn't notice much of the way in food in the fridge."

"I thought I might have some toast later," Gary said defensively.

Rhian sniffed to show what she thought of that. She took out her mobile and flicked through the menu.

"Hello, Frankie, are you busy?"

"Not especially, why?"

"Could you come over to the pub, stopping off at the shops to pick up some groceries for Gary? He's hurt himself and can't get out."

"Hold on there, Rhian," Gary said.

"What does he need?" Frankie asked.

"Everything, Frankie, he's a man so he needs bloody everything," Rhian replied, ringing off.

"This is embarrassing, Rhian," Gary said. "You can't just get your landlady to do my shopping."

"Rubbish," Rhian said. "She will enjoy fussing round after you."

"Do you think so?" Gary asked.

"Sure of it," Rhian replied. She looked Gary over. "Come on, Gary, give. What really happened?"

"I told you, I fell down the stairs." He avoided her eyes.

"My father used to come home drunk and give my mother a good beating. I've seen bruises like that before. You don't get fist marks from falling down stairs."

"Okay, I was mugged. They didn't get much and I wouldn't recognize them again, so let it drop."

"Mugged, right, Gary, do you think I'm stupid? No, don't answer that," Rhian said.

He gave her a wan smile. "No, I've never thought you stupid. A little naive sometimes, but nothing life will not cure. Okay, Charlie Parkes sent a couple of his boys round to make a point. Your, ah, friend, Max . . ."

He stopped and looked at her curiously, silently inviting her to clarify her relationship with the man.

"Go on," Rhian said.

"Max pissed him off by beating up his boys. It's a matter of face, you see. Charlie can't have people thinking that he can't run his own manor, or they would start taking liberties. He accepted I had nothing to do with it or I'd be in hospital or worse, but an example still had to be made, and as Max wasn't available . . ."

Gary shrugged, which caused him to wince again.

"I get the picture," Rhian said.

She was angry, blazingly angry. Parkes and Max could play boys' games with each other all they liked, but how dare they involve her boss. Gary was a decent bloke who did not deserve this. Something would have to be done, she told herself.

"You might warn your friend Max to make himself scarce for a while," Gary said.

"Max can look after himself," Rhian said, tight lipped.

"Yeah, well, I saw that he is pretty handy with his fists, but Parkes' boys will probably be tooled up next time they go looking for him."

"What?"

"Tooled up, you know, with shooters."

"They had a go last night," Rhian said. "Someone did a drive-by at Max and me after we left the pub. He took a bullet."

"Bloody hell," Gary said. "Is he all right?"

"Oh, sure, just a minor wound, it won't bother him much."

"Right," Gary said, looking puzzled.

"Max was, ah, tooled up himself, so he shot up their car. It was dark, but he says he got the gunman."

"Oh, dear God," Gary said, putting his head in his hands.

At that point there was a knock at the door. Rhian let in Frankie.

She arrived like Christ come to cleanse the temple, except that Christ probably didn't carry Asda shopping bags.

"That was quick," Rhian said.

"I was out in Mildred so I came right over," Frankie said.

"Mildred?" asked Gary.

"My Morris Minor."

"Good Lord, does it still run?"

"Most of the time," Frankie replied.

"Where are you parked?" Gary asked.

"Right outside," Frankie said.

"You ought to move her. This is a double yellow no-parking zone."

"No problem, I have a disabled parking badge," Frankie said with a grin.

"That's all very well, but Charlie Parkes has the clamping concession in this borough. The sort of goons he employs would clamp an invalid carriage with the invalid still in it."

"They won't touch Mildred," Frankie said, confidently.

Gary still looked doubtful, but Rhian suspected that Frankie had put some sort of aversion spell on the Morris.

"I've fresh bread, milk and butter, some cold meats, cheese, mincemeat, pasta, and fruit. I also brought a four-pack of Guinness to build up your strength," Frankie said.

"That's very kind, but we do have rather a lot of stout downstairs," Gary said with a smile.

"Oh, yes, I suppose you would," Frankie said vaguely.

"It being a pub," Rhian added, helpfully.

She showed Frankie the kitchen. After the groceries were safely stowed, Frankie cooked pasta while Rhian updated her on the problem. They left Gary in the lounge watching a repeat of a 1970s sitcom. The plot involved a market gardener whose tomatoes would not ripen and the allegedly hilarious attempts by him and his "kooky" friends to rectify the problem and get them to market. Gary was fast asleep when they brought in lunch. There was nothing like a 70s sitcom to help you drift off.

"Up you get," Rhian said, assisting Gary to the table.

"You are stronger than you look," Gary said.

"So I'm told," Rhian replied.

While Frankie clucked around Gary, Rhian keyed a contact on her mobile. It rang five times before a digitally recorded voice said. "I'm busy, leave a message after the tone."

"I don't care how bloody busy you are, sunshine. I want you round at the Black Swan bloody quick, like now."

She hung up.

"He won't be able to come until after dark," Frankie said.

"Why, is he a vampire or something?" Gary asked, with a chuckle.

The food, or maybe having two women running around after him, had done wonders for his mood.

"Or something," Frankie replied.

He looked at Frankie with a smile, which faded when Frankie failed to return it.

"Well, you've seen him in action," she said to Gary.

"You shouldn't involve him," Rhian said.

"He's already involved," Frankie said. "He's met you, and me, and Max. The way things are going, all of East London's going to be involved."

"Involved in what?" Gary asked.

"Max is a daemon," Frankie said, conversationally. "Think of him as a vampire if it helps, but he's not really. Although he does drink human blood."

"This is a wind up, right?" Gary asked, uncertainly. "You're yanking my chain."

"You've seen Max," Frankie said. "How would you describe him?"

"Very fast, very strong, but . . ." Gary's voice trailed off.

"And he shrugs off bullet wounds," Rhian added.

"I feel like I've fallen down the rabbit hole," Gary said. He looked at the women as if they were mad. "So what are you? The two witches, or have you left a mate back at home to watch the cauldron?"

"Ha, bloody ha," Rhian replied. "Of course I'm not a witch. Frankie is the witch."

She paused and ran a hand through her hair. "Frankie's right. What you don't know won't protect you but ignorance could kill. I involved you the moment I took a job here. The connection with Max, or something like him, was inevitable. I'm so very sorry, Gary, that I didn't think things through."

"Look," Gary said. "I am sure you nice ladies are quite sincere about all this Wicca stuff, but I'm Church of England myself. Well, I would be if I ever went to church. Max may well be a scary guy, but East London has always been full of scary guys. My grandfather met the Krays once, and let me tell you, they were bloody terrifying. They made the Charlie Parkeses of this world look like Mormon missionaries."

"I'm really sorry, Gary, but I have to convince you for your own good," Rhian said.

"Stop! Think about this, Rhian," Frankie said, warningly.

"He's my responsibility so it's my problem," Rhian said, sadly.

She was aware that what she was about to do would change her relationship with Gary forever. Perhaps destroy it altogether, but she had to do what she had to do. Rhian reached inside of herself and summoned her alter ego, the wolf.

The world spun and morphed around her. It was so easy to change after Frankie's magic. This must be what Boudica experienced. The world settled down, monochrome and flat but alive with three-dimensional scents and sounds. She heard Sheila rattle some glasses downstairs. When a pigeon on a ledge outside the building cooed, she heard it. She smelt it.

Gary froze.

The wolf stalked around the room. It knew Frankie as one of Rhian's pack and it accepted Gary as harmless by feeding off Rhian's emotional responses. After two circuits, the wolf was bored so she sat down and scratched an ear. She offered no resistance when Rhian pushed her down and was Rhian again.

There was a long silence.

"So you're not a witch, you're a werewolf," Gary finally said.

He was remarkably calm, all things considered.

"She's not really a werewolf, but . . ." Frankie said.

"I can think of her as one if it helps," Gary finished the sentence for her.

He put his head in his hands. "This is a dream, right. My barmaid is a werewolf, her landlady is a witch, and one of my customers is a vampire. Anything else you want to tell me?"

Rhian shook her head.

"No, are you sure? Is this where you tell me that David Icke is the son of God and the world is run by shape-shifting alien lizards from Draco? Are Peter Pan, Tinkerbell and Wendy really living in a meaningful *ménage à trois* in Neverland? Does every rainbow have a pot of gold at the end? Can I expect Lord Lucan to pop in for a quick one on Sherga later or maybe H.P. bloody Lovecraft to ride Great Cthulhu down my bleedin' chimney?"

His voice had risen to a near shriek.

"Be quiet," Frankie said, cracking the words like a whip. "You're frightening the girl."

"Sorry, Rhian," Gary said.

He paused. "What am I doing apologizing to a werewolf for frightening her?" he said, wonderingly.

"I'm not a werewolf," Rhian said, somewhat plaintively. "I just look like one."

"If it quacks like a duck," Gary said. He held up a hand to placate Frankie.

"I'm only joking. You must admit, this is a lot to take in. I trundle happily through life with nothing but Head Office, Charlie Parkes and the obergruppenführers from Customs and Exercise to worry about, and suddenly I am lost in a horror story."

"Hmm," Frankie said. "There is also the problem that someone is opening gates to the Otherworld, letting in elves."

"Elves don't sound so bad," Gary said.

"These are sorcerous psychopathic elves that feed on human pain and death."

"Oh, right," Gary said. "I suppose they would be."

The Jaguar had "a do not attempt to drive this car" notice stuck under a windscreen wiper when Jameson and Karla returned to pick it up. Further investigation revealed a large yellow metal plate clamped to the offside front wheel.

Two large beefy men leaned against the front of the white van parked behind. One, hiding behind large black wrap-around sunglasses, had his arms crossed. The other sucked on a fag, his open sleeveless leather jacket displaying his chest hair and arm tattoos to full advantage.

Jameson gestured at the wheel clamp. "I suppose this is something to do with you?"

"You're illegally parked," said black sunglasses.

The other just sneered, quite a decent little trick that he managed without removing the cigarette from the corner of his mouth. There was, Jameson reflected, always one that talks and one that sneers. He wondered if they were recruited in pairs because they possessed those skills or whether such job specialization was the product of a long training course. He was reminded of the old KGB street thugs who went around in threes: one who could read, one who could write, and one who kept an eye on the intellectuals.

"Didn't you see the police card on the top of the dashboard?"

"The motor don't look like no jam sandwich," black sunglasses said. "Where's your duke box?"

British police cars were no longer white with an orange stripe down the side, but "jam sandwich" was soaked into London English. Jameson fished out his special branch warrant card and stuck it in front of the sunglasses.

"Well you know now, so get the bloody thing off."

"Can't do that, squire," black sunglasses said, arms still crossed. His mate practiced another sneer.

"The only way you get that clamp off of the Jew's canoe, sunshine, is to cough up a monkey," said black sunglasses.

Jameson ran a quick translation from London into English. A monkey was five hundred pounds sterling but Jew's canoe was a new one on him.

"Five hundred quid, you must be having a giraffe," said Jameson, getting into the vernacular, giraffe being laugh.

"A monkey if we take it off now. If we leave and have to come back, it'll be another two hundred sovs for the call-out charge."

"I haven't got time for this crap," Jameson said, losing patience.

He opened the car's boot and rummaged around. He tossed a pair of heavy-duty bolt cutters to Karla, who caught them casually in one hand.

"Fat lot of use that will be on a wheel clamp," black sunglasses said. "What is she, superwoman or something?"

"Or something," Jameson replied. "Cut if off, if you please, Karla."

"You tell him, love. The bastard clamped my son when he came to see me." An old woman's head was stuck out of one of the upper windows.

"Piss off, you old bat," black sunglasses said.

"Don't you talk to Edna like that," said an old man sticking his head out of a window further along on the same level. "I fought a war for you."

The redbrick building might have offices on the lower floors, but there were clearly flats above.

A loud twang drew everyone's attention back to the Jag. Powered by Karla, the cutters sliced through the clamp like Challenger tanks through an Iraqi firebase. Karla proceeded to use the cutters to bash back a flap of metal so she could get at the rest of the plate.

"Oy!" Black sunglasses came off the van and started forward. Jameson pushed him away.

"That'll learn you," Edna said, crowing.

The talkative thug removed his sunglasses with a flourish, tossing them into the van without taking his eyes off Jameson. Unfortunately, the window was still up, so they bounced back into the street. This somewhat spoiled the coolness of the gesture.

"Now you've done it," said the thug with the sneer to Jameson.

"It speaks," Jameson said, with a show of astonishment. "Does this mean you are due for promotion?"

The thug looked at him open-mouthed. His fag rolled down and lodged in his bare folded arms. He shrieked and brushed himself down. Jameson had the distinct feeling that he was not facing exactly Premiere League opposition. The unarmed instructors at the security services would have wept real tears over these two.

The first thug charged Jameson and launched a massive roundhouse swing. It would have ended the fight there and then had it landed. Jameson had graduated with a poor degree because, apart from partying and rowing, he had secured a boxing blue representing Cambridge in a bout against the old enemy, Oxford. He moved inside the swing and caught the thug with two left jabs to the chin. A step to the right and he landed a solid right on the thug's ear.

"Lovely, jubberly, keep your guard up and jab," said the old man, demonstrating so vigorously that he nearly fell out of the window.

"Kill the bastard," advised Edna.

The thug whirled around for another try.

Arms enfolded Jameson from behind. He had lost track of the sneering thug and the swine had his arms pinned. The two had probably pulled off this maneuver before. Thug number one grinned and swung a massive fist. Jameson rolled his head aside and a fist like a pile driver scraped his cheek. A heavy ring opened up a cut. A loud smack indicated that the fist had found a target, and then Jameson was free.

Thug number one opened his mouth. The world will never know what pearls of wisdom he intended to impart. Jameson jabbed him in the aforesaid mouth with another left before he could get started. The thug took a step back, raising his arms to protect his face. That opened the way for a hard right below the belt. Jameson gave it everything he had and his fist sank into flab.

The thugs doubled over with a wheeze. Like a lot of bullies, he had relied too long on size to intimidate. He had let himself go. He should have spent more time in the gym and less in the boozer.

Jameson was aware that the second thug was still somewhere behind. He needed to end this right now and to hell with the ninth Marquess of Queensberry. He hadn't done Oscar Wilde any favours. Time to stop fannying around, Jameson decided. He grasped the first thug's shaven head with both hands and used his whole body weight to push it down. Then he jumped off his right leg and smashed his right knee into the bastard's face. The thug's nose broke with a crunch and he went over backwards in a spray of blood.

He didn't get up.

Jameson whirled around to locate the sneering thug—and relaxed. The man was on one knee holding his chin in both hands. Thug number two tried to rise when Jameson walked over.

"I believe I owe you one," Jameson said pleasantly.

He kicked the thug in the mouth. The man would need some extensive dental work before he could adopt a good sneer again.

"I hope you are registered with an NHS dentist," Jameson said solicitously. "Private treatment can be so expensive."

A Rastaman on the pavement watched with disapproval, shaking his dreadlocks sadly at the brutality and wickedness of old London Town.

"Babylon, man," he said.

"Yah," Jameson replied.

Karla started to clap, a theme taken up by Jameson's elderly audience. There were more of them at the windows, like spectators at a match. There must be a bloody old people's home up there. Jameson wondered which idiot in the Council's Planning Department thought it a good plan to house old people in upstairs flats. He inclined his head in appreciation of their appreciation.

Karla sat on the bonnet of the Jaguar. What remained of the yellow clamp was slung up against the building.

"I don't suppose it occurred to you to give me a hand," Jameson asked.

"I've been reading up on the health of men of a certain age," Karla said, seriously. "You've the life expectancy of mayflies at the best of times. The book stressed the dangers of lack of exercise. I thought you could benefit from a workout."

Jameson was speechless. He got in the car and started the engine. Karla barely managed to jump inside before he drove off. He noticed the logo on the side of the van, but it rang no bells. London was full of chancers he had never heard of Charlie Parkes Security Services.

Max's mobile Teutonic status symbol drew up outside the pub not long after the Sun dipped gratefully below the horizon, leaving. The Wicked City slipped into the long north European twilight as a prelude to another night's carousing and general mayhem. Max would drive a BMW. The initials were rumored to stand for Bloody Minded Wankers in London, that being a fair description of the drivers. Nice cars though, Rhian noticed, as she slipped into the passenger seat. The machine pulled smoothly away, gathering speed quickly.

"Is everything ready?" Max asked.

"Gary did as you said," she said. "But I don't understand why you wanted him to warn Parkes that we are coming?"

"He will assume that we will be mob handed and will do likewise, calling in his soldiers."

"And we want that?" Rhian asked, confused.

Max put his hand on her knee, and she removed it.

"Certainly, that way we get them all together and deal with the matter once and for all."

"I suppose it does get Gary off the hook from any more retaliation from Parkes' thugs."

Max laughed. "Parkes won't be a problem for your friends after tonight."

Rhian began to get pangs of doubt. She had summoned Max because she did not see why he should not clear up the mess he had made for Gary. She was bloody angry at the time and not thinking. She hadn't wanted to start a war. Now she had cooled off a tad, she wondered whether she should have warned off Parkes herself. She mentally shook her head. Warn off Parkes herself? What was she thinking of? Rhian didn't warn people off, let alone East End gangsters. Something was happening to her.

"I don't want any deaths," she said.

"Sure," Max said easily.

Too easily, Rhian regarded him with deep suspicion. "I mean it."

"I know," Max replied, cheerfully.

He appeared to be looking forward to the evening's entertainment. Rhian dreaded the whole business and just wanted to get it done. Max checked his satnav and turned off the main road.

"We can't be there yet?" Rhian asked.

"Shortcut," Max replied. "The traffic will be hellish at the Fairwater Roundabout."

The traffic was bloody awful anyway. It always was in London. The city was a conglomerate of small towns and cities that had spread out to touch, and the road system had grown organically from tracks designed for local traffic. The local traffic at the time of building consisted primarily of pedestrians and horses. The only routes that could be said to be at all car-friendly were the radial highways to the provinces: the A1 to the north, the A2 to the Channel, the A3 to the south coast, and the A4 to the west.

Max threaded the powerful motor quickly through the crush, making the most of its superb handling and brakes. He was an aggressive driver, other motorists backing down rather than contest a gap.

"Have you ever heard the phrase Bloody Minded Wanker?" Rhian asked.

"Who do you think started it?" Max replied, flashing a grin at her.

They arrived outside a yard surrounded by high walls that failed to hide a hill of piled-up rusting car bodies in one corner. Max parked outside and they looked the place over from the car. A sign announced they were at Charlie Parkes Security Services & Scrap Metal Dealership. Despite the hour, the gates were open.

"It seems we are expected," Max said.

He laughed and drove straight in.

❋◗❋

"It's good of you to see us so quickly," Jameson said. "And at this late hour."

"Not at all, I often work late on operationalization issues. So, you're a Special Branch Commander," said Shternberg. "Presumably you want face-time to progress disambiguation of security outcomes?"

Jameson blinked. Karla gazed at Shternberg the way a patent officer looks at the latest design for a perpetual motion machine.

The man was not quite what Jameson had expected. Shternberg was tall and well-built, with the toned body that comes from time in the gym or enthusiastic tennis. He had bright blue eyes, a pale complexion, and a shock of blond hair that was short-cut at the sides but stood up on top. He looked more Nordic than East European.

His grasp of the English language was perfect, in its way, and accentless. This immediately marked him out as overseas. Everybody in the British Isles had an accent that gave away their initial social class and the region within which they grew up. His voice was cold and precise, like a foreign actor that had learned to speak with an all-purpose "English" accent. Unfortunately, someone had also taught Shternberg Master of Business Administration-speak.

He leaned back in an expensive executive chair in front of a modern desk that was all chrome and polished wood. The top looked like a parking lot at an English seaside town in January—large, black and empty. A wireless flat screen and keyboard sat at one edge beside a small metallic arrangement of pipes and leaves in silver and gold. Jameson wondered whether it was an executive toy or a piece of modern art.

The other chairs in the office were low so that Shternberg looked down on his guests. Jameson considered whether this was some cunning ploy to intimidate or simply an expression of the man's overweening sense of superiority. Jameson suspected the latter, and his suspicion rapidly hardened.

"My knighthood, of course. Presumably you are here to discuss security measures for my safety."

Shternberg spoke slowly, like a man explaining something to a small and exceptionally retarded child. Jameson had only been in the man's company for a minute and already he despised him. Special Branch would be more concerned with the safety of Her Majesty than some narcissistic jumped-up money lender. Shternberg's false assumption did explain why he and Karla had got past the botoxed deceptionist in Shternberg's outer office so easily. Receptionists existed to receive visitors and usher them into the presence of the Great Man. Deceptionists served the opposite function.

"No, I was not aware that you are on the next honors list. Congratulations."

"Thank you."

"For what will you be awarded a knighthood?" Jameson asked, politely.

The real answer to that was a massive "campaign contribution" to a prominent politician or one of the major political parties. "Campaign contribution" was the accepted political speak for a backhander. Under Prime Minister David Lloyd George, the selling of honors by politicians had become such a scandal that the scam was made illegal, not that making something illegal ever changed anything. Politicians just had to find some fig-leaf of respectability to cover up the real reason for the award.

"Services to education," Shternberg replied, smugly.

Jameson did not reply and let the pause in the conversation drag out. He had interrogated many suspects, from IRA terrorists to magic-using crooks. Silence was the interrogator's weapon. The subject became more and more stressed until the urge to speak was overwhelming. You could learn so much about how a subject chose to break the silence. It could tell you what they most wanted to hide and what they feared you knew.

Shternberg said nothing, just waited with a half-smile, his hands flat on the desk. This suggested to Jameson that he was a pro. Jameson wondered who had trained the man: the Ukranian SZRU, Estonian KAPO, Latvian SAB, Lithuanian VSD—the list of potential sponsors was endless. Shternberg was so polished that his instructors could even have been the best of the best, the lads from Lubyanka Square. The good ole boys of the Russian FSB evolved out of the KGB. A new name, but customers got the same old friendly service, as the old joke goes.

"I want to ask you about Fethers," Jameson finally said.

Tactic two for an interrogator was the shock approach. Drop your best factoid to imply that you know more than you do. He watched Shternberg closely and was rewarded with a flicker in his eyes. Only a slight flicker, gone in a microsecond, but it was nevertheless suggestive. Not that it proved Shternberg summoned daemons, of course.

"Fethers, Fethers—is that a person or a company?" Shternberg said.

"He was arranging a bailout for Go-Girls," Jameson said.

"Indeed?"

"Until he was killed."

"Oh," Shternberg said with utter disinterest. "Now you mention it, perhaps I do recall the name being brought up in a mind-share at the bank. I believe he was a potential duck shuffler."

"Duck shuffler?" Jameson asked.

"Duck shuffler," Shternberg repeated, tracing out a straight line in the air with his hands. "You know, you get all your ducks for a deal nicely in a row and then someone upsets the apple cart."

"The apples knocking over the ducks," Jameson said, the surreal image floating across his mind's eye.

"Precisely," Shternberg said, with a mirthless smile.

"So Fethers' death was convenient?" Jameson asked.

"Moderately so," Shternberg replied. "I doubt he had the bandwidth to seriously disturb our battle-rhythm."

"What made a bankrupt retail chain worth having?" Jameson asked.

"Go-Girls own a number of their own shops in key high-street sites."

"So you'll asset-strip the company by selling the premises?" Jameson asked.

"We will certainly leverage our investment across the business units to realize their capital value," Shternberg replied.

"You will still be left with a bankrupt retail chain."

"The paradigm is to bucketize the components to core competencies, while right-sizing the administrative resources to reinforce the net-net."

"You mean fire the admin staff to cut costs?"

"You've a talent for succinctness."

Shternberg smiled, not the type of smile to encourage small children. The expression one imagined was what one might see on the snout of a great white upon encountering a surfer, or a game-show host faced with a contestant whose hearing aid has failed.

"The technical services will be bangalored, the empty suits downsized, and half the sales staff promoted to customers."

Jameson translated that as farming out the IT jobs to the third world, and firing the management and most of the shop employees.

"Further traction can be gained by pencil-whipping the accounts with creatalytics."

Or cooking the books, in other words.

"Before selling off the rump of the business as a going concern."

"And I suppose profits are considered capital gains rather than income, so you will be paying a lower rate of tax than your secretary on your profits."

Shternberg made another disturbing movement with his mouth that could be construed as a grin if one was feeling charitable. Jameson was not inclined to be.

"Oh dear, surely you are not that vanilla, Commander Jameson. Only little people pay taxes. Greyfriars is owned by my wife, who lives in Monaco, and I'm non-dom so I've no tax liability at all."

Non-dom stood for non-domiciled and was a special status originally offered to attract foreign plutocrats to live in London without officially living in the United Kingdom, taxwise. They paid tax only on money acquired in Britain, which did not include earnings laundered through offshore tax havens like Monaco. The arrangement was so convenient that British nationals who were rich enough were now arranging non-dom status. One generous non-dom British benefactor to a political party had even become ennobled and taken a seat in the House of Lords. Jameson recalled that he voted to up the rate of tax on British citizens—the non non-dom ones, that is.

Jameson paid fifty percent income tax on the top end of his civil-service salary, so he was presumably classed as one of the little people.

"That does not seem very fair or equitable," Jameson said softly.

Shternberg tilted back his head and laughed out loud.

"You don't make money with all that kumbaya stuff. Wealth creators like me must be above the morality of the common herd."

Jameson opened his mouth to point out that vulture capitalists like Shternberg created wealth only for themselves, but the man talked over him.

"You know what drives the financial markets, Commander,

fear—fear and greed, but mostly fear. Look up the Fear Index on the Vix, the Chicago Board Options Exchange Volatility Index."

He rotated the swivel chair.

"Well, you've used up your time allotment. Unlike you state employees, I've work still to do. If you need to dialogue with me again, contact my secretary, but I warn you that my availability is limited."

Shternberg leaned forward and turned to the computer screen, completely ignoring Jameson and Karla is if they had ceased to exist.

Jameson got up to go. He kept his face impassive at the rudeness. He was damned if he would give Shternberg the satisfaction of a response, but inside he was seething. Karla, of course, felt what he felt. She walked up to Shternberg's desk. He continued to ignore her so she leaned over and tapped it with her nails, making a metallic click. Shternberg glanced up and Karla smiled at him. He rocked back in his chair, eyes wide.

"Thank you for your cooperation, sir," Jameson said.

They left the office, ignored by the minimal staff that Greyfriars employed. Jameson waited until they were out on the street before talking.

"I suppose, he was human?" Jameson asked.

"I think so," Karla replied. "He smelt human and not a magic user."

"I suppose," Jameson said. "It rather depends on your definition of human. In my opinion, the man is a bloody psychopath."

CHAPTER 14
NIGHT OF THE WOLF

Security lights snapped on from various directions, bathing the yard in harsh light. Through the glare, Rhian could just make out figures closing the gates behind the BMW. Max slipped the car in neutral and coasted to a stop in front of the Portakabin office at the far end of the yard. Car scrap and trucks formed mazes of metal on each side.

"Ding, ding, everybody out," Max said.

His eyes glittered. He is enjoying every moment of this, Rhian thought. Somehow his buoyant mood lifted her out of her anger and she found herself smiling back.

"Let's give them a scare," she said, jumping out.

"A scare, right," he said.

The BMW doors closed with solid thumps that would have brought a round of applause from the workers in the Bayerische Motoren Werke.

"There's at least two hiding on the right and another bunch in among the scrap metal on the left," Max said.

Charlie strutted out of the Portakabin, followed by a goon.

"We're shut," he said.

"You'll be shut permanently if you don't keep your nose out of my affairs," Max said. "You stay clear of the Dirty Duck in future and all who sail in her. Got it?"

"It's called the Black Swan," Rhian said.

Rhian caught flickers of movement to their flanks. Charlie's goons must be closing in. Why didn't Max just get on with it? He stood, legs apart, head back, right hand in the pocket of his long black mac. Charlie Parkes squared up to him, smiling humorlessly.

"And you'll make me, will you?" Charlie asked, spreading his hands to exaggerated effect. "You haven't brought much in the way of backup."

A willy-waggling contest, Rhian thought. The mayhem couldn't start until the right challenges had been delivered and rejected. Max was enjoying himself immensely, and so was the wolf. She was close to Rhian's mind, watching through Rhian's eyes, leaking her feelings into Rhian's psyche.

"Sure I have, I've brought Snow White," Max said, indicating her with the back of his left hand. "She'll be plenty backup just to sort out the local iron and his collection of mincing wooftahs."

Rhian was not entirely sure what an iron was, let alone a mincing wooftah, but from the jaw-dropping expression on Charlie Parkes face, she confidently assumed that it was uncomplimentary.

Parkes' mouth worked but no sound issued.

"I would have let her give you a kicking on her own, but when one is a gentleman . . ." Max adopted a suitable expression and spread his hands to convey a sense of noblesse oblige.

"Kill the bastard," Parkes said, "but save the girl for me."

The goon behind Parkes stepped round him and leveled a shotgun. Max gave Rhian a hard shove to the shoulder that pushed her to the ground. The shotgun discharged both barrels in rapid succession. Flare and concussion punched past Rhian, and she had a flashback to the subway where she first met Max, a lifetime ago. She rolled onto her paws and surveyed the world through flat monochrome, like the image in a sniper's night sight.

Max moved to the right, out of the line of fire. He held a pistol in both hands, arms outstretched. Two sharp cracks and the goon with the shotgun went over backwards. No killing, Rhian thought, I wanted no deaths on my conscience. What was she doing here?

The wolf growled and gave a cough that sounded like a laugh. Max changed aim but Parkes dropped out of sight into one of the pools of shadow.

The wolf smelled people all round, smelled their tension, their fear, their lust to kill. Rhian and the wolf's mind integrated smoothly. Frankie had worked a miracle with her magic, unpleasant though it had been at the time. Rhian could not exactly control the wolf, but she could influence it emotionally. She could guide its choices. She conveyed her fear of guns to the wolf, so it bounded after Max into the shadows among the scrap.

One of those transient tangential thoughts that the brain comes up with under stress floated across Rhian's mind. If she could emotionally influence the wolf, could the wolf influence her? Had her personality changed since Frankie's spell in the graveyard? Was she more aggressive than when she had been plain old Rhian? Would the old Rhian have fronted Charlie Parkes' gang, or would she just have run?

Max had his back to a half-crushed hatchback that had another perched unstably on top. He held his pistol close to his chest, barrel pointed skywards. She skidded to a stop beside him and he glanced down at her.

"Heel," he said, with a grin.

She snarled at him.

"You look quite dashing in a fur coat," Max said, unmoved by her flash of teeth.

The wolf heard two metallic clicks on the other side of the wrecks, which Rhian interpreted as a gangster pulling back the hammers on his shotgun. Max stuck three fingers under her nose, using them to count down. At zero he reached up and pushed the top hatchback, causing it to rock.

Taking a firmer grip on the sub chassis, he lifted the wreck up before pushing it firmly away. Metal ripped and protested with grinding shrieks and the hatchback slid off its perch. It rolled over and tumbled down the other side. A man screamed but was abruptly silenced, like someone had turned off his microphone.

The wolf jumped up on the first wreck in a single bound. It smelled fresh blood and leapt to the second car, finding a body pinned under the twisted metal.

"Wayne, Wayne!"

A gangster knelt by the corpse, trying ineffectually to pull it clear. He looked up wide-eyed when the wolf landed with a thud, and for a split moment they stared at each other. It could only have been a microsecond. To Rhian, it stretched out like the start of a summer holiday. The man broke the spell by reaching down for his shotgun.

For the first time, the reality of what was about to happen sunk home. They were going to kill everybody in the yard. That was what Max had meant by solving the problem once and for all. Rhian shut down in shock and the wolf took over.

The wolf leapt.

She hit the gangster hard, catching his face in her jaws and wrenching around his head until the salty taste of warm blood filled her mouth. Movement caught the wolf's eye. Without hesitation, she dropped her victim and jumped to the right. A shotgun blast rattled the car wreck. The wolf jinked left to avoid the second shot, which tore up the ground where she had been standing.

This gunman was made of sterner stuff than his colleagues, calmly breaking open his weapon to eject the spent cartridges as if he were doing nothing more dangerous than a grouse shoot. He behaved like a professional, an ex-soldier maybe, smoothly reaching into his coat pocket for reloads. The wolf gathered her back legs under her body. The gunman pushed the cartridges home and snapped the weapon shut as she charged.

In two more bounds the wolf would have him, but the muzzles of his levelled shotgun opened wide before her like the entrance to the Blackwall Tunnel. He pulled back the hammers when she was just two miserable meters away. It might as well have been a mile.

She saw the twin flash before she heard the concussion. Max knocked the shotgun up, the shot whistling over her head. The wolf took the gunman's throat, dropping him when he stopped moving.

Shots punched through thin metal car bodies and clanged off engine blocks. The wolf bounded across the floodlit yard, jinking left and right. Bullets hammered past her.

A gunman's nerve broke and he tried to run. The wolf hit him in the small of the back and the gunman fell, arms outstretched, as if he was appealing to a deity for divine protection. He was an easy kill.

The wolf bit into the back of her victim's neck and he went limp. She shook him a few times, puzzled that something with the arrogance to try to kill her should die so easily.

She and Max moved through the scrapyard, hunting, keeping to the shadows. The wolf was aware of Max close by but ignored him. He was of the pack, a member of the hunt.

"Lenny?" a voice asked from the other side of the yard. "Have you got them?"

"Lenny's lost his head," Max replied, adding a low chuckle that might have crawled out from a crypt.

A fusillade of wildly aimed shots from a variety of weapons spanged through the scrap. Max watched coolly, gun extended in one hand in the classic target-shooter's stance. He fired a single shot that elicited a cry of pain.

An automatic weapon replied with a sustained burst.

The night belonged to the wolf. She put her head up and howled, filling the yard with throbbing sound. Moonlight broke through the London clouds as if Morgana heard the cry and blessed her with a shower of silvery light.

"Jesus Christ!" said a voice from across the yard.

The wolf cleared the BMW in a single bound. Her powerful haunches drove her halfway across they open center of the yard before the first ill-aimed shot sounded. More followed, but she thrust forward, paws only briefly in contact with the ground. Her heart pounded, pumping oxygenated blood from her lungs to her heavy musculature.

She focused on her objective, a breakdown truck with a rounded bonnet and cab and an open rear. A shotgun blasted burning scraps of wadding from its barrel. A grey blur shot past her nose, leaving a spinning column of air in its wake.

A kiddies' toy, a plastic gonk, was wired to the bonnet of the truck as a mascot. Two men behind were silhouetted against the yard lights. She used the gonk as a target marker and jumped. The wolf skidded across the metal and crashed into a man standing on the other side. They hit the ground together with the wolf on top. The man cracked his head and lay still. She whirled and jumped for the second gangster, who dropped his gun and ran. The wolf pulled him down by ripping into his calf muscles until he rolled over screaming.

Her nose warned her of a human behind, so she leapt sideways. A shotgun blast tore through the air where she had been, and her last victim went quiet. Chunks of his torso decorated the truck. The shotgun wielder gazed in horror at the gore-spattered vehicle. The wolf ripped out his throat before he could fire the second barrel.

Something burned her shoulder and she snapped at the wound. Diving under a truck, she shuffled on her belly towards a set of legs on the far side.

"Where's it gone?" a voice asked in panic.

His knee joint crunched in her jaws and more screaming started. A man turned to flee, but she caught him and bit through the spinal cord in the base of his neck.

The night was awash in noise: shouts, cries, and the sharp brisance of discharged firearms. The wolf heard a new sound, a rhythmic *whump, whump, whump* approaching from the sky. She ignored it, fearing nothing that flew.

A man stood upright behind a cube of crushed car metal, paralyzed like a frozen corpse in a glacier. He stared at her, face a rictus of fear, gun forgotten in his hands. His throat tore open between teeth like carving knives.

Shots blasted from three men standing in the back of a tow truck. One of them had an oversized pistol that fired bursts of automatic fire. Flame flickered from the barrel, driving the muzzle up and to the side, spraying rounds wildly.

The flyer slid overhead. Blasts of wind lifted dust through the yard, stinging the wolf's eyes.

"I can't see," a man in the truck cried.

The wolf jumped into the back of the truck. She grabbed the arm that held the machine pistol. It triggered a long burst, stitching a man from right hip to left shoulder. He dropped without so much as a sigh. She bit down hard, bones snapping between her teeth, until the machine pistol fell away still clutched in a hand. A chunky gold bracelet slipped off the severed wrist, glittering as it fell.

Ignoring the screaming gangster, she searched for the next threat.

He threw himself head first over the side of the truck to escape her, but she bit hard into his groin and thigh and pulled him back in. She shook her head to tear through flesh. Hot gushing blood soaked her fur. The man's screams faded into liquid gurgles—and he died.

Something whimpered behind the wolf, so she turned lightly on her paws. A gangster knelt, left hand wrapped around the stump of his right arm, trying to stem the blood. He whimpered again, staring at the floor of the truck. He wasn't a threat, so the wolf lost interest.

Rhian remembered all the times that men like this had scared her, bullied her, made her run. She had the power now. If she pushed, the wolf would finish him.

Wind blasted as the flyer came back for a second low pass.

"Fuck off, you bastards," Charlie Parkes' voice sounded over engine and rotor noise. He triggered a long burst into the sky causing the helicopter to sheer off.

Rhian knew that this had gone on too long. You can't have gunfights in London. It just wasn't done. The helicopter was merely the first sign of police interest, and the Met had a well-deserved reputation for being trigger happy. You couldn't get a Brazilian plumber not for love nor money in London during a terror alert. Armed response units would be on their way filled with nice young men like the one on the tube train. Rhian didn't want to kill nice young men. She didn't want to kill anyone. It had to end.

The wolf picked up the feeling behind the thought. It had to end. She jumped from the truck and headed for the Portakabin, keeping a pile of car engines between it and her for cover. She found Max kneeling down behind the scrap.

"So there you are, Snow White," Max said. "It won't be easy to winkle him out of there. This is what we'll do . . ."

The wolf was not interested in listening to Max talk. When in doubt it attacked, instantly, without warning.

"Wait!" Max said, as she broke cover and raced for the Portakabin.

Parkes appeared at the window and fired a short burst at her. Max fired back. The gangster ducked down. The wolf ran, her world shrinking until dominated by the window. It was thrown wide open. Bright aluminium gleamed on the Portakabin wall where the handle had chipped the paint.

Parkes popped up and pointed an AK47 at her. Max's pistol fired twice, punching silvered stress holes in the aluminium. Parkes swung the gun and triggered a burst at Max before retargeting her. The momentary distraction was all the wolf needed. She jumped high, a burst from the assault rifle passing beneath her.

The wolf landed on the Portakabin's flat roof with a loud thud. Parkes sprayed a long burst through it, smashing wood into fragments. The wolf was already away, diving into the darkness behind the 'kabin. Wood splinters stung her haunches. Max's gun sounded again, and

Parkes switched his attention back to the vampire. His inability to concentrate on a single target was a weakness.

The Portakabin was in darkness but the wolf could see Parkes inside, silhouetted against the yard lights. Space between the 'kabin and the yard's back wall was tight, but the wolf pivoted on her back legs. She dived through the window, exploding into the room in a shower of glass shards. Parkes had his back to her, still firing at Max.

The wolf touched down on a table, claws scrabbling. Parkes turned slowly, as if he was rotating in syrup. The wolf could get but slight purchase on the smooth surface, but Parkes was only a meter away so it sufficed. She bit hard into his shoulder, shaking her head to tear through flesh and tendons. His arm disengaged from its socket. Parkes screamed like a cathedral castrato. The rifle dropped to the floor, unloading a few rounds into the end wall.

Parkes lay on his back, the wolf's front paws on his chest. His eyes were wide with fear and his throat lay temptingly within reach. The wolf could see arterial vessels pulse and smell the blood dripping from his shoulder. She opened her jaws for the kill.

Rhian wrestled with the wolf, demanding control. She reluctantly conceded Rhian's right to avenge the attack on her pack.

Rhian, human Rhian, knelt on all fours on Parkes' chest. She cocked her head.

"Still want to take me out, lover boy?" she said, with a smile that she didn't feel.

Charlie's eyes rolled up in his head and he fainted.

Rhian heaved herself up and opened the 'kabin door, stepping into the yard. Max sat in the open, reloading his pistol. Behind him a truck burned fiercely, flames spitting from something volatile in the back.

"Why is it," Max asked, rhetorically, "that every time I take you on a date I get shot?"

"We don't go on dates," Rhian said automatically.

She felt numb. She couldn't think. She didn't want to think. She wasn't sure what had happened. It was blurred, unreal, like a dream.

"And talking of getting shot," Max continued as if she had not spoken, "you should have called out before walking through that door. How do you think friendly fire accidents happen?"

Rhian helped him up. A blood-stained tear in his coat over the heart marked the passage of a bullet. The wound obviously bothered him, as he leaned on her shoulder.

"Can you drive?" Rhian asked.

"No problem," Max replied.

"Good, I never learnt and the police must be close."

She helped Max towards the car. They passed down a line of broken and mutilated bodies. Gore spattered the yard, marking her kills—her kills, not Max's. One gangster had dragged himself two or three meters before expiring from loss of blood. She remembered biting his hand off. She remembered the taste of blood in her mouth. She remembered it all.

The greasy smell of burning rubber mixed with roasting meat filled the yard like the emanations from a dodgy kebab shop. Someone's remains must be in the burning truck. She felt sick. Horror dripped into her consciousness like acid. She relived each act of violence and brutality. At the time, they were just a sequence of events forced on her by circumstance, by the gangsters. Now she saw that the butchery was the result of her choices, her decisions. She felt sickened to the lowest quanta of her soul.

Max chuckled.

"You are hell on tracks when you get going, little witch," Max said, admiringly.

Rhian threw up. Max held her while she shook and vomited until there was nothing left to heave but thin bile.

"You are such a conundrum, Snow White, so powerful and yet so squeamish. You kill without hesitation but go into shock at the sight of a few bodies. You really are the most interesting human I have met for centuries."

The BMW had no obvious damage. Rhian climbed into the passenger seat beside Max.

"Ouch," she said.

"Problem?"

"I think I've got a wood splinter in my bottom."

Max squeezed her knee. "No problem, I'll get it out for you later."

Rhian removed his hand, which seemed to amuse him for some unaccountable reason. Max drove steadily, without obvious hurry, but the sports saloon covered the ground quickly. Rhian wondered where the forces of law and order had got to.

"They'll set up a perimeter around the yard and faff about with health and safety for hours yet," Max said, noting her anxious looking around and guessing the reason.

He was still chuckling at his own joke when they rounded a bend to find the way ahead blocked by two police cars staggered broadside on across the road. She thought he would run the roadblock, but Max slowed down.

The policemen had carbines slung across their chests on black leather straps. Rhian tensed, noticing that their right hands curled around the pistol grips.

"Let me do the talking," Max said, touching her leg to steady her.

The BMW's window slid down smoothly and silently, another demonstration of the superiority of Bavarian engineering.

"Can I help you, officer?" Max asked the policeman who approached.

Max's accent was clipped English upper class, entirely fitting the car he drove and the expensive clothes he and Rhian wore. Neither looked like a policeman's expectation of a gangster.

"Yes, sir, may I ask your identity?" the policeman asked.

"Sir Max Emmerman, my card."

The policeman examined it then looked at Rhian.

"This is my personal assistant, Miss Olegeva Leggova. She's Lithuanian and doesn't speak much English," Max said. "She's been assisting me in going over some figures."

"I see, sir," the policeman said, looking where Max's left hand rested casually on her thigh.

It did not seem to occur to the policeman to ask why a wealthy businessman would have a young female assistant who didn't understand English. In fact, Rhian had the impression that the man was smirking. She could only see the back of Max's head, but she suspected that he had winked at the officer, and she felt her cheeks burning red. The copper smirked some more as if he and Max were part of some male club, all bloody boys together.

"I don't suppose you've seen anything unusual?"

"Indeed not, officer, Miss Leggova and I have been busy."

By now Rhian thought she was way beyond embarrassment,

but Max always managed somehow to take matters one step further. Leg-over, dear God!

"Sorry to trouble you, sir. Have a nice evening."

"I intend to, officer."

Another smirk hovered on the copper's lips, demonstrating that claims of the elimination of canteen culture sexism from the Met were wildly optimistic.

Max manoeuvred between the patrol cars and drove away.

"Are you really a knight?" Rhian asked.

"Amongst other things," Max replied. "It depends what identity I adopt."

He gave her thigh a squeeze, reminding Rhian that his hand was still inappropriately placed, so she removed it.

"I think I handled that rather well," Max said, back on his default setting of smug.

"Have I mentioned how much I dislike you?" Rhian asked.

"Often," Max replied.

He seemed to find the exchange funny.

CHAPTER 15
ROLE PLAYING

Jameson's racing-green Jaguar came to a halt by the curb near silently. He and Karla climbed out.

"Parkes Security Services & Scrap Metal Dealership," Jameson read the sign out loud. He had the impression that he should know that name but couldn't quite place it. A uniformed copper held his hand up to prevent them entering through the open gate.

"Crime scene, sir,"

"That's okay, constable. We'll wait while you get the officer in charge," Jameson said.

The constable looked doubtfully at Karla's black leather jacket and trousers but clocked the hundred-thousand-pound sports car, not to mention Jameson's immaculate Savile Row suit and Guards' officer accent.

"Yes, sir," he said. "Please wait here."

Jameson lit a cigarette while Karla looked on disapprovingly. Her researches into increasing the lifespan of the human male had indicated that smoking was frowned upon so she had a campaign to wean him off them. Jameson was digging in his heels. She was not his wife, not even a woman. Why did their relationship increasingly feel like a marriage?

The officer returned. "I am afraid Superintendent Bates is too busy to see you, sir."

"Indeed," Jameson said.

Very deliberately, he dropped his cigarette after a last deep inhalation and crushed it. Then he took out his Metropolitan Police Special Branch Card and held it up for the officer to see.

"I'll find him myself."

"But sir—," said the constable, as Jameson and Karla swept past him.

The yard was like a back street in Beirut on a bad day. Socos—Scene of Crime Officers—in white plastic suits that left only their faces uncovered, photographed and sampled bodies and debris. The place stank of burned rubber and spilled diesel.

"Oy, you, what're you playing at?" asked a man in a strong Scottish accent.

He strode over and thrust his face into Jameson's, breathing whisky fumes strong enough to mask all other smells. "Get out before I nick you."

"Commander Jameson, Special Branch," he said, holding up his ID.

"Get out before I nick you, sir," Drudge said. "This case is under the Sweeney's jurisdiction."

"And you are?"

"Inspector Drudge."

"Anything and everything is under my jurisdiction if I so choose, Drudge," Jameson said. "Let's see your warrant card."

Drudge handed it to Jameson, who examined it before passing it to Karla, who flicked the card back to Drudge without bothering to look. It bounced off Drudge's chest and fell onto the ground. A plainclothesman with Drudge bent down.

"Leave it," Drudge snarled. His face turned red and a vein in his neck throbbed with a strong pulse. Karla examined it with interest.

"And who the hell is she?" Drudge asked.

"My, ah, associate, Miss Scarlet," Jameson said.

"She got an ID card?" Drudge asked.

"Indeed, she has," Jameson said. "But you won't be seeing it. Miss Scarlet is a civil servant, but she does not normally disclose her Department."

Drudge blinked. Civil servants who were instructed not to disclose their Department usually worked for the Foreign Office or the Home Office or, to put it another way, were spooks at MI6 or MI5.

A large man, whose barrel chest strained against buttons fastening the tunic of a senior officer in the Met, joined the group.

"What's going on, Drudge?" he asked, looking at Jameson and Karla with distaste.

"Commander Jameson, Special Branch, and a Miss Scarlet from the, ah, Civil Service, sir," Drudge said.

"You are Superintendent Bates?" Jameson asked, casually.

Bates eyes flickered and his face set into a bland mask. Jameson sussed him immediately. Bates wasn't a cop but a bureaucrat, one of the new breed of political officers who had risen through the system like a bubble in a lava lamp. They were promoted from rank to rank, leaving no trace of their passage. He would have a career based on lip service to the right policies, shuffling the correct documents but never, ever, rocking the boat. He would always support the current management initiative until the next fad was rolled out.

P.G. Wodehouse had satirized the system wonderfully after three years in Hollywood, where he was paid a great deal of money but not allowed to do anything. It was all about yes-men and nodders. The current megalomaniac in charge throws out some opinion in committee and the yes-men all say yes according to seniority before the nodders are allowed to nod in order of rank. Bates would have started as a junior nodder on something like the Minor Criminal Self-Esteem Enhancement Committee. Eventually he would become Chief Yes-Man at the dizzy heights of a Health and Safety Awareness Task Force. In the meantime, he might even catch the odd criminal, provided they had no embarrassing political connections. Arresting criminals was not actually frowned upon by promotion boards, just not considered obligatory or even particularly useful.

"What can I do for you?" Bates asked, more politely.

A policeman who messed with spooks could find himself manning a hut in the Romney Marshes for the rest of his career, even if he was a Superintendent.

"Just a few questions, if you don't mind," Jameson said blandly. "What did your officers see of the gunfight?"

"Nothing, of course," Bates said. "We have only just arrived ourselves."

Jameson was astonished. "I thought the incident started just before midnight?"

"Yes, well, it takes time to assemble an armed response," Bates said huffily. "We had to find enough officers to man a perimeter while we assessed the health and safety issues. By then the gunfire had died away, so I decided to wait for dawn before moving a team in to assess the situation."

Jameson knew he was looking at Bates as if he was something found behind the skirting board of a genetics lab, but he couldn't control his expression. He would not have believed it had he not read in *The Times* that a woman in Scotland had died of hypothermia at the bottom of a hole, while two senior officers from the local fire brigade had stood around the top for eight hours arguing whether the health and safety regulations allowed them to use the winch on their engine.

Above them, a police helicopter went by, beating the air with a characteristic whump, whump, whump.

Jameson was back in Afghanistan, retreating step by step along gullies in the unyielding mountains of the Hindu Kush, followed rock by rock by ISA-backed irregulars. The British Guardsmen returned fire with their SA80 rifles. Designed to fight Russian infantry at long ranges, the rifles were incredibly accurate. At point-blank range they were less useful than combat shotguns. The troopers snap-shot from the hip at fleeting targets that seemed to spring from the solid rock.

When the Guardsmen reached the flat landing zone, they turned and drove Terry Taliban back with aimed fire until they gained enough distance from their pursuers to disengage and move safely across the open ground. They regrouped in the shelter of some boulders on the far side, where a cliff fell vertically into the valley below.

The mountains were so high that the Chinook had to climb up to meet them. Its rotors strained for lift in the rarefied mountain air. Terrys appeared among the boulders on the far side, spraying erratic bursts from their AK47s. Guardsmen would already be dead if Afghans could shoot straight. The soldiers returned aimed fire. Some Terrys dropped. The rest faded back into cover.

A soft, slow American voice drawled in Jameson's earphones. "We see you, Zulu One. Stand by for extraction."

"Zeta Nine this is Zulu One. Abort the extraction. The landing zone is compromised. Repeat, the landing zone is compromised."

"Hell, Major, I never expected to live for ever. It's a long walk home. Y'all be ready now, as I'll perch off the edge like a sparrow on a wire."

American chopper pilots all seemed to hail south of the Mason-Dixon line for some reason. They were also utterly deranged.

The huge aircraft pivoted over Jameson's men, blasting dust in all directions. Its tail ramp was already lowered when the pilot dropped the back wheels on the cliff edge. He held the plane level on the rotors with the front wheels dangling over the sheer drop. A crewman at the rear beckoned for them to embark.

Jameson's men scrambled aboard. He stayed on one knee, searching the Taliban position through the scope of his rifle, but the whole area was obscured by swirling dust. The scope caught a shadow that resolved into the outline of a man. The Terry got off a wild volley before Jameson dropped him with a double tap to the chest.

The American crewman screamed something that Jameson couldn't hear above the roar of the twin turboshaft mounted on the tail. The crewman waved his arm extravagantly for emphasis, indicating that Jameson should get a bloody move on. The helicopter suddenly tilted forward, dragging the ramp across the ground to the cliff edge. It was already a meter off when Jameson leapt the gap. The crewman caught him and punched the button that closed the rear door.

"You sure left that late," the crewman screamed, straight into his ear. "Another second and you'd have been flying back on your own."

"Most amusing," Jameson replied, but was doubtful if the crewman heard him. The noise was like being inside a steam boiler while a phalanx of mechanical navvies beat the outside with shovels. Jameson hated choppers.

The Guardsmen sat exhausted on the floor, heads down, while a medic worked on one who had taken a round on his body armor. Jameson shot him an inquiring look, and the medic gave a nod. The armor had held.

Another soldier shook so hard he had to place his rifle on the deck. Jameson put his mouth close to the man's ear so he could hear.

"Buck up, Perkins. Every one you walk away from . . ."

"Yes, sir," Perkins mouthed, attempting a weak grin.

"Good man."

Jameson absentmindedly pulled out a packet of cigarettes. The crewman shook his head, drawing a hand across his throat. Jameson put them away, holding one hand palm up by way of apology. Jameson really hated helicopters.

He made his way to the front, patting his men on their shoulders and murmuring meaningless platitudes that they couldn't hear, until he reached the hatch into the cockpit.

"Brilliant flying, Zeta Nine . . ."

The copilot looked up at Jameson, tears running down his face.

The pilot lolled forward. A single bullet from the last burst had run the length of the cargo bay. It had managed to miss everyone and everything until it punched a hole in the back of the pilot's helmet.

Zeta Nine had made his last extraction.

Bates stepped back in alarm, his eyes wide. He half-raised his arms as if to ward off a blow. Jameson forced himself to unclench hands making tight fists. At that moment he hated the Chief Superintendent so much that he could cheerfully have killed the man. This mincing filing clerk had the audacity to wear the uniform of one of Her Britannic Majesty's officers. Karla took a step forward, nails lengthening and hardening. She felt what he felt, even if she didn't understand his reasons. Actually, she didn't care what his reasons were. It was enough that he hated.

Very deliberately, Jameson suppressed his emotions. He forced them down into a toxic little core, emptying his soul in the process. That was why lovers left him. He was a hollow man with a frozen void for a heart. The alternative was worse. Feeling left him reliving events every night in his dreams. Karla didn't care but Karla wasn't human.

"So there is no eye-witness evidence," Jameson said.

"We have camera footage from a helicopter," Bates said.

"Indeed?"

"But it doesn't show much, as the yard was erratically lighted. All you can see are running men and gunshots."

"Don't you have thermal imaging on those things," Jameson jerked his thumb at the police helicopter that was circling the yard.

"Oh, the images weren't from a police helicopter, good gracious, no. It's news footage from a TV company. We couldn't send a police aircraft over a gunfight, far too dangerous. We have a duty of care to the crew."

Bates checked his watch. "I have to chair an important meeting, Drudge will look after you," Bates said.

"Health and safety?" Jameson asked.

"What?"

"This meeting, is it the Health and Safety Committee?"

"No, Human Resources, to consider the psychologist's report on the best color to paint customer waiting rooms in police stations. The idea is to ensure a tranquil atmosphere."

"That is important," Jameson said.

"Yes," Bates replied.

The man was beyond sarcasm so Jameson gave up. "Miss Scarlet and I will just have a wander round. I'll call you if I need you," Jameson said to Drudge.

The inspector thumped off, grinding his teeth, bawling out a subordinate to relieve his anger.

Jameson went over to where a forensic team were taking swabs from a body, stopping a meter away to avoid contaminating the crime scene.

"What killed him?"

"Well, it's early days," the technician said. "But I fancy the two holes in his chest had something to do with it."

"Are all the deaths by gunshot wound?"

"No," the technician paused and grimaced. "Some of them have been ripped open by a chainsaw and died from shock and blood loss."

"A chainsaw or a large predatory animal?"

The technician shrugged. "Could be an animal, but we aren't talking someone's pet pooch. The wounds could have been caused by a team of bloody great Rottweiler guard dogs, I suppose, or maybe something escaped from London Zoo."

"I see," Jameson said, glancing at Karla.

She wandered around the yard while Jameson lit a cigarette.

"Smoking is forbidden on duty," Drudge said from behind Jameson.

He took a lungful of nicotine and exhaled it skywards before turning to face the Inspector. "I shall try to keep it in mind," Jameson said.

"Bloody Special Branch, you think you really are special, think the rules don't apply to you," Drudge said quietly, so he couldn't be overheard.

"Yep," Jameson said, taking another drag.

"Jameson, over here," Karla said.

He walked over to where she knelt beside a patch of spilled oil that had caked into tar. An animal had run through the mess, leaving pawprints across the concrete.

"I'm no aboriginal tracker, but that is a dog," Jameson said, lifting an eyebrow.

"A dog with large paws," Karla said.

She got up, brushing the dust off her knees, and paced out the tracks. The dog must have been running fast, as all four feet touched the ground close together. Karla had to leap to match the bound indicated by the tracks.

"A dog with large paws and a long stride," Jameson said.

"A very large dog," Karla said.

"Did the yard have guard dogs, Drudge?" Jameson asked without turning round to repay the Inspector's incivility.

"The TV footage of the attack showed a dog," said Drudge.

"So was there a guard dog?" Jameson asked again.

"Mister Parkes didn't need no guard dog," said a new voice, with a thick nasal twang.

A man appeared from amongst the scrap metal. His nose was held in plastic strips that were stuck down to his cheeks.

"The thug who could talk," Jameson said with delight. "Of course, Parkes, I knew I had heard the name before."

"How's your mate's teeth?" he said solicitously to the thug.

The thug snarled and took a step towards Jameson with his fist raised. Jameson smiled and the thug thought better of starting something. Probably wisely, as it hadn't turned out so well the last time.

"That's the bastard toff who broke my nose and beat up Dermont," the thug said. "Why don't you arrest him, Mister Drudge?"

The detective hesitated then shook his head.

"Mister Parkes won't like it," the thug warned.

Drudge looked like Odysseus faced with sailing between Scylla and Charybdis or a man trying to choose between staying for a visit from his mother-in-law or taking a cycling holiday on the Yorkshire Moors. He took a step forward.

"You intend to arrest a Special Branch Commander on the witness statement of a tin-pot thug?" Jameson asked, softly.

Drudge shook his head.

Karla laughed out loud.

Drudge gazed at her in sheer hatred, trying to intimidate her with the policeman's glare. Everyone quailed before the policeman's glare, running a quick mental check through their various offenses. Everyone had at least one black spot on their conscience. Karla held his gaze and gave a sardonic grin. Her conscience was spotless, largely because she didn't have one. Drudge looked away first. Karla could outstare a Siberian tiger.

"I guess we're done here," Jameson said.

He and Karla walked back to the Jag.

"Maybe it was no more than the underworld settling a business dispute in the traditional way?" Jameson asked, rhetorically.

"Perhaps, but dogs aren't the only animal to leave tracks like that," replied Karla. "It could have been a wolf."

"Wolves aren't that big."

"Werewolves are."

Rhian slept late the next morning, but she still rose exhausted. The ground tilted when she levered herself up, so she steadied herself with a hand upon the wall. Her bed was a tangled mess. She remembered little of her dreams, little except for the crunch of teeth on cartilage and bones, and the taste of hot salty blood. She shuddered at the memory, her face drawn and wan in the bathroom mirror. Dark panda-shadows circumnavigated her eyes.

She was a mess. Could she have gone down with 'flu?

Frankie sat clutching a mug of tea when Rhian dropped carefully onto a kitchen chair. Without a word she poured a mug for Rhian and added two sugars, waving away Rhian's protests that she didn't use sweeteners.

"I know you don't, but drink it anyway," Frankie said. "Magic costs, and you need to replace the energy."

"I don't do magic," Rhian said.

Frankie snorted.

"You might not do magic, but magic certainly does you. Where do you think the wolf gets its power from?"

Rhian took a sip of the sweet, liquid and felt sick. Her head throbbed, so she rested it carefully in both hands, a precaution to prevent it falling off her shoulders.

"The wolf feeds on your life force." Frankie answered her own question. "You used to sleep it off when you changed back. Now you can flip back and forwards, you will feel the full impact." Her voice softened. "Take these."

She plonked two aspirin down in front of Rhian, who knocked them back with a gulp of the revolting tea.

"Don't you have any magic spells for hangover symptoms?" Rhian asked.

"Hmm, not a good idea," Frankie replied. "I can suppress the symptoms, but that will only delay matters and build up the blood debt. Aspirin is safer. And the wolf was busy last night."

"What makes you think so?" Rhian asked.

"Well, apart from your condition, I saw you on television."

"What?" Rhian snapped her head up. She immediately regretted giving way to the impulse. The top of her skull kept going when her head stopped. It snapped back with a lurch that gave her double vision.

"Come and see," Frankie said. "You're on Sat News. No, I'll carry your tea for you. I don't want it all over the carpet."

Frankie switched on the TV in the lounge and they sat down to watch the rolling news. There were a couple of items on the latest economic disasters and an interview with a politician trying to explain why her husband had charged the hire of pornographic movies to her Parliamentary expenses. Then Rhian was on, or rather the wolf was on.

"Slaughter on the London streets," claimed the anchor woman with the usual accuracy of the press. "Gang warfare turns our city into a battlefield," her male co-author added. Why did they have to do a bloody irritating double act? Why did it take two presenters to read the autocue and why was there always one of each sex? And why was she wasting her time on *why* questions?

The channel moved into film footage taken from the air showing figures moving indistinctly through the shadows of the scrap yard, scurrying quickly across the lighted zones. Flashes marked out gunshots, the sequence ending with a burst of automatic fire straight into the camera.

"Our brave reporters were repeatedly fired on," said the anorexic and over made-up presenter, silicone-enhanced bosom heaving with excitement.

The next video sequence showed a truck burning in the distance.

Then they ran it all again in slow motion with little circles picking out men who were running, firing, and falling.

"Astonishingly, a large fighting dog was involved," said the male presenter.

A new set of blown-up fuzzy sequences showed the wolf jumping into the back of an open truck and attacking three men. Gun muzzles flashed, but all three men went down. They repeated the sequence in slow motion at least twice.

Rhian ran for the bathroom and talked to Hugh on the big white telephone. She only had the tea to throw up so was soon dry-heaving. She washed her face before carefully removing the blade from her lady-shave. Slowly and deliberately she sliced the blade across her arm, welcoming the pain of punishment.

"Where's Karla?" Randolph asked.

"I left her in the underground car park," Jameson replied.

"I suppose she is terrorizing the security staff," Randolph said.

"She's asleep in the car," Jameson said, somewhat defensively.

Actually, Karla never slept, but she did need to shut down every now and then. Jameson thought that this was when she sifted and catalogued the memories in her head, like defragging a computer drive. Just how much information could she store before the disk was full and memories had to be deleted?

Randolph's office was a model of Spartan efficiency, neat shelves of hard copy in cardboard sleeves and a line of civil service light-grey filing cabinets. One glass wall looked out over the Thames, Jameson could see a twin jet Airbus in the red-and-blue livery of British Airways climb steeply out of London's City Airport. The runways were sandwiched between the Royal Albert and King George V docks, so the airport was almost an island.

The small airliner passed over the tower which housed the Commission. The building's sound proofing was so good that the jet seemed to fly silently, like an airship. It would refuel at Shannon in Ireland and then head out to Kennedy Airport in New York, an air bridge that spanned the ocean between the financial districts of the North Atlantic's twin cities. The planes used the old Concorde flight numbers. They consisted entirely of business-class seats so the "masters of the universe" were not exposed to the *hoi polloi*.

Jameson jerked his attention back, aware that Randolph was speaking.

"What?"

"It amazes me how you've lasted this long, Jameson. You have the attention span of a crested newt."

"Sorry," Jameson said.

"But then, I must admit you have a good minder," Randolph said. "I asked you about the Martin Street Massacre, as I believe the drunken halfwits in the press have dubbed last night's incident."

"It seems to have been just an outbreak of gang warfare," Jameson said. "Although there was one singular observation."

"Oh, yes?" Randolph lifted his head.

"A large dog was involved."

"A guard dog," Randolph waved a hand dismissively.

"Apparently not."

"One of the attackers had a pet pit bull?"

"Possibly," Jameson replied.

"We have enough problems without creating phantoms to chase."

Randolph was right, of course, but something about the incident bothered Jameson. He had some half-recollection of an old case, but Randolph was talking again.

"So tell me about this Shternberg fellow?" Randolph said.

Jameson marshalled his thoughts. "Rich city fat cat, ruthless, intelligent, unemotional, narcissistic with a massive sense of self worth—he is probably a functioning psychopath."

"I see. He sounds like a fairly typical financier. Do you think he would be capable of killing?"

"I think he could be capable of anything, if he thought it in his interest and that he could get away with it," Jameson replied. "And I suspect his overweening sense of superiority leads him to conclude that he could get away with quite a lot."

"Right," Randolph scribbled some notes on a pad with a pencil-thin silver fountain pen. "I suppose he is human?"

"Yes, Karla was certain, and he had no smell of magic about him."

"So he didn't personally summon a daemon," Randolph said. "It wouldn't astonish me if Shternberg knew where to hire a hit man, but how the hell would he know how to find a sorcerer capable of opening gates on the scale we've measured?"

"It would help if we knew more about his background," Jameson said. "Our enemies in MI5 must have a file on him."

Randolph gave a hollow laugh. "They would hardly tell us. The only people MI5 have ever voluntarily shared information with are their friends in the KGB."

He tapped the silver pen on his teeth, and Jameson looked out of the window. A turbo-prop short-haul airliner descended steeply down to the runway. Landing gear extended, it looked like a stooping hawk.

"He's the only lead, so we'll prod him a little and see if we get a reaction," Randolph said. "We'll start by triggering a revenue investigation into his affairs. Nothing puts the wind up a corporate like the tax man."

"I doubt you'll find anything. He strikes me as too fly to commit tax evasion."

"I'm sure you're right, but the investigation will tie him in knots."

"Maybe, and if it doesn't?" Jameson asked.

"Then we apply direct pressure."

"If he's sorcerous connections, the reaction could be unpleasant," Jameson said.

Randolph smiled like Sweeney Todd, the daemon barber of Fleet Street. "Nothing you and Karla can't handle, I'm sure."

CHAPTER 16
DR. FAUSTUS AND OTHER PROBLEMS

Jameson was seriously pissed off, well and truly miffed. He accepted that a pension for a Commission field operative was largely a theoretical concept because he wouldn't live to collect, but he never expected to die of boredom. He also hated getting up in the early morning. In fact, the list of things he hated about the current operation would fill a Kindle. He fidgeted in his car seat, playing with the radio. The popular classic station was playing Wagner, for the fifteenth time that week. Radio 3, the BBC serious music channel, was broadcasting an experimental symphony for massed lawn mowers and typewriter. BBC Radio 2 fielded a chat-show presenter reminiscing about his upbringing in rural Ireland. You had to be seven or have had a frontal lobotomy to like BBC Radio 1.

Reluctantly, he put on Radio 4's morning heavyweight news analysis. The formidable BBC journalist, Jeremy Paxman, was skewering a politician to the proverbial wall. Jameson wondered why they all bothered. The politician was lying, he knew he was lying, and he knew that the listeners all knew he was lying. What was the point? Even Paxman sounded bored.

"You know what gets me about corporates?" Jameson asked. "It's their weird need for money-based status symbols that make their lives difficult. Take Shternberg here. He locates his business in the Docklands financial center, the most expensive office space in London, East London. Then he insists on living in a country mansion in the fashionable green belt west of London, so he has a horrendous commute. The only sensible way to get into the city is by train, like the lumpen proletariat. So does he do that? No! He takes a car from his estate north to a light airfield, where he boards a helicopter. Helicopters aren't allowed into City Airport, so he has to land in a disused power station coal yard in West London, on the wrong side of the river. He then grinds by car through the traffic jams all the way to Docklands. I mean, where's the sense in that? It takes four times as long as the train and is a lot less comfortable. The only advantage of the helicopter is that it wastes an obscene amount of money."

He paused for breath before continuing.

"Surely, there are less inconvenient ways of showing off your wealth. Julius Caesar built a luxury villa at huge expense then pulled it down at first viewing on the grounds that he didn't like the color scheme of the master bedroom. Now that's conspicuous consumption. All it cost him was one day. And a shedload of cash, but he'd borrowed the cash. Karla, Karla?"

Jameson was ranting to himself. Karla had put her seat back and switched off. Jameson looked at her enviously. She had many qualities; even when switched off she could vitalize in a microsecond if her keen senses detected potential danger. But she didn't do routine surveillance, so he had to. He could not even lose himself in literature.

He had promised himself the pleasure of a reread of *Marlowe's Tragicall History of the Life and Death of Dr. Faustus*. In it Marlowe addressed the Calvinist world picture of absolute predestination. The idea was that God marked out the damned from birth and there was nothing they could do to alter their fate. Free will in this philosophy was a delusion. This was an important theme when Marlowe was up at Cambridge in the 1500s.

Jameson wished he had paid more attention to his tutors when he was there. Sin, damnation, and death were vague concepts to a young man more interested in girls and sport. They meant rather more to him now.

Faustus was thrice damned, first by God, then by Satan, and finally by his own choices.

"If we say that we have no sin,
We deceive ourselves, and there's no truth in us.
Why then belike we must sin,
And so consequently die.
Ay, we must die an everlasting death."

Faustus' sin was greed, the academic's sin of greed for knowledge beyond mortal reach. It ended with a pact with the devil. Jameson had it on good authority, the Library, that Marlowe's Dr. Faustus was a thinly disguised parody of Dr. Dee.

Marlowe was too good an artist to answer his own question but left it for every man to consider for himself. Predestination or free will? Jameson looked fondly at Karla. How much free will did she have? She seemed to choose, to show free will, but she was eternally bound in a love geas to him. Theologians might argue that she had no more soul than a cruise missile, so free will, sin, and redemption were theoretical concepts in her case.

But what about Jameson, how much free will did he have? His class and talents predestined his life: public school, Cambridge, an indifferent degree, sports blues, Sandhurst, the Guards, combat tours, and finally, The Commission. Had he chosen this life, or had it chosen him? Faust ended up ripped to pieces by a daemon and his soul consigned to Hell. Jameson was not sure he believed in Hell, other than the one we all lived in, but he believed in daemons. By God, he believed in daemons. It was all too likely that he would end his life, like Faust, on a daemon's claws.

The arrival of Shternberg's helicopter snapped him out of it. The little corporate toy flew down the Thames and circled the empty shell of Battersea Power Station, disappearing for a moment in the rising sun. It flared, pitching up its nose, and settled slowly onto the circular helipad in the empty coal yard. Shternberg was out and running to the waiting Bentley while the rotors still turned.

"*Sweet Karla, make me immortal with a kiss,*" Jameson said, taking a startled Karla in his arms and carrying out the act with passion. He was delighted to have something to do other than watch an empty concrete pad. He dropped her and started the Jag's engine.

Shternberg's chauffeur closed the door for his boss and doubled around the car to the driver's seat. He moved off while still clipping on his seatbelt. Jameson swung in behind the Bentley, making no attempt to be discreet. After all, the whole idea was to make Shternberg sweat a little.

Randolph's attempt to use the Inland Revenue had been an utter failure. He had been blocked. MI6 apparently had Shternberg under their protection for reasons unknown. Randolph surmised that he was seen as an information asset, but MI6 weren't telling, so The Commission moved to Plan B.

The cars crossed Battersea Bridge and turned east along the embankment. Jameson used the power of the Jag to hold like superglue to the Bentley. He ran a red light, sliding through the junction in a blare of horns from outraged motorists on green. Shternberg looked back out of the rear window. Jameson winked at him and semi-quoted.

> *"Sweet Karla, make me immortal with a kiss.*
> *"Her lips suck forth my soul: see, where it flies!—*
> *"Come, Karla, come, give me my soul again.*
> *"Here will I dwell, for heaven is in these lips,*
> *"And all is dross that is not Karla."*

"Oh, Marlowe," Karla said, dismissively.

"Dr. Faustus," Jameson said.

"It's Helen, not Karla."

"I was improvising," Jameson said. "Was this the face that launch'd a thousand ships, and burnt the topless towers of Troy."

"Illium, not Troy."

"You've been reading my books again."

"No, I remember seeing the play. Marlowe invited me. Now there was a devious sod. The secret service chopped him after Walsingham died."

Jameson gave Karla a sideways glance. At that moment, the traffic ground to a halt and he had to slam on the car's brakes to avoid mating with the Bentley in front. A Mercedes van pulled alongside. The slob at the wheel flicked ash out of the open window. He could look down into the Jaguar from his vantage point. He put his head out of the van to drink in Karla, who was dressed in her working clothes of tight-fitting black leather jacket and trousers.

Van-man said something to his mate, who also slid across for a leer. Karla was always conscious of attention, so she turned to look at them. Van-man made an obscene gesture, indicating what he would like to do to her. Karla smiled at him, showing her teeth, indicating what she would like to do to him. He turned white and rolled up the window. The traffic started to move and van-man stalled the engine. His vehicle was soon lost behind in a sea of maneuvering cars and blasting horns.

Rhian returned to work at the Swan. As she had feared, it was not the same. Gary was polite enough, but the wolf hung between them like a steel bulkhead. Gary stayed mostly in the office when she was working. She told herself that it was because of his injuries, but she knew she was lying. Taking a deep breath, she decided to take the mountain to Mohammed. She stuck her head around the office door. Gary sat at his desk, adding up figures on a calculator.

"Gary," she said, putting her hand on his shoulder.

He looked up at her and flinched, pulling away so her hand dropped free.

"Oh, Rhian, what did you want?"

"Nothing, Gary," she said dully. "You just answered my question. I'll work my shift and then leave. No need for any unpleasantness or embarrassment. You can send my last paycheck to Frankie."

"Service," said a querulous voice from the bar.

Rhian grabbed the chance to leave the office. "Coming, Willie."

She poured Willie the Dog's half pint of ordinary while blinking back tears. She thought she had found a home here, but somehow it never worked out for her. It would be easy to blame the wolf, but this was the pattern of her life. She burned out her welcome wherever she went.

The pub door opened with a ding of the bell and a group of students walked in. One of them waited at the bar while she took Willie's money.

"Rhian, could I have a word?" Gary asked from behind her. "In private, if you please."

"Sure," Rhian replied.

"Hey, I'm waiting to be served," complained the student.

"So wait, your mother had to and life's a bitch," Gary said.

Rhian blinked; rudeness to a customer was most unlike Gary. She followed him into the office, where he handed her a tissue.

"You're crying."

"Hay fever," she replied. "I'm allergic to something."

"Yes, a stupid, selfish, gutless boss," Gary said. He put his arms around her. "All the management training courses I've been on, and that's quite a few, insist that hugging young women staff guarantees a trip to the Industrial Tribunal. I'm going to live dangerously and do it anyway."

Rhian burst into more tears.

"Um, I was trying to be nice," Gary said in alarm, releasing her.

"You are," she replied. She hugged him hard, causing Gary to wince. "Sorry, ribs still tender?"

"A bit," Gary replied. "You're stronger than you look. I suppose that's the, ah . . ."

"Yes, I suppose so."

Gary laughed, a little forced, but Rhian was pleased he made the effort. She wiped her eyes and went out to serve the student. She took the order and poured the drink, but he hesitated after paying, staring at her.

"Is there anything else?" Rhian asked.

He straightened with a visible effort.

"Yes, there is. Don't hang around when your shift ends. I'm taking you clubbing and I don't like to be kept waiting," the student said.

"What?"

"I, er, don't like to be kept waiting," repeated the student, taking a step backwards.

"Of all the arrogant . . ." Rhian ran out of words.

A tubby blond with brown eyebrows at the students' table gave a peal of laughter.

"What that girl needs is some firm handling," she said, lowering her voice an octave to imitate a man. "You'll see she'll respond to a real man who shows her who's boss."

The other students sniggered and Rhian's would-be escort flushed.

"I think you'd better sit down," Rhian said, her voice dangerously calm.

"Good advice, son," Gary stuck his head around the office door. "The last suitor to try the ole cave-man act with our Rhian is still in intensive care having his arm reattached."

Everyone laughed, including Rhian. She didn't care for the joke, but she was delighted that the old Gary was back. She still had a place.

He joined her at the bar.

"The pot in the bet to take you out must be getting pretty substantial," Gary said.

"How did you know about that?" Rhian asked.

"I'm the landlord. I know about everything that goes on in my pub," he replied.

Jameson parked the Jaguar in a clearing amongst the woodland that ran around the periphery of Shternberg's country estate. Karla's eyes glowed metallic green in the dark. Her body cycles peaked naturally in the early hours of the morning.

The estate was surrounded by a high wall so Karla made a stirrup with her hands and boosted Jameson up. A thin wire ran along the top, held clear of the brickwork by insulated hoops. He clipped a cable to the wire and connected it to his phone.

"Why am I waiting?" Karla asked. "Can't you get a move on?"

"Hang on a sec," Jameson replied. "I just have to take out the security system."

"Meanwhile, I'll just stand here, shall I, holding you up?"

"If you don't mind," Jameson replied, politely.

He keyed the analysis program on the phone. It looked like an ordinary Android device from the outside but had a number of unusual features, including a security analysis and defeat package. Your average burglar would have happily paid a year in the nick to own one. Eventually the wait symbol stopped flashing and a green icon showed the mobile had the systems sussed. Jameson unclipped it and cut the wire. He hovered for a second, but there were no flashing lights or bells.

Hauling himself over the wall, he dropped down the other side. Karla vaulted the wall as if clearing a five-barred gate.

"Show off!" Jameson said.

She smiled at him, flashing long needle-pointed teeth.

The drive up to the front of the mansion was brilliantly lit. The rear, where they entered the garden, was in shadow. Rhododendron and other bushes were tastefully arranged to form a semi-wilderness containing winding paths. Jameson avoided these, pushing his way between the bushes. Paths were obvious places to site some sort of detection mechanism.

"This is going to play hell with my clothes," he said.

"Wassock," Karla replied succinctly.

She had a nice line in archaic insults, acquired during a very long life. Wassock, pronounced "wazzok," was an old rural north-country expression for a traditional village idiot. It had a brief resurgence of use among public schoolboys, which is how Jameson knew what it meant.

"I begin to see the advantages of a black leather suit like yours," Jameson said. "But I suspect that although you look cute in it, I really would resemble a wassock."

The bushes ended at a cleared grassed area a few meters from the house. Large French windows gave access to the lawn. The room behind was dark and empty. Jameson considered entry through the French windows but rejected the idea. Instead, he chose a small door on the left of the building that was presumably used by the servants. Both the French windows and the kitchen door were protected by security cameras, presumably low-light models.

"That's what you get for employing bloody amateurs," Jameson said.

"What?" Karla asked.

"Both the cameras are mounted above the left corners of the doors," Jameson replied. "Don't you see? The cameras both point the same way. The left camera covers the right one as well as the door, but is itself vulnerable."

He moved into the blind spot.

"Dear God, they haven't even buried the cable in the wall."

He pointed to where the cable from the camera was clipped to the outside of the brickwork. Dropping on one knee, he pulled out a tuft of grass.

"Give me a lift up."

"I think you only bring me along to act as a human ladder," Karla said.

"Certainly not," Jameson replied. "You aren't human."

She shoved him up the wall a little more vigorously than required. Jameson decided not to complain in case he got accidentally dropped. His colleagues thought that Karla had no sense of humor, but they didn't know her. She had a sense of fun, in the same way that the Emperor Caligula could be a laugh a minute. Like when he was deciding who to toss to the lions.

Jameson carefully smeared mud all over the camera lens. The exposed cable was tempting. Using his phone, he could corrupt the system to show anything from an empty doorway to the BBC News, but that would take time. Sometimes the old ways were the best. When they came to review the tapes, all they would see was a malfunctioning camera.

"Okay, let me down."

Karla took her hand away and he dropped like a share price. She caught him before he hit the ground, but this was payback time for the ladder crack. She knew how much he disliked her demonstrating her strength on him. He decided to maintain a dignified silence on the matter. She sniggered, showing that she was not fooled at all.

The door lock was a nice new modern digital pad system that offered no protection at all to Jameson's phone. He had been concerned that Shternberg might have left on the old-fashioned mechanical lock. Now they could be really tricky. A few seconds of digital magic and the door clicked open. He closed the burglar app on the phone and ran the magical field-protection app through its cycle. It detected nothing. Jameson looked at Karla questioningly. In his experience, she was far more reliable than any artificial detector. She shook her head, concurring with the mobile, so he entered.

The inside of the house was in darkness, so Jameson took a pencil torch from his inside pocket and shone it around. He found a scullery with an old-fashioned sink, draining boards, boot racks, and couple of shotguns propped against the wall in the corner. He passed through an inner door, into the kitchen which was a strange mixture of the old and new. An Aga shared space with microwave ovens. Most of the space in the kitchen was taken up by a large wooden table. Traditional kitchen sideboards lined the walls. Rows of stacked plates, pots, and pans filled the shelves.

Jameson pressed on into a corridor and began trying doors at random. He discovered the broom cupboard and a stairway down to the cellar. A quick reconnaissance revealed nothing but Shternberg's collection of wines. Jameson would not have minded trying one or two. The man had good taste and deep pockets. The next door was more promising. It was locked. He searched through his pockets for his picklock until Karla tapped him on the shoulder and handed it to him.

"Thanks, I forgot I'd given that to you."

Bingo, the room was some sort of office, with filing cabinets and a computer on a desk in the corner. He turned the computer on, looking through the filing cabinets while he waited for it to boot. The cabinets contained cardboard folders full of receipts and spreadsheet printouts. Jameson had the impression that he was looking at the household accounts. Nevertheless, he plied his phone into a USB socket on the front of the computer and initiated a data dump. He looked around the room while the hard drive disgorged its secrets, but found nothing further of interest.

The final room on the rear of the ground floor was a sitting room. Although comfortably furnished, it was not luxurious, so he concluded that it was for the servants' use. A door separated the functional areas of the ground floor from the main entrance. Jameson checked with his phone but could find no sign of electrical or magical alarms, so he pushed open the door and shone his torch into the hallway.

Light reflected off the back of a man wearing silver clothes like a spacesuit. Jameson took two or three steps forward and raised his hand to chop at the back of the neck. Karla laughed softly and he realized that it was a suit of armor. The hallway was lined with them.

"Bloody Shternberg, typical of a nouveau riche asset-stripper to have suits of armor lying around like some poxy lord of the manor," said Jameson, feeling foolish.

He heard something behind him and swung round, shining the torch. Karla leaned against the doorway with her arms crossed. She would never mistake an inanimate object for a person no matter how dark it was. She could sense her prey's feelings, smell his sweat, hear his heartbeat.

A grand staircase gave access to the first floor. If the mansion had a typical layout, the master's study and living rooms would be on this floor. Jameson slowly and carefully climbed the stairs. He placed his feet on the side of each step so it would not creak. Nevertheless, the fifth depressed silently under his weight. Jameson cursed under his breath and activated the security search on his phone, something he should have done before using the stairway. It was a natural place for an alarm. He was getting past this sort of thing, getting too old and too careless.

A red icon flashed on the phone's display.

"Oh, bugger, silent alarm," Jameson said to Karla, as there was no further point in being quiet.

"I can hear people moving about," Karla said.

"Okay, out, mission accomplished," Jameson said.

He quite deliberately pulled open the front door, setting off an audible alarm. Exiting, he and Karla circled around the house to the back. Somebody threw back a window on the first floor and leaned out. Jameson had a quick impression of a long stick. He knocked Karla over and dived the other way, a split second before the double blast of a shogun. Pellets chopped through the bushes behind them.

Jameson landed on his hands and rolled over onto his back, pulling a pistol from the holster under his left arm. He was armed with a Glock 26 subcompact pistol for this particular operation, not his usual railgun with its distinctive bolts. He had not expected to encounter paranormal entities.

He snapped off two shots at the shadowy figure in the window. The gunman returned fire, shooting each barrel separately into the garden. The pellets went wide of Jameson and Karla, confirming that the gunman was not sure where they were. Light snapped on in the rooms at the rear of the house, illuminating the man. He was loading new shells into the breaches of his weapon. The man half turned to yell at someone behind him. "For Christ's sake, turn that bloody light off."

Jameson grinned, "Tough luck, sunshine."

He had all the time in the world, like he was on a firing range. Sighting carefully down the barrel, he put a double tap into the lit window. The gunman dropped without a sound. The shotgun fell out of the window, clattering down the wall. Jameson regained his feet and ran into the bushes, pounding along the decorative paths.

The dogs made no sound. Guard dogs barked, but hunting dogs, killers, were silent. They ran in so fast that Jameson had no chance even to count them. He had an impression of teeth, and then the crack of his Glock. He pulled the double-weight trigger as fast as he could without aiming. He fired from the hip, getting off three, maybe four shots before the first dog hit him and knocked him into the bushes. He smashed his elbow on a root, badly jarring the ulnar nerve. The ulnar is the largest nerve in the human body protected neither by muscle nor bone. Presumably evolution will one day fix the problem. In the meantime, like the appendix, the design fault continues to plague the human body. The pistol dropped from suddenly nerveless fingers and he cursed.

He pushed at the dog, trying to keep its teeth from his throat. The animal made a strange noise, halfway between a gargle and cough. It spewed blood all over his chest and died. At least one of his hastily fired rounds had smashed through the dog's lungs. He searched frantically for the pistol, but it was lost somewhere in the undergrowth.

Snarls, growls, and smashing sounds of splintering wood indicated that Karla was fighting for her life. Cursing, he staggered to his feet to offer what help he could. A dog writhed on the path. It whimpered in pain, back bent at an impossible angle. Karla rolled on the ground, a dog clamped to each arm by its teeth. Jameson ran in and kicked one in the ribs. It yelped and attacked him. He backed off raising his arms like a boxer to cover his chest and face. It bit into his arm, the heavy body pulling him round.

He struggled to keep his feet. He had to prevent the animal pulling him to the ground. Then it would have a significant advantage. He smashed his free fist into its head, but it was like striking a wooden block. Changing tactics, he jabbed it in the eye with his thumb, gouging deep until it released him.

Berserk with rage, foaming at the mouth, the dog sprang again. Jameson desperately raised his arms, but the attack never came. A clawed hand sank into the back of its neck, halting it in mid-air. It crashed onto its back. Karla was lightning quick, stamping on the animal's throat before it could roll back onto its legs. It choked to death from a crushed windpipe. Jameson looked round for the third dog and found it on its side, throat ripped out. Blood soaked the gravel path.

"You're hurt," Karla said, in concern.

She gently lifted his arm and licked at his blood. Jameson wondered where the hell the dogs had come from and who had released them. That was the wrong question. That the bloody things were dead was what mattered. That and the fact that his arm hurt.

"We have to go," Jameson said. "The idea was to put the wind up Shternberg, not get found in *flagrante delicto*."

Karla had to haul him over the wall.

"You drive," Jameson said.

"Really, I can drive?" Karla asked.

"I'm afraid so," Jameson replied. "I don't think I'm up to it."

Karla was as pleased as a kid on Christmas morning eyeing up a newly delivered sack from Santa. She got Jameson into the passenger seat and slid over the bonnet to take the wheel. She put her hand on the electronic control unit on the dashboard and the engine started. The Jaguar shot off, tail wagging and back wheels spinning.

"Will you turn the thrice-cursed traction control back on, please?" Jameson asked.

"It's more fun with it off," Karla replied.

"Fun for whom?" Jameson asked. "It's no bloody fun for me."

Karla pouted and glanced at the control panel. The drive configurations system flashed icons in colored succession and the wheels stopped spinning. The rear of the car stopped wagging like a Labrador's tail and dropped in line with the front.

"Better," Jameson said. "While we're on the subject, how do you do that? The car just seems to know what you want."

Karla didn't reply, but she did smile at him. Her teeth were extended at the excitement of driving.

"And put your teeth away," Jameson said, his arm hurting. "You'll scare someone to death, probably me."

He searched the side compartment by his seat until he found an analgesic and antiseptic spray. He took off his jacket, not without some difficulty. He rolled up his sleeve and sprayed his arm. The chilling liquid almost immediately took away the pain. A doctor had once told Jameson that the effect of painkillers was nine-tenths placebo. Not that Jameson gave a damn, as long as they worked.

Karla pulled onto the main road behind an articulated lorry. Without hesitation, she pulled out and rocketed down the side of the long vehicle. They slipped around the front just before an oncoming car shot past in a blaze of flashing headlights.

"And you," Karla said, making a rude gesture in a direction of the car.

Jameson lowered the seat back and closed his eyes, thinking he might try to get some sleep. His mind drifted over the events of the evening.

"Oh shit!" Jameson sat bolt upright, ignoring the throbbing arm.

"What?" Karla asked.

"I've left the bloody gun behind."

CHAPTER 17
PRESSURE

"So let me get this straight, just so there is no misunderstanding," Randolph said. "You decided to carry out a little amateur burglary on Shternberg's country house to 'speed things up.'"

"We weren't getting anywhere following him around," Jameson said defensively. "So I thought we should ratchet up the pressure a little. You know, prod him a little and see what reaction we got."

"*You thought*, you thought?" Randolph said. "If you'd thought, you wouldn't have left evidence behind?"

"Ah, yes, the Glock," Jameson said.

"The Glock," Randolph mimicked. "The Glock with the serial number issued to Her Majesty's Metropolitan police force and hence traceable to us."

"I was a little preoccupied at the time," Jameson said. "What with fighting off a pack of killer dogs intent on ripping out my throat."

"Daemon killer dogs?" Randolph asked hopefully.

"Just the normal kind," Jameson replied.

"Did you find any sign of unsanctioned paranormal activity?"

"No."

"Or bring back any useful intelligence?"

"We did clone a hard drive. The Library are going through the data, but it looks like household accounts."

"Household accounts," Randolph repeated, his voice leaking

sarcasm like sump oil from an old motor. "Do you have any idea how many strings I had to pull, how many favors I had to call in, how much political capital I had to expend with Special Branch to get that serial number expunged from the record?"

"Sorry about that," Jameson apologized. It had been unprofessional.

"And all for nothing."

"It's early days yet," Jameson said. "Let's see what reaction we provoke."

"No more burglaries," Randolph said.

"Right," Jameson replied.

"We can but hope that Shternberg uses magic rather than a Russian Mafia hit squad to eliminate you," Randolph said brightly. "Then at least I'd know that we are on the right lines."

When Rhian came off evening shift, Frankie was sitting at the kitchen table gazing gloomily at various stacks of official-looking papers. She held a glass of wine in both hands, elbows resting on the table. The bottle was open beside her. From the level, Frankie had been hitting the giggle water hard.

Rhian took a glass from the kitchen cabinet and emptied what was left of the wine into it. She didn't particularly want a drink but thought that Frankie had already had enough. It did not seem to have improved the woman's mood.

"Everything okay?" Rhian said.

Frankie put the glass down carefully, the way drunks do when they want to appear sober.

"That pile there," Frankie said, pointing, "are the outstanding utility bills."

Rhian noticed quite a lot of red ink, but Frankie had already picked up a document from a second pile.

"This is a letter rejecting my application for a credit card, which is unfortunate as I was hoping to use it to make minimum payments on the three cards I already have, seeing as how they are maxed out."

Frankie rummaged a bit until she produced a letter, which she waved vaguely in Rhian's direction. "This is a letter from my bank manager inviting me in for a little chat."

Frankie picked up a glass and stared at it intently. Finally registering that it was empty, she attempted to pour more wine from the bottle.

"I doubt if it is a social invite, so I expect the matter of my overdraft to come up in conversation. But this is the one that really worries me." Frankie pushed her glasses back up her nose and focused unsteadily on yet another document. "I'm three months behind with the mortgage, and I don't know how I'm going to pay it off. The bastard bankers are threatening to foreclose on my flat."

Rhian got up and found another bottle of wine. She unscrewed the cap and refilled the glasses. Frankie was right; this wasn't a problem to be faced sober.

"There must be a solution," Rhian said.

"Oh, there is," Frankie said. She picked up the check that Rhian had obtained from Max and waved it vaguely in the girl's direction. "All I have to do is pay this in to get the bank off my neck. Of course, there is a dunside."

She concentrated carefully. "Downside—the dunside being that we'll be working for a bloody vampire."

"But vampires don't exist, you said so," Rhian said.

"Shouldn't believe all you're told," Frankie said, waving a finger drunkenly at Rhian.

"You said *we*?" Rhian asked.

"What?"

"We will be working for a vampire?"

"Damn right," Frankie said. "Don't see why you shouldn't be a full partner in the business, seeing as how you got the contract. I'd have gone bankrup' without you. But bankrup's not so bad. Might be better'n working for a sicker."

Frankie concentrated hard again and raised one finger in the air. "A sucker," she said, triumphantly.

"Come on, I'll help you to bed," Rhian said, taking Frankie's arm.

She helped Frankie to her feet, checking her tendency to sway.

"Full dammed partnership," Frankie said, voice slurring. "The vampire, the witch, the werewolf, a partnership made in hell. All we need is the bloody wardrobe."

✹

Jameson made one of his rare visits to his office. Settling himself comfortably in his leather chair, he lifted his feet onto the desk and proceeded to go through the files on Shternberg. It was possible that might find something hitherto overlooked. The information provided by Inspector Fowler was particularly detailed, but, unfortunately, most of those details would be irrelevant. The task that faced him was like looking for a yellow peg in a sea of ripened wheat.

One little nugget of information caught his eye. Shternberg was a Freemason. This was not in itself suspicious. Many small-town businessmen, tradesmen, professionals, and local administrators spent a great deal of time exchanging funny handshakes and doing each other favors down at the lodge but Shternberg was not a small-town sort of person.

Freemasonry had been innocent of involvement with paranormal entities or magic for some centuries, since Adam Weishaupt's Illuminati lodge was suppressed in 1784 by the Elector of Bavaria. Adam Weishaupt was of course an alias—Adam, the first man, and Weishaupt, wise head. His real identity was unknown, but he was definitely buried in Gotha. Suggestions that he was also known as George Washington were pure conspiracy theory.

Shternberg was a member of Lodge 492, known as the Guild of Bankers. That was unsurprising, given his line of work. However, he was also a member of the Badford Lodge in Essex, motto *alter ipse amicus*—a friend is another self. Jameson wondered why a city financier would bother with a bunch of Essex Masons who would be concerned mainly with flogging each other dodgy Fords from the Dagenham Works. He also wondered why Fowler should have drawn his attention to the matter. He had learned to trust Fowler's instincts.

He glanced idly down the list of other lodge members. Many of them were members of the Metropolitan Police serving in East London. Of course, like taxi drivers, many East London policemen lived in Essex. There they could afford to purchase their own homes, something impossible in London on a policeman's salary. He was not surprised to see Inspector Drudge on the list, nor the name of Charlie Parkes. Gangsters and Met policemen had an unfortunate tendency to belong to the same lodges. Campaigning journalists exposed this fact every decade or so, and politicians tutted. Not that it did the slightest good.

Fowler had put a star by one name, Frank Mitchell. Jameson thumbed through to the appendices at the back of the report, where he found an entire section on Mitchell, including photos. Officially, he was a pillar of Badford society, living in a gruesome detached luxury modern mansion in Chingford. It was a style which would have looked more at home in Dallas, the television program, not the city.

Unofficially, the man was better known as Mad Mitch, or Fearsome Frankie. He was the head of the Essex Mob that ran the recreational drug business from the West End to Southend, that is, from the sublime to the ridiculous. They controlled the import, transport, and retail of cocaine and ecstasy from the continent through small Essex ports into London. Anyone doing business of a certain brand in East London paid a tithe to the Essex Mob, in blood if not cash. Generous contributions to unofficial police hardship funds kept the authorities off their backs.

Jameson laughed out loud. Shternberg's value to the spooks at MI6 was obvious. He must have the black on half the people in The City by supplying them with Colombian marching powder. Shternberg would be the financial backer behind the Essex mob. No doubt the man's original and mysterious source of wealth lay in the drug trade.

Shternberg kept a private light aircraft at City airport and had a pilot's license. They must have been very useful when he started out and had a more "hands-on" engagement in the drug rackets. Light aircraft were a ridiculously easy way of moving packages and people across the Channel without unduly adding to the workload of Her Majesty's officials by going through Customs.

Not that this got Jameson any further forward. There had always been corruption and crime in London, and there always would be. None of this was The Commission's problem. Jameson closed the file with a sigh. It was getting late, and Karla would be getting hyper and bored. A bored Karla was likely to get into trouble, so he decided to call it a day.

Rhian's world settled into cozy predictability over the following days. Frankie paid in the check and kept a roof over their heads while picking up the odd commission, while Rhian worked at the Black Swan. It couldn't last, of course. It never did.

She was working an evening shift when the next crisis erupted.

The pub was empty, as it was early. Rhian was killing time by attempting to clean the coffee machine. Lack of use had gummed the thing up. She unscrewed everything that unscrewed and soaked the bits in hot water and detergent. She was puzzling how to put it back together and wishing she had taken notes, when her phone chimed.

The flashing icon indicated that Max desired to speak to her. With a sigh, she keyed the icon.

"Snow White, I've got a job for you, right away," Max instructed in his best alpha-male manner.

"It's not convenient at present," she replied.

"Tough," Max said, "I need you now."

She considered telling him to go and rotate on it but remembered whose money was paying the mortgage.

"Very well, I'll see what I can do," she said. "I'll ring you back."

Gary had installed an intercom between the bar and his flat after recent events, so Rhian keyed it.

"Gary, can you release me from my shift tonight; I've something to deal with." Rhian asked.

"It's hardly convenient at this short notice," Gary replied. "Can't you reschedule it, whatever it is, to some other time?"

"It concerns Max," Rhian said.

"Ah, I'll be right down."

The bell over the door dinged, and the first students of the evening drifted in.

"What can I get you, gentlemen?" Rhian asked.

"You're the famous Welsh barmaid," one said, in delight.

"What?" Rhian asked.

"Your photo is on the notice board at the student union—pint of bitter, love."

"Someone has posted a photo of me?" Rhian asked, outraged.

"Easy enough to do with a camera phone," the student replied.

"I suppose it's something to do with that stupid bet?" she asked, pouring his drink.

"The pot gets bigger all the time," he replied.

He paid in small change that he sorted from a small leather purse. A man with a purse was one of those novelties with which Rhian became acquainted only after moving to London. She did not approve.

Women used purses for purely practical reasons, lacking trouser pockets. A man with a purse implied a meanness of character.

"Do you know what a Welsh rarebit is?" he asked, switching subjects.

"It's a traditional dish made by pouring a savory melted Cheddar cheese sauce over toast, usually flavored with Worcestershire sauce," she replied, fixing him with a gimlet eye that just dared him to add the punch line.

"Oh, right," he said, and scuttled off.

Gary appeared. "So, he didn't have the nerve to suggest a Welsh rarebit was a Cardiff virgin."

"Apparently not," Rhian replied.

"Not surprised, you are rather scary," Gary said.

Rhian looked at him in astonishment—her, frightening? Rhian the little Welsh mouse who was pushed about until she slipped away? Had the wolf changed her that much, or was it simply events molding her character into—what?

"That's why the pot on the bet to take you out is so big. Who dares wins, only the brave, and all that," said Gary.

"I'm really sorry to ruin your evening," Rhian said.

"Not a problem, you can take my shift tomorrow. You watch yourself around that Max character, Rhian."

"I will," Rhian replied.

She got her coat and walked outside before phoning Frankie. She hoped the woman hadn't been on the river water.

East London was getting to her. River Ouse equals booze. When did she start thinking in rhyming slang? When did she become a Londoner? What was next, dressing up as a Pearly Queen, doing the Lambeth Walk, or rioting at regular intervals? Nobody riots like the London mob, who over the centuries, have brought down kings and prime ministers.

Frankie's landline rang and rang. Come on, Rhian thought. She was about to ring off and try the woman's mobile when the line clicked.

"Yes?"

Frankie sounded sober.

"I've had a call from Max."

"Ah!"

Why did everyone say "ah" at the mention of Max's name? This was going to be seriously irritating if it carried on.

"We have an immediate commission," Rhian said.

"Oh goddess," Frankie moaned.

"I suppose you don't want to give the money back," Rhian said, nettled.

"You suppose correctly," Frankie said, pulling herself together. "Since I no longer have it."

"I'll ring Max to get the details while you drive over to pick me up," Rhian said. She redialed. "Okay, Max, it's set up. So what's the job?"

"I want you to close an Otherworld gate that will open shortly at the ExCel Exhibition Center in the Royal Docks."

"Oh, right, an Otherworld gate," Rhian repeated, trying to be blasé but getting that "through the looking glass" feeling that seemed to occur so frequently lately. A thought occurred to her. "This gate, there's nothing coming through, is there? Nothing dangerous, that is?"

"Nothing you won't be able to handle, I'm sure. I've every confidence in you, Snow White," Max said.

Patronising git, Rhian thought. What she said was, "And our fee?"

"Five thousand sovs," Max replied.

Sov was the street word for one of The Bank of England's Pounds Stirling, but Rhian half-wondered whether Max was using the original meaning of Sovereigns. She had this mental image of the urbane Max down by the shore digging up a chest of gold coins, probably with a parrot on his shoulder—and a crutch. She giggled.

"What?"

"I said—each?" Rhian asked, brightly.

"Don't push your luck, Fido."

The line went dead before she could think of a suitably witty reply.

Rhian googled the ExCel Exhibition Center on her phone while sitting in Mildred on the way to the job. She had never been there so was curious. It was also a distinct advantage to be distracted from monitoring Mildred's erratic progress through the heavy traffic. She steadfastly refused to look up, even when car horns blared nearby.

The Center was not quite what she expected. At the back of her mind she held a vague preconception of redbrick and Victorian chimneys interspersed with 1960s concrete crap, but it was nothing like that at all. ExCel was huge, ultramodern, avant-garde even. It looked like a giant rectangular white tent with a roof hung from pylons. She was not entirely surprised to read that it was owned by an Abu Dhabi company. It would not have looked out of place on the coast of the Persian Gulf, an air-conditioned chip reflecting brittle white sunlight across the desert. It was as out of place on the banks of the Thames as a Mayan pyramid.

Frankie drove around the inner lane of a roundabout twice to get her bearings. Spotting a sign, she cruised majestically across the front of an articulated lorry. It nearly jack-knifed under braking to avoid them. She exited the roundabout on the south road, towards the River.

Rhian recognised landmarks, like the Whitechapel University Campus and the overhead pylons of the Docklands Light Railway. They also passed an old and imposing three-story Victorian building that she could not recall seeing before. It was completely isolated on a patch of wasteland by fast carriageways, cut off on all sides. Rhian was not surprised to see the windows and doors boarded up.

She GPSed their location to discover whether it had a name. It did, the Admiral's House. Intrigued, she Googled to find the building's story. Everything in London has a story if you dig deep enough. The admiral in question was the commanding officer of the old Royal Dockyards. It was a listed building so could not be demolished, but it had no function in this new landscape of university campuses, hotels, and yuppie flats. Its preservation was, she reflected, such a very English compromise. The English mixed a sentimentality that refused to sweep away the past with a hardheaded pragmatism that would not allow a penny to be wasted on conversion. So there it sat, a sad and useless relic, now just a forgotten backdrop to the vibrant new East London Docklands.

Battersea Power station in the west had suffered a similar fate. No longer wanted, it was an architectural white elephant, but its four chimneys were such an iconic part of the river frontage that it was listed. The gutted shell of the largest art deco brick-built building in Europe had slowly decayed for half a century. It was near collapse through neglect.

Rhian sighed, thinking that she was in no position to criticize. What were the Welsh, if not siblings of the English in Celtic sentimentality but devoid of the strand of Germanic realism that ran though English culture like a Roman road. Her people clung to the past with a hysterical grip as if to a comfort blanket. They persisted in speaking a language so minor that it no longer ranked second or even . third on the island.

Frankie swung off the carriageway onto the ramp that ran down to the Exhibition Center car park, mounting the pavement at the apex of the corner. Mildred's unyielding 1960s suspension faithfully transferred the energy to Rhian's bottom. The shock wave catapulted her against the seatbelt, breaking her mood of morbid introspection.

"Whoops," Frankie said, adjusting her glasses.

They deposited Mildred under one of the railway pylons. Frankie produced the bright yellow steering lock from under the driver's seat, but, noting the expression on Rhian's face, put it back. She hauled two rucksacks out of the back and handed one to Rhian, who slipped it over one shoulder, wearing it like a bag.

Frankie took out a single L-shaped wooden divining rod from the second. The smaller length of the L fitted loosely into a copper tube that doubled as a handle, allowing the rod to move freely.

"Don't you need two of those?" Rhian asked. "One in each hand?"

"How would I carry my rucksack?" Frankie countered.

"Good point."

The rod swung gently back and forth like a radar dish. Rhian was not sure whether it was moving on its own or Frankie was gently swinging it. She didn't like to ask.

"There's no hole in reality here," Frankie said.

"Oh good, easy money, we can go home and write out an invoice for Max," Rhian said.

"But the area is awash with magical potential," said Frankie, as if Rhian had not spoken. "Come on."

"There must be an exhibition on," Rhian said, as they walked down the packed rows of vehicles. "I wonder what?" She took out her mobile and tapped it to run a search. "It's not working."

"No, I told you, the place is awash with magic," Frankie said.

"Right."

Rhian gazed at the phone's screen, which had snapped on to show a swirling psychedelic pattern in purple and pink. It was like looking at an episode of *Top of the Pops* from the 1970s. The colors shifted to the red end of the spectrum, light and darkness almost conveying an impression of a face. Rhian quickly clicked the off switch. The image was no doubt simply in her imagination, but it didn't look like a hippy flower child—too many teeth, not to mention the forked tongue and staring eyes.

"That's all I need, a daemonically possessed telephone," Rhian muttered to herself.

"What?"

"Nothing, just thinking out loud."

The car park was at the rear entrance to the center and it was a long walk. A steady procession of people flowed past. Rhian noticed that most were male but that they could be grouped into two quite separate categories. The first category was slim, thin even, carrying lightweight shoulder bags and wearing trainers. They bounced along like they were suspended from sky hooks by elastic threads. The second category sported beards, rucksacks, and impressive beer guts that could only have been achieved by sustained and rigorous consumption. They rolled from foot to foot like a stately vessel in heavy seas.

Entering the center was like being dropped into a vast arcade lined with shops. The broad center aisle was filled with bars, restaurants, and sales booths. People wound through the complex singly, as couples, and in groups. A large red banner announced the imminence of the London Marathon. Arrows directed athletes to the checking-in booths, which explained the athletic looking types.

Frankie had her eyes fixed on her divining rod, muttering Latin phrases. She walked briskly through the crowds the same way she drove, with a complete disregard for everyone else. Miraculously, people moved aside for her. Perhaps they worried that her particular brand of madness was catching. Rhian walked behind, smiling apologetically, trying to convey that she was only there to prevent a mad relative from coming to harm.

The rod guided Frankie to a seating area around a booth selling genuine eel pies and mash, and a variety of continental lagers at ludicrously inflated prices. A party from France were examining the Olde Englishe Fayre with a kind of fascinated horror. They looked like condemned souls who had heard about living conditions in Hell but were nonetheless astonished to find imps with real pitchforks when they got there.

"Hm, I think I've lost the signal," Frankie said, waggling the divining rod. "There is so much energy swirling around. I just need to reboot."

She removed the wooden rod and kissed it, smoothing it down gently with her hand while crooning a lullaby in Latin.

Frankie replaced the rod and did some more waggling. Pursing her lips, she said, "Right, you've asked for it."

She banged the rod vigorously on one of the pie shop's plastic tables, yelling, "Work, you bastard or I'll use you as a firelighter."

The customers at the table leaned back in horror, one spilling a hot tea in his lap. Leaping to his feet, he danced around, pulling faces and screaming like a New Zealand rugby player performing the Haka. Rhian put her hand over her face as Frankie reengaged the rod and tube.

"Ha!" Frankie exclaimed in delight as the rod flipped to the right, and she was off.

The rod guided them to a large entrance guarded by men wearing red tops emblazoned with a logo boasting that the wearers were South London Warmakers. Rhian had to double check to make sure she had read the last word correctly.

"What are those people exhibiting?" Frankie said, eyes widening.

"Maybe it's a wargame show," Rhian replied.

"Wargames, is that where corporate human resources make middle-aged, middling obese middle managers run round in circles firing paint balls at each other, ostensibly as a team building exercise?"

"But really in the hope that some of them will have cardiac arrests and save the cost of redundancy payments?" Rhian asked.

"Precisely."

"I don't think so," Rhian said. "I suspect it's more about orcs and elves."

"They make them dress up as orcs and elves and hit each other with swords?" Frankie asked in horror.

"No, I knew this bloke who collected little miniature figurines of orcs and elves. He spent hours painting the models and mounting them on little stands that he decorated with bits from the garden."

"Why?"

"So he could line them up and fight battles with them against his mates."

There was a pause while Frankie considered this. "Just when you assume you've plumbed the depths of male stupidity, they come up with something new. I suppose it's better than lap-dancing clubs."

Apparently, Frankie still hadn't forgotten Suze with an "E."

"Only one step more ridiculous than Gary's trains," Frankie said.

"So you know about them," Rhian said, looking sideways at Frankie.

"He, ah, invited me up to see them."

"Makes a change from etchings," Rhian said, straight-faced.

Frankie went beetroot-colored. "We'd better go in," she said, hurriedly.

They handed over ten pounds each to a spotty youth who stamped the back of their wrists with ink marker. He handed them each a plastic carrier bag colored a particularly revolting shade of orange. After some wrangling, Rhian secured a handwritten receipt from said youth in order to exploit the "plus expenses" part of their agreement with Max.

The first thing that struck Rhian was the enormous size of the show space. Aircraft hangars were modestly proportioned in comparison. It was filled with beards and beer guts, some trailed by bored looking women carrying stuff. A pervasive fug of testosterone filled the air with the scent of rugby player's jockstrap. She had never before been in an enclosed space with so many men. It was like a wildlife park where you could observe the male of the species in its natural habitat—geekville.

Rhian peered into the carrier bag and discovered a map of the event, which she passed to Frankie. She also discovered a model of a large-breasted space girl in skin-tight clothes, clutching a ray gun that looked like a hair dryer. The space girl needed the weapon to ward off a 1950s robot who menaced her with pincers on concertina arms. The intense fascination that large-breasted space girls in skin-tight clothes inspired in robots and weird aliens was never adequately explained in the story plots.

She recalled a discussion with another girl about the future as depicted in sci-fi movies. The girl had gloomily noted that very good legs would be needed as the skirts were so short. Rhian had countered that large breasts were of equal importance. How a girl was supposed to grow ginormous mammaries while keeping slim, toned legs was a mystery until technology came to the rescue with silicone implants.

The divining rod started to rotate slowly through 360 degrees in Frankie's hand.

"There's magic everywhere but no focus," she said.

"Which means?" Rhian asked.

"There's no open portal to the other world, but the whole area is leaky, like something is thinning the walls of reality."

"Deliberately?" Rhian asked.

"Very deliberately," Frankie replied. "But I can't do anything unless there is a focus, do you see. I need something to fasten on."

"So we wait for something to happen?" Rhian asked.

"Precisely," Frankie replied. "Of course, if we are lucky, the problem will fix itself and nothing will happen."

Rhian looked at the woman sharply. From Frankie's anxious expression, she did not believe that for a moment.

"In that case, we may as well look at the show," Rhian said.

CHAPTER 18
WEIRDNESS

The display covered the equivalent of four kitchen tables and depicted a bright blue seascape as seen from the air. It included part of a mountainous mainland covered with tropical foliage. At the sea's edge a port complex was modeled with cranes, warehouses, and docks. They were in a much smaller scale than Gary's trains but still beautifully painted.

Airships of various designs rose from the dock on wire stands to defend against a similar armada swooping in across the ocean. Some of the flying machines looked like zeppelins with various combinations of balloons. Others were more like ironclad battleships. A vicious melee swirled around volcanic islands. Burning airships dropped from the sky trailing black and white smoke. Wreckage floated in the sea or lay scattered in the island jungles.

Rhian leaned over to examine the brightly colored models and found that the defenders sported little Stars and Stripes whereas the attackers were decorated with the Rising Sun of Japan. An idea hung at the back of Rhian's mind like a waterlogged branch floating just below the surface. The battle reminded her of something but she could not quite remember what.

She sought out a spotty youth who was part of the display team and tapped him on the shoulder.

"Excuse me, is this display inspired by an actual event?" Rhian asked.

The youth looked at her in horror, spooked at being spoken to by a girl. An older-beard-and-beer gut moved him gently to one side.

"It's Pearl Harbor, reimagined as a steampunk campaign," the beard said.

"Pearl Harbor was . . ." Frankie began.

"I know," Rhian replied, somewhat nettled. "I am not completely ignorant, you know. I saw Ben Affleck in the movie."

"It was a real battle as well as a movie," Frankie said dryly.

Rhian turned her back on Frankie and walked away.

A disembodied voice over the tannoy announced that the Buckinghamshire Bravehearts were looking for Gary, who was supposed to be bringing the eight-sided dice and the rubber dragon.

Interspersed among the displays were stalls selling all manner of models and gaming accoutrements. Rhian was quite gobsmacked at the range. She saw Roman soldiers, vampires, Egyptian chariots, aliens, panzergrenadiers, dinosaurs with ray guns, Confederate cavalry, and even some orcs and elves.

She stopped in front of a stall that just sold dice, thousands of different sorts of dice in all colors, shapes, and sizes. Dice sets made from semiprecious stones caught her eye: purple amethyst at fifty-two pounds, for seven, black obsidian for forty pounds and pale green and red unkite. The last was a snip at twenty-five quid. Were there really people willing to pay seventy-five pounds for a handful of dice in green-white jade? Apparently there were, as the stall was two deep in customers.

Rhian found a model of a werewolf in a glass display cabinet alongside vampires, ghouls, and less recognizable monsters. It depicted a girl in the moment of transformation. The miniature girl leaned forward, pulling off a cream blouse to display more front than Blackpool. Her head was tilted back in agony, or ecstasy. Long blonde hair streamed down her back. Her legs, projecting from a miniskirt, were wolflike. The figure was mounted on a stand that included the stump of a twisted tree and an old cracked Gothic tombstone leaning over at a crazy angle.

"How much is the werewolf model?" Rhian asked, pointing to it.

"Seven fifty," replied the stall keeper, so she handed over a ten-pound note.

The man produced an unpainted shiny metal model in a ziplock bag and tried to give it to her.

"No, I meant how much for the painted model," she said.

"That's just for display," the man said, disapprovingly. "You have to assemble and paint your own."

"I'll give you twenty quid."

"Done!"

The stallholder removed the model from the display cabinet and wrapped it in paper for her, in exchange for another note.

"Present for the boyfriend is it, love?"

Rhian nodded. It was easier than trying to come up with a reason why she wanted the piece.

"Lucky boyfriend," the man said.

Rhian had walked away before parsing the ambiguity of the remark. Men didn't notice Rhian, except for James, of course. He didn't count because he was special. She wondered what was different about her now. She pushed the thought away into the sealed box marked forbidden territory.

She moved on to a display marked "The Battle of Blenheim" on a table that must have been near six meters long. The banner proudly announced that it was on a one-to-one scale, which somewhat confused Rhian. Six meters was impressive, but hardly one-to-one. She was reminded of a Blackadder scene in General Melchett's château thirty-five miles behind the line. Captain Darling proudly displayed a two-foot scale model of the ground captured in the last Big Push. That was at a one-to-one scale, as she recalled.

She wormed her way through the crowd to take a closer look. The table was covered in thousands of tiny little figures only a few millimeters high. One-to-one referred to the number of men represented by each model. She recognised the Redcoats, but not the uniforms of the other nationalities.

"How long do you think they took to create?" Frankie asked.

"Months and months," Rhian replied, shaking her head. "Each one must have been painted using a magnifying glass. Look, you can see the white crossed straps on the Redcoats."

"If one could just harness all that obsessive male behavior and attention to detail to something useful, we might have starships by now, or a cure for cancer," Frankie said.

"Or silicone breast implants that don't leak," Rhian said, sardonically. "It is men and their interests we are talking about."

Frankie laughed and the ice between the women melted.

"I'm sorry about that Pearl Harbor crack, Rhian. I tend to get snappy when I'm nervous."

"That's okay, I've had the misfortune of a modern British education, but I do read the occasional book," Rhian replied.

"Things are hotting up," Frankie said, diplomatically changing the subject. "Look!"

She stood close to Rhian to mask the divining rod. It was pointed towards the center of the hall, quivering gently as if excited.

The center of the arena was roped off and a poster announced it was an orc encampment created by the Royal Tunbridge Wells Fantasy Reenactment Society. Or, to put it another way, a bunch of weirdoes dressed up as monsters.

An attempt had been made to create a monster camp with the sort of wooden tepees that can be bought as children's play houses. They had a campfire underlit by red bulbs to give a mock flame effect. Re-enactors sat around in animal fur costumes, pretending to sharpen swords. An orc with a gigantic plastic battle axe consumed a Pret-a-Manger low-calorie vegetarian-option, sandwich which somewhat spoiled the effect. So far, so caveman but what really added to the weirdness was the monster masks that covered the top half of their faces and heads—and the green-skin makeup.

"They look like that Finnish monster rock band that won the Eurovision Song Contest," Frankie said.

"Not something I watch," Rhian replied, with a shudder.

"I don't either, of course not. It's just that sometimes one sees articles, in the Sunday *Guardian*," Frankie wittered.

It was, Rhian reflected, an English middle-class conceit that one never watched television, except for the odd improving program on the BBC. Television was for the proles. Nevertheless, English middle-class ladies all seemed to know the plots to the soaps and the winners of the various game shows. No doubt it leeched in by osmosis since, of course, they never watched such lowbrow stuff.

Frankie walked around the encampment, following the guide rope. Rhian stayed put and watched. It looked about as menacing as a children's tea party hosted by the Teletubbies, but the punters seemed to like it. The group were doing a roaring trade having their photos taken with customers who got to wave the swords and, if pretty girls, be abducted over a monster's shoulder. Apparently being a monster gave one a certain license. One of the re-enactors came over to Rhian, waving clawed hands and generally pretending to threaten her. To keep in the spirit of the event, she shrank back, squeaking in mock terror.

"Har, har, a fair young maiden for the cooking pot," said the monster, "or I could take you out for dinner after the show if you give me your telephone number."

Rhian laughed and shook her head. "There are enough monsters in my life already," she said.

She was starting to enjoy herself, despite the silliness. Frankie reappeared, having made a circumnavigation of the encampment.

"Rhian," she said in an urgent hiss, "this is serious."

"Har, har, another maiden for my harem," said the monster in a booming voice. Putting his hand around Frankie's waist, he attempted to lift her over the rope.

"Will you get off!"

Frankie struggled free, disheveling her hair and showing far too much leg. She pushed her glasses back on and smoothed down her skirt in an effort to recover her dignity.

"It's about to kick off," Frankie said.

"So I see," Rhian said.

"I'm serious, look at this."

Frankie showed her the divining rod, which thrashed and coiled around Frankie's arm like a pet snake. The end lifted towards Rhian, and, just for a moment, she saw two eyes and a flickering tongue.

"The rope around the encampment show makes a perfect delineated area for a magical circle," Frankie said.

"To do what?" Rhian asked, having a shrewd idea what, but wanting to hear it confirmed.

"To contain the magic, to concentrate it and raise a cone of force that will open a portal deep into the Otherworld. So deep that it links to places human beings can't go," Frankie replied.

The air thickened with static, something Rhian now associated as immanent to magic. Frankie grabbed the rucksack off Rhian and removed a chip of chalk rock from a side pocket. Kneeling, she carefully drew a thick circle on the plastic-coated floor around them, going over any thin sections as necessary to reinforce the line. She placed four candles, red, yellow, blue, and green equidistantly around the circumference of the circle.

"Sylphs of air fly to the circle," Frankie lit the yellow candle.

"Undines of ocean depths, swim to me," Frankie lit the blue candle.

"Salamanders, dancing on fire, join us," Frankie lit the red candle.

"Gnomes of the earth, link the power of your tunnels to my cause," Frankie lit the green candle.

There was something incongruous about a witch in large glasses invoking a magical ritual as old as mankind, especially as she used a cheap see-through purple plastic lighter.

"Har, har, we have a witch for the burning, boys," said the man in the monster mask on the other side of the rope.

His voice sounded deeper and garbled, as if his teeth were too big. Rhian looked at him carefully. The silly plastic mask stuck closely to his face, looking more real, like a proper film prop. The man was bulkier than she remembered, his arms a little too long, his legs a little too short.

"Um, Frankie," Rhian said, touching the woman's shoulder.

Frankie pushed her off, placing little heaps of some herbal mix in between the candles. She set alight each pile, not with the gas lighter but with her finger. They burned with steady green flames without the herbs being consumed.

She raised her arms and head to the ceiling and spun clockwise, "Orbis."

The green flames from the herbs and yellow from the candles shot upwards to knee height, swirling around the chalk circle clockwise in green and yellow rings.

"I say, the special effects at these shows are getting better," said a wargamer holding handfuls of carrier bags.

"Nah, seen better," said his mate, who was clutching a box full of plastic battleships.

"I've bought us some time," Frankie said. "The circle I've cast won't hold for ever but, I hope, long enough for me to raise my own cone of power. Make sure you stay within the ring."

The air inside the roped-off encampment thickened, forming into translucent grey tendrils that drifted clockwise, linking and amalgamating to form bubbles like the wax in a lava lamp. Reenactors shambled and grunted, swinging their swords at some invisible barrier around the encampment. It rang like a bell with each strike.

Frankie stood with her eyes closed. She posed with her arms out to the side and her elbows bent at ninety degrees. Her hands were open and flat, palms up. She reminded Rhian of pictures of princesses and queens in Egyptian tombs. Frankie had often said that all Western religious and magical ritual traced back to Egypt, the ultimate source of arcane knowledge. She chanted something in a fluid language that sounded Romantic. It was full of words ending in "o" and "a." No linguist, for all Rhian knew it could be Spanish, Italian, or even Romanian itself.

The floating blobs and tendrils solidified and pinkened. Rhian felt a subsonic snap in her chest. The floaters rushed together into a tiny pulsating ball in a pink color too rich to exist naturally. Then it exploded with a pop like the cork from a champagne bottle.

Hundreds of chittering, leaping things appeared from nowhere at the edge of the rope. They scuttled outwards into the hall like an upended basin of cockroaches. Mischievous rather than dangerous, they jumped on the display tables, kicking over the models. They ripped up books and magazines, throwing the pieces into the air to create an artificial snowstorm. They flipped up women's skirts to make them scream.

One flung itself at the flame barrier around Frankie's magic circle. The humanoid thing hung there, gibbering angrily, scrabbling with clawed hands and feet. Bright red eyes glared at Rhian from a pink face and body. Pointy ears waggled and it poked its tongue out at her in a manner that was decidedly obscene.

"Um, Frankie," Rhian said, patting the witch's shoulder.

Frankie shook her off without opening her eyes.

"Don't distract me. The portal only links to superficial layers of the Otherworld at the moment, but someone is trying to drive it deeper."

The pink goblin burst into green flames. It leapt off the magic circle, screaming in a fluting voice. It fled across the hall seeking the security of fellows, managing to set light to others in its panic-stricken flight. When it was consumed, it left nothing but pink ash drifting in the air. The green flames spread quickly and lethally amongst the goblins without anything else catching fire. The goblinoids never seemed to learn, clustering together in their terror. They were all destroyed, leaving chaos as their epitaph.

"Now you have to admit that was good," said the wargamer with the carrier bags.

"Seen better in 1970s Doctor Who episodes," said his hard-to-please mate with the plastic battleships. "And they had wobbly scenery to boot."

"Be fair, it would wobble if you booted it."

Rhian filtered out the inane conversation and focused on the encampment. Grey tendrils and blobs were reforming and rotating clockwise, slowly turning rust red. The color pulled into the center. It thickened, spinning faster and faster, like when an ice dancer pulls in her arms. A vortex of seething energy formed. The funnel continued to squeeze and wriggle until it spat out a monster.

And what a monster—Five meters long, it looked like a flattened ice-cream cone. The ice cream end, the head, was smooth and the color of old bones, but the segmented body was rust red. Lateral deep purple projections that were as long as the body was wide stuck out from each segment.

Rhian couldn't get her head around the physics of the thing. How did something so bulky float in the air like a zeppelin? She tapped Frankie on the shoulder.

"What! I told you not to bother . . . Ye gods!" said Frankie on noticing the beast.

"What in the name of Hell is that?" Rhian asked.

"A monster from the Otherworld," said Frankie, helpfully.

The tentacles rippled in sequence, like a series of Mexican waves. The monster slid through the air, picking up speed.

"That is impossible," Rhian said. "Those tentacles . . ."

"Parapodia," Frankie interrupted.

"What?"

"Parapodia, like on the side of segmented worms," Frankie said.

"These *parapodia* things cannot possibly move enough air to generate motion," Rhian said.

"Not according to the rules of our world," Frankie said, "but who knows how things work where it comes from. The portal opening has moved deep within the Otherworld."

"What are we going to do about it?" Rhian asked.

"Close the hole," Frankie replied. "Cut off the energy from the portal, and the monster can't exist here. Nothing that far away from our physics could. The more you distract me, the longer it will take."

Frankie readopted her ancient Egyptian princess stance. She closed her eyes and resumed chanting. The monster circled the display hall, ten or twenty meters up.

"Now that is cool," said the wargamer with the carrier bags.

"It's just a radio-controlled balloon," said his mate. "I was at the Riddlington Riflemen Show when they flew a twenty-foot zeppelin round the room. Silly sods couldn't afford helium, so they filled it with hydrogen that they made themselves. A spark from the electric motors ignited the gas. The whole venue burned down. The Sea Scouts were pretty miffed."

"The Sea Scouts, why?"

"The show was in their Scout Hut."

On the second pass, Rhian noticed that the monster had five bright red eyes wiggling on little stalks at the front. The slit under the chin was presumably the mouth. It circled a third time, watched by the admiring crowd, and seemed to come to a decision. The pattern of *parapodia* oscillation changed and the nose dipped. It picked up speed.

The monster leveled out at about two meters height and turned to head for a group of wargamers watching from an open area. The slit under its head opened and a long, segmented cable as thick as a man's thigh snaked out. On the end was a hinged claw like a serrated beak. The spectators scattered and the monster changed direction to follow one individual. The claw turned sideways and opened.

Rhian jumped over the flames and out of the magic circle to find the very air fizzing with magical energy. She recalled the subway where she met Max—and the elves. By the time she hit the floor, she landed on four feet and the world was monochrome.

There was a moment of disorientation, then the wolf howled. She gave it her all, a special howl, a challenge. She screamed the cry of an alpha female detecting an interloper in her hunting grounds, "a get out of my face or else" sort of howl. She ran after the floating monster. Pushing between the wargamers, she sent them flying. Plastic battleships sailed through the air, but the wolf was gone by the time they crunched on the floor.

"Well, really," a voice said.

The monster left a pervasive scent, like rotten seaweed spiced with nitric acid. The youth targeted by the floater ducked under the claw and fled. It snapped shut on thin air. The floater lifted its nose and climbed hard, killing speed by translating it into height. It then stalled, rotating as it dived to change direction, and reorientated on the youth.

"Well, I'll be damned, an Immelman Turn!" somebody yelled.

What struck Rhian was how little panic the audience showed. One or two people were backing away nervously, mostly women. They demonstrated yet again the superior intellect of the female of the species. Most of the wargamers gawped as if at a strip show.

The monster had plenty of other potential targets but seemed incapable of flexibility once committed to a particular prey. As a predator it was very, very dumb, albeit big and dangerous. Unlike the wolf, who was very, very smart, as well as dangerous. She changed direction at full speed, claws digging into the plastic, proving the superiority of ground traction. She cut across the angle of turn rapidly, closing on the floater.

The youth began jinking from side to side, hollering in terror, or perhaps excitement. The floater quickly caught him up. He finally did something sensible and tried to dive under a stall, but left it too late. The claw on the cable snaked in after him and pulled him out, screaming, by his ankle. Blood splattered across the floor where the deeply serrated claw bit into his flesh, and the monster lifted the youth. The extra weight badly affected the floater. It made heavy weather of climbing, giving the wolf a near stationary target.

She reached the monster and jumped. She snapped at a *parapodium* near the rear, but her teeth closed on spongy flesh that tore easily. The wolf dropped back to the ground. The floater ignored the attack. It continued to pull the struggling youth into the air until only his arms touched the ground.

Their combined flight path crashed the pair into a display, and the youth had the gumption to grab the leg of the table, which Rhian thought was impressive, as his foot must be agony. The floater took the strain and pulled, upsetting the table and spilling plastic star marines and alien predators all over the floor. Its claw scraped along the youth's leg like a wire stripper, peeling back flesh to the bone. The youth fainted from shock, losing his grip on the table, and the floater began to climb again. It reeled in the cable like an electrical extension lead on a drum, pulling the youth towards the gaping maw.

The wolf leapt onto the floater's back and tried to bite into one of the ridges along a segment. The monster's body was heavily armored, like a crab, so her teeth failed to penetrate. Giving up, the wolf ran along the back to the head and tore off one of the stalked eyes. Sour ichor filled her mouth. She spat the monster's flesh out in disgust and savaged another eye.

The monster let go of the youth, who hit the floor with a nasty thud. The loss of weight caused it to buck, throwing off the wolf, who turned in mid-air to land on her paws. The floater climbed to about ten meters and slowly circled.

Rhian felt the wolf's excitement and lust for the kill. She was swept along with its fierce emotions and uncluttered motivations. She forgot the youth as if he had never existed. The floater was out of reach for the moment, but if it came down—when it came down—the wolf snarled viciously. She would have the bugger. Nothing hunted her territory without her permission, not while she was alive. All the thing had to do was keep high and go after easier prey, but it was stupid. Its little pea brain clicked to a decision and it angled down.

The wolf stood her ground, muscles so tense that she quivered. Her senses fixed on her target, watching and tracking its flight path. She listened for the faintest change in air turbulence over the parapodia that might indicate a maneuver. She smelled not just rotten seaweed but also the acrid ichor that ran down the monster's armored head from its torn eye stalks.

Down it came and the wolf didn't move, not even when its underslung mouth gaped wide, showing the tip of the claw. She waited, until Rhian was almost screaming, wanting her to dodge or attack or something, anything, to relieve the tension.

The claw shot out on the end of its cable so lightning-fast it must have been a blur to the humans. Still the wolf waited until the large clumsy monster was utterly committed to the strike. Then she made her move.

She skipped sideways at the last moment. She moved aside mere centimeters. The horizontal claw raked down the side of her flank. The serrated edge ripped out fur, drawing blood. The wolf whipped around and sank her teeth into the cable behind the claw. She shook her head, ripping out flesh. It tasted like engine oil and had the consistency of power cables.

The floater flexed its segmented body in pain but failed to utter a sound. Perhaps it couldn't. It vented gallons of oily liquid that smelt of diesel from hidden spouts under the *parapodia* and shot towards the ceiling. As well as upward-facing aluminium pylons on the outside of the building, the roof was supported by downward-facing equivalents on the inside. The rapidly rising floater impaled itself on one. The aluminium point punched through its armor like a warrior's spear.

The monster thrashed its *parapodia* in random sequences as it tried to escape. The pylon pinned it like an insect on an entomological display. It shrank, folding in on itself like a concertina until only tattered remnants remained. These dropped from the pylon and disintegrated into fine dust that dissipated before reaching the ground.

The wolf howled again, the triumphant howl after a successful hunt to call the junior members of the pack to feed. There was no pack, and nothing to feed on, but it was the principle that mattered. Some rites are so important that they must be observed, irrespective of trivial details.

The wargamers started to clap, to the wolf's satisfaction. She strutted, enjoying the tribute rightfully hers. Rhian reminded her that their packmate, Frankie, was still fighting and that worse monsters stood poised to invade her realm. The wolf acknowledged the latter point by bounding back to the center display.

Frankie hadn't moved. She sang, eyes closed, hands on fire with green flames like the ones delineating her magic circle. Rhian was alarmed to see a new vortex spinning over the orc encampment.

Misty shapes slowly coalesced around the edge of the circle, shadows of humanoid figures. There must have been a dozen or more. They flickered like distant images in the desert, solidifying like the picture on an old analog television when you adjusted the fine tune.

Rhian had hoped for another monster: monsters could be fought and killed. With monsters, she and the wolf had a chance, but she knew she wouldn't stand an earthly chance against a dozen elves. It had taken the combined strength of Max and the wolf to overcome a couple. What could a dozen do?

The wolf felt her fear and laughed—well, snarled, but it was the equivalent of a laugh. Had she expected to live forever? What better way to die than in the company of a packmate, fighting for your lands? New strength fortified Rhian's resolve. She would do all she could for Frankie and her fellow humans. She could do no more.

When it came right down to it, what else was there in life? It was a far better way to go than the drooling decay of old age in a care home for the senile, so sedated that she couldn't remember her name. Assuming a car crash or cancer didn't get her first. She would fight, she would die, and she would join James with her head held high.

The figures were almost stable, almost fully in phase with the world. They were definitely elves, with perfect scent and elegant bodies. Their beautiful eyes gazed at the wolf with latent cruelty.

"Be gone!" Frankie yelled in English, attracting Rhian's attention.

The witch was wreathed in flames that twisted around her head in a cone of magical force. When she stepped from the circle, the magic went with her. The Siths' heads snapped around as if noticing Frankie for the first time. She thrust both hands out towards the orc encampment. Streams of fire ran down her arms. They poured off her fingers like a flamethrower, striking and engulfing the vortex.

An elf made a sign, and a pulse of black nothingness flicked out to strike at Frankie. The darkness knocked her back, bending her double in agony. The woman screamed, but straightened. She kept the flow of magical flames going, never hesitating no matter how they hurt her. Fire tightened on the vortex, compressing it down. The elves shrank as if they were being pushed away into the distance on a plane outside of the normal three dimensions.

Another symbol and another pulse of blackness, but this one was so weak that the wolf could see right through it. The attack barely rocked Frankie. She gripped with both hands.

A violent but soundless explosion threw the wolf off her paws. The world flared and compressed into a small green ball surrounded by blackness. Rhian's last image was of Frankie lying sprawled on the floor, blood flowing from her scalp.

CHAPTER 19
FRATERNAL RITUALS

"I think we might take a run out to Essex," Jameson said, getting into the car. "To see a lodge about a man."

"Essex is boring," Karla replied. "Wet, flat, and full of chavs."

"The north is quite pleasant," Jameson protested, "around the old Roman capital at Colchester."

"Are we going to Colchester?" Karla asked.

"Ah, no, Badford."

Jameson turned his phone off and checked the satnav was in receive only mode so that Randolph could not track him. He wanted a purely private enterprise after the last fiasco. What The Commission didn't know couldn't be held against him. He checked the new Glock that he had wheeled out of Stores before starting the car and heading east, and put a spare magazine in his pocket. He wasn't expecting to use the pistol anytime soon, let alone start a major firefight, but hard-won experience had taught him that the best time to check one's weapon was before one needed it.

It was midnight before the Jag crossed under the M25, the largest ring road in the world. The Jag powered out into the flat countryside. One knew one was in Essex when one passed the first burned out old Ford decorating the center of a roundabout like an obscure piece of modern sculpture.

Their running counterparts filled the road, especially Ford STs, the hot hatches that were Essex-man's answer to Ferrari. Jaguars had a peculiar effect on ST drivers. The mere sight of a Jag in a rearview mirror caused them to downshift and push the throttle to the floor. If ST drivers had a motto, it was "they shall not pass—especially in a bloody Jaguar."

Jameson enjoyed the thrill of the race, weaving the big sports car in and out of the lines of traffic in hot pursuit of a bright orange ST. In heavy traffic the agile ST was quicker, but as soon as a lane opened he was able to use the endless pull of the big V-12 to power past the four-in-line Ford. He was quite sorry when he turned off to Badford. The car's satnav guided him to a modern, blocky concrete building located well out of town in the marshes down by the river. The windows were dark, but the front was dimly illuminated by an exterior light. Jameson suspected that there would be additional security lights activated by motion detectors to scare off the local riffraff.

A long gravel drive ran up to the front of the Masonic Hall across flat, featureless land. Jameson drove on past to where the map showed a lane that led to a waterside pub. He left the car at the back of the near-empty car park. The hostelry was still open, presumably catering to a few hardy regulars who were no doubt cronies of the landlord. Mostly the business would rely on lunchtime trade, families if the swings and slides outside were any indication. The map showed the rear of the Hall was but one or two hundred meters from the pub across country.

He and Karla climbed over a gate and set off across a grassy field. He set his small electric torch to diffuse illumination so as not to draw too much attention. A large lump resolved into a cow lying down. It lifted its head to look at Jameson with disinterested eyes, mouth moving rhythmically on the cud.

He backed away slowly and adjusted the torch to throw a tighter beam that reached further. The light revealed more resting bovines. Jameson plotted a weaving course that stayed as far away as possible from the cows. He was a city dweller and found large beasts with horns disturbing. If they weren't dangerous then they looked as if they might be. Actually the cows did him one favor, because without the longer reach of the torch, he might have fallen down the steep bank into a water-filled drainage ditch that was not shown on his map.

"Flat and wet, Essex," Karla said in his ear, with the gloomy triumph of someone whose most pessimistic forecasts have proved accurate.

Tossing a mental coin, which landed vertically in a virtual cow pat, he turned left at random and walked along the ditch. After fifty meters or so he found an earthy ramp over the ditch, gated to keep in the cows. Climbing over the bars, they headed back towards the Hall. It seemed further away than when they started.

Jameson stepped into a small drainage channel that ran at right angles to the ditch. Water and mud splashed as high as his knee. He was beginning to regret his cunning plan to sneak in around the back.

"I will shoot you if you mention the topography of Essex again," he said to Karla.

By the time they reached the Hall, he had tramped through so many pools and channels that he had given up trying to avoid them. He squelched with every step. His shoes were ruined and his suit fit only for the dry cleaners.

At the back of the Hall, Jameson cracked open a window with a small aluminium jemmy that he had taken the precaution of bringing.

"You know," he said softly to Karla, swinging his legs over the sill, "if there is such a thing as a burglar and petty housebreakers guild then I must by now be eligible for a fellowship."

He shone his torch around a decent-sized room. It was furnished with leather arm chairs and resembled the lounge bar of a genteel provincial hotel. Broadsheet newspapers were carefully placed on occasional tables. Jameson had never been a Mason. The thought of standing with one trouser leg rolled up, left breast bared, a noose around his neck, chanting things like "so mote it be" was not something that appealed. God knows, Cambridge sporting clubs had been bad enough for stupid traditions, mostly involving alcohol, and, if you were lucky, girls, but at least you were not required to pay homage to a supreme architect. Nevertheless, he had read up on Masonic ritual to prime himself for the night's jaunt, and the room was not entirely what he had expected. He pushed open a door and entered a large space with a high ceiling done out like a medieval great hall.

"This," he said to Karla, "is more like it."

They entered to the right of a stage, on which stood a throne. There was just no other word adequate to describe the high-backed wooden chair upholstered in rich blue leather and fronted by two pillars. Wooden benches ran along the walls to the sides, shields decorated with coats of arms above. A formal double door opposite opened onto the front entrance. So far it might have been the senior common room at a Cambridge college, except that the Master was not usually enthroned. There the similarity ended.

The floor was tiled in a blue-and-white diamond pattern, with a blood-red star in the center. Concrete beams lent the room a pseudo-classical feel, like a Greek temple. The red neon light shaped like a G hanging down from the roof was a wonderfully tacky addition to the décor.

From his research, he knew that the room was supposed to resemble the middle section of King Solomon's Temple, although he doubted the neon light was an entirely authentic touch. It would be laid out east-west with the Master's seat facing east to the rising Sun. The clock behind would always be stopped at midday, when the meridian Sun was overhead.

Despite his cynicism about boys' secret societies, the hall room had a certain grandeur. He could understand how someone could become lost in the intricacies of the ceremonies in such a room.

"What exactly are we looking for?"

Jameson jumped, as Karla had spoken in a normal conversational tone that was at complete variance to his mood.

"God knows," he confessed, shining the torch on her. "Anything out of the ordinary, I suppose."

"Out of the ordinary," she repeated, eying the neon G.

"Just so," Jameson replied, walking down the walls to examine the coats of arms.

He was not really expecting to find anything. The real purpose of the break-in was to ratchet up the pressure on Shternberg. His perambulation took him back to his starting position at the west wall behind the Master's throne. He was struck by the Egyptian motifs, a pyramid and the all-seeing Eye of Horus emblazoned in gold leaf on the wall behind the throne. It reminded him of American bank notes. Egyptian-style gods, flat perspective drawings of human figures with animal heads, made offerings on each side.

"I thought Freemasonry used biblical symbols," Jameson said. He was speaking to himself, as Karla had zero interest in human ceremony or religion. She seemed to be preoccupied by something, her head tilted to one side.

He mounted the stage and poked around the throne and lectern, but found only a variety of sacred books, including the King James' Bible, the Koran and the Talmud. Freemasonry was marvelously ecumenical, so no doubt they could produce a Norse Edda or Hindu . . . his brain jammed. He was sure Hindus had religious writings, because they were written in Sanskrit, the oldest of the Indo-European languages, but he blanked on the name.

It was, Jameson thought gloomily, another senior moment, another marker on life's inexorable escalator to enfeeblement. He made a mental note not to mention it to Karla, or she would be back on the internet to research some new horror to keep him fit. It would probably involve dried seaweed or something equally execrable.

While he was exercising the inalienable right of an Englishman to wallow in gloom and self-pity, he noticed a torn scrap of paper on the floor behind the throne. Presumably only the grand high wizard, or whatever the high mucky-muck in charge was called, got to sit on the throne. The scrap must have slipped down unnoticed.

He picked it up and had a quick glance, but Karla interrupted him.

"Jameson, someone's coming," she said, urgently.

He thrust the paper in his pocket just as the main doors flew open, admitting five men. One snapped on the lights.

"Well, well," the one in front said, the one with a semi-automatic pistol pointed at Jameson's chest. "The Worshipful Master calls it correctly again. He said we might have visitors."

"Inspector Drudge," Jameson said, recognizing one of the newcomers. "Oh, you are in a world of trouble when I report that you are consorting with armed criminals."

"What makes you think you'll be reporting anyone, *Commander*?" Drudge said, laying sarcastic emphasis on the last word. "Good job I had his car number logged on the police computer, Frank. The traffic cameras tracked him all the way to Badford."

The thug in the expensive clothes must be the gangster Frank Mitchell. He didn't look much like his prison photo.

"Sure, you did your bit. I'll let the Master know," Mitchell said.

"Right, I'll be off then," Drudge said.

"Like hell you will!" Mitchell flashed a sharklike grin at the detective. "You'll get your hands dirty with everybody else, just so's you don't get no ideas about grassing."

Drudge looked unhappy but held his tongue. This didn't look good to Jameson.

Jameson weighed his chances. He assumed that they all had guns, even though only two were visible. If they ran to the form of the normal London villain they would be abysmal shots but you were bound to hit something if you fired enough rounds. Currently, the guns were pointed at Jameson, who must appear to be the more dangerous of the two. A natural assumption, but one that could get the gangsters killed.

"I guess we should be going," Jameson said, looking at Karla.

Mitchell laughed, apparently with genuine amusement.

"Not until we have a little chat, matey, about what you are doing in . . . The Temple," Mitchell said, fronting the last couple of words with capital letters.

"I was considering joining your happy band of scouts so I thought I'd have a look round first to see if the décor suited," Jameson said.

"And did it?"

"No, the place has the ambience of a Burmese brothel," Jameson sneered at Mitchell, trying to make him angry. An angry gangster might be a careless gangster.

Mitchell's face twisted in raw hate and he took a step towards Jameson, who tensed, but the man's temper stopped as if it had been switched off electronically. His face reverted to an easy smile. Jameson had met many killers over the years, the cold-blooded, the angry, and the barking mad. Not all of them had been on the other side. Mitchell struck him as a thorough-going psychopath.

"Naughty," Mitchell said. "We shall have to teach you the manners needed when addressing a Senior Warden."

The man was one of your new breed of gangsters, all flash clothes, slicked-back hair and fake country-club vowels. He probably had a trophy wife and a daughter who competed in the local gymkhana. Jameson readjusted his footing so his jacket swung slightly more open, facilitating access to the Glock.

"Uh, uh." Mitchell shook the gun slightly from side to side. "The Master said you would be tooled up, so take out the shooter very slowly and place it carefully on the ground."

The other two gangsters produced pistols, so Jameson, under four guns, did exactly as he was told. Drudge was apparently unarmed.

Mitchell examined Karla, who was dressed in her usual working clothes, a skintight leather cat suit.

"I can see you're not armed, sugar tits—well, not with a gun anyway."

He beamed at her and the men relaxed, laughing at their leader's vulgar wit and lowering their weapons. Apparently they were under the understandable but unfortunate misapprehension that their prisoners were helpless.

"Now, I suppose you think that you are a big strong man, and keen to prove it to sugar tits here. You won't break just because we kick you around a bit," Mitchell said to Jameson. "But I know you officers and gentlemen. Suppose we have some fun with your girlfriend instead. You got your little toy, Mikey?"

"Sure, boss." Mikey produced an old-fashioned cutthroat razor and opened it.

"Mikey here is a little strange. You see, he likes to hurt women, don't you, Mikey?"

The thug just grinned.

Seeds of doubt sprouted their first fragile shoots in Mitchell's eyes, as this was not going to the usual script. Jameson should be begging and Karla wetting herself in terror, but the two showed no reaction at all.

"I'm not kidding around here," Mitchell screamed, trying to shake them.

There was a moment of silence, then Mitchell's psychopathic smile switched on.

"Okay folks, you apparently need persuading that I'm serious. Mickey, why don't you go over to the little lady and cut off that outfit. Try to be careful now; we don't want her sliced too badly. I wouldn't want her to lose a nipple or anything."

Drudge licked his lips and edged backwards, stopping when Mitchell shot him a filthy look.

Mickey walked slowly to Karla, making sure she saw the light glinting off his blade. Jameson eyed the Glock, planning every move carefully in his head. The gangsters' eyes were on Karla, the air heavy with sado-sexual anticipation. Mickey put his free hand on her shoulder and drew her slowly towards him, lifting the razor.

Gravity is such a miserable little power, by far the weakest of the four natural forces that rule the universe. Jameson dropped in slow motion, thrusting his hand down, fingers reaching for the Glock.

Karla was quicker than gravity. Unbound by the normal laws of physics, she moved so fast she blurred. Her left hand reached up and grasped the wrist holding the razor. She squeezed. Blood spurted from cracking bones and springing tendons. Mikey opened his mouth to scream but managed little more than a whimper before her right hand exploded upwards to catch his chin in her palm. She followed through, slamming his jaws together, smashing teeth and cutting off the tip of his tongue. Her arm straightened, forcing his chin up. She bent his neck back until something snapped with an audible crack.

Mikey stopped trying to scream, his attention fully taken up with dying. The gangsters were slow, minds numbed by the impossibility of what they had witnessed. Mickey weighed sixteen stone, Mikey had a razor, and Mikey liked to hurt women, but Mikey was a bleeding corpse in Karla's hands. They just could not grasp the reality. Instincts cut in eventually and they lifted their guns to fire at her.

Loud explosions detonated in the concrete building. Jameson grasped the Glock and rolled over onto his front. Karla used the remains of Mikey as a shield. The corpse jerked with each hit. Karla hurled Mickey's mortal remains at the gangsters. Jameson rose to one knee, shooting into the mass of flesh. A bullet smashed into the battery of switches by the doors, shorting them out with a blue flash.

All the lights went out.

"You gave me one hell of a scare. I thought you were a dead 'un," Rhian said.

"Sorry," Frankie said. "Closing so powerful a portal . . ." She shuddered. "I'll be alright with some rest and a glass of wine."

"You had one hell of a nosebleed," Rhian said. "Not to mention the blood weeping from your eyes and ears."

"Yes, yes, I know," Frankie said. "You don't have to remind me of the gory details. I had enough trouble fighting off that lackwit with the first-aid kit."

Rhian laughed. "He was only trying to be helpful."

"You try having a bandage wrapped around your head, over your eyes and ears," Frankie said.

Rhian studied her anxiously, noting the deep lines in her face, the dark smudges under her eyes, and the pallor that draped her like a cloak.

"Are you sure you're alright?"

"I will be," Frankie said. She experimented with a wan smile. "You don't get owt for nowt. It's the prime rule of the universe, and it applies as much to magic as the laws of thermodynamics apply to the material world."

"What exactly are the Laws of Thermodynamics?" Rhian asked.

"Not exactly sure," Frankie confessed, "but I know they are important and mean that everything costs."

"Your spell was rather spectacular," Rhian said.

"Wasn't it just?" Frankie replied, proudly. Her smile vanished as quickly as it came. "Did you see what was left of the re-enactors caught within the portal vortex?"

"Yes," Rhian said briefly.

She got a brief glimpse of skeletons covered in white ash before she concentrated on helping Frankie. She made sure she did not look again.

"I wasn't fast enough to save them," Frankie said, sorrowfully.

"You did what you could. We both did."

They walked slowly along the bank of the Thames outside the Exhibition Center, returning inconspicuously to the car park at the back. The Center swarmed with police asking questions and paramedics treating the injured.

"You really should rest before driving home," Rhian said, not being entirely altruistic.

"Not on your life. I'll manage," Frankie said. "I want to be gone before The Commission arrive."

"They'll surely hunt down the witch involved," Rhian said, obliquely.

"They won't have to. I'll phone in a full report to Randolph—tomorrow—when I'm feeling better. I can't face bloody Jameson looking like this."

There was a pause.

"I meant feeling like this," Frankie said, coloring.

The flush in her cheeks was an improvement, but Rhian thought it impolitic to comment. Cranes were laid out at regular intervals along the bank like sculptures, and Rhian stopped to examine one, partly to give Frankie a rest. The crane didn't look right. Rhian made no claims to be an expert on dockside engineering, but it was too flimsily constructed and not quite big enough.

"They are a sort of modern sculpture," Frankie said, reading her thoughts.

"There must be dozens of them," Rhian said, somewhat exaggerating. "How much did this lot cost?"

"Money no object," Frankie replied. "This is The City. Think of them as an allegoric symbol of the insidious conversion of London's Docklands from a vibrant, functioning industrial port to a superficial sham based on virtual technology and the movement of invisible assets."

Rhian looked at her. "Are you sure you are feeling better?"

"I read that in the *Guardian*'s art page," Frankie confessed.

Rhian leaned against the "crane" and looked up the river eastward towards London. Light blazed from the Docklands towers because money never slept. The computers would be digitally ticking through the night, buying and selling options on everything from copper to olive oil. A war there, a famine here, a glut of guano somewhere else, all data input and output, all to be traded. Inexorable logic squeezed a profit out of human hope and fear. A green laser marked the sky above the Millennium Dome, the giant plastic tent built by Tony Blair to commemorate the fact that the current calendar had clocked up a number with three zeros on the decimal system.

A footbridge crossed high over the river by the Center. Steps and a lift in towers on each bank gave access, lending the structure the appearance of a double-glazed modern Tower Bridge. The other side of the river was mostly unlit. Large sections were still wasteland, but the blocks of low-rise yuppie flats on waterside frontages encroached further every year. An open area was covered by the curved plastic roofs on pylons that were a feature of Docklands architecture. Rhian wondered about its function: a car park, a trendy open air market, or somebody's idea of landscaping?

"That was a nasty one?" Frankie said.

Rhian nodded. "The last monsters were elves."

"I guessed. The potential portal was so huge that it might have persisted for days and flooded the area with energy from their part of the Otherworld. And all those people." Frankie shuddered. "Every death would have added to the potency of the spell, prolonging the event. We closed the hole just in time, but what about next one, or the time after that? They only have to get lucky once. We have to stop this at source and someone, somewhere not too far away, is controlling this."

"So how do we find them?" Rhian asked.

"I don't know. They will have a place, a coven gathering to carry out the necessary rituals for the spell. It will be well screened by a thrice-blessed circle. It could be in that old building there and we wouldn't know."

She pointed at a derelict sugar warehouse across the river lit up by the lights along the river bank footpath. You could still make out the Tate & Lyle brand name of the importer. The building was as out of place among the new East End as a condom in a convent.

"Maybe we ought to look?" Rhian asked, waving her hand vaguely in the direction of the footbridge.

Frankie shook her head. "That was just an example. No doubt it's just an old listed warehouse, scheduled for redevelopment into upmarket apartments or sound studios or whatever makes the developer the most profit."

The women walked slowly along the embankment to the car park, Frankie deep in thought. Rhian kept her counsel, having nothing useful to contribute. Frankie paused before unlocking the car.

"The Commission has the resources we lack. That's why we are going to going to contact them in the morning. I just hope we won't regret getting involved with my old employers, the Goddess rot their blackened souls."

"Boss, the lights have gone out," said a plaintive voice. "Boss, boss?"

"Shaddup, you arse. I can see the fuckin' lights are out."

Damn, so Mitchell was still alive. Jameson hoped he had shot him in the brief exchange of fire. He dropped flat and rolled to change position, firing as he moved to where his memory placed the targets.

"Shit!" said a voice.

A storm of shot came downrange, intermittently lighting up the far end of the hall. Jameson took careful aim at a half-glimpsed shadow and rapidly fired three times, exhausting the magazine. A grunt and thud signaled a hit.

He rolled to the right seven or eight times. Ejecting the old magazine, he pushed a new one home. The slider jacked up a new round with a click that sounded louder than a pile driver. He smeared himself against the floor, waiting for another burst of fire that never came.

A loud scream trailed off into a gurgle and obscene sucking noises. Daemons like Karla could see in the dark. The mechanism had never been tied down; Karla flatly refused to cooperate in any investigations. Maybe she saw into the infrared or maybe it was something else entirely. Whatever it was, she was a sighted predator in the Kingdom of the Blind.

The surviving gangsters scrambled for the door, not caring that they were silhouetted against the outside lights. Jameson considered dropping them as punishment for their stupidity, but sorting out London's underworld was not part of his remit. Randolph frowned on too high a body count as it created administrative problems. He grinned, as the thought occurred that the gangster's therapists would be on overtime.

"Time to go, Karla, before they call reinforcements," Jameson said softly. "Karla?"

Something stroked his cheek causing him to jump clear of the ground. "Jesus, don't do that!"

She put her hand on his shoulder and laughed with genuine amusement.

"I might have shot you," he said, trying to regain some dignity.

"No, I wouldn't have let that happen," she said, in all seriousness.

He was still remonstrating with her as their beat the retreat out of the back window of the Temple. They had covered about ten meters across the wetland when a powerful torch snapped on, illuminating Karla from behind. The flat crack of pistol shots sounded. She gave a little cry and fell down into darkness.

"Bastards!"

Jameson pulled his Glock and fired two double taps at the torch, which spun and dropped onto the mud, flicking off.

"I'm gut shot," a gangster moaned.

"Tough shit," Mitchell replied callously. He raised his voice. "It's just you and me left, pretty boy. Let's see what you're made of."

Mitchell advanced, firing his pistol. Jameson walked towards the gangster, waiting for his eyes to readjust as his night vision recovered from the torch-light. He held his fire, ignoring whip-snaps from the bow waves of passing supersonic projectiles. An outraged moo and the sound of a heavy body blundering through the pasture suggested that one of Mitchell's rounds had struck home, albeit not on the intended target.

Mitchell's gun clicked and refused to fire, either empty or jammed. Jameson kept walking a few more steps until the man was clearly outlined against the background orange light of Badford town center. Mitchell struggled with the recalcitrant gun, then he stopped fiddling with his pistol and glared at Jameson. His expression showed not a shred of remorse or fear, just burning hatred. Jameson shot him through the heart twice. Mitchell dropped silently. Jameson walked right up to the gangster and shot him again through the face. He'd had his chance.

He found Karla sitting up, examining her torn leather jacket.

"The bastards shot me," she said.

"Are you okay?" Jameson asked.

Karla didn't answer, engrossed in examining her wound. She grimaced and caught something that dropped from her clothes, passing it to Jameson. It was a spent round.

"The other two passed straight through," she said casually, wiping her hands on her trousers and climbing to her feet, using Jameson's shoulder as a crutch.

"Are you going to carry me?" she asked, playfully.

"I might," Jameson replied. "For a suitable reward."

But Karla didn't reply. Cocking her head to one side, she seemed to be listening to something he couldn't hear.

"Jameson, I think we should get out of here," she said.

"Why?"

"Something's coming, something of the marsh, something attracted to the spilling of blood."

She straightened. Abandoning the wounded maiden routine, she pulled him along after her.

"This isn't the way back to the car," Jameson said.

He looked towards the ditch, on the far side of which was the pub. It is never truly dark in southeast England, as the lights from a dispersed complex of twenty million people leave a residue of background illumination. Against this dim glow, Jameson imagined he saw tentacles emerging from the stagnant water. A thump of hooves and moos signalled that the cows were on the move.

A scream sounded from near the Temple. Jameson stopped, and, hearing more cries, took a few steps back towards where the gutshot man had fallen.

Tentacles burst from the temple roof, hoisting a figure into the night sky. He screamed for help. The screams choked off when the tentacles tore him to pieces. Jameson was halfway convinced the screams were in a Scottish accent.

CHAPTER 20
THE BLACK MUSEUM

Jameson and Karla made a low-key entrance to The Commission building the following afternoon. He would have avoided the place until Randolph cooled down, but he wanted to consult Kendrics about the scrap of paper liberated from the Temple at Badford.

The geek's office was a showpiece for creative chaos. He sat surrounded by desks and tables piled with modern and obsolete computer equipment. Servers, in various states of repair, were piled along one wall, and most of the floor space was stacked with printouts and magazines. Coffee mugs occupied every free space, and a solitary pizza takeout box lay abandoned on a stack of copies of *Digital Witchcraft & Wicca* magazine.

"Randolph has put the word out that he wants to see you," Kendrics said, peering over what looked like a pile of old capacitors.

"I am not here. You've not seen me," Jameson said, very deliberately.

"Okay, what do you want?" Kendrics asked, eying Karla doubtfully.

"Does this mean anything to you?" Jameson replied, handing the torn paper over.

Kendrics examined it owlishly.

"It looks Egyptian," he proffered.

"Do tell," Jameson said. "What gave it away? Look, is it a genuine copy of an ancient Egyptian script, something modern written in

Egyptian hieroglyphics, or just a geek code that has nothing to do with the Pharaohs?"

"Is that all you want to know?" Kendrics asked sarcastically, tossing the paper down.

Karla looked up from examining fungal growth at the bottom of a mug that she had found on a filing cabinet. It was emblazoned with the logo "Geeks do it with Gadgets," which at least had the merit of honesty.

"You are not being particularly cooperative," she said, without any detectable threat. But Kendrics still recoiled.

At that point his phone rang, and he grasped it the way a man seized a letter he hoped would be announcing the cancellation of his root-canal appointment. He stiffened upon hearing the caller.

"Yes, sir, no, sir, yes sir, he's here now, sir," Kendrics handed the phone to Jameson with a degree of malice.

"I want to see you—my office, now," Randolph said.

"It's not entirely convenient," Jameson replied, but the phone clicked, indicating that Randolph had already cut the connection.

Jameson reflected on who in the building might have dobbed him in. His thoughts must have shown in his expression because Kendrics looked anxious.

"I'll scan the hieroglyphs and run them through the databases while you are with Randolph. Shouldn't take long," he said, helpfully.

Jameson nodded his thanks and went to collect his bollocking.

"Do correct me if my memory is lapsing in my dotage, but I seem to recall forbidding you to carry out further larceny on Shternberg," Randolph said.

"Ah yes, but . . ."

"And yet when we have a red flap on and I try to call you, I find your phone switched off," Randolph beamed. "Now why would that be, do you think?"

"Sorry, must have forgot to charge it," Jameson replied unconvincingly.

"Indeed, I find that not only can you not support the Gamekeepers and Cleaners clearing up one mess, but you have created an entirely new one for us to deal with, simultaneously."

Karla laughed.

Randolph raised an eyebrow. "Something amusing you, monster?"

"I was just thinking that we found the proof you wanted. Shternberg was master of a daemon-raising cult, a cult that we destroyed."

"You destroyed the cult, not the daemon." Randolph said, crushingly. "The entire Coven had to be activated to put that down."

Karla shrugged. "That's what witches are for."

Jameson decided to intervene before matters got out of hand.

"If the Coven were in Badford, who dealt with the Dockside incident?" he asked.

"Fortunately one of our resting," Randolph pronounced the word as if it were distasteful, "employees handled the matter."

"Frankie?" Jameson asked.

"The same."

"She was the best we had."

"Until her breakdown, and that was also something to do with you, as I recall."

Jameson wasn't going to answer that.

"She tried to phone in a report, but I wasn't having that. I got her in here where we could subject her to a truth spell."

"She permitted that?" Jameson asked.

"I convinced her that it was in her best interests to cooperate."

Randolph pressed a button. A screen on the wall flickered on and played back Frankie's interrogation. Jameson watched the whole thing without saying a word.

"I apologize, sir. That was far more serious than I imagined. I should have been there."

Mollified, Randolph waved the apology away. "We survived."

"A massacre would have powered enough blood magic to tear a massive hole in space time. We're running out of time. Frankie's right, they only have to get lucky once."

"So kill him," Karla said.

Randolph shook his head. "It's not that easy. I agree, Shternberg is probably in this up to his greasy neck but killing him might not stop it."

"We could interrogate him robustly before his execution," Jameson suggested, looking Randolph straight in the eyes.

"Tempting—but no, he has too many friends in both Whitehall and Westminster," Randolph said. "He also has 6's protection, remember. The Secret Intelligence Service would love to get the leverage to take us over."

There was a long silence. Jameson looked at the screen, which had frozen at the end of the video showing Frankie staring at the camera. He noticed a petite, short-haired girl in an expensive business suit behind her. She sat primly, legs crossed. Her face was pale under hair as dark as a vampire's crypt.

"Have we got someone new on the payroll?" Jameson asked, pointing at her.

Randolph twisted around to see. "That's Appleyard's personal assistant, not one of ours. You wouldn't think freelance witching would pay well enough to hire staff, but apparently it does."

"So Frankie's got a PA? What's her name?"

"Hmm," Randolph tapped on his computer keyboard. "She's a Miss Jones from Welsh Wales, a Rhian Jones."

Something stirred in the depths of Jameson's memory, something about that name, but he couldn't quite put his finger on it. No doubt it would come to him in the fullness of time.

Frankie sat propped up on cushions in a comfy chair in her dressing gown. Gary gazed at her earnestly from a chair by the window.

"It's nice of Gary to come over and cheer you up," Rhian said innocently.

"Outstanding," Frankie replied, giving Rhian a look that would strip paint.

No doubt all Frankie wanted was to slob out in front of a costume drama on the television. Preferably one where the heroine died of consumption and the hero was tall and dark and vowed a life of celibacy unless saved by the love of a good woman. Instead, she sat trying to look elegant while dressed like her grandmother. It was difficult not to have a bad hair day after the Excel adventure. Magic did frizz it so.

"I don't see where you picked this virus up, Frankie," Gary said. "No one else has it."

"Yes, it's a puzzler," Frankie said.

"You look terrible," Gary said sympathetically. "All hollow eyed and wan."

"Thank you," Frankie replied, shooting Rhian a silent plea for help.

"You know, I really think you should get some sleep now," Rhian said, standing up.

Gary put down his cup and saucer. "I should go."

"Are you sure?" Frankie asked with phony regret.

"You shouldn't get overtired," Rhian replied, playing her designated role.

"No, that's right. I can come back tomorrow," Gary said.

He turned and recovered his jacket where it was hung on the back of the chair.

"You don't see many of those in these parts," Gary said, looking out of the window.

Rhian took the few steps across the room to join him.

"Have you got a rich friend?" she asked.

"What?" asked Frankie.

"A Jaguar sports has pulled up outside. Must have cost a hundred grand at least," Gary said.

"Oh joy!" Frankie said, with feeling.

Rhian watched as a man and woman got out of the motor. They made an incongruous couple. He was middle-aged, forty at least, but lean and fit. His companion jumped lithely out of the car. She was only a couple of years older than Rhian. Whereas he wore a conservative dark blue suit that screamed old money, she had on what Rhian could only describe as a black leather cat suit. She looked ridiculously old-fashioned, like a 1960s actress in an action TV series—*Department Z*, the *Enforcers*, or something. She also looked as sexy as hell.

They walked around the side of the flat, and the doorbell rang a few moments later.

"You answer it," Frankie said to Rhian, with a groan.

Rhian opened the front door. "Yes?" she said.

"Ah, the redoubtable Miss Jones, from Welsh Wales," he said, in an upper-class English drawl.

It has often been observed that an Englishman has only to open his mouth for half his fellow countrymen to form an instinctive dislike for him. Listening to that accent, Rhian began to understand how this might come about.

"We're here to see Frankie, and you," he said. "Can we come in?"

"Frankie is unwell," Rhian said, not moving from the doorway. "I can take a message."

"Let them in." Frankie's voice was raised to carry from the lounge.

Rhian reluctantly stood aside to allow them access. The mouth of the Durham Cathedral door knocker twisted. Its eyes opened and followed the woman.

"Beware, daemon," it said in a hollow voice.

Rhian blinked; it had never done that before. She followed the visitors into the lounge, noting that they seemed to know the way.

"Hello, Frankie, you're looking knackered," the man said, cheerfully.

"Let me introduce you to Major Jameson of The Commission," Frankie said, ignoring the jibe. "And Karla, who is . . . how do I introduce your friend?"

Frankie smiled at him with sweet venom.

"Partner will do," Jameson replied.

"Partner." Frankie drew the word out.

Gary and Rhian exchanged meaningful glances and Gary firmly sat down with the air of one who is not to be moved.

"We've met your assistant, Miss Jones," Jameson said, pleasantly. "And this is?"

He looked at Gary and raised an eyebrow.

"Gary Hunter, a friend of mine," Frankie said.

"I see, a friend," Jameson said, drawing the word out.

"Mister Hunter manages the Black Swan," Rhian said. "I work for him."

"Oh the Dirty Duck," Jameson replied. "I thought they would have bulldozed it by now."

"Not quite, Major," Gary said.

He rose and shook Jameson's hand. The men stood for a moment, gripping each other's hand in some unspoken male communication that passed Rhian by.

"Call me Jameson, I'm retired from The Army."

"Gary."

"So Miss Jones works for both of you. She is a lady of many talents. That must be how she can afford the designer clothes."

"You wanted something specific?" Frankie asked. "Or is this a social visit?"

Jameson retrieved a silver cigarette case from an inner jacket pocket while looking meaningfully at Gary.

"It's a delicate matter," he said.

"You can talk in front of Gary," Frankie said.

"Ah, a close friend then," Jameson said, tapping a cigarette end on his case while fishing through his pockets for a lighter.

"I'd be obliged if you'd refrain from indulging your disgusting habit in my flat," Frankie said. "I realize addicts find it difficult to control their cravings, but I can do without the smell."

"Ah, right."

Rhian hid a smile, forty-thirty Frankie.

"Tell me about the Excel job," Jameson said.

"You've read my report, I suppose."

"Yes, but I want to hear about it again. I need to know your impressions, your intuitions. All the useful details not found in one of Randolph's antiseptic bloody files."

"Hold hard, are you talking about the pyrotechnic disaster at Excel that was in the news? All those people burnt?" He stopped, looking at each face in turn. "That wasn't a special-effects accident, was it?" He turned to Frankie, "You don't have flu."

"Not that close a friend, then," Jameson said, to no one in particular.

Love all, Rhian thought.

"If this is a confidential meeting then perhaps I should leave you to it," Gary said in a neutral tone, but Rhian saw the hurt in his eyes.

So, apparently, did Frankie.

"No, please stay, Gary. I could use your support."

"Okay," he said, sitting down.

Frankie took Jameson though the full details once again, omitting only the wolf. Gary looked at Rhian thoughtfully, no doubt wondering about her contribution. Fortunately he kept his own counsel about his barmaid's alter ego.

At the end of Frankie's story, Jameson asked, "Have you got a drink?"

Rhian found some wine and glasses and handed them round. Karla smiled at her but shook her head.

"So there's no doubt this was the big one, an attempt to fix a major portal open using blood magic?"

Frankie shrugged, "Why else a target like that? There must have been five thousand people in the wargame show alone. It's later than we think. More people in London every year, more ticking minds weaving stories in the Otherworld, more release of entropy with every death, more power flowing through the digital networks, more energy added to the stew of two thousand years. The Commission is fighting a losing battle, Jameson. How long can you fire-brigade? How long can you hold it all together, papering over the cracks in reality before London goes up like a psychic Krakatoa?"

"We do what we have to. What else is there?" Jameson changed tack. "How did you just happen to be in just the right place at just the right time, Frankie?"

"I was hired by a client to protect the area."

"And the name of this client?"

"Confidential."

"Lawyers, doctors, and private eyes can plead client confidentially. Frankie, you are no Sam Spade. Surely you understand that I need to know how they knew?"

Frankie shook her head.

"We could force it out of you, but you wouldn't be good for much afterwards."

"Now wait a minute," Gary said.

"It's okay. Jameson is just wind-bagging," Frankie said. "They might need me again."

Jameson finished his wine in one gulp.

"You did well, Frankie. You always were the best, but you're getting too old for solo missions like this. Come back to us and the Coven can support you."

Frankie firmly shook her head. "Absolutely not, I'm done taking orders."

"But perhaps you weren't entirely flying solo. Perhaps you've been using unlicensed help."

Jameson turned to Rhian.

"Do you have a nickname?"

"Like what?" Rhian said.

"I don't know, but let me have a guess. Let's see, something suitable for a Welsh girl with raven hair and pale North European skin, Snow White perhaps?"

Rhian's face tightened despite her best efforts. How did he know? How much did he know?

"Max thinks you're a witch, doesn't he, Rhian?"

This time Rhian kept poker-faced, but Jameson knew. He saw something in her eyes, or the way she held her hands, or something.

Jameson glanced at Karla, who walked up to Rhian and smeled her.

"She smells of magic," Karla sniffed again. "But it's secondhand. She's not a witch, not a daemon either, but there is something."

Karla undid the buttons on Rhian's blouse to reveal Morgana's pendant. She reached out for it. When her hand was still a few inches away, a bright blue spark arced from the silver to her finger.

Karla screamed and leapt back, unsheathing her claws and teeth. The wolf surged within Rhian. She leaned forward, balling her fists and snarling at Karla. Gary jerked, his chair going over backwards. Rhian fought to control the wolf. Before Frankie's spell took effect she wouldn't have had a chance. She would have transformed and attacked the vampire, but now she was in control, if only just.

"Did I mention that Jameson's partner was a daemon?" Frankie asked Gary, calmly sipping her wine.

Go girl, match point, Rhian thought.

"It must have slipped your mind," Gary said, recovering his chair and his dignity.

"I've always had an odd taste in women," Jameson said meaningfully.

Love all, Rhian decided, Jameson having returned serve with a lob.

Gary and Rhian exchanged another look, both thinking that one suspicion was confirmed. Frankie and Jameson clearly had a history that went deeper than merely work issues. No one was that bitchy about a colleague. An old flame was another matter. In Rhian's limited experience, the degree of bitchiness was directly proportional to the intensity of the original relationship. On that scale, Jameson and Frankie must have had a screaming affair that ended very badly. Frankie was the one driving the exchange. Jameson must have meant far more to her than she meant to him. Rhian hoped Gary had not picked up on that.

She wondered whether the affair was before or after Pete, or maybe during. Perhaps Pete had reasons for running off with Suze-with-an-E that Frankie had not thought it necessary to expand upon.

"That answers one question. Max is your confidential client,"

Jameson said, breaking Rhian's train of thought before she got really catty.

Jameson had a closer look at Rhian's pendant, handling it without fear.

"That's a heavy-duty protective amulet on your assistant. You usually employ herbal magic so why use a Celtic brooch?"

"She's Welsh and she has a sentimental attachment to things Celtic. It makes the spell more potent, as it can feed off those emotions," Frankie said casually.

"She'll need good protection if you are working for suckers," Jameson said. "Especially if she fronts them like she just did Karla."

At that moment his phone chimed and he examined the message.

"You'll have to excuse us. Don't get up, we'll see ourselves out."

Jameson drove, which didn't please Karla much, but he had enjoyed enough excitement recently. He keyed the phone on its dashboard rest and told it to contact Kendrics. The security systems took a little time to convince each other that they were friends, but eventually Kendrics' number rang. He picked up after just one ring.

"You wanted me," Jameson said, changing down to kick in the turbo and overtake a bus. The driver attempted to "shut the door" on the Jag, as they say in racing circles, but stood no hope.

"Yes, that is, no," Kendrics said. "I'm transferring you."

There was a click.

"What the hell have you got us into now?" Randolph asked.

"What?"

"Those Egyptian hieroglyphics that you gave Kendrics. Why the hell didn't you bring them to me first?"

"I hadn't realized you were an expert on ancient civilizations, sir," Jameson said, politely. "I thought you read politics at the LSE."

The London School of Economics, founded by George Bernard Shaw and Sidney and Beatrice Webb, was a college of London University. Its alumni included the lead singer of the rock group Bankers Bad Breath, James Bond's father, and Eliza Doolittle, as well as prominent politicians such as President Bartlet and Prime Minister Jim Hacker.

"Don't give me any of your Light Blue crap," Randolph said, referring to Jameson's appearance in the Boat Race for Cambridge.

"Of course not, sir," Jameson said, smiling broadly and getting a return smile from a flustered housewife of a certain age riding in the back of a black cab. "The LSE is a notably good university, especially given its short existence."

Oxford was founded a few years after the Battle of Hastings. It was about the time William the Conqueror's son, William Rufus, was King of England. Randolph knew when he was batting on a sticky wicket, so he moved the conversation on.

"Kendrics found nothing in The Libraries' records, so he extended the search out to other government databases," Randolph said.

There was a pause while Jameson negotiated two youths on an overloaded moped who seemed to be under the impression that traffic lights served only to decorate the streets.

"And presumably he got a match," Jameson said, when he had the Jaguar back under control.

"I don't know," Randolph replied. "Nothing showed up, but ten minutes later I had The Black Museum on the phone accusing me of crossing departmental boundaries and threatening unspecified retaliation."

"I see," Jameson said.

"Can you imagine how many favors I had to call in to buy them off?"

"Well . . ."

"No, of course you can't, or you wouldn't have dropped me in it so deeply that only my ears are clear of dung. The Black Museum have consented, actually demanded, to see you and Karla immediately. Get over there, but don't give the slimy bastards an inch."

The phone went dead.

Karla smiled. "Randolph is wasted as a man."

"What makes you think he's human?" Jameson asked.

The Black Museum was an eternal thorn in the Commission's collective flank. It had started as a sub-department of Anthropology at the British Museum dedicated to the curation of unusual artifacts connected with ancient religious beliefs. "Unusual" was a euphemism for disturbing, obscene, or blasphemous. The gentlemen who ran the British Museum were academic enough to forbid the destruction of any items in the National Collection no matter how horrific, but

Victorian enough to keep them off display. They might corrupt weak minds such as women, servants, or the lower orders.

Both the BM and The Commission were independent entities that predated the formation of the modern Civil Service. When they learned of each other's existence there was no overarching body to arbitrate the resulting turf war. The Commission's Library took the view that the BM's paranormal collection should be transferred to their control for safekeeping. The Museum took the view that The Commission could get stuffed. For the last hundred years or so a standoff had prevailed. Hostilities had been reduced to sniping from fortified positions across the barren wasteland of British Civil Service procedures.

An invitation to visit, even one framed as a summons, from The Black Museum to Commission enforcers was as likely as finding the Staffordshire Hoard of Saxon treasure with a twenty-pound metal detector. It was theoretically possible but one didn't expect it to happen in one's lifetime.

Jameson parked the Jag in Bart Street, just south of Bloomsbury Way, taking care to display his Special Branch Parking Permit.

They walked the short distance into Bury Place, to a round concrete windowless shell a couple of meters in both diameter and height. Structures like this served a variety of boring but essential utilities all over central London. They were so commonplace that the populace no longer noticed them. This one was covered in illegal posters announcing pub concerts, street sales, and the services of ladies sporting exotic underwear and whips. The only free area was where a brass plate greened with age was sunk into the door. At various times posterers had tried to utilise this attractive freehold, but their posters had mysteriously caught fire.

Jameson put his hand on the plate, which shone silver at his touch.

"Major Jameson, The Commission. I believe I am expected."

"And your companion," said a disembodied voice.

"Karla. I'm with him," she said, putting her hand on the brass plate in turn.

This time it turned dull rust red, the color of dried blood.

"Come in," said the voice.

A solid metallic click sounded from the lock and the door slipped outwards by a few inches. Jameson pulled it open for Karla to step over the concrete sill. Following her, he pulled the heavy door to, shutting them into a steel cage. The floor dropped and a high-speed lift carried them down under London. Lights showed the walls sliding by faster and faster as the lift accelerated.

Abrupt heavy braking pushed Jameson down when the lift stopped. He found himself face to face with a slim man in a dark business suit set off by a salmon-pink tie.

"Director Bellevue," Jameson said, inclining his head. "I had not expected to be welcomed by you personally."

The man examined Jameson with an expression of faint distaste.

"Welcome is not quite the word I'd employ, but no doubt it will suffice."

Jameson slid back the cage door and followed Karla out.

"My associate, Karla . . ."

"Is a daemon, I know," Bellevue said coldly. "We have taken the appropriate measures, or she would not have got this far without being destroyed."

Bellevue turned on the heel of his black leather shoes and stalked up the corridor, which had an arched roof of red brick. The walls were plastered and painted in the insipid pale green that Jameson associated with government buildings. The Civil Service must have bought a job lot of several hundred thousand gallons back in the early twentieth century.

"Follow me," Bellevue said over his shoulder.

The corridor curved gently, dropping downwards until they came upon a black cat sitting licking its paws. It ignored Jameson but arched its back and spat at Karla.

"We discussed this, Mike. I don't like it any better than you," Bellevue said.

The cat spat again, then stalked up the corridor with its tail straight up in the air.

"You will have to excuse Mike. Deep down he is convinced he's the Museum Director, and he has an aversion to daemons. He doesn't much like Commission officers either."

"And Mike is?" Jameson asked.

"A cat, what does he look like? He's Mike, The Museum Cat," Bellevue pronounced each word with a capital letter. "You must have heard of Mike?"

Bellevue looked at Jameson.

"You never read Mike's biography, written by Budge? Good grief, what do they teach you people in The Commission?"

"E. A. Budge, the Egyptologist?" Jameson asked.

Bellevue nodded.

"But that would make the cat a hundred years old."

"At least and the rest," Bellevue said. "Mike has patrolled the Museum catching and killing vermin since its earliest days."

He looked speculatively at Karla. "Rats, pigeons, daemons, it's all the same to Mike."

Karla grinned at him. "I am pleased that you have such a dangerous beast under control."

They entered a much larger tunnel with a gravel floor that was used as a storage area for wooden crates and steel containers. A three-rail line ran along one side, disappearing around a curve into blackness.

"Does that link up with the tube system?" Jameson asked, pointing.

"Useful for moving larger artifacts," Bellevue replied.

"How on earth did the Museum afford all this? How did you excavate your own tube line without anyone noticing?"

Bellevue smiled, obviously pleased that Jameson was suitably impressed. "It was not as difficult as you might think. Haven't you guessed where you are? For God's sake, man, this is the British Museum tube station."

"There isn't one."

"There was. Part of the deep Central Line opened in 1900. The nearby High Holborn station was built by a competing train company It was only a few yards away overground, but unconnected underground. When the system was rationalized into a single network, it made sense to add a deep Central Line station under High Holborn. That left this station superfluous, and it was acquired for the Black Museum. The collection was originally in the basement of the British Museum building off Great Russell Street. Space became increasingly problematic as the National Collection expanded. The Natural History Collection decamped to South Kensington, and we came here. The Museum was glad to get shot of us after the infamous plague of newts during the 1911 great tea trolley disaster."

Bellevue's lecture was drowned out by the deep rumble and roar of a train passing through a nearby tunnel. Everything in the decommissioned station shook. Bellevue made a lunge to stop a cardboard box sliding off the end of a crate. Karla got there first and secured it until the vibration stopped.

"Of course, there are disadvantages," Bellevue said.

Jameson noticed an old sepia-faded poster on the wall indicating the direction to First Aid.

"The public sheltered down here during the Blitz," Bellevue said, observing his interest.

"You let the public into the Black Museum?"

"Of course not, we moved in after the war. Oh, I see what you mean. I was referring to the first Blitz, in World War One."

They passed through an arch, where the platform had been, and climbed a spiral staircase. At the top, a door took them into a room with chairs along one side and a desk at the other. Behind a computer on the desk sat a slim woman of indeterminate age. Jameson was vaguely disappointed not to see a vintage Civil Service black typewriter. The computer rather ruined the ambience.

"Miss, ah, Trenchfoot, my secretary," Bellevue said.

She lifted her glasses from where they hung around her neck on a chain, and, placing them on her nose, examined the visitors carefully.

"I have their passes, Director," she said.

Jameson smiled broadly at her as he took the plastic card from her hand and clipped it on his lapel, but she was immune to his manly charms. She did recoil when Karla took her ID.

"I am beginning to feel unloved," Karla said to Jameson, laughing.

"You are the first daemon allowed access to the Black Museum," Bellevue said. "I must say, you are not quite what we expected."

"I could snarl and drool a bit if that would help," Karla said.

"No interruptions, Miss Trenchfoot?" Bellevue asked, ushering his guests into his office. Like Jameson, he automatically stood aside to let the lady go first. It was easy to forget that this lady was a blood-sucking monster. Bellevue's room was a clone of every corporate management office that Jameson had ever seen, apart from the lack of a picture window. Hidden lighting filled the room in a comfortable glow. Even the air smelled fresh, or what passed for fresh in London. Presumably there was a circulation system somewhere. The man was a bureaucrat, not a museum curator, a product of the new style public sector management. The gentlemen were out and the players were in. Trouble was, it was often not quite clear what game were they trained to play.

They all sat down.

"So where did you get this?" Bellevue placed the crumpled, torn sheet of hieroglyphs on his desk and smoothed it out.

"In a Masonic temple," Jameson replied. "In Essex."

"Essex?" Bellevue looked shocked.

"Badford to be precise."

"It just gets better and better." Bellevue scratched his chin. "Tell me the context, please."

"Not relevant, if you'll just tell me what it is and why it concerns the Black Museum," Jameson countered.

"That is confidential," Bellevue said stiffly.

"It seems we have an impasse," Jameson said, unwilling to blink first in a bureaucratic showdown with one of The Commission's mortal enemies.

"What fools you people are," Karla said, looking up as if for information. "Your complete destruction is possible and all you do is play chimp games, beating your chests and waggling your willies at each other. How do human women put up with it?"

Bellevue turned beetroot red and huffed. Jameson only smiled, being used to Karla's directness.

"Now listen," Karla said. She ran through an abridged and admirably succinct version of events to date. Bellevue listened intently, turning pale when she mentioned elves. "So," Karla asked, "are you going to stop pissing around and tell us what we need to know?"

Bellevue pressed a button on his phone.

"Sir," Miss Trenchfoot's voice was tinny on the little speaker.

"Ask Professor Fairbold to join us at his earliest convenience."

"Yes, Director."

"And bring in some tea please."

Jameson relaxed; tea indicated a temporary truce in the Civil Service lexicon of interdepartmental infighting.

"What do you know about the Egyptian Book of the Dead?" Bellevue asked.

"It's the Ancient Egyptian Bible or Koran," Jameson replied.

"That is the popular view, and, as usual, the popular view is misleading. It isn't called the Book of the Dead, and it isn't even a book.

The real name is untranslatable into modern English, but would be something like The List of Emerging Forth into the Light. It's actually a compendium of spells."

"Like a Wicca's Book of Shadows," Jameson interjected.

"Yes, but a rather specialized list used in funeral rites. The spells are to help the dead person's Ba."

"Ba?" Jameson asked.

"Their soul, if you will, although the word is untranslatable as we don't have the cultural references. Ba means something more tangible than a soul, more like a clone, almost a total copy of the deceased. Anyway, the spells allow the Ba to enter the Otherworld and proceed safely through its various regions to the Field of Reeds, the Egyptian Heaven. Each list is different, individually created for the owner."

He picked up the scrap of paper.

"These hieroglyphs depict a spell from the Book."

"So what? I can go and buy a copy of the Book of the Dead in the British Museum bookshop. What's the big secret about that?" Jameson asked, pointing at the scrap of paper with its hieroglyphics, and trying to deflect what was turning into a lecture on Egyptian culture. Maybe Bellevue had gone native and was becoming an academic.

"I am coming to that," Bellevue said, refusing to be distracted.

There was a knock at the door and Miss Trenchfoot entered with a tray. "Professor Fairbold is on his way, Director."

Bellevue ignored her and carried on with his explanation as if she wasn't there.

"You've heard of Wallis Budge?"

"The famous British Museum Egyptologist—of course."

"He smuggled the Papyrus of Ani out of Egypt for the National Collection. The Papyrus is the most complete collection of *The Book of the Dead* ever found. It contains spells unknown in other copies. The Egyptian authorities and the French got wind of the matter and locked him up. Fortunately, Budge got away. Just as well, I shudder to think what might have transpired if the French had got the Papyrus."

Bellevue tapped the scrap of paper liberated from Essex.

"This is one of the forbidden spells that we have censored from the version of the Papyrus of Ani on general release to academia and the public. That is why we were so concerned to find out that The Commission had a copy, because there are no copies!"

"Until now," Jameson said. "It seems you have a mole."

"Impossible," Bellevue shook his head. "My people are entirely reliable. Someone must have stumbled on another version of the Book in Egypt."

A knock on the door announced the arrival of the summoned professor before Jameson could tell Bellevue what he thought of that explanation. Maybe Bellevue believed in the tooth fairy as well.

"Ah, Fairbold, take these two down and show them the original of this," Bellevue handed the professor the paper and rose to his feet to indicate the interview was over. "Answer any questions they might have."

The black cat sat outside. It regarded The Commission agents with an expression of supercilious disdain, turning its head to watch them leave. It was licking its paws again when Jameson looked back. He noticed one of them had a white flash.

CHAPTER 21
I MEET THEREFORE
I AM

Professor Fairbold reassuringly resembled an archetype Museum curator, from his white-flecked beard to his worn leather shoes. He even wore a lab coat that had once been white. Fairbold led them through a maze of tunnels to a study. Benches loaded with reprints of academic papers, journals, and documents ran along the walls. At one end was a sink with a kettle. He shooed a black cat off the chair against the desk, where it had been sleeping. It jumped down as if it had intended to do so all along and that Fairbold's hand-waving was a complete coincidence. Jameson noticed that it had one white front paw.

"Tea?" Fairbold asked.

"No, thank you," Jameson said, wondering if the Civil Service bulk-bought the stuff from the same place they got the paint.

"Sit down."

Jameson moved a skull of a small mammal from a chair and sat. Karla preferred to stand. A low moan sounded through the door, tonally rich in depressive harmonics to an extent that made Jameson's teeth clench.

"Take no notice," Fairbold said. "When we were in the BM's basement people said it was the ghost of Pharoah Amon Ra haunting

299

his coffin. Total nonsense, of course, the moans are much louder here than Bloomsbury."

"Of course," Jameson replied.

"It's actually echoes from the Holy Land."

"The Holy Land?" Jameson asked, thinking Israel was a long way off for an echo.

"The St. Giles Rookery," Fairbold replied. "We are right on top of the stew here. The slum wasn't the biggest or the worst in London but it was right next door to the gentility in Oxford Street and the West End. They say that a watch stolen at eleven o'clock had changed hands three times and was being chawed in St. Giles by twelve."

"Chawed?" Jameson asked, wondering if he was going mad.

"Old Romany word for fencing stolen items, like 'totty' meaning a pretty girl or 'chav' a low-born youth. There's lots of Romany in vernacular Southern English."

"Fascinating as this is, Professor Fairbold . . ." Jameson said.

"All totally harmless, although I have to say that the hauntings have become more prolonged and frequent in the last few weeks."

"Professor . . ."

"And you're a genuine daemon, my dear," Fairbold said to Karla, taking her hand. "I've never seen one in the flesh before, so to speak. We academics lead such sheltered lives in our studies." He beamed at her. "I'm told you are one of the blood-sucking kind."

Karla leaned towards Fairbold. Jameson made to stop her, but she put her face close to the professor's and extended her teeth.

"Fascinating. May I take a closer look?" he asked, producing a small magnifying lens and holding it over her mouth.

Karla looked very confused. Prey was supposed to recoil in terror, not try to study the hunter's fangs.

"How rude of me not to offer you some blood, my dear," Fairbold said, rolling up his sleeve.

"Professor, please!" Jameson said, despairingly. "We've eaten. Now about *The Book of the Dead*."

"Ah yes," He sat back, reluctantly putting away the glass. "Well, you may have read that Budge cut the Papyrus of Ani into thirty-seven pieces to smuggle it out of Egypt, irreparably damaging it in the process."

"Go on," Jameson said, unwilling to admit he knew no such thing and cared even less.

"Utter nonsense, of course, Budge was a Museum man through and through, not Indiana Jones. The Papyrus was cut up here in the Museum to disguise the fact that we were excising certain sensitive sections. One of them was the Coming Forth into the Light Spell. We have the only copy ever found, that is, until you people showed up. It has quite shaken the Director, I can tell you."

Fairbold tittered, apparently amused at the Director's consternation. There was little love lost between the academics and the management in most academic organizations.

"You are sure?" Jameson asked.

"Oh yes. Now where did I put that key? Trust Howlet to be missing when I have visitors."

Fairbold fumbled through the drawers built into the side of his desk.

"Howlet?"

"My assistant, he's not the most reliable of fellows, but good at finding things. Ah, here it is."

Fairbold produced an ancient brass key with a double-loop handle and trotted over to a bench. On it was an antiquated iron press of a design new to Jameson. It looked the sort of thing that might have been used to grill steaks or press trouser creases. The curator put the key in the lock at the front and strained on it without success.

"Allow me," Karla reached over him and clicked the key through a complete turn.

"My, you're strong for a little thing," Fairbold said.

Karla smiled at him and gave Jameson an "is this nut for real" look.

"I suppose it's because you are a daemon."

"Professor, is it supposed to do that?" Jameson pointed to the press. The tension had come off the plates and white vapor was rolling from between them as if carbon dioxide was melting inside.

"It's just water vapor. The Papyrus always decreases entropic levels, lowering the temperature sharply in its immediate vicinity. It's not dangerous, take no notice."

Whatever he professed, Jameson noticed that Fairbold donned a pair of latex gloves before pushing back the top plate on a rear hinge. Yellow light streamed from inside, imparting a golden glow to the study. Fairbold averted his eyes until the light dimmed. He put the paper beside the press and stepped back to give Jameson access.

"See for yourself."

A rectangular section of papyrus was held down by a plate of glass. To Jameson all Egyptian writing looked alike. Figures with strange perspectives, legs sideways, chest flat, some with animal heads, marched in columns carrying unspecific objects. He picked up the Badford paper and moved it across the papyrus, looking for a match. His eyes ached and he found it difficult to focus. The papyrus hieroglyphs seemed to squirm and fade into the distance when studied. The check took longer than he had expected, but Fairbold was right. The match was exact.

He could hear distant shouts and assumed that the ghosts from the Rookery were active again, but the cries seemed more joyful. The figures on the papyrus were splashing in the water and hunting wildfowl with nets and sticks. How had he thought Egyptian art cartoony? These pictures were rounded, vibrant and highly colored. He could hear the beat of the bird's wings and the slap of the river against the hull of his reed-boat.

"Don't fall in," Karla hauled him back, fingers gripping him so tightly that they hurt.

"I'm okay." He wanted to rub his shoulder but forced himself to stand still.

"I should have warned you," Fairbold said, in concern. "People with active imaginations can get sucked in, mesmerized, if you like. Did you see the Field of Reeds, Heaven?"

"Something like that," Jameson replied. "Professor, what does this spell do?"

"Hm, thought I said. It is The Coming Forth into the Light."

Jameson looked at him uncomprehendingly.

"It's a spell to allow the Ba to safely open a door from the Field of the Reeds into the living world. So he can take up offerings and gifts from his living relatives and do favored people good. Conversely, the Ba might want to play cruel tricks on his enemies and curse them and their possessions, smiting them and so forth."

"In other words, it's a magic spell for opening a door from deep into the Otherworld to the material world," Jameson said.

"That is correct," Fairbold said, beaming.

"Oh shit!" Jameson replied.

"Yes, but surely it's not dangerous?" Fairbold asked.

"You think?" Jameson replied. "The ability to open a hole in space-time into the deep Otherworld isn't dangerous? What, in your view, might be dangerous, the Sun going nova?"

"But the spell won't work for a modern sorcerer," Fairbold replied, speaking quickly so Jameson couldn't interrupt. "I know, you want to tell me that all Western magic originated in Egypt, that even the sorcerers' wand is a representation of the Goddess Weret Hekau, Great in Magic, who was depicted as a cobra."

Actually, Jameson wanted to ask something quite different.

"Our world view is so different from the Bronze Age that ancient Egyptian is not translatable, so the spell won't work in a modern language."

"So, just use Ancient Egyptian for the ritual." Jameson said, finally getting a toe hold on the conversation.

"We don't know Ancient Egyptian." Fairbold held up a hand to block Jameson's protest. "Did you know that Egyptians had two words that we translate as magic, *heka* and *akhu*? The difference was important to them. It described two quite different types of sorcery, but we can't make head nor tail of the distinction. We can more or less translate hieroglyphics where their meaning has some analogy in modern thought, but we have no idea how the words were pronounced or what gestures should be used while invoking the magic. And, as I keep trying to explain, we don't follow the concepts clearly enough. For example, Thoth was the god who stood with Ma'at on Ra's boat as it travelled across the heavens. But if Ma'at was his wife and associate, why was Seshat his feminine equivalent and how was she vital for maintaining the universe? Even the name *Thoth*, is Greek, not Egyptian."

"What is his Egyptian name, then?" Jameson asked.

"It's translated as *Dhwty* in the modern alphabet and may, note *may*, be pronounced as something like *dee-hauty*, but who knows?"

"I begin to see," Jameson said, thoughtfully. "Thank you, Dr Fairbold, you've been most helpful."

"One thing before you go," Fairbold said. "Would you be interested in the parallel spell from the Papyrus of Ani, for closing the door to the Field of Reeds?"

Jameson had a distinct feeling of déjà vu. Randolph chaired the meeting, Kendrics and Miss Arnoux squabbled, Karla gazed at the ceiling, and he got increasingly frustrated.

"None of this makes any sense," Miss Arnoux kept repeating. "No one would copy out an Egyptian spell to create a portal to the other world. Fairbold is right to say that it probably wouldn't work, and why should anyone bother? There are other rituals that do work and are well understood."

"I suppose the fragment I found was copied from the Black Museum?" Jameson asked.

"Fairbold's assistant has been found in a pub car park in South London with a hatchet in his head," Randolph said. "In the boot of a Ford Focus stolen from Essex."

"The Mitchell gang tying up the loose ends," Jameson said.

"Presumably, although the style of killing has also been the modus operandi for a gang of corrupt police running a murder incorporated out of Catford Nick. Maybe Frank Mitchell's mob subcontracted to the Met. Mitchell himself and an Inspector Drudge have disappeared," Randolph said. He smiled fondly at Jameson and Karla, or as near to the expression as he got.

"Shternberg is The Worshipful Master of The Badford Lodge, so why don't we ice him?" Jameson asked.

"We have been through this," Randolph said. "He has protection at the highest levels."

"He might have an accident or just disappear," Jameson replied.

"That thought had not escaped me," Randolph replied, putting his hands together as if in prayer. "And I would not hesitate to sanction the kill, whatever the political fallout, if I was convinced it would solve matters, but would it?"

"Well, we have to do something. Without Frankie's intervention that last portal would have resulted in a mass killing. The sudden rise in entropy might have stabilized the hole in space-time, giving the Sith a permanent door into London," Kendrics said.

"I wouldn't have used those precise terms, but Kendrics is correct," Miss Arnoux replied, somewhat unwillingly.

The room fell silent. Jameson poured himself a glass of water and took a sip. He didn't really want it but it gave him something to do. He would have liked to pace up and down but he knew it irritated the hell out of Randolph.

"Maybe we are looking at this from the wrong angle," Jameson said. "What about motivation, as dear old 'Ercule would put it? Let's use our little grey cells. Why would anyone short of a raving lunatic want to let the Elves in?"

"They think they will get power," Kendrics replied, hesitantly.

"Sith would share about as much power with a human as a hungry man would with a lamb curry," Karla said, making one of her rare interjections.

Jameson was addicted to curry, but Karla loathed the meal. She found all forms of human food disgusting but especially disliked heavily spiced dishes like curry, chili, or sofrito. He had often wondered whether that was the source of the old superstition that garlic would repel vampires.

"Maybe we are looking at this all wrong," Jameson said thoughtfully. "Maybe contact with the Sith was an accident caused by someone who didn't have access to modern Western magic and was trying to achieve something else."

"Like what?" Randolph asked the obvious question.

"If we knew that, we would be halfway home," Jameson said. "Miss Arnoux, what were the main properties, perhaps I should say preoccupations, of Egyptian magic?"

"How long have you got?" she replied. "Much of it was what we would call daemonic magic, to control or placate various gods and daemons. That is one reason we have lost knowledge of Egyptian magic rituals. The medieval Church had a downer on magic generally, even harmless healing spells, but daemonic magic really riled them."

She sighed.

"Not that it mattered. Most of the ancient knowledge was already destroyed by then, the great fire in the Library of Alexandria, the burnings of magic scrolls ordered by the Emperor Augustus, and the Islamic conquests. The Church just flushed away the last remnants."

She grimaced, and Jameson suspected she was thinking of all the witches who had been tortured and killed by the clergy, but, being a professional, she kept to the point.

"Many of the spells concerned the afterlife in the Otherworld, which, as you know was an Egyptian obsession."

"How about spells to affect the real world?" Jameson asked.

"There was a variety of magic to protect individuals against magical or natural harm, like an attack by crocodiles, and, conversely, spells to harm an enemy. They even used what looks to us as voodoo-doll magic, pins and all."

Jameson shook his head. "Why go to a lot of trouble to hurt someone by magic when you can just put out a contract on them? It has to be something more grandiose, more all-encompassing to interest the likes of Shternberg."

"Some of the spells try to force a god to act. I recall a headache-cure spell that threatens to kill a sacred cow in the forecourt of the Temple of Hathor, the cow-goddess."

"And now we have aspirin," Randolph said.

"Yes, but some spells threaten sacrilege on a grand scale. Magic designed to cause truly cosmic disaster, such as plague, famine, or the Sun not rising. The magician would protect himself from divine retribution by using a form of words that blamed the god for the disaster, not himself. He had to avoid payback because such a powerful invocation worked by disrupting *maat*."

"*Maat*?" Randolph asked.

"*Maat* was a goddess but also a concept, a kind of divine order of justice, truth, and harmony. Much of Egyptian religious magic involved strengthening *maat*."

"As above, so below," Jameson said, quoting one of the seven principles of Hermeticism.

"Quite!"

"Fascinating as all this is—" Randolph's tone indicated that he did not find it at all fascinating—"how does this get us further forward?"

"I don't know," Jameson confessed, "but I do know that Shternberg is the key to all this, and I'm not going to get any answers sitting here."

He rose from his seat. "Come on, Karla, we have work."

Not all that far away, a second meeting was taking place in a less salubrious part of town; to wit, the saloon bar of the Black Swan public house. The assembled members were considering the same problem, albeit from a different angle. Frankie had flatly refused to let Max into her flat, however much he was paying, so they met at the Swan.

Gary had insisted on joining the sit-down to "look after the girls' interests," and, rather to Rhian's surprise, Frankie had agreed with only a token protest. This was so astonishing, given Frankie's current attitude to men, that Rhian was beginning to have dark suspicions about her boss and flatmate.

"I don't understand the motivation behind opening these portals to the Sith," Frankie said, unconsciously echoing Jameson. "*Cui bono*, as Cicero so succinctly put it."

"What?" Rhian asked. From Gary's expression he hadn't a clue either.

"Latin, honey, for 'Who benefits.' Cicero was . . ."

"Stuff Cicero," Max said firmly. "It beats me how you humans achieve anything given your endless prattle around the subject. I don't give a toss who benefits or why. The point is that we came that close to disaster this time."

He held his hand up, thumb and forefinger almost touching, to indicate the thinness of their escape.

"Thanks to Frankie and Rhian," Gary said sharply.

"They were paid," Max said.

"And humans will do anything for money or love," Sefrina said huskily. "What will you do for love, handsome?"

Sefrina was just as Rhian remembered her, a different designer outfit but otherwise unchanged. She blasted sex appeal like radiation from an H-bomb. Frankie gave her a sour look.

"We were fortunate. Max is right," Frankie said. "We can't hope to be lucky all the time. We need to stop this at source."

"Correct, which is why I've summoned you," Max said.

Frankie noticeably bristled at the word *summoned*. An infinitesimal grin slid across Max's face, unnoticed by everyone except Rhian. She glowered at him warningly and received a beaming smile in return.

"I am surprised neither of you wondered how I knew where a portal would open in London," Max said.

"That's hardly difficult," Frankie replied, still peeved. "The psychic shock waves from an open door to the Otherworld spread out in a ripple and are easily detected by sensitives like The Commission's Coven."

Rhian realised that Frankie had rather missed Max's point.

"But he knew in advance," she said, pointing at Max.

"So he did," Frankie replied. "How did you do that, daemon? Suckers aren't magically sensitive."

"Show them one of your little toys, Sefrina," Max said.

She reached into her bag and produced a small electronic gadget with a dark face, which Rhian recognised immediately.

"It's a phone," she said. "Just like the one you gave me."

"I buy them in bulk," Max said.

Rhian felt a little let down. She had assumed that he had bought her mobile especially for her.

"Yes, it's a mobile, but a rather special one. Sefrina here is rather special, even for one of our kind. She is more than usually vicious, treacherous, and self-centered but, she has one astonishing skill that makes her worth tolerating. She possesses an astonishing rapport with human digital toys."

"Like Karla with Jameson's Jaguar," Frankie said.

"Really, I didn't know that," Max said, casually.

Frankie bit her lip, clearly regretting volunteering the information.

"Sefrina talks to mobiles, and they listen and they learn, so when she's finished they have new skills."

"Such as?" Frankie asked, taking the phone from Max's hand.

The phone snapped on to show a picture of a troll head with burning orange eyes.

"Such as detecting the emanations from a forming portal, you stupid witch-whore," said the troll thickly.

His mouth twisted in the attempt to form intelligible words. Frankie dropped the phone and Sefrina laughed, a sound as light as the first delicate snows of winter dancing on a breeze. She picked up the mobile then leaned back, crossing her legs, slowly sliding one against the other.

Gary's eyes widened and he swallowed hard. Frankie shot him a "wait 'til I get you on your own" look.

"Give it a rest, Sefrina," Max said wearily. "With two million men in London, why do you have to torment this one?"

"Because it amuses me and because the witch thinks she owns him. That amuses me even more," Sefrina said.

Gary froze and Frankie turned pink, soliciting another of Sefrina's tinkly laughs. It had always puzzled Rhian why Max showed an interest in her when he had this walking sex machine at home. Of course, she was always puzzled what any man saw in her. She never understood why James was so besotted. Stop! That was a forbidden thought. Fold it up and place it in a deep trunk in her subconscious.

The wolf snarled gently, amused at her confusion. The wolf was rarely confused, seeing, wanting, and acting being a natural chain that cascaded without hesitation.

"Sefrina has managed an upgrade," Max said, clearly proud of remembering the technical term. "She can now teach . . ."

"Program," Sefrina said, "and infest, corrupt, contaminate and possess."

"Program," Max repeated, sourly, "phones to detect the thaumaturgic power behind the spells."

"The source," Frankie said.

"Precisely," Max beamed. "Scatter a handful of these around East London and we can pinpoint the source. So instead of closing each opening portal in turn until we eventually miss one, we kill the sorcerer and destroy his enchantment, thus ending the matter."

"Fine," Rhian said, "but where do we come in?"

"There's a complication," Max said.

Frankie groaned. "Isn't there always?"

"To receive early warning of the spell powering up, the bewitched mobile phones must be placed in the London Otherworld. By that I mean the human-created parts of the London Otherworld."

"I begin to see," Frankie said. "And you need humans to do the placing?"

"Exactly," Max beamed. "If Sefrina or I do it, our perceptions of the Otherworld will inhibit proper placement. Humans are powering the spell, so only humans can properly detect it."

"I suppose that follows hermetic logic," Frankie said, slowly. "How many mobiles require placing for accurate triangulation?"

"Five to six should suffice," Max replied. "The phones will be programed with a guidance spell so they will take you where they need to go."

"Why can't you just tell us in advance and let me sort out the travel arrangements?" Frankie asked.

"Perception again," Max replied. "A mobile is essentially a human device."

Frankie nodded. "So we will be going in blind. Hardly ideal, but I suppose Rhian and I can manage that."

"There is the matter of their fee," Gary said.

"Ah, yes, shall we say five hun—" Frankie said.

"Thousand pounds a phone," Gary said.

"What are you, their agent?" Max asked.

"Precisely," Gary said, in imitation of Max.

Rhian sat back and waited for the explosion, but Frankie accepted Gary taking over like a lamb. Maybe the woman was learning when it was in her interests to keep quiet, or maybe . . . Rhian's eyes narrowed at the other possible reason for Frankie's sudden meekness.

Sefrina laughed loudly, throwing her head back.

"It seems you have competition for control of your little pets, Max," she said.

Back at his flat, Jameson selected Mahler on his player. Something about Mahler helped him think. The contrasts in the musician's work were astonishing. His music jumped from child-like to a complexity that defied rational analysis, from discord to sweet harmony, from key to key, even from loud to soft. Such juxtapositions inspired Jameson to make counterintuitive leaps of logic over insufficient or contradictory data. Mahler helped him to the truth.

Karla wandered in from the bathroom. She dried her hair on a towel that was her only covering. She was not exactly assisting his concentration.

"Yuk, German music," she said.

"Austrian-Jewish, actually," Jameson said, loftily.

Karla gave him a "whatever" pout and glanced at the player. It immediately selected Florence + the Machine. The lyrics of "Kissed with a Fist" filled his apartment over the harsh edge of electric guitars.

> You hit me once
> I hit you back
> You gave a kick
> I gave a slap.

He hit the mute on his remote control. It was not so much that he disliked Florence as that she did not inspire thought.

"You could sit quietly and read poetry," he suggested, hopefully.

She examined him as if to check whether he had finally succumbed to senility.

"You haven't been out for a while," he said.

"Trying to get rid of me," she replied.

"Yes," he responded, truthfully.

"I haven't been out on my own recently," Karla said reflectively. "Don't wait up."

She dressed in their bedroom and left without saying goodbye. "Goodbye" was a fairly meaningless convention to a daemon who lived almost entirely in the present. He gratefully switched Mahler back on and tried not to think of how Karla might be amusing herself in the London night.

Jameson piled his files on the coffee table and poured himself a scotch, another essential tool for inspirational thought. With a sigh, he started going through the documents from Fowler covering what little was known to officialdom about Shternberg's life. He tried a technique that had worked from him before. He related the bald facts of the case to his perception of the individual's psychology.

Daemons, like Karla, tended to have straightforward motivations. They were so simple as to be almost useless at predicting their behavior. She did whatever amused her at the time with little care for consequences. Her behavior was whimsical and haphazard, responding to each new input and emotion that crossed her mind.

Humans, on the other hand, were complex, with long-term planned goals that made their behavior rational. A rational behavior was a predictable behavior, provided, and this was the rub, one understood the subject's goals and the world picture underpinning their rationality.

So what were the keys to Shternberg's mindset? He was clever, certainly sociopathic, and probably psychopathic, a vain man who recognized no boundaries to his actions or objectives. He had no conscience or constraining code to advise him when he was going too far. Such a man was often spectacularly successful. Ultimately they crashed in flames, often taking many unfortunates with them.

What was Shternberg's ultimate goal? Almost certainly power—money would be merely a tool for acquiring power. That made him different from many corporate fat cats to whom power was a tool to increase their personal wealth. Power was why the man had arranged a knighthood, not because it got him a better table in fashionable restaurants or prettier totty on his arm. Knighthoods opened doors along the corridors of power. No doubt a peerage would follow in the fullness in time, oiled by a few more campaign contributions.

Something struck Jameson about Shternberg's knighthood, some half-remembered memory. He checked back through the files to confirm his recollection. Shternberg's honor had been for services to education. Now why did Shternberg give a tinker's fart about education? Shternberg had endowed Whitechapel University with a substantial grant to research economic psychology, whatever the hell that was.

Why Whitechapel, when he could have endowed Oxford, Cambridge, or one of the better London University colleges such as Imperial or UC? Any of those would have given him a seat at a much more prestigious top table. And why psychology as opposed to, say, economics, which would have been much more appropriate for a financier? It made no sense, which meant that the motivation was not obvious. Jameson poured himself another scotch with the mounting excitement. He was sure he had found a chink in an enemy's otherwise impregnable armor. Whitechapel University merited closer study.

He fished out his phone to check his e-mails. Amongst the offers for introductions to broad-minded ladies, Canadian drugs, or techniques for enlarging his sexual organ, he found a message from Inspector Fowler. Jameson had asked him to run the name Rhian Jones through the police computers.

She had no criminal record nor was she suspected of criminal associations, although she had been the victim of a serious crime. He sipped his scotch and opened the attached file, not expecting too much. The police had funny ideas of what constituted serious crime, depending on the latest political initiative. He was surprised to read that she had been hospitalized in an assault that had also killed her boyfriend. Reading between the lines, rape was the likely motive.

She was the only survivor, the assailants apparently being ripped to pieces by a pack of feral dogs that had never been traced. It was, he supposed, not impossible for some domestic dogs given too much latitude to run free and form a pack. It happened not infrequently in lambing country like Wales. Farmers were legally permitted to shoot dogs straying onto their land. The girl had been bloody lucky to be unconscious when the dogs struck.

Jameson read the next paragraph twice just to make sure he had not consumed too much scotch. The attack had taken place in Ealing.

A pack of feral dogs in suburban West London was about as likely as a street gang of bishops. Actually less likely, now he came to think about it.

Fowler had added a note. The detective sergeant who dealt with the case was an old mate, so he had given him a ring for the off-the-record story. Apparently a property speculator was trying to remove protesters off some land for development. It seems likely that he hired the gang to carry out the clearance and that they brought fighting dogs with them. Off the record, Fowler's mate surmised that the dogs had turned on the gang in the excitement.

No further action was taken because the girl clammed up, probably preferring to forget what had happened to her. She was found naked, her clothes torn off. Plus no one was left to charge. The gang were all dead and the speculator's corpse was discovered a few weeks later in a car park. Presumably one of his own dogs had turned on him. The animal was never traced, but, under the circumstances, little effort was expended and the case was closed.

Jameson closed his eyes, recalling the large attack dog at the gangland massacre in the scrapyard. He flicked through the file on the ExCel shambles to refresh his memory. As he thought, some witnesses talked of a dog attacking the "robot drone" before it exploded.

It seemed that where Miss Jones went, a fighting dog was not far behind. Karla would have detected if the girl was a werewolf or some other kind of daemon. She had to be human, which only left one possibility. Frankie had lied to him. The Celtic brooch wasn't a protective spell, and Frankie hadn't given it to Rhian. It was something old, from Wales maybe. It had infected the girl with daemonic possession. Karla wouldn't have been able to detect that when Rhian was in human form.

He poured himself another scotch and reflected. His duty was to inform The Commission so that they could eliminate the problem. That meant eliminate Rhian Jones. But she didn't seem to be berserk. She hadn't harmed anyone, at least not anyone Jameson gave a fig about. Gangsters, gangers, and the bent businessmen that hired them were fair game as far as he was concerned. He had topped quite a few lowlifes himself over the years.

And the girl did have Frankie's help, the witch being another consideration. Rhian was more than Frankie's assistant. Jameson had not missed their close relationship, and Frankie did not have many friends.

He listened to the end of Mahler's third, drinking scotch and remembering old times. Then, very carefully, because he was not entirely sober, he pressed the laptop's delete-and-shred button.

CHAPTER 22
LONDINIUM

"Okay, toots, are you sure you don't want to have a bath or rub yourself down with virgin olive oil?" the mobile asked. Or rather, the daemon on its front screen said, with a salacious grin and a wink. "You can use me to take a few photos."

"Is that thing for real?" Rhian asked.

Frankie regarded the phone with distaste.

"I'm afraid so. I've tried turning it off but it won't stay switched off. I should have paid more attention to Sefrina. You recall she used words like *possess* and *contaminate* as well as *program*. I just assumed it was geek jargon, but she meant them literally."

"Five thousand quid is starting to look like a modest sum for having to put up with this," Rhian said.

"How about you, cutie?" the daemon asked Rhian, sticking a 3D holographic head out of the phone to eye her up and down.

"How about I try turning you off by pounding you with a brick," she replied sweetly.

"I'm too important," it said smugly.

The phone stopped speaking but made a disgusting slobbering noise instead. Frankie placed it face down on the table.

"I suppose we ought to go," Frankie said.

"Promise me you won't take any risks," said Gary, taking hold of Frankie's hand.

"I'll be fine," Frankie said. "I've got my bag of magical tricks and wolf-girl at my side. What can go wrong?"

Gary looked unconvinced. He seized Frankie by the shoulders and held her tight, kissing her hard on the mouth. The phone groaned and made wet sucker noises while Rhian looked at the ceiling. She would have thought that Gary and Frankie could have restrained themselves at their age. It was bad enough putting up with that bloody machine, without a couple of randy geriatrics unsettling her stomach.

They took a taxi to the Museum of London since they were on expenses. Frankie had extracted their destination from the mobile. She wrapped it in a hand towel in her shopping bag to deaden any noises it might choose to make on the journey. Nevertheless, it did its best to embarrass them by screaming out muffled homilies such as "take me harder, big boy" and "I need to go wee wee." The taxi driver examined Rhian and Frankie carefully in his mirror, but they gazed stonily and silently out of the windows. He seemed to decide that he was hearing things.

At the Museum they bought a couple of tickets for the Roman Fort Experience and waited for the tour to start outside. They leaned on a rail and looked down into sunken gardens overgrown with weeds and yellow buttercups at the exposed remains of the Old London City Wall. A tourist information board informed them that this had originally been the western fortification of the Roman Fort that had stood in the north west corner of Londinium. Only the lowest levels were original, the rest being medieval reconstructions on top of Roman foundations.

"The wall was six meters high and two point four meters thick. It ran for one point nine miles around the city," Rhian read. "It was built in 110 AD. Apparently there are more sections exposed across the road in Noble Street."

"Do tell," Frankie said, less than bowled over.

The guide appeared, leading a small crocodile of tourists, including Americans in the inevitable baseball caps and Chinese with multiple camera gadgets festooned around their necks. The guide was a young blonde woman with an Oxbridge accent. Her badge indicated that she was a volunteer. Their ranks were traditionally made up of coffin dodgers finding something to do between stopping work and taking up permanent residence in a senile dementia ward. The girl probably had a good degree in history and hence was unemployable.

"Names in London often have ancient provenance. For example, in 1969, eight dog skeletons were unearthed from the Roman layer in the trench outside the eastern wall at Houndsditch. However, memory of the Roman fort seems to have completely disappeared until it was discovered during modern building works," the guide said. She sounded bored.

"Typical of the English to remember their pets and forget their soldiers," said a tourist in a Germanic voice.

Frankie and Rhian tacked themselves onto the group well to the rear. They tried to ignore muffled noises like a Brontosaurus breaking wind erupting at irregular intervals from Frankie's bag.

The guide took them to the next batch of wall in Noble Street, a part that was much better preserved, with a turret at least five meters high.

"The difference between the Roman stonework and the later medieval is clear on this section," said the guide. "Note that the Roman stone has a red tile layer."

She walked across the well-maintained lawn to indicate the horizontal tile layer. Photoflashes bounced off the wall behind her.

"Only the outer skin of a Roman fortification would be dressed stone, with the intervening space filled with rubble and concrete. The tiled layer was to box off a section and provide stable foundations for next story. This design added rigidity, which was useful if you had a bunch of unruly barbarians hitting the wall with battering rams."

She paused, waiting for laughter which failed to materialize.

"Now we will proceed to the remains of the fort's west gate, which is preserved underground. Please follow me through the medieval archway beside the turret."

Frankie and Rhian dutifully obeyed, keeping station at the end of the crowd. A spiral staircase on the other side of the archway dropped them a level into a large vault that looked as if it had once been a cellar. It smelled dry and dusty like an old tomb. The floor had been removed and dug away to reveal foundations and brickwork. A recorded tour-guide spiel started up from hidden speakers somewhere in the roof. Spotlights lit up various sections in turn as the voice explained the meaning of the excavations. The illuminations gradually led the tour party around the vault towards the far side.

Frankie pulled Rhian behind a wall so that they were hidden in shadow. She waited until the tourists had left the vault by another staircase and they were alone before getting out the mobile. The light from its screen was their only illumination.

"Right, you're supposed to be our guide, so guide us," Frankie said to the daemon-face.

"Climb down there," it said, sulkily.

"Oh great, I just knew it," Frankie said, scrambling down into the excavation. Rhian followed, sliding the last few feet and trying not to think what it was doing to her Armani jeans. She wondered whether she could charge a replacement pair to expenses.

The daemon pointed silently ahead, towards the remains of one of the gate towers. It was slow progress as the floor was uneven and stonework projected randomly. Rhian caught more than one crack across the shin. Reaching the tower, they entered the ruins through a small ruined archway. A spiral staircase of stone dropped into the darkness.

"Go down," the daemon said, so they did.

They went down and around in the gloom until Rhian had completely lost her bearings.

"I don't understand how this could be here," Rhian said. "We must be down to the upper tube levels by now."

"Uh-uh, no tubes, we have left the real world behind. This is the Otherworld, Rhian. Can't you feel it?"

Rhian felt tired, but otherwise normal.

"Shouldn't we have passed through a portal or gate or something?"

"That's the human way using magic. We are following a daemon path. Daemons can walk between the worlds and take attuned humans with them. Isn't that so, phone?"

"Just get on with it," the daemon replied.

They went deeper, until Rhian spotted light filtering up from below. Two more twists of the spiral and they emerged through a door onto packed earth beneath a large arch. Rhian blinked in the sunlight coming in from behind them, and gazed at herself in astonishment.

The Armani jeans and smart jacket had disappeared, replaced by a long, pale blue woolen dress belted below her breasts in a high waistline. It was fastened by a metal brooch on top of each shoulder.

Under it she had a sort of off-white, long-sleeved chemise in linen that dropped to her knees. The clothes were bulky but not uncomfortable.

She looked at Frankie and did a double-take. The woman wore a sleeveless pure white silk ankle-length dress also fastened with shoulder brooches. A scarlet strip threaded with gold wire decorated the hem. She had a scarlet cloak fastened over her left shoulder and hanging off her right hip. Frankie's hair was most un-Frankie-like. The style wound it up in a complex beehive held in place by a jeweled gold band at the front. Rhian noticed that the brooches fastening Frankie's clothes were made of silver and studded with gems, while her own were cheap metal.

"Is there a problem, lady?"

The speaker was a man in a scarlet tunic. He had a broad leather belt around his waist supporting a sword in a brown leather sheath on his left side. The weapon looked functional rather than decorative.

Frankie held out her hand with the shopping bag, which still looked like a shopping bag. When Rhian failed to respond, Frankie said, "Splish, splosh, girl," without looking at her.

Rhian took the hint and the bag.

"Not at all, Centurion, I was merely considering how much safer I feel protected by such well-built fortifications manned by such estimable soldiers," Frankie said, lowering her head and fluttering her eyes. "One never knows when rebels may strike."

"You needn't concern your pretty head about the ghastly little Brits, lady. We've thrashed them so soundly that all they are good for is slaves."

He nodded in Rhian's direction, without taking his eyes of Frankie. The penny dropped. Rhian had assumed she was dressed as Frankie's younger friend or maid because her clothing was inferior. It hadn't occurred to her that she was slave to Frankie's Roman lady. And as a Welsh girl she wasn't ecstatic about the 'ghastly little Brits' tag. Bloody English, she thought, before remembering that the centurion was a bloody Roman. The English would be living in a bog somewhere on the continent. One pack of arrogant bloody imperialists was, she reflected, not unlike another.

"Well, I must be on my way," Frankie said.

"If there's nothing further I can show you," the officer said reluctantly.

Frankie swept out from the arch. Rhian glanced around curiously before following her. The arch was a gateway, and behind them was a straight track to another gateway that was closed. To each side were two-story buildings with sand-colored walls and red corrugated roof tiles. The rest of the space was filled with one story, long narrow buildings in precise rows: barracks, she realised.

She hurried after Frankie, passing between two sentries who stood at attention holding Roman curved shields and spears. They had swords in sheaths on their right sides, but no helmets or armor. They were dressed in off-white knee-length woolen tunics.

One of them winked at her. He probably would have had a comment to make had the officer of the guard not been present. From the outside, the top of the gate was marked by alternating white and red stone to make an archway. The gatehouse was also a tower, with little square windows on the second floor. Each had its own decorated archway of alternating colored stone. The fort was intended to inspire shock and awe, not just by its strength but also by its sophistication. The "ghastly little Brits" in their wooden shacks would have seen nothing like it.

A sentry stood guard on the top battlements. He must have an amazing view all the way up the Thames to the west and to the hills that delineated the Thames basin. The same hills marked the boundaries of modern London. He leaned over, caught Rhian's eye, and wolf-whistled at her. She stuck her nose in the air and turned away, reflecting that the behavior of the London male was unchanged over two millennia.

An earthen track ran due west from the fort. She was a little disappointed not to see a famous Roman road. Presumably they had not yet all been built. She noticed a cluster of small white constructions about the size of a garden shed lining the track some distance away. Some were pyramidal and others like squat columns.

"Frankie, what are those?"

"Tombs of wealthy citizens. Roman law prohibited burial of corpses within city limits for hygienic reasons. That's how archaeologists know that Roman cities were abandoned as going concerns long before English immigrants moved into an empty land. They found corpses were buried within the city walls."

The Welsh tradition remembered English barbarians swarming over British land and had another explanation for the corpses.

"Frankie, why are we dressed like this?" Rhian asked.

"Because these are the clothes one would wear in Roman London."

"I had Armani on and you wore British Home Stores," Rhian said plaintively. "So how come I am the slave and you the lady?"

"Ah, I hoped you wouldn't pick up on that. I suppose the answer is superior breeding," Frankie said, with a smile. "You're native British from the badlands to the west, and my ancestors were from within the Empire."

Rhian let that one go.

"So why are you holding a very un-Roman mobile phone, and why didn't the centurion comment?"

"It has no equivalent here, so for him it didn't exist."

"He noticed the plastic shopping bag," Rhian said, raising it up to display its seventies psychedelic artwork.

"Yes, but he will have seen something more Roman-like. I don't know, maybe a weaved basket or some such."

Rhian digested this for a moment.

"Frankie."

"Yes, Rhian?" Frankie said, somewhat tetchily.

"Why was he speaking English if he was Roman?"

"What makes you think he was?"

"What?"

Rhian replayed the conversation in her head. The centurion had suggested she was a "ghastly little Brit," but he had used a single word. She focused hard. *Britunculi*, he had called the natives *Britunculi*. It seemed that language was mutable here and you heard the meaning, not the words.

Frankie consulted the phone, which called her a clumsy bitch before telling her to go into the city and find London Bridge.

Rhian gazed out over the swampy marshland of what would one day be the West End, the costliest real estate on Earth. Right now you couldn't give it away. In front of them the River Thames meandered across the landscape. It was much wider than its modern equivalent and its banks were not well defined. Mudflat islands amongst riverlets that left and joined the main stream became increasingly drier and more grassy inland until they became marshy ground rather than muddy water. Small boats plied up and down the waterway. Some of the larger had single masts with square sails.

A small river on their right flowed down to the Thames. That, Rhian thought, must be the River Fleet, as in Fleet Street. The modern road was presumably located where a wooden bridge crossed the water just a few meters upstream from the Thames on the first truly dry ground. The Fleet was one of London's lost waterways, subsumed into the sewage system of the modern city.

The women followed a dry, hard-packed path that followed the wall, deviating between pools protected by combat air patrols of thousands of midgies.

"I bet this place is riddled with malaria," Frankie said darkly.

"Shouldn't we have brought flyspray?" Rhian asked.

"It isn't real, honey, remember that. Sure, we can be killed here and we really would die, but we can't bring a disease home with us."

"That is so reassuring, Frankie. Thank you for sharing."

"Don't mention it. Here's Aldersgate."

The city gate was much smaller than the one into the fort and was open and unguarded. They entered Londinium unchallenged.

With a little digging, Jameson unearthed the research project application in economic psychology funded by Shternberg. Unfortunately, it was written in a torturous jargon that might as well have been ancient Hittite for all the meaning he could discern. He recalled an acquaintance at college who had read psychology and economics before securing a highly lucrative position in The City. What was his name, Wartly something? Wartly-Trumpton, that was it. His friends called him Tethers, for some reason. A few phone calls and he had tracked the fellow down. The Old Boy Network still counted for something.

They met over a staggeringly expensive lunch that his banking friend insisted on paying for. Jameson was inclined to let him, knowing it would probably be charged to expenses. This decision was confirmed when his companion ordered a bottle of wine costing a couple of thousand pounds. Eventually they came to the brandy and coffees, and societal norms allowed them to get down to the business at hand.

"So what are you doing these days, Jameson? I heard you had gone into Intelligence after leaving the army, spooks and all that."

Which was surprisingly accurate, Jameson thought. The Old Boy Network cut both ways.

"Don't answer that question," Tethers said. "I wouldn't want you to have to kill me."

Tethers laughed uproariously at his own joke, making Jameson seriously wish he could kill him. The man stopped laughing and looked at him with sharp eyes that belied the hail-fellow façade. Wartly-Trumpton had been one of the shinier knives in Cambridge's academic drawer. No doubt that was why he had risen so high in the bank.

"Business good?" Jameson asked politely, not giving a damn about the answer.

"Never better, sport, we have a new axis at the Bank to unload on the muppets before freefall. Lots of burning of the old midnight oil."

"What?" Jameson asked, wondering whether Wortly-Trumpton had shoved too much white powder up his nose.

"Axes are shares we are pushing and muppets are potential investors," Wortly-Trumpton replied. He saw that Jameson was still in the dark.

"Look, you buy up the derivatives of some asset, tangible or intangible. It could be the value of the euro or the price of tin. Currently we have cornered the market on wheat. That creates a shortage and drives up the price. At that point you dump the whole lot on your clients. The price drops faster than a tart's knickers when you flood the market. Then you buy in again when the muppets panic and try to cut their losses."

"Isn't that what used to be called a pump-and-dump?" Jameson asked.

"Certainly not." Wortly-Trumpton was affronted. "Pump-and-dumps are criminal, while derivative trading is perfectly legal. The art is to rip the other guy's face off before he can do it to you."

"And you still have clients?" Jameson asked.

"Certainly, they always hope to find a bigger fool to dump the crap on before it plummets. Often the little people with their over-mortgaged suburban semis fill this role, or, if all else fails, the taxpayer. Pretty much the same group, really."

Jameson remembered something else about Wortly-Trumpton. Not only was he bright, but he was also a complete and utter four-letter shit. He was the sort of guy who follows you into a revolving door but comes out in front, who is first into the pub but the last to reach the bar and buy a round.

"Have a look at this, Tethers, old chap, and tell me what you think," Jameson said, handing over the research application.

He indicated to the waiter for another coffee, while Tethers skimmed through the document.

"Clever, but it won't work," Tethers said, throwing the application on the table.

"Please explain."

"They are trying to put together a model to predict movements in the markets. The approach is new but still pointless."

"Go on."

"Back in the eighties, natural scientists started using computer models to analyze and predict natural events. It occurred to the chaps in the city that these models might be able to predict when share prices were going to move up or down and how far. But it all went tits-up, of course."

"How so?"

"Natural science models are probabilistic. They deal fine with large-scale events. They tell you nothing about small-scale events, which are not probabilistic but chaotic, and hence unpredictable—see?"

"No," Jameson said.

"Okay, look at it this way. Ask a climatologist what the average temperature of London will be at midday over the course of a decade, he can give a pretty accurate estimate. Ask him what the temperature will be on midday on the first of June, 2020, and he can only make a wild guess. It depends on too many imponderables. A model can tell when the market is over-depressed or inflated and is ripe for correction, but anyone can do that. It can't tell you when that correction will be triggered. That depends on unpredictable events, such as an earthquake in Japan, a terrorist attack in New York, or a war in the Middle East. And it's the timing that is important, to know when to buy and sell. The trick is to sell to a bigger fool right at the peak of the market. Everyone knows a collapse is due but not when, you see. You don't want to get left holding the baby when the music stops," Tethers said, mixing his metaphors.

"I see."

"This outline," Tethers tapped the application, "tries a new approach of measuring the psychology of the investors. It is based on the observation that the market collapses when more investors take fright and try to sell, then hope to find a bigger fool and keep on buying."

"You're saying that the market crashes when traders unconsciously decide to crash it as a group."

"Correct, and that depends on imponderables, as the trigger can be anything. Even something relatively unimportant, like a rumor, can start a crash."

"You know what drives the financial markets, Commander, fear, fear and greed, but mostly fear," Jameson muttered.

"What?"

"Just something someone said," Jameson replied.

"Well, your friend is right, and Whitechapel University—strange place for a university—are trying to model mob psychology as it pertains to financial markets. Won't work, they might as well try to predict the future. How could you know when something will happen that causes the market to take fright?"

"Sounds like a plot for a thriller."

"Yah, but not in real life, unless you can arrange an earthquake under London or the Great Storm of '87 on cue."

Jameson's imagination lurched down a horrific route before common sense re-grounded him. Why would anyone bother playing the markets with that level of power at their disposal?

Tethers finished his brandy.

"Nice to see you again, Jameson, but I've got to go. There must be an old lady with some savings somewhere that the bank hasn't yet stolen."

And with that, Tethers Wartly-Trumpton was gone, leaving before Jameson realized that he had been stuck with the bill.

A huge cheer erupted from a large oval wooden structure that towered over the north of the city, just to the southeast of the fort.

"Tottenham Hotspur must be playing a game at home," Rhian said.

"That's the gladiatorial amphitheatre," Frankie said. "The Romans didn't play team games. They preferred blood sports."

"I do know that, Frankie. I've seen *Gladiator*."

"Sorry, I can be a bit didactic at times."

Rhian would probably have agreed if she knew what didactic meant.

"And you've never seen Millwall play if you think football isn't a blood sport."

"I don't know much about football. I did once have a boyfriend who took me to rugby matches. That was quite fun."

That figured, Rhian thought. Football was the Welsh national sport, but in England it was the working-class sport. The upper classes played rugger. What was the English saying? Football is a gentlemen's game for louts, and rugby is a louts' game for gentlemen. Best change the subject.

"Did you see *Gladiator*, Frankie?"

"Certainly did. Not a bad movie but unhistorical, so unhistorical that I had to see it three times to confirm my first impressions."

"Yeeees," Rhian said. "Russell Crowe does look quite fit in a kilt and armor."

Rhian was surprised how much wasteland the city walls enclosed. The area directly in front of them contained only badly built native roundhouses. Long thatched roofs hung almost to the ground like ill-fitting wigs. Animals grazed between them: goats, chickens, and a few sheep. A quick mental calculation suggested that St. Paul's Cathedral occupied this space in modern London.

They passed by a construction site where a building was going up. The main two-story section was complete except for the roof. A polyhedral tower with a cross section not unlike a fifty-pence coin was still being raised at the rear. Men worked, clad only in loincloths under the supervision of a foreman who wore a fawn short-sleeved tunic that reached to his knees. He had a sort of horizontal cross on a pole with weights hanging off on string that he was using to check wall alignments.

"Are those men slaves?" Rhian asked, slightly shocked.

"Yes, but in this place so are you, honey. Half the population of the city or more are slaves, including the doctors and clerks. Some of the latter will have bought themselves out and be freedmen, occupying the middle ground between the free and enslaved."

They walked on in silence. The buildings were clustered more thickly towards the center of the city and along the river. These followed a pattern of white-plastered walls and red-tiled roofs but otherwise came in different sizes and shapes. Some had inverted

V-sloped roofs while in others the roof fell only to one side. Most were two stories high and only had narrow slit windows on the upper floor. Each one was like a little fort. This was a frontier town on the edge of the civilized world.

"It must be gloomy inside these places," Rhian said.

"They probably have central courts or light wells," Frankie replied.

"It would be amazing to see an interior," Rhian said wistfully.

"Not a good idea, honey. We should keep our interaction with the locals to a minimum to avoid being sucked into this reality. Did I tell you not to eat or drink anything?"

"No."

"Well, I'm telling you now."

Ahead of them was a large square structure. The northern wing towered over the rest of the city, being three or four stories high.

"That'll be the Basilica and Forum on Lombard Street. It's like the central market and town hall all in one complex. I think we'll avoid that, too many people, too many chances of an incident."

She took her bearings.

"If that's Lombard Street, then we are on Cheapside, and that must be the Cheapside Public Baths."

She gestured to a two-story building on her left inside a walled compound that had a rounded white roof like a Byzantine church. A large glass window on the end of the second floor added to the resemblance, although it was not colored.

"If we turn right at the bathhouse, we should hit the river at about the bridge."

The streets were narrow, with people coming and going in tunics and yellow ochre cloaks. They had to stand to one side to allow an eight-man slave team in loincloths to carry a litter past them. Curtains stopped the curious peering in, but voices suggested at least two passengers.

"I had the Governor in the back of the litter once," the foremost slave said to his opposite number on the front of the other pole. "He was a fat git and no mistake. I asked him when he was going to do something about paving the streets. How about putting a proper gutter in the middle for sewage like a civilized city instead of letting it run everywhere when it rained, I said. He told me to shut up or he'd cut out my tongue."

"We're in a culture with no motors of any kind, but human labor is cheap," Frankie observed, watching the litter lurch up the street. "That was a London black cab."

The ground floors of many of the buildings were shops. They sold clothes, leather, wooden and metal items, everything from jewelry to saws. Most of all there were food shops and what looked like bars selling wine, beer, and fast food that stank of fish, even when it wasn't. Customers perched on stools at the bars or sat at tables, which spilled into the street.

In the middle of it all, Frankie's phone rang.

CHAPTER 23
SAYING GOODBYE

Rhian moved back a few steps to give Frankie token privacy, as one would on a London street. The conversation grew quite animated, with much arm waving on Frankie's side. This was largely ignored by those around her, although they tended to give the woman a wide berth. It seemed the citizens of Londinium were no more curious about their compatriots' foibles than the citizens of London.

"Pssst."

A hand tugged at Rhian's sleeve, a hand attached to a short, thin man with dark hair and a goatee beard without the moustache.

"Your mistress is talking to her hand," the beard said.

"She is highly creative and is often struck by one of the muses," Rhian said, on slightly dodgy ground as she was not sure what a muse was. The Greek she appeared to be speaking guided the sentence for her.

"Ah yes, ladies and gentlemen of quality are often a little too creative," Beard said.

It was, Rhian perceived, one of those irregular verbs in English. I am creative, you are eccentric, she is barking mad. Of course, class also played a part. When the members of Oxford University's Bullingdon Club got merry on champers and smashed up a restaurant, it was held to be high spirits. When youths from Scumbag College, Grimthorpe, got rat-arsed on lager and smashed up a pub, it was three weeks without the option in one of Her Majesty's Holiday Camps. Still, anyone who expected life to be fair was destined for disappointment.

"My master, Paresseos, trained as a doctor in Alexandria and is well versed in treating highly strung gentlefolk. He has helped the wife of the Governor—not the old one, the new one," the beard said hastily. "Tell your master, Paresseos, at the yellow house in front of the Forum."

With that, he disappeared into the shifting bodies.

"What did he want?"

Frankie had finished her conversation.

"Nothing. Who was on the phone?"

"Max, who else, the signal strength isn't good enough for a call from my mum," Frankie said somewhat sarcastically. "Apparently Sefrina, the bitch, forgot to warn us that the phones will guide us to moments of high entropic release, as they use the energy to communicate."

"Oh, right," Rhian said.

"Entropic release is geek-speak for emotional hot spots, like when lots of people are terrified and die."

"Excellent!"

Frankie looked around. "It seems peaceful enough."

"The man I was talking to did imply that the governor had recently changed."

Frankie shrugged. "Roman governors served fixed terms, so they were always changing. Let's not hang around."

Frankie seemed to know what she was talking about, so Rhian let it go. But she was uneasy nonetheless. The doctor's slave had been quick to disown any connection with the old governor.

They moved through the winding streets heading for the Thames. An alley dumped them into a paved courtyard surrounded by the windowless backs of buildings and high walls. The path ran along the edge to an exit under an arch. At the back of the courtyard was a blocky flat-roofed building fronted by Doric columns like a Victorian city hall. The two tall, brilliantly white marble doors in the entranceway were firmly shut. A single engraving cut into the doors depicted a giant warrior, naked except for a helmet and holding a bull by the horns. Muscles bulged as the warrior strained to break the powerful animal's neck.

The courtyard was empty of people and silent. The sparrows

squabbling over spilt food had vanished. Rhian hadn't consciously taken note of the friendly little birds until they were conspicuously absent. The sterility of the courtyard had a disquieting quality, like an empty, disused morgue.

Rhian and Frankie were halfway across the yard when the doors slowly opened with a noise like boulders being hauled across rock. The interior was dark and gloomy, lit only by flickers of deep red. The mouth of the temple expanded like a window on a smart screen except that it stayed the same size. Something propelled Rhian and Frankie inside—despite them not moving. The basic laws of space-time distorted under some powerful enchantment, and the temple enveloped them.

Lava flowed from pools of boiling magma. Flames writhed over molten rock, illuminating the cave in flickering light that cast red and orange shadows. Hot air shimmered in the heat, distorting outlines so the very stones seemed to dance in partnership.

Heat radiating from the magma should have burned off her skin and boiled the blood in Rhian's veins, but she felt nothing. She was a ghost observing hell. A gleam of yellow-brown metal in the distance caught her eye. It came closer, expanding into a giant made from highly polished bronze, except that it didn't move like a robot or any kind of machine. It flowed like living liquid metal.

The giant held a round shield on his left arm and a sword in his right hand. Silver and gold leaf patters radiated out from the center of the shield like a stylized sun. It gazed at them and its mouth curled.

"Women, the weaker vessel, in my sanctuary. What vile heresy is this?" it asked, voice booming and echoing off the walls.

Golden flames sprung along the sword as if someone had turned on a gas tap. Frankie dropped to her knees, pulling Rhian down beside her.

"Great Mithras, we beg pardon. We are travelers from a far country on an important errand for your worshippers," Frankie said.

"My worshippers are soldiers, merchants, men of power and substance. What need have they of help from weak and feeble womanhood. Back to your homes and children, to await your husband's pleasure."

"There's someone looking for a smack," Rhian said under her breath.

"But we bring a gift, Great Mithras. To enhance your majesty and glory, we bring the gift of northern fire," Frankie said.

"Show me," the giant said.

Frankie's lips moved in a soundless chant and she cupped her hands. When she opened them, blue flames sprung from a white ball resting on her palms. She threw the ball clumsily with both hands, like a schoolgirl. Rhian expected it to drop to the ground after a few feet, but it floated weightlessly across the courtyard. The ball splattered on the statue's shield, cascading blue fire over the surface. The statue tilted the shield, seemingly mesmerized by the crawling flames.

"Come on, while it's distracted. Don't look back."

Frankie jumped up and pulled on Rhian's arm and they were outside the cave, back in the courtyard.

They made a run for the courtyard exit, even the motherly witch managing to put on a fair turn of speed. Outside the courtyard Frankie stopped and bent over, panting and holding her side.

"What, in the name of all the sexist pigs rotting in hell, was that?" Rhian asked.

"That was a god, or a daemon if you prefer, Great Mithras by name."

"God of what, women-hating?"

Frankie laughed, the laugh turning into a coughing fit as she was still out of breath. Rhian thumped her on the back. Eventually Frankie pushed her off and carried on.

"Mithraism was another of those Middle Eastern monotheistic religions, like Christianity or Islam. You may have noticed none of them is exactly keen on women, but Mithraism took it to its logical conclusion and banned them altogether. The Mithraics also prohibited slaves and even men from the lower orders joining. They had ranks and degrees, like Freemasonry, so were popular with the army for a while. They lost out badly against Christianity, which took anybody and everybody indiscriminately."

"But walking metal giants waving flaming swords?"

"This is the Otherworld, honey, reality is mutable."

"How did you know it was Mithras, so you could placate him with flames?"

"There were certain clues: the death of the sacred bull, the underground cave, but, most of all, the fact Mithraism's London temple was discovered ages ago off Queen Victoria Street. I recalled Mithraism involved flame-worship. We need to press on."

"Are you up to it?" Rhian asked.

"Oh, sure, I was just a bit winded from running. The magic was nothing, just a conjuring trick really, but I'm glad it worked. I would not have relished a thaumatological duel with a god."

"If you're ready, hotpants," said the daemon in the phone. "Follow the brook."

"I didn't notice you offering much help in there," Frankie said.

The mobile blew a raspberry at her.

The brook was the Walbrook, another of London's lost underground rivers. It split Londinium in half. The women walked down to a wooden footbridge and crossed to the other side. They reached the Thames by the side of a complex of buildings in a low-walled compound. Clerks in tunics, soldiers with the wide military belts, and the odd official in a toga signified that they had found the governmental heart of the city. It was a sort of Roman Whitehall.

The riverbank was lined with wharves used by river boats, everything from a one-man coracle to a flat-bottomed sailing barge. The Thames was so much wider than in modern London, even allowing for the fact that the tide was in, and Southark, on the south bank, seemed to be an island among mud flats.

They stayed clear of the bank, which was an anthill of activity. In amongst the loading and unloading of river boats, slaves and masons were building a city wall along the river. Carts full of white Kent stone crossed the Walbrook by a wooden bridge on their way to the building area. Nobody paid the slightest attention to health and safety protocols.

"The riverside wall was put up much later than the land side, at the end of the third century," Frankie said, half to herself. "That was an unsettled period."

"Yeah," Rhian said. "It would be. I mean you don't spend money on military defense in peaceful times."

London Bridge was downstream a hundred meters or so. The parts above water were made entirely of wood, even the pillars supporting the structure being layers of stout logs. The bridge was wide enough for carts to cross. High railings, supported on crossbeams, lined each edge. Only the entrance ramps at each end were stone, or more probably earth banks lined by stone.

The tide was on the ebb, and the river swirled around the wooden supports angrily as if Old Father Thames was trying to remove the interloper from his domain. Heavy wood piles broke the water in front of the supports.

The protective rails were essential, as there seemed to be no road rules, and carts and people jockeyed for position. While she watched, two carts collided amid much yelling and fist waving that took the attention of a small detachment of soldiers to resolve. They did this by beating both carters indiscriminately with the hafts of their spears.

To reach the bridge they had to walk back into the city to the start of the ramp. Crossing involved some fancy footwork to avoid pedestrians, carts, and the occasional bodyguards clearing the way for someone important and his hangers-on.

Larger fat-bodied ships, half as wide as long, were moored on the seaward side of the bridge in the main channel. A single mast in the center supported a crosspiece for the main sail. A smaller mast projected over the bows, holding a smaller crosspiece. The ships were decked and a large rectangular hatch gave access to the hold. Rhian was fascinated by the vessel's alienness.

Two steering bars, connected to the side rudders, projected into a railed wooden platform at the stern. No doubt Master and helmsmen navigated from this position. Rhian noticed that the furled sails were dyed a pale browny-green that blended with sea and sky.

The ship immediately behind the bridge carried white Kentish stone. A gang of men unloaded the cargo into flat-bottomed river barges to ferry the blocks to the wharf. They swung the stone over the side of the ship slung under a wooden crane rigged on a temporary tripod. The work looked hard and dangerous.

"Okay, phone, we're on the bridge, now what?" Frankie asked.

"Go to the Southwark end and place me on a vacant display pole, then you can bugger off."

The south end of the bridge had spears lashed to the railings, upon which were stuck rotting heads. The first head looked at them, but not with eyeballs. They had long since rotted away or been pecked out by crows. Little orange sparks flickered deep in the blackened sockets.

"I was Recinus, Governor of Londinium, who opposed the revolt of Carausius. Look on me and see the fruits of loyalty," the head said, in a hollow voice.

"I was Carus, Commander of the Fort, who plotted with Carausius. Look on me and see the fruits of treachery," said a second head.

"I was Carausius, Imperator, Lord of the North, Ruler of Britain and Gaul. Look on me and see the fruits of ambition."

There were more but Rhian shut them out, since none of the names or events meant much to her. Frankie stopped at the first free spear.

"You didn't by any chance bring some tape, Rhian?"

"'Fraid not."

"Just put me on the top and say the words, you silly cow. I will do the rest," said the phone.

Frankie gave it a filthy look but did as she was bid, holding it in place with outstretched hands while chanting a spell. The phone morphed into a head, just as rotten and decayed as the rest.

"Max said you'd guide us home without the need for me to open a gate," Frankie said to the head.

"Just walk back along the bridge to London. Even you two bimbos should be able to manage that."

Frankie opened her mouth to snarl a reply but was beaten to it by a rough voice.

"Oy, what're you bints doing?"

"Just examining the traitors," Frankie replied calmly. "As my Lord Allectus commands."

"Oh well, right, sorry, ma'am," the soldier dipped his head in a slight bow of respect. "But it's not safe for a lady of quality this side of the bridge without an escort."

"Indeed, no, thank you," Frankie said, turning and walking away.

Rhian hurried to catch up, ignored by all and sundry. Apparently her lowly status rendered her invisible.

"Who the hell is Allectus?" she asked.

"I've worked out where we are. This is the fag-end of the Carausian revolt. Carausius set himself up as Emperor of northern France, the Low Countries, and Britain. He executed officials and officers loyal to Maximian, the western Emperor. He did okay for a while until he lost prestige when the new western Caesar, Constantius, recaptured Boulogne. Allectus was one of Carausius' henchmen. He mounted a coup, assassinating Carausius and starting a new wave of purges, hence the heads. These are troubled times and it's going to get worse."

"Oh, why?"

"Allectus was a financial officer, a bean counter with no military experience. He will be soundly beaten in a battle somewhere on the south coast by an army sneaking ashore in thick fog. His defeated Frankish troops sack London before Constantius gets a fleet up the Thames."

"Um, Frankie, have you noticed the weather?" Rhian asked, pointing downstream.

Thick banks of fog rolled across the water, spilling out across the marshy countryside. The east wind had got up and there was a distinct chill in the air.

"Oh goddess, it's later than I thought. Come on!"

Frankie grabbed Rhian's arm and started to run.

Something was on fire in the City, a house or other building, judging by the thick trail of black smoke that twisted into the sky before dissipating to the east. It solidified into a giant bronze figure of Mithras, who waved his sword and shield. He screamed something that Rhian didn't quite catch about the whores of Babylon and thrust the sword towards London Bridge. Bolts of golden lightning flashed from the tip and headed in their direction.

Rhian screamed, put her arms out protectively and waited to die. A blue haze covered her and Frankie, a shield that caught the lightning and absorbed it, radiating the energy away over the city. Quanta of blue power shot over Rhian's head like a stream of tracer bullets. Mithras raised his shield and they bounced off, but the impact forced him to his knees.

A giant figure of an ancient Egyptian queen stood over Southwark. A ribbon held back her black hair. Brick-red, it matched the color of her ankle-length dress. She held an ankh in her left hand and a long steel rod in her right. The ankh was the source of the blue energy. The strangest thing about the goddess was her hat, which resembled a stylised throne. She looked straight at Rhian. A deep calm soaked into Rhian's soul like a cool breeze on a summer's afternoon, like the smell of new baked bread, like the caress of a lover's hand.

Oh, James, how I miss you, she thought but not with the usual bitter guilt and pain. Under the jet-black eyes of the goddess she felt regret and sadness rather than hurt. Mostly she experienced such joy that once she had been loved unconditionally, beautifully, by someone who sacrificed his life for her.

"Isis, Great Mother, Queen of heaven, we thank you," Frankie said.

The goddess lowered her rod. The weird bifurcate end played silver flashes over Mithras. He snarled with rage and cowered under his shield.

The fog reached the bridge and rolled under. It piled up, higher and higher, until it spilled over the edge and the first tendrils flowed around their ankles. In seconds the mist covered Rhian and Frankie completely and they lost sight of the divine duel.

The bridge vanished from under Rhian's feet. She fell into the river and water closed over her head. She wished she had learned to swim.

CHAPTER 24
OVER THEIR HEADS

Buildings with roofs that resembled giant plastic tents suspended on aluminium pylons no doubt looked just spiffing in Dubai or other desert sheikdoms, but whoever thought them appropriate for the ambience of East London had to be seriously deranged or an aficionado of wacky baccy.

Jameson was not surprised that Whitechapel University had long outgrown the Victorian building in Whitechapel that had housed Whitechapel Technical College. This was the name by which the seat of learning had been known when it trained competent plumbers and practitioners in similar essential trades. The University had long abandoned such mundane studies. Now it offered honors degrees in such groundbreaking subjects as kite design.

He parked the Jag in the visitors' car park, took a deep breath, and headed for the plastic tent that housed the Department of Commercial Psychology and Investment Studies. He and Karla followed the sign to reception. There he flashed an identity card at the receptionist that identified him as a senior official in the Department for Innovation, Universities & Skills, one of Prime Minister Gordon Brown's more lunatic reorganizations that provided activity in lieu of actually having any ideas.

She and Karla were suitably equipped with little plastic ID cards to clip to their clothes. They were then allowed to penetrate the hallowed halls of Whitechapel University without being mistaken for Al Qaeda bombers. After observing some of the posters on the student noticeboard, Jameson decided that Al Qaeda would be more interested in recruitment opportunities than terrorist operations at the college. The management must be worried about someone trying to nick the computers.

A series of confusing directions had them process up and down endless identical corridors. Eventually, they located a door marked Professor Pilkington, Chairperson of Psychology and Economics, which seemed near enough to Commercial Psychology and Investment Studies to be their objective.

Pilkington was a round man with a beard and rather wild hair whose magnificent stomach strained the buttons of his short-sleeved shirt. Jameson had always distrusted people in short-sleeved shirts as trimmers. Halfway fashions were the preserve of people trying to suggest individuality but who were frightened to go the whole radical hog and don a T-shirt with an anticapitalist logo.

"I was not expecting someone from the Department or I'd have been more prepared," Pilkington said.

"My name is Jameson, from the Assessment and Enforcement Section," he lied, flashing a humorless grin. "We like to drop in unannounced."

"Ah," Pilkington said, nervously. "What would you like to know?"

Jameson opened his black civil service briefcase and took out a file. "You received a substantial private grant from Mr Shternberg to research mass psychology and its economic impacts."

"Ah yes," Pilkington said, blinking.

"We would like to know how the project is proceeding."

"I believe the Department has returned the normal reports," Pilkington said.

"Yes, but it is quite unusual for a new university to be supported so handsomely for such a strategic research program. It has become something of a test case for us in DIUS, as the Minister is keen to support universities other than the traditional elitist Russell Group."

"Indeed," Pilkington said, brightening.

"Should the project go well, the Minister might be minded to divert research funds from Oxford, Cambridge, or London to energize new nonelitist colleges such as Whitechapel."

"I see," Pilkington said, eyes defocusing as dreams of untold riches floated across his mind.

Complete bollocks, of course, as no politician would want to take on the big three. They could call on too many allies and alumni in high places, but it sounded the sort of thing a chippy politician might say in the eternal quest for votes.

Pilkington pulled down one of those stiff cardboard boxes that only academics seemed to find useful and tipped the contents out on his desk. A few minutes of desperate scrabbling, and he had located a file.

"Yes, right, well, the project is on schedule. A substantial tranche of the capital outlay has been spent on the necessary computer equipment and software, notably a Beowulf Cluster for parallel processing."

Pilkington looked at Jameson, who nodded as if he had a clue what the man was talking about.

"Data examination and input has been completed and initial statistical analysis undertaken. The project is on time and into stage three, model formulation and testing. Doctor Vocstrite is the project leader. He could no doubt tell you more."

"Fine, take me to him," Jameson rose.

"Ah, that might be a problem," Pilkington said.

Jameson sat down again.

"The project was at a critical stage and Vocstrite found the university atmosphere distracting. Mr. Shternberg kindly arranged to supply resources for the team to take a sabbatical somewhere quiet where they could really focus."

"And where would that be?" Jameson asked.

"I don't actually know," Pilkington said shiftily.

"Some of your staff are on sabbatical and you don't know where?"

"There was a mix-up," Pilkington replied defensively, "and the necessary travel file and health and safety assessment seems to have been deleted."

"Does he have a mobile phone?"

"Well, yes, but he seems to have switched it off—on sabbatical—you see."

"E-mail?"

"Not picking them up."

"Shternberg?"

"He, ah, has been very busy lately and not returning our calls?"

"And this doesn't worry you in any way?"

"No doubt they will turn up."

"I want to see Vocstrite's labs and offices," Jameson said.

"Is that really necessary?"

Jameson just looked at Pilkington, not commenting.

"I'll get a passkey."

Jameson and Karla spent a fruitless two hours taking the rooms apart without finding anything useful. There were empty spaces in the cabinets suggesting missing files, and when he tried a computer, he discovered that the hard drive had been removed. In short, the college had been "dry-cleaned" by security experts, no doubt people working for Shternberg.

"I can smell perfume," Karla said, when they sat down to consider what to do next.

"Maybe one of his assistants was a woman," Jameson said.

"But this is Vocstrite's office," Karla replied.

She could be so innocent about the convolutions of human existence. It gave her a charming naivety for a monster who drank blood and could rip a man in half with her bare hands. She sniffed around the room like a bloodhound. Karla had astonishingly acute senses that could track a moth flying in pitch dark. He was not so surprised when she fished out a business card from behind a used coffee mug. He dutifully took it, loath to crush her enthusiasm, and read it. He read it again.

"Bingooo," said Jameson to Karla. "I could kiss you."

The thought was father to the act, so he was busy for the next few seconds.

"I take it I did good," Karla said, letting him come up for air. She didn't really need the stuff except for talking.

"KM Ferndale, Ph.D. Senior Lecturer in Bronze Age History, Kings College London, oh yes, you did good alright. Let's get out of here and give Doctor Ferndale a ring."

Rhian panicked and thrashed, swallowing water, not knowing up from down. She reached for the wolf. It shrank away, frightened and unable to help. It didn't like water, either. A hand grabbed Rhian by the collar of her jacket and pulled until her head broke water into blessed light and air. She struggled, trying to grab something, anything, for support.

"Stop it, Rhian, lie still or you'll drown both of us," yelled a voice in her ear that a rational part of her brain identified as Frankie.

With a tremendous effort of will she forced herself to calm down and relax. Frankie swam, towing Rhian on her back like a Thames waste barge. Water sloshed against her face and she swallowed more of the river. The swim seemed to go on forever. All she could see were clouds and the looming mass of London Bridge, the modern concrete version.

"Grab hold," Frankie said.

Rhian turned her head, which caused her to sink. She threw her arms out in panic and hit something solid. Scrabbling hands found rope, and she hauled herself up until her head and chest were above water. The rope ran along the edge of a floating wooden landing, supporting fenders to protect docking boats. She got both arms up on the pontoon and coughed up water.

Frankie pulled her completely onto the wood, and she got up on her hands and knees. Hacking coughs racked her body, turning into retching until she brought up more of the river.

After the final heave she became aware that Frankie was saying something.

"Pardon?" Rhian said.

"That fecking bitch, that evil, stupid fecking bitch," Frankie said.

Rhian was a little shocked as the prim middle-class Frankie never swore.

"Which bitch?" Rhian asked, wondering if she had anything more to spew up.

"Sefrina, the evil, fecking, sucker bitch," Frankie said. "She could have arranged for us to transit home anywhere in Southwark or London, but she had to do it halfway across London Bridge."

"I don't understand," Rhian said. "So what?"

"Londinium's bridge was not in quite the same place as the modern one. I suppose we are lucky it was downstream. Upstream, we would have been sucked into the whirlpools around the bridge supports and drowned. We nearly did anyway. It was sheer bloody chance that the tidal flow pushed us within reach of a floating pier."

"Sefrina set us up," Rhian said, turning the idea over in her mind. "She actually tried to drown us, but why?"

"For the hell of it, because it amused her, because she doesn't like witches, because Max values you: take your pick. That's why suckers don't rule the world. You can generally rely on fear and self-interest, if nothing more noble, to get human beings to cooperate in a crisis. Suckers combine total self-absorption with a vicious sense of humor."

A woo-wah announced the arrival of a blues and twos meat wagon. An interested crowd of rubberneckers examined them from the embankment. Paramedics trotted purposefully down the wooden ramp that connected the landing platform to terra firma. They had the air of people with a job to do and the determination to do it properly.

"Oh no," Frankie groaned to herself before appealing to the paramedics. "We're fine, really. We just need to get home where a hot bath and a cup of cocoa will set us as right as rain."

"You've been in the Thames tidal estuary," said a woman paramedic, wrinkling her nose.

"Well, yes."

"You and six hundred thousand tons of sewage poured in annually, mostly after heavy rain overloads the sewage system."

"Yes, but . . ."

"Like the heavy rain we had last night. 'Course, cholera's not been a problem since the nineteenth century, which only leaves dysentery, meningitis, and legionnaire's disease. You remember David Walliam's charity swim down the Thames?"

"Well, yes, but my inoculations are up to date."

"Really, got your medical card with you?"

Two paramedics marched Frankie up the ramp. Rhian walked behind, still coughing up the odd centiliter.

"Walliams had a full suite of inoculations and antibiotics before his swim but still went down with Thames-Tummy. This is not as fun as it sounds, unless you like running a high fever while throwing up for twenty-four hours. *Escherichia coli* and *Cryptosporidium enteritis* are not best mates with the human body."

Frankie managed one more feeble protest. "You can't take me in to casualty against my will."

"I can section you if I conclude that you are of severe mental impairment—such as might be indicated by jumping in the Thames. Do you want to spend six weeks in the funny farm trying to persuade the trick cyclists that you're sane?"

The paramedic carried on remorselessly as her male colleagues stuffed Frankie into the meat wagon.

"I haven't even got to diseases like Rat Catcher's Yellows."

Rhian paused as she was about to climb in behind Frankie. "That doesn't sound good," she said anxiously.

"Rat Catcher's Yellows is also known as Black Jaundice, Fort Bragg Fever, or *Leptospirosis* to the medical trade. No, it isn't good. We can't inoculate against it, but a large injection of a heavy dose of penicillin should provide some protection."

"Why's it called Rat Catcher's Yellows?" Rhian asked.

She knew it was the sort of question you never asked medical people but she just couldn't help herself.

"Because you turn yellow just before you die. You catch *Leptospirosis* by swallowing the rat's pee in the river."

At that point Rhian cleared her stomach of the last of the river water by throwing up violently all over the ambulance steps.

Jameson hadn't piloted a helicopter for months. It wasn't like riding a bike, you really did forget. Even a modern chopper with sophisticated electronics that combined the cyclic and collective into a single control was a tricky beast to handle. The Commission's runabout was a heavy two-engine job. The law required two engines to legally operate over London. Nevertheless, the treacherous crosswinds over the mountains of North Wales tossed the aircraft about like a microlite. He cut the throttle to ride out an updraft when it promptly became a downdraft and he had to climb frantically.

"Perhaps we should have taken the train," Karla said.

He was too busy to think of a witty reply. They staggered on erratically through the air like a drunk walking back from the pub. Finally, they left the mountains and he could descend onto the coastal plain and into relatively calm air. Jameson concentrated on landing. It was a bit bumpy, but . . .any one you walk away from is a good one, as the moustachioed Brylcream boys of the RAF used to say. By the time he put the machine down, he was exhausted and the sweat running down his face had started to drip onto his shirt collar.

"Too many cigarettes, too many whiskeys, and not enough exercise," Karla said disapprovingly.

Jameson ignored her and took off his headphones.

"Why can't bloody academics hold their meetings somewhere civilized, like Kensington High Street? Why do they have to find some God-forsaken hole on the periphery of human civilization? And why don't they ever switch on their mobile phones?"

"Humans are too complex for their own good, and academics are complex humans. What do you expect, common sense?"

The helicopter blades stopped turning with a final whine and Jameson released his harness by hitting the central button. He opened the door and jumped out, narrowly missing a cow pat. He'd landed in a field by the sports lodge that was proudly hosting the International Society of Bronze History annual bunfight.

A desk was set up in reception to hand out badges and programs. It also sold memorabilia, such as T-shirts announcing that Bronze Age historians did it with ground radar, which must have seemed achingly funny and ever so daring to the assembled academics. Jameson flashed his Special Branch card to the two bored female undergrads on the desk and asked for Dr. Ferndale.

One of the students shot off while the other examined Jameson thoughtfully. Karla gave her a look, whereupon she busied herself sorting T-shirts in a box under the counter. Jameson eyed Karla suspiciously, wondering what that was all about. She gave him a radiant smile of perfect innocence and put her arm through his.

Doctor Ferndale turned out to be an astonishing elderly lady of tiny proportions and short grey hair. She had a large amber necklace that seemed way too heavy for her neck. Jameson thought she would be in danger of blowing away in a light breeze, let alone the bracing Welsh sea air.

"I'm sorry to drag you away from your meeting, Doctor Ferndale," Jameson said, showing her his card.

"Think nothing of it, young man," she replied, her manner measured and precise, that of someone who chooses words carefully. "You've saved me from having to sit through Professor Rontogeist's annual lecture on Hittite legal procedure in the event of divorce. His faculty won't give him the money to attend unless he gives a lecture. Unfortunately, he hasn't produced anything new for a decade so we get the same slides every year. He's a nice old stick and so enjoys these get-togethers. Nobody has the heart to disappoint him by rejecting his paper. It does get a little dull, though, after the sixth or seventh time of hearing."

"Er, yes," Jameson said, who thought it sounded as if it would be balls-achingly boring the first time.

Doctor Ferndale was not quite what he expected. She might be a bit doddery but she had bright, observant eyes like a sparrow. He had the impression that she didn't miss much.

"Is there somewhere we can talk privately?" he asked.

"The coffee bar will be empty until the midafternoon break. We can go there."

Jameson obtained a couple of coffees, which he had to pour himself from vacuum flasks set up in the corner. It took him a little time to find milk, sugar, and little plastic swizzle sticks. He carried the refreshment back to a table in a recess where Karla sat with Doctor Ferndale. Karla flashed him a grateful look when he arrived.

"I've been chatting to your companion. Such a pretty girl, but I suspect she is older than she looks," Ferndale said blandly, raising her coffee cup to her lips.

Jameson gave Karla an inquiring look and got a rather helpless shrug in silent reply.

"Now what would Special Branch, no less, want to talk to me about so urgently that they fly up from London in a helicopter? How exciting. I shall be invited to every party and pumped for information. I must think up some way of hinting at exciting derring-do around the pyramids. Possibly I shall invent a story involving spies or some such, since I assume that you will wish our talk to be confidential."

"Ah, yes," Jameson replied, thinking it was time he reclaimed the conversation. "I believe you've had contact with Doctor Vocstrite of Whitechapel University."

"Indeed, concerning Ancient Egyptian religious beliefs."

"Could you be more specific?"

Ferndale dabbed her lips with a paper tissue and examined the complimentary biscuit on the saucer before putting it carefully to one side.

"He was interested in the spells in *The Book of the Dead*, and other tracts, concerning the Egyptian concept of *maat*."

She looked at Jameson quizzically.

"Are you familiar with the term?"

"More or less," Jameson replied. "It concerns divine order, truth, and justice personified by the goddess of the same name."

He felt like an undergraduate again, giving a stock answer in a tutorial and waiting for his tutor to expose the shallowness of his intellect.

"Like all translations from Ancient Egyptian, the English words fail to convey the real significance."

"I know, Professor Fairbold explained the difficulties."

Ferndale raised her eyebrows.

"You know Fairbold, well, well. *Maat* was another name for the human universe, which could only be sustained and protected from chaos by the proper observances and rites involving religion and magic. The temples were like power stations or beacons to create order from madness. The main duty of the pharaoh was to use his divine power to arrange balance and order among the gods by means of magic and ritual. As I said, it doesn't translate very well. Our civilization works on the assumption that the universe does its own thing all too well according to its own laws, with or without our participation."

"And what did Vocstrite want?"

"Translation help to code the hieroglyphic scripts in such a way that they could undergo statistical analysis. I understand they had some idea to describe *maat* in mathematical terms and compare it to modern models of mass psychology."

"I see. Did you know they were funded by a City financier?"

"I didn't, but I'm not surprised. It had to be that or the military."

"What makes you say that, Dr. Ferndale?"

"They were working on Egyptian curse spells to disrupt *maat* by threatening or bribing gods. Only generals, bankers, or James Bond villains have an interest in stirring up mob reactions and access to the necessary funds. I discounted Blofeld on the grounds that he was either dead or at least one-hundred-and-thirty-one, which only left bankers or generals."

Jameson laughed.

"Bankers might think they could clean up by knowing just when induced irrational fear would crash the markets," Ferndale said. "It's all nonsense though. *Maat* is a meaningless term in the modern world, so any value it ever had as an insight into mob psychology is lost."

"So why did you help them, if you thought their project was hopeless?" Jameson asked.

"All knowledge can be useful. No Egyptologist would ever get the computing power and mathematical assistance to carry out such an intensive study of ancient writings. Who knows what they might turn up?"

"Who indeed," Jameson said, thoughtfully. He stood up abruptly.

"You've been most helpful, Doctor Ferndale, thank you."

"Not at all, young man, and thank you for introducing me to your fascinating companion. I have read about such beings, but never expected to meet one."

Rhian and Frankie found Max and Sefrina waiting at a table when they tottered into the Black Swan wearing National Health Service paper bathrobes. The hospital had insisted on disposing of their clothes as a biohazard. Gary appeared from behind the bar.

"We've been in the river," Frankie said.

"We know," Gary pointed up at the TV screen in the corner of the pub. It was tuned to the rolling news.

Some bastard had taken a phone video of them crawling out of the Thames. Another clip showed paramedics frogmarching a protesting Frankie into the ambulance. In fact, from the amount of material, there must have been a whole suite of amateur Hitchcocks at the Thames. The news people spliced the clips together into an entertaining ten-second loop that was the cause of much merriment to the pancake-makeup-coated bimbo acting as anchor.

Rhian elected to stand but Frankie settled into a chair, slowly and carefully as befitted someone whose rear end had been used as target practice by a trainee nurse with a horse syringe.

"What were you doing in the Thames?" Max asked.

Rhian gave him a sharp look, but he seemed genuinely puzzled.

"Swimming! At least I was swimming; Rhian was drowning. That fecking useless toxic homicidal bitch there," Frankie pointed at Sefrina, "set us up and nearly killed us."

Max's eyes narrowed.

"Is that true, Sefrina?" he asked quietly.

Sefrina laughed, her voice tinkling as pleasantly as a tuning fork falling through a forest of icicles.

"Perhaps, just a little," she said. "Still, no harm done."

Rhian remembered struggling in the river, her panic as the water entered her mouth and her terror. Rage hit her like a thunderbolt and she snarled. All her life people like Sefrina had bullied and frightened her, but she wasn't just meek little Rhian anymore.

The wolf cleared the table without knocking over a single glass. Sefrina was fast, with reactions like a cheetah, but the wolf hit her before she had more than half risen from her seat. The vampire went over backwards, her chair splintering under their combined weight. The wolf rode Sefrina into the floor like a surfboard, ignoring the clawed hands digging at the iron-hard muscles in her shoulders.

Sefrina opened her mouth wider than any human being could to extend fangs like a velociraptor, but the wolf clamped her jaws across the vampire's throat. She bit, razor-sharp teeth sinking a few millimeters into Sefrina's flesh, just tight enough to hold her, just loose enough to threaten without delivering instant death.

The sucker froze, face expressionless. The wolf could smell her fear and exulted in her terror. How do you like it bitch? Rhian thought. How do you like being helpless in the face of a terrible death? Not laughing now, are you? She closed her jaws another millimeter and Sefrina's eyes flickered.

"We need her, Rhian, to program the phones," Frankie said, her quiet voice filling the silence.

Everyone was frozen into place like actors at the end of a soap episode.

"Of course we do, Frankie," Rhian said, turning her back contemptuously on the vampire, walking casually away on two legs.

She leaned against the bar and smiled at Gary. He put his hand on her shoulder and squeezed. Rhian liked the human gesture and patted his hand. Sefrina found a chair and sat down again at the table, massaging the punctures in her throat. She glared venomously at Rhian, eyes like bottomless pits of evil.

Max moved too fast for Rhian the human to see. He had Sefrina by the hair, head down on the table, her face turned up.

"I warned you to leave Snow White alone, that she belongs to me,"

Max said. "If you ever do that again, I will destroy you, even if she doesn't. Have I made myself clear?"

"I belong to no one but myself," Rhian said softly.

No one heard, but that didn't matter. It only mattered that she knew it to be true. Once she had belonged to someone else, but that was then. Now she was mistress of her life.

"Yes, Max," Sefrina said.

"Good," Max released her and turned his attention to Frankie. "She has the next phone ready. Time is not on our side, so if you are recovered . . ."

He left the sentence unfinished.

"Oh, super," Frankie said. "I am charging a new outfit to you on expenses."

"Fair enough," Max said, with a grin.

He snapped his fingers and Sefrina retrieved her bag from under the table. Extracting a mobile, she tossed it over to Frankie with every sign of bad grace. Frankie turned it on to check it was working and a daemon's face appeared on the screen. It opened its mouth to say something obnoxious but took one look at the expression on Frankie's face and turned itself off.

"The last one led us on a song and dance halfway across the city before we reached the deposition point. Couldn't it take us into the Otherworld nearer the critical point?" Frankie asked.

"Sefrina?" Max asked, looking at her carefully.

"Not always possible," Sefrina said, shaking her head. "It will guide you in as close as possible, but the entry point and the best surveillance position have different properties."

"Is that true?" Max asked, showing his teeth.

"Yes," Sefrina said sulkily, breaking eye contact first.

Max rose from his chair. "We'll eat together, Snow White, when you get back," Max said.

"My name's Rhian, and we don't eat the same things."

"Nevertheless." Max bowed and left, taking his pet monster with him.

Frankie also rose, albeit more gingerly than Max.

"Why didn't you destroy Sefrina?" Frankie asked Rhian. "Was it because of my warning that we still needed her help?"

"Not really," Rhian shook her head. "It's not that she hadn't asked for it, and it would have been so easy. Just one little snap, like biting the head off a jelly baby, but I'd have enjoyed it. That's why I didn't kill her, because I'd have enjoyed it."

Frankie hugged Rhian.

"I am so pleased, so very pleased."

"I passed some sort of test, did I?" Rhian said, catching on.

"Power can be corrosive, particularly when granted to someone who has never had it before. And you were such a little mouse when I first met you, Rhian," Frankie said, somewhat elliptically.

"If I had started killing because I could, for pleasure, would you have handed me to The Commission for elimination?"

"No, I couldn't bring myself to do that, not after what we've been through together," Frankie said. "I'd have killed you myself, before taking my own life in atonement to try to balance the karma in my soul."

CHAPTER 25
BLITZ

The Sun was dipping when Rhian and Frankie set off to plant the second daemonic mobile. They motored up the Mile End road in queues of traffic heading out of the city. Past Bow Church, the phone guided them off the Bow Road to the northern approach of the Blackwall Tunnel under the Thames. They left the main road before reaching the river by turning left into a dimly lit housing estate.

Frankie turned on Mildred's lights. The antique motor had barely adequate headlights at the best of times, but tonight they seemed as useful as an iPod in torch mode. Frankie peered through the windscreen, and it seemed to Rhian that they were driving through mist.

She relayed directions to Frankie from the daemonic face on the mobile's screen, ignoring the leers, suggestive remarks, and various lecherous noises. Sefrina had insisted that the lewdness was an unavoidable side effect, but Rhian was unconvinced.

Mildred was never exactly a smooth runner at the best of times. Tonight her engine sounded increasingly rough as they drove further into the estate. Frankie slowed and changed down, leaning on the lever with all her weight to get the car in gear. She forced the cogs to mesh with a noise like an iron bar dragged across railings.

"I never learnt to double declutch," Frankie said. "Crash gearboxes were well before my time, although my grandmother talked about them."

Rhian wondered what the hell she was talking about. It came to Rhian that Mildred was strange, her proportions not quite right. Everything about the car was very vertical and boxy. She smelled of old leather and engine oil. When had that happened?

The lights of the estate houses faded away, and they drove down a one-track lane with trees and bushes on each side. After two or three hundred meters, the lane ended abruptly at a canal. Rhian climbed out, noting that the door opened the wrong way with the hinges at the rear. Mildred's rounded wings over the front tires had become independent mudguards, like you find on a bicycle. Although mist swirled around their feet, the sky was clear and starlight provided some light. You couldn't normally see stars in the London sky.

"Now what?" Frankie asked.

The phone was uncharacteristically silent.

"There's a boat parked down there," Rhian replied, pointing to the canal.

"Docked," Frankie said, automatically. "You park cars but dock boats."

"Whatever," Rhian said.

A footpath took them to a narrow boat alongside the towpath. The daemonic mobile was strangely subdued, like a small-town hoodlum who finally runs into the real thing after arriving in the big city.

They stepped straight into the shadowy well at the rear of the barge. Rhian stumbled when the deck turned out to be further down than she anticipated. Frankie caught her.

"Careful, honey, the counter is deeper than you think."

"Counter, right," Rhian replied, not surprised that Frankie was familiar with the intimate anatomy of a canal narrow boat. That was just like the woman. No doubt she had lived on one at some time while going through a hippie phase.

A dark figure in robes and cowl, like a cross between a monk and a hoody, stood silent and unmoving at the rear. He rested one hand on the tiller but stretched out the other arm, the sleeve falling back to reveal a gnarled hand, palm upraised.

Frankie ransacked her bag. "I can't find my purse. Have you got a silver coin?"

Rhian checked. "Will a pound coin do? It's shiny, albeit gold rather than silver."

"Fine!"

Frankie took the coin and placed it in the gnarled hand without making flesh contact. The bony fingers closed slowly over the coin. Rhian tried to see the boatman's face, but it was too deep within the cowl. The boat started to move away from the bank. It quickly picked up speed until it moved at what felt like a fast walk or jog-trot.

What Rhian found spooky was the complete lack of engine noise, but she could hear a rhythmic clip-clop from the bow. She stuck her head out to have a look. A dapple grey carthorse walked along the towpath, pulling the barge. She was sure it had not been there when they boarded. How could you miss something the size of a carthorse? And shouldn't there be a driver or rider or something? How did the horse know where they were going? Come to that, how did the boatman know where they were going? Nobody had given him directions, or spoken to him at all, come to that. Frankie and Rhian hadn't even exchanged a word between themselves after the first whispered exchange about the coin.

Rhian kept remembering a song about a ferryman. She tugged Frankie's arm and whispered in her ear.

"I thought you shouldn't pay the ferryman before he gets you to the other side?"

"That's Chris de Burgh," Frankie replied. "You paid Charon a coin in advance to ferry you over the River Styx."

"Where to?" Rhian asked.

"The land of the dead. Charon was a psychopomp in Egyptian and Classical religions, you see."

Rhian didn't see, but she had not been reassured by any of the answers that she had got so far, so she elected to stay in blissful ignorance. She could always look up Charon, River Styx, and psychopomp later on her phone, preferably over a nice cup of tea and a biscuit.

"We're heading north," Frankie said. "Back up the canal system to the Bow Road."

The narrow boat pulled into the bank and came to a halt so that the women could alight. The boatman turned his head to watch them leave. Rhian half expected the whine of electric motors or the sound of grinding stone, but there was nothing. The psych-whatsit didn't even tell them to have a nice day. Rhian got the phone out and checked with the daemon, who seemed as pleased as her to be off the boat. It pointed down the towpath, where they found some steps up to the streets.

The houses looked much the same as in modern London except that most of the rooms were in darkness. Others were dimly lit in red or yellow flickering lights. Street lamps were only found on corners, and they were dim. Only the edges of the street were paved, the road being hard-packed dirt. They passed very few people, mostly men in suits with beards and whiskers. The few women wore bonnets and high-waisted dresses that fell to just above the ankle. Rhian and Frankie were similarly garbed. Frankie even had a small folded parasol. They saw no vehicles but heard a motor passing nearby. The daemon guided them through side street after side street. Rhian wondered where they were but decided that the key issue was not "where" but "when."

"When are we?" Rhian asked, suppressing a giggle when she realized that she sounded like a Doctor Who assistant.

"I don't know. Somewhere around the turn of the nineteenth and twentieth centuries, I suppose. This isn't really my period. Why are you laughing?"

"We must be careful not to fall and sprain an ankle," Rhian said solemnly. "Overused plot devices for girlies, sprained ankles."

"Right," Frankie replied, clearly wondering whether Rhian had all her circuits connected.

Beams of light speared the sky, tracking backwards and forwards.

"They look almost like lasers," Rhian said. "Do you think there is a festival on tonight?"

"I don't think so," Frankie replied. "I'd have said that they were searchlights but this can't be the blitz. It can't be 1940s London, so where in hell are we? I don't like this, Rhian, come on."

Frankie increased speed from her usual comfortable ramble, occasionally darting a glance up at the night sky.

They had no warning. The first blast was less than a hundred meters away. More exploded around them. A house at the end of the street disintegrated. The front façade and part of the roof fell into the garden. Somewhere a woman screamed, her voice full of terror. More explosions erupted further away. Rhian was covered in dust, and her ears sang as if she had spent all evening at a Quo concert.

Frankie pulled her up and pointed at the sky. She was saying something, but Rhian's ears were still singing. High up, the searchlights had converged on a silvery cigar-shaped object. Rhian had seen artists' impressions of UFO motherships that looked similar. Her hearing began to recover and she caught Frankie's words.

"It's a bloody zeppelin. We're in the middle of the first blitz of London, in the Great War."

The thump of anti-aircraft cannon sounded, and a few seconds later, explosions racked the sky. The zeppelin sailed serenely on, as untroubled as a swan threatened by midges. Another batch of explosions far away indicated that it had dropped more bombs.

Down a side road they found an antiaircraft gun mounted on an old-fashioned lorry with a square cab and mudguards over the wheels. The gun was short-barreled and fixed on top of a high iron pedestal. Four or five men worked it, passing up shells while a gunner aimed by squinting down the barrel. Rhian found it hard to believe that they could shoot down an airship with such a ridiculously primitive device.

As it turned out, they couldn't. The gun fired, creating a blast of hot air that made Rhian's chest thump and her ears ache but had no effect on the zeppelin.

"Look," Frankie said, pointing at the sky.

A stream of glowing balls bathed the rear of the zeppelin. They came from somewhere underneath the airship. Rhian couldn't see anything, but a small plane must be attacking. Glowing sparks showed that the airship crew were returning fire, but the little fighter would be an impossible target in the dark. Another hose of fiery balls vanished into the zepplin's rear until it began to glow red inside, like a Chinese lantern. Slowly it folded into a "V" shape and dropped. Naked flames spewed from the hull.

Rhian wondered how many crew it carried, a dozen, two dozen. And she didn't think they had parachutes in The Great War. But how many men, women, and children were in the bombed houses, and they weren't even soldiers.

"This is the place," the phone daemon said. "Attach me to a wall."

A corner pub had taken a direct hit and imploded. Men were pulling at the wreckage looking for survivors, and someone was screaming that his grandpa was missing. They infiltrated the wreckage, pretending to be rescuers. Frankie slapped the mobile phone on a wall and it stuck, becoming just another gable. She muttered the activation spell.

"What are you doing?" asked a voice.

"She had a torch! She was signalling to the Hun, telling them where to drop their bombs."

"Spies! Babykillers! Get them!"

The rescue party turned into a vengeful mob at the drop of an accusation.

"Oh, Goddess. Leg it!" Frankie said.

Their pursuers started at the far side of the ruin, giving Frankie and Rhian a head start. Frankie was not built for speed, especially in a ridiculously long Great War dress. They could not shake off the hue and cry, and Frankie was soon exhausted. Rhian looked over her shoulder to find three men only meters behind. Their faces twisted in exertion and hate. One held a piece of broken floorboard like a club, another a razor.

"Keep going, I'll meet you at the boat," Rhian said.

Fortunately Frankie was too tired to argue, which would normally have been her first reaction. Rhian summoned the wolf and spun around. She gained momentum in three long strides and smashed through the men like a speeding car. She used her weight to bowl them over. Turning so fast her claws dug up the hard-packed dirt, she reengaged. The one with the club got to his feet, but she knocked him right back down. The razor man took a panic-stricken slash at her. She caught his wrist in her jaws. Exerting just a modicum of pressure, she swung him round until something cracked in his arm. His eyes turned up in his head and he dropped in a faint from the pain.

The other two began to run back up the street and the wolf harried them, nipping at their heels like a sheepdog. The trio rounded a bend and ran straight into the main party of vigilante spy-catchers. The wolf snarled, bit, and shoulder-charged, creating chaos. Shots rang out and a man fell with a little cry. The wolf smelled gun smoke, so she ducked among the crowd for cover.

There, on the other side of the street, a soldier, an officer by his peaked cap, stood holding a pistol like a target shooter. He aimed down the length of his arm. The wolf gathered her hind legs beneath her body, ready to explode out of cover and bring the soldier down before he could take an aimed shot.

Rhian exerted all the willpower she had to check the wolf and persuade her to flee. This man is not our prey, she emoted, not our problem. He only seeks to protect his territory and his cubs. The wolf took off after Frankie, keeping the mass of people between her and the soldier as long as possible. She jinked from side to side to put him off his aim. A couple of shots followed her but whined harmlessly into the night. She lost the pursuers at the next junction.

Rhian had no idea where she was or in which direction the canal was to be found, but the wolf knew. She had a hunter's map in her head like a satellite navigation system. It was not long before she picked up Frankie's scent. When she arrived at the landing, the narrow boat was gone. The scent trail vanished at the bank, so Frankie must have boarded.

Rhian urged the wolf to run south down the towpath, assuming that the ferryman would be heading back to Mildred. After a few moments the wolf's sensitive hearing picked up the sound of Frankie's voice. She sounded as if she was having a right old strop.

"Stop this ship immediately, you hear. You're supposed to wait for Rhian, you numbskull."

The wolf bounded forward and the part that was Rhian gave a metaphysical grin. The ferryman would be regretting starting the voyage precipitously. The wolf gave a burst of speed, catching the narrow boat and pacing it. Frankie failed to notice, busy as she was hitting the unresponsive ferryman with her parasol. The wolf howled.

"There she is. Put into the bank you cretin," Frankie said.

A shot cracked out, then another. The soldier had found them, but he had discharged all the bullets from his pistol, so his head was down while he reloaded. The wolf accelerated and leapt for the boat. She didn't have a decent run up and misjudged the distance in her haste, hitting the side of the covered cargo space. For a moment she scrabbled on the edge of the roof, sliding backwards towards the water. Frankie took a firm two-handed grip on the fur around her neck and pulled with all her weight. It was just enough to tip the balance and they fell into the open rear counter.

The ferryman smelled like a decaying corpse to the wolf. She looked under his hood with her monochromatic night vision to see a head like a dried mummified skull.

❋◉❋

"I am getting," Randolph said sourly, "a sense of *déjà vu* about these meetings. The same people sit around the same table having the same discussion. Everyone explains how clever they've been, but we are no further forward. Or am I missing something?"

"That's not entirely fair," Jameson said. "We now have a good idea what exactly created this crisis."

He counted off on his fingers.

"Shternberg somehow got wind of the forbidden sections of Budge's copy of the Book of the Dead. He had the bright idea of using the magic spells to disturb *maat* to precipitate financial crashes in which he could clean up. He bribed or coerced Pilkington's assistant to provide copies. He gave one to a bunch of academics for modern computer-based analysis, academics which he had already bought with a generous grant. The bloody project worked only too well but with unforeseen results. That's what one would expect of a load of bloody amateurs playing around. They bored a hole deep into the Otherworld to the Sith, who by now probably control the system. They may still do odd favours for Shternberg, like the Fethers murder, to keep him onside until his usefulness is exhausted."

"Excellent," Randolph said. "And when we have a full-blown apocalypse in London with millions dying it will be just chocolate soldier to know why it happened. It would be rather more convenient to stop the disaster before we get to that stage, don't you think?"

"We do have a counterspell worked out from the Book of the Dead that should negate the source, the magic engine powering the portals—once we find it," Miss Arnoux said.

"Once we find it," Randolph repeated sarcastically, "once we bloody find it. That, of course, is the rub. And are we close to finding it?"

There was a silence while Randolph searched each face in turn.

"I've half the Met working on it," Jameson said. "But Shternberg covered his tracks well. The man himself has gone to ground somewhere. Our accountants have taken his company apart but can find no trace of a likely address. We are still questioning the staff, but I'm not hopeful that will produce any information of value."

Randolph stood up.

"We need to find where the missing Whitechapel academics have their damned computer systems and shut them down before they create a stable portal to Sith-land. They must be somewhere in East London. Find the bastards!"

"Yes, sir," Jameson said.

"Why don't you store me next to the skin? I could vibrate to give you silent instructions, one buzz for left, two for right, and a screaming orgasm for stop now," said the third phone.

Rhian ignored it, experience teaching her that arguing with a daemonically possessed mobile was about as productive as a debate with a satnav. Mildred trundled sedately down the Mile End Road towards the city of London.

"I suppose most of these phone placements are likely to be in the Square Mile, within the old London walls or very close by?" Rhian asked.

"Yah, that's where the people were, before modern London expanded in the last few hundred years. On the other hand, we might be heading for Southwark on the south bank or Aldwych."

"Why Aldwych?"

"It's the third of the three cities that made up London, well, four if you count Southwark. When the Anglo-Saxons started to build towns again after the collapse of Roman civilization, they tended to seek greenfield sites. They were bothered by the thought of ghosts hanging round the old Roman ruins. So they built Lundenwic a little way upstream. They didn't move back into London until the Viking raids, Vikings being infinitely more scary than ghosts. They repaired the Roman walls and rebuilt London Bridge to create Lundenburgh. The 'wic' bit signified a trading post but a 'burgh' is a fortification."

"Fascinating," Rhian said utterly insincerely.

"Sorry, honey, I do tend to lecture."

The mobile was blissfully silent for a while, and the Mile End Road became the Whitechapel Road and eventually Aldgate. Here the eastern gate had once pierced the defensive wall.

"Turn left off the main road and go down Jewry Street when you get to Houndsditch, cuties," the phone said.

The road system around Aldgate Tube Station had been turned into a complicated one-way network. A large 'no entry' sign indicated that they would have to leave the main road and take a loop to the north. Frankie sailed up to the sign, driveling happily on about the history of the area. Rhian had learned to let Frankie's stream of consciousness pass over her. When Frankie was nervous she talked about inconsequentials. To Frankie, that meant not hairstyles or the latest doings of TV celebs, but London historical trivia.

Odd phrases drifted over Rhan's head as she eyed the rapidly approaching sign: Jewish immigration, Oliver Cromwell, the Jewish Cemetery, and so on. By the time that Mildred had passed the point of no return in its lunge up a one-way street the wrong way, there seemed little point in Rhian yelling. Distracting Frankie probably wouldn't help.

A red double-decker bus passed them on the right, the driver goggling at the women as if Mildred was being driven by Martians. Frankie was engrossed in describing some battle between Mosley's blackshirts and Jewish ex-servicemen after the war. None of which made any sense to Rhian, as she thought that Mosley was something to do with motor racing.

A black cab appeared right in front of them. Rhian gripped her seatbelt hard and put one foot up against Mildred's metal dashboard to absorb the impact. The taxi driver hauled desperately on the steering wheel. He dodged to the right, narrowly missing a builder's truck. He shook his fist as he passed within centimeters of an outraged Frankie.

"Sodding hell," said the phone daemon.

"Did you see that?" Frankie asked, indignantly.

"Yes," Rhian replied, her voice so high up the tonal register that she squeaked.

"He was on the wrong side. Bloody taxi drivers think they own the road. Stick a light on their roof and they think the normal rules don't apply."

They cleared the one-way system back onto a normal road and Frankie turned into Jewry Street. She stayed on the road when it became Crutched Friars.

"Stop at St. Olaves," the phone said.

St. Olaves was a blocky church on the corner of Hart Street and Seething Lane. A very Italian-looking tower made it quite unlike a normal English church. Frankie parked on the double yellow no-parking lines outside Seething Gardens. They got out, retrieving their rucksacks from the boot.

"Go into the church and find the pulpit," said the mobile phone.

The entrance to the churchyard was through a Romanesque arch, which, on close inspection, was not at all in a classical style but more medieval macabre. Three grinning skulls decorated the panel under the archway, with two more on blocks at the corners. A plaque underneath recorded a date, the eleventh of April, 1658. Frankie paused to examine it.

"St. Ghastly Grim," she said.

"What?"

"I just remembered. That's what Charles Dickens called this graveyard in one of his books."

"How come you are such a mine of useless information about obscure details of London history?" Rhian asked, half convinced that Frankie made most of it up just to annoy her.

"If you practice witchcraft in London, the past has a nasty habit of intruding on the present. It doesn't hurt to be forewarned with a little knowledge."

Rhian felt a little ashamed as well as resentful, which did not improve her mood. She marched into the graveyard with Frankie on her heels. It was silent and peaceful like a garden, not at all a ghastly grim. A songbird called, but Rhian couldn't see it.

"Chip, chip, chip, chooee, chooee, chooee."

A child's voice lifted in harmony.

"London Bridge is falling down,
"Falling down, falling down.
"London Bridge is falling down,
"My fair lady."

Rhian shivered, feeling suddenly cold. Her grandmother would have said that someone had walked on her grave. A large black bird hopped onto the path. It looked at her with intelligent black eyes and clacked its beak.

"Isn't that a raven from the Tower?" Rhian asked.

"Good grief, I believe you are right. There will be hell to pay if one of the seven ravens has gone AWOL."

"Nevermore," said the raven.

The two women exchanged a silent glance.

"Probably one of the Beefeaters taught it that to spook the tourists," Rhian suggested, hesitantly.

"Quite," Frankie replied. "Let's go in."

Large, mostly clear gothic windows allowed plenty of light into the small church. The women were quite alone. Rhian was not a religious person but she always had this sense of awe in one of London's historic churches. The atmosphere made her want to whisper and tread lightly. A table by the door displayed postcards and a leaflet with a short history of the church. Rhian slipped a pound into the honesty box and picked up a leaflet.

"The church is mostly new," Rhian said in surprise, reading the leaflet. "Although it goes right back, the current church was rebuilt in 1950 after it was gutted by bombing in the Blitz."

"Is that so," Frankie said. "Old Adolf really had it in for London's churches and cemeteries."

"It says here that the Reverend Augustus Powell Miller oversaw the restoration. Listen to this quote from him, Frankie."

Rhian read out loud.

"In the quiet and silence of this sanctuary we can know that we are compassed about with a great cloud of witnesses and that the past mingles with the present and can inspire us for whatever tasks the future has for us."

"Let's hope that's prophetic," Frankie replied.

"The church is famous for its nine bells," Rhian read out. "Noteworthy people buried here include Anthony Bacon, elder brother of Francis . . ."

"Who was a spy in Sir Francis Walsingham's espionage network," Frankie said.

"How did you know that?" Rhian asked, crossly.

"Walsingham created The Commission. The Commission in question came from Queen Elizabeth the first."

"Other residents include Mary Ramsay, who brought the Black Death to London, and Mother Goose, who was buried on the fourteenth of September, 1586," Rhian said. "Mother Goose?"

"An archetype," Frankie replied. "She is also buried in Boston and several other places."

"Now here is someone really famous buried in the church," Rhian said.

"Samuel Pepys?" Frankie asked.

"How did you know," Rhian said, now quite nettled.

"Because I'm a rich seam of useless information. The old naval office where Pepys worked was just outside where Seething Gardens are now. Some people still call it Pepys Gardens. This would have been his parish church. I was also tipped off by this memorial."

Frankie pointed a bust on the wall of a woman dressed in a classical style. Rhian went over to examine it. The writing was in Latin but the name was clear enough: Elizabeth Pepys.

"Is there any mention of the Great Fire of London in your potted history, Rhian?"

"Um," Rhian flicked through the pages. "Not much, the fire got within one hundred meters of the church but was turned back by a sudden gust of wind."

"How convenient," Frankie said drily. "I am getting a bad feeling about this, Rhian. We know that the mobile will need to be fixed in an Otherworld location created by major human trauma. The dramatic event most associated with Samuel Pepys is the Great Fire."

"Are you bimbos going to talk all day?" asked the phone daemon.

Rhian jumped; she had quite forgot she was holding it.

"Where do we go?" Frankie asked.

Rhian thought she sounded tired.

"Go through the pulpit," the daemon said.

"The wooden pulpit is an original carved by the celebrated sculptor Grinling Gibbons," said Rhian, consulting her leaflet.

"Never heard of him," said Frankie.

The pulpit was decorated by a sculpture described in the leaflet as an angel, but which looked to Rhian more like a head with a set of wings where its ears should be. A large Bible sat on a lectern made in the image of an eagle. The bird's head jutted out like the dragon prow of a Viking long ship.

Frankie walked into and through the pulpit, disappearing into the grain of the wood. Rhian did likewise.

CHAPTER 26
LONDON BRIDGE IS FALLING DOWN

The one-room wooden building was a mess, the floor littered with smashed wood and debris. From the smell, it had been used as a toilet. A smashed cross lay against a wall.

"Surely this isn't a shadow of eighteenth-century London," Rhian said, looking around.

"Hardly," Frankie said.

She stood by a wall where she could look out through a split in a plank. The split wasn't natural. It looked as if it had been made by a sizable axe, or a chainsaw.

"Have a look."

Rhian joined her, picking her way carefully through human feces. She saw a devastated city. The Roman city walls stood, but only stubs of ruins showed where stone buildings had once been. Rectangular wooden huts with thatched roofs were scattered around seemingly haphazardly, although Rhian fancied she could see traces of the Roman road layout.

A group of men, warriors, ran past the church carrying spears and round, colored shields. They wore dyed woolen tunics and trousers, and most protected their heads with conical steel helmets. The leader had mail armor and a sword but otherwise was indistinguishable from his men. He glanced at the church and Rhian froze, scared that he could see right through the wood. He waved a sword to rally his men.

"Faster, whoresons, the Norse come in dragonboats. To the bridge, to the bridge!" the swordsman called.

Frankie grabbed the phone off Rhian and spoke to the daemon. "Listen, creep. No bloody messing around, as this is dangerous. Where do we plant you?"

"Near the entrance to the bridge," it replied. "Not on the bridge, mind."

"Right, daemon. Rhian, this is what I want you to do. We are in Lundenburgh in the middle of a Dark Age battle. There is no way we can blend into the locals, so we will do the opposite. We will stand out so conspicuously that we will be untouchable. You," Frankie shook the phone, "Will be a raven and sit on my shoulder. Got it?"

The daemon sullenly nodded assent. Frankie closed her eyes, muttered something. Her dirty ragged peasant dress vanished. She was clad in a long-sleeved rust-brown dress that fell to the ground. Over it she had an off-white woolen jumper decorated with red zig-zag patterns on the neck and cuffs. Sophisticated gold and amber jewelry hung from her neck, giving a strange mix of civilized and barbaric. She placed the phone on her shoulder. It clung on, as a raven.

"I suppose I'm a slave girl again," Rhian said grumpily.

"No, Rhian, you will be the wolf. Stay close to me and act as magical and humanlike as you can. Don't precipitate violence, but be aggressive and prepared to dish it out as hard as you like. These men respect only strength."

Frankie walked out of the desecrated church like a queen come to judge her subjects, a raven on her shoulder, a wolf stalking alongside. When the light caught her necklace it fluoresced with inner fire.

Rhian took a moment to become used to the world as seen by the wolf. Lundenburgh stank, not of engine emissions, concrete, and chemistry, but of animals, waste, and the stink of unwashed human bodies. The coastal strip around the bridge had wharves and large two-story wooden buildings that must serve as warehouses. The city was not a capital in any sense, but it was still a mercantile center.

The bridge was largely unchanged from the Roman era. Maybe the pattern of the wooden rails was somewhat different, but heads still decorated poles at either end. A large fleet of longships approached from downstream on oars, square sails furled. Armed men poured across the city to line the seawall and the bridge. Dark clouds rolled in from the west and the wind sharpened.

Frankie and Rhian rounded a long building and bumped into a group of warriors arming themselves with bundles of javelins handed out through a hatch. Frankie walked through them, not breaking stride or acknowledging their presence. The men backed away, eyes wide. The wolf growled deep in her throat and showed her teeth. A man turned and ran and they all fled.

"Where are those womanish raven-starvers off to?" asked a voice from within the building in a bellow that would have shamed Brian Blessed.

A man in mail with a helmet richly decorated in gold shot through a door and shook his fist. "Goat dung, come back or I'll eat your livers and throw your entrails to the dogs!"

He noticed Frankie and pushed his helmet back so he could see more clearly. Frankie was forced to stop as the man was right in front of her.

"Well," he said, "so it's to be that sort of battle."

He was joined by a second bareheaded warrior who pulled a long knife from a sheath hung from his belt. The wolf moved to intercept him. Frankie raised both arms to the sky.

"My Lord Odin."

Sunlight lanced through a gap in the clouds, illuminating Frankie and reflecting golden light off her amber necklace so it seemed to burn.

The warrior in mail knocked his companion to the ground with a single blow.

"Put the knife away, idiot. Do you not see who she is? She wears Brisingamen, the chain of fire."

He looked at Frankie quizzically, head to one side.

"What service can I do for you, My Lady? What brings you to this place?"

Frankie chanted slowly, not taking her eyes off the man.

"The ninth hall is *Folkvang*, where bright Freyja decides

"Where her warriors shall sit,
"Some of the slain belong to her,
"Some belong to Odin."

She paused for breath.

"Odin, my Lord, has granted me my pick of the bravest warriors of the Danes and the Norse who fall in noble battle at this place as my half, to sit beside me and at my command in *Sessrumnir*, great and fair hall. He has granted me Fenrir to smell out cowards," Frankie gestured at the wolf, "and Muninn to spot the deeds of the valiant. Muninn will watch by the Bridge, missing nothing, guiding the Valkyrie in their harvest," Frankie said.

The warrior bowed.

"In that case, noble Freyja, Queen of Magic and Battle, I shall escort you to the Bridge myself in the hope that I may win a warrior's death and a seat at your table."

And that was how it was. Frankie progressed to through the city with an ever-growing escort of warriors and perched the "raven" on a warehouse near Lundenburh Bridge. She and Rhian retired as the Norse longships collided with the bridge. Danish warriors rained missiles into the longships. The Norse had ripped thatched roofs from buildings further downstream and they employed these as shields. The air was filled with the clash of iron on wood and the screams of men.

The Norse swung iron grapples on ropes and threw them at the bridge. Some men fell, but other warriors rushed to take their place. Frankie and the wolf retreated back into the city as the longships backed water. The ropes attached to the bridge stretched taut, shedding water in fine sprays that formed little rainbows. The structure collapsed with a groan of rending wood, hurling many of the Danish warriors into the Thames. Black clouds rolled across the sky, darkening the ground.

Rhian was back in St. Olaves churchyard, as Rhian, on two legs. The soft red pastel light of a North European sunset filled the garden. As the women walked through the arch, a child's song drifted from the gardens.

"Build it up with iron and steel,
"Iron and steel, iron and steel,
"Build it up with iron and steel,
"My fair lady."

Rhian half thought she heard a voice croak "nevermore," but she probably imagined it.

The IED was hidden in a culvert by the road, but he couldn't explain that to the rest of the squad however hard he tried. They pushed on, ignoring him. He was insubstantial, a ghost or a whisper on the wind. He shouted and pulled at their clothes, pointing to the electronic bomb detector that ticked ominously in his hand. A soft tone sounded, indicating they were now in the blast zone. Jameson woke up covered in sweat, the duvet twisted around his body. He picked up the phone by his bed.

"Jameson, is that you?"

"Kendrics, what time is it?"

Jameson squinted at the phone, trying to read the time through sleep-fuddled eyes.

"Two o'clock in the morning."

The last clause was unnecessary, as Jameson's body clock told him that much.

"What the hell do you want, Kendrics?"

"That, ah, data you brought back from Shternberg's country house."

"Yes," Jameson gripped the phone tighter.

"The household accounts."

"Yes, get on with it, man."

"Well, it occurred to me that although the records in Shternberg's office had been well sanitized that there might be some tangential evidence in the accounts. So I looked for something that appeared harmless but was nonetheless suggestive."

Kendrics paused. He really had the most annoying mannerisms.

"And was there?" Jameson asked, encouragingly, trying to hurry things along without flustering the man. Yelling at him would only slow things down.

"Yes, I noticed a series of receipts from Shternberg's chauffeur claiming for filling up his car repeatedly from the same petrol station in East London. It caught my eye because it is only a few miles from Whitechapel University but is not in a commercial zone. The area just has private flats and hotels except for a boarded-up listed building isolated on some wasteland."

"Empty, boarded-up, and isolated, that is interesting," Jameson said.

"Yes, so I checked ownership. It took time to work through a series of shell companies in the Bahamas, but I believe that ultimately Shternberg owns it."

"What's Randolph doing?"

"I, um, haven't told him as it's late, so I thought in the morning, you know . . ."

"Ring Randolph now," Jameson said. "Tell him we'll need the Gamekeeper on-duty crash team and a witch ready to perform the Egyptian Closing of the Way. Karla and I will meet the team at the petrol station. Now, Kendrics, phone him now. Oh, and Kendrics?"

"Yes?"

"You've done bloody well, bloody well indeed."

Jameson put down the phone.

"So the game's afoot," Karla said, walking into his arms as he stood up.

He hadn't noticed her come into his bedroom. She was at her most active at night, but he needed sleep, which he wouldn't get if she prowled his bedroom.

"Yah, you've ten minutes to get ready. Put some clothes on, Karla. You're distracting me and I need to think."

She laughed lightly and departed after giving him a kiss.

Jameson pulled on his clothes, wondering where she had picked up the Sherlock Holmes phrase, before deciding that he didn't want to know.

Rhian also dreamed, but unlike Jameson, her dreams were tranquil. She and James were together, not doing anything special, but together. It was wonderful. She felt a great loss when her mobile beeped gently in her bedroom. It took a few minutes to track it down to where she had dropped it under her rumpled blouse.

"I would have woken you with a kiss like old times, Snow White, but I can't get in your house without permission. That odious doorknocker has it in for me, but all you have to do is proffer the invitation."

"And why the hell would I do that, Max?"

"Because I've a job for you, little witch, along with your scary friend."

Rhian had trouble classifying Frankie as scary, but she could see how Max might think so, or at least pretend to. You never knew with Max.

"Can't it wait until morning?" Rhian asked.

"Nope, the phones have dialed in. They have a fix, little witch."

"I thought you needed six operating, and we have only placed three."

"Six is optimum, but three will do to triangulate, especially when the energy release is off the scale. The magic source has fired up again and it is going for the big one, a permanent gate to the Land of the Sith."

Rhian went cold, remembering that terrible, perfect couple.

"Hold on, I'll wake Frankie."

She dragged on a T-shirt and jeans and banged on Frankie's bedroom door, eliciting a muffled squawk from inside.

"Max is outside and he needs us to smash the magic engine."

Another squawk.

"Can't hear you properly, look, I'll come in."

Rhian opened the door and flicked the light switch down. Frankie and Gary sat bolt upright in her bed, blinking at the sudden glare. A trail of discarded clothes, both male and female, marked the path from the bedroom door.

"Well," Rhian said, "how long has this been going on?"

"I can explain," Frankie said.

"I'm waiting," Rhian replied.

"It's not like it looks," Gary said.

Rhian raised an eyebrow.

"Frankie and I went out last night for a quiet drink, and she invited me in for a nightcap and . . ."

"One thing led to another?" Rhian asked.

"Yes . . . No, it was late and with all the excitement around this manor lately, she thought it would be safer for me if I slept here."

"I see," Rhian said deadpan, trying not to laugh at Frankie's hot flush and Gary's guilty face. "But was she safer with you sleeping here?"

"It's not like it looks," Gary said feebly, reduced to repeating himself.

"Bollocks, it's exactly like it looks," Frankie exploded. "Can't you see the little minx is winding you up. She's got us making stupid explanations like a couple of teenagers caught in the dorm after lights out."

Rhian couldn't contain herself anymore and burst out laughing until she cried. Truth to tell, she felt pleased for them. It couldn't be easy finding companionship at their age. She was pleased and perhaps just a little jealous.

"Go and make yourself useful in the kitchen with a pot of tea while we get dressed," Frankie said, trying to reestablish some dignity as the senior partner in their relationship.

"Okay, but get your kit on as quickly as you got it off, because Max is without," Rhian replied, slipping out and shutting the door behind her.

A thud suggested that she had been just in time to avoid whatever Frankie had thrown.

They assembled outside on the street ten minutes later. Frankie was adamant about not letting Max into her home, muttering something about bloody Karla being daemonic enough for one lifetime. Max outlined the situation.

"Okay, we need to stop by my lock-up so I can put a kit together and fetch my car," Frankie said.

"And we'll have to drop 'round the pub so I can pick something up," Gary said.

"There's no point you coming, Gary," Rhian said. "It will be dangerous and there's nothing you can do."

Gary's lips set in a tight line.

"Rhian's right," Frankie said.

"I'm not discussing it. I'm telling you. I am going to keep an eye on you two and that's the end of the matter."

"Yes, Gary," Frankie said meekly.

Dear God, Rhian thought, it must be lurve.

"And the ladies' fee is twenty thousand up front, with a bonus of a further twenty on successful completion," Gary said. "The terms are nonnegotiable, but I come free."

"If you've quite finished pratting around, can we get on?" Max said. "Apocalypse, death and destruction, end of life as we know it."

Rhian jumped into the front passenger seat of the BMW, leaving the back to Gary and Frankie. She pretended she hadn't noticed they were holding hands like lovestruck teenagers. Max squeezed her knee.

On arriving at the lock-up he took one look at Mildred and decided that they would all go in the BMW. Frankie hummed and hawed, selecting various herbs and artifacts until Max nearly lost it. Fortunately, Gary was in and out the Black Swan in two shakes of a dirty duck's tail. He chucked something in the car boot that Rhian didn't see, but from the noise it was probably his baseball bat. She didn't tell Max who might go ballistic at being diverted to fetch a stick.

Max set a new speed record through the empty streets down into the docklands, and Rhian soon began to recognize landmarks.

"You haven't told us where we are going," she said.

"You won't know it. The magic source is in an old boarded-up house . . ."

"I bet it's the Admiral of the Royal Dockyards' grace-and-favor home," Rhian said. She watched the illuminated campus of Whitechapel University slide by. It looked even weirder at night.

"Yes, how did you know that?" Max asked, shooting her a look.

"One gets to hear things," Rhian said, casually.

It wouldn't hurt to let him wonder.

"You are always full of surprises, Snow White," Max said patronizingly. "I'm so glad I decided to keep you."

Bloody man had an answer to everything and knew just how to wind her up. She searched for a suitable reply.

"Stop and turn round," Frankie suddenly said, interrupting her thought processes. "Go back to that garage."

Such was the urgency in her voice that Max did as he was bid without argument. The petrol station was an unmanned all-nighter. A single large black people carrier with darkened windows waited in the shadows by the closed shop. Max pulled in behind it.

"We have company," he said.

Rhian turned around to see a Jaguar sports car stop behind them, boxing in the BMW.

"Oh great, Tweedledum and bloody Tweedledee," Frankie said as Karla and Jameson got out.

Men in dark combat suits with guns on slings debussed from a sliding door in the side of the van and took up a position in front of the BMW. They didn't point the guns at anyone but held them purposefully, like a plumber holds a wrench when examining some dodgy pipework. When they got out of the BMW, Rhian noticed that

Max had his right hand in his pocket. She prayed that he wouldn't start anything. He might be bulletproof, but the other three weren't.

"Karla," Max said. "I see you brought your people to the party after all. Well, the more the merrier."

"What are you doing here, Max?" Karla asked.

"Trying to protect our flock from Otherworld wolves, same as you, I expect," Max replied.

"Never thought I'd see the day that you'd stoop to working for a sucker," Jameson said to Frankie.

"You're in no position to cast the first stone," Frankie said, nodding at Karla.

"Can it, the lot of you," Rhian said, rather surprising herself at her assertiveness. "We don't have time for all these petty feuds. You all keep telling me how dangerous and impossible it is to stop . . . whatever's going on." She paused because she wasn't sure she did know what was going on, "so why don't you start behaving like adults and cooperate."

"The young lady makes admirable sense, unlike the rest of you idiots."

"Miss Arnoux," Frankie said. "Surely you are not their magic support?"

Unnoticed by Rhian, an old woman had alighted from the carrier.

"Thank you for your vote of confidence, my dear," Miss Arnoux said. "I realise that my life force is not what it was thirty years ago, but I have not yet found a witch of a suitable talent to train as your replacement. Perforce I must do the job myself."

"Not tonight," Frankie said, shaking her head.

"I hoped you'd say that, Francesca. I've a spell prepared that you can use. Come with me and I'll teach it to you."

Gary wandered over to Jameson and was soon deep in conversation. Rhian edged towards them to eavesdrop but was intercepted.

"Hello, girl on the train," one of the armed men said to Rhian, pushing his visor up so she could see his face.

"The fake ticket inspector!" Rhian said. "So you're not an SAS man."

Gaston laughed.

"Parachute regiment and then The Commission," he said. "You weren't far out."

"The last time we met you were having a panic attack. You never did ring me," Gaston said accusingly.

"It's complicated," Rhian replied. "I did keep your number."

"By Abbadon's left testicle, can't you humans keep your mind on the job for more than a second?" Max said.

"I rather think I did have my mind on the job," Gaston said with an innocent smile that made Rhian blush.

The loosely aligned combat teams ditched the vehicles on the carriageway. Rhian examined the old house in the glow cast by the streetlights. It was one of the strangest buildings she had ever seen. It had always stood independently, never part of a typical London terrace. It was roughly square, with four tall windows on each side now boarded up. The lower half was typical London red brick, but the upper was covered in red slate. The grey-tiled roof sloped steeply to a point as high as a third story. The building's strangest feature was the hexagonal three-story tower with its own pointed roof sunk into one corner of the main building like a medieval alchemist's laboratory. Large windows circled the top of the tower so the presiding admiral would have had a grand view over the docks and river.

Elaborately carved wooden posts supported a wooden balcony around the middle story of the tower. There presumably had once been rails around the edge, but now it held only rolls of barbed wire to keep out intruders. It must have been such an elegant working home once.

They vaulted the crash bars at the edge of the road and walked cautiously towards the house on ground uneven and poorly lit. Rhian was tempted to call the wolf to enjoy the advantage of four legs and better night vision, but she was reluctant to activate it except in dire need. She stumbled, but a hand gripped her elbow.

"Do you need a hand?" Gaston said. "We have low-light cameras built into our visors."

"Lucky you," Rhian replied, tetchily.

Gary stayed close to the women, carrying a double-barreled shotgun.

"I didn't know you had a gun in the pub," Rhian said, sidling up to him.

"It's for sport, really, not a weapon," Gary said. "I find a baseball bat far more useful in an East End boozer. Guns up the ante and can lead to unfortunate results and recriminations, especially with the police. A smack from a bat is not considered worth getting worked up about, let alone reporting to the gendarmes. They probably would officially ignore the complaint anyway. Guns, though, guns are heavy metal."

"What do you shoot with it?" Rhian asked.

"Clay pigeons, I've never been into killing things," Gary replied.

"Neither was I," Rhian answered obliquely.

The door to the property was solidly wooden with an impressive lock. Max's team stood back to let The Commission boys do the biz. Karla declared it free of magical defenses, so one of Gaston's boys tried an electronic scan.

He shook his head. "Nothing, guv, must be purely mechanical."

"Okay, boys, use the universal key," Jameson said.

Two of the gamekeepers smashed at the door with a metal battering ram swung between them. The lock splintered but the door held, indicating some heavyweight antiburglar protection, probably iron bars that slid into the masonry when the door locked.

"What do you expect to find inside?" Frankie asked Jameson.

"The source of the magic is a powerful computer system called a Beowulf cluster. No real idea what that is, but it's some sort of way of linking computers together into a single device."

"You tried cutting the electricity supply to the building?" Frankie asked.

"Obviously, but that had no effect. The system will be possessed. It probably can draw energy from entropic potential differences between different universes."

Rhian, who was listening, translated that as "magic."

The door crashed in. It had resisted to the last, but the masonry on each side was made of weaker stuff.

"Okay, let's go," Jameson said, leading the way.

CHAPTER 27
ISLE OF HARTY

Rhian was not sure what she was expecting, but it was not a windswept marsh in winter with light levels barely above twilight. The wind howled in buffets that hit like a succession of boulders in an avalanche. It was cold, very, very cold. Low black clouds scudded across the sky at a crazy speed. Behind her was a doorway to normality, positioned ten centimeters off the ground. Ahead, the track was as straight as a die for three or four hundred meters to an embankment.

The air smelled of salt water laced with an accent of decaying mud and seaweed. Drainage channels ran along each side of the track. Feeder streams wound through pools and tufts of coarse marsh grasses until they lost themselves in a main ditch. A low head of twisted, wind-swept bushes marked the edge of the path.

High-pitched cries sounded in the lulls between wind blasts, although Rhian had to strain to see any wading birds. A seagull balanced on the wind, wings half retracted into upturned V's. It flicked sharply from bank to bank to maintain stability. The bird dropped towards the ground and was lost to view. A head, covered in long, shaggy brown hair and armed with wicked curved horns, lifted to stare at Rhian.

"A hairy cow with horns—where are we, Scotland?" Rhian asked, yelling to be heard over the wind.

"Can't be," Frankie replied, shaking her head. "We must be

somewhere in the shadow cast by the Thames Estuary into the Otherworld."

"Have you any idea of the trope?" Jameson asked.

Frankie shook her head again, sparing her voice from an unequal contest with the wind.

They moved down the track. The Commission gamekeepers adopted a combat formation. They walked well-spaced, three at the front, one on the left, and two on the right, avoiding the center of the path. The fourth took up the rear, repeatedly walking backwards to watch behind them.

There was a sucking noise, loud enough to carry over the wind. A grey hoop pushed into the sky from a pool several hundred meters away. It slowly unfurled into a tentacle. The size was difficult to judge against the grey sky, but it must be attached to something truly enormous. The tentacle probed the marsh gently, dipping in like a sonar buoy from a helicopter searching for submarines.

It struck without warning.

After a brief struggle it pulled up a newt-shaped creature colored a blotchy grass green. The animal's four stubby legs thrashed and clawed at the tentacle, which squeezed until the newt stopped moving. The tentacle retracted, doubling back into a loop to push its capture down into the mud. It disappeared altogether with a last obscene slurp.

"Keep moving," Jameson said, utterly unnecessarily in Rhian's opinion, as everybody's pace had already picked up.

They reached the embankment without further mishap to find it was a flood defense. A wide river flowed slowly from left to right, except that it wasn't freshwater. Rhian could see seaweed on the exposed shingles, and the smell of sea air was stronger. They must be looking over a creek at an island. As they watched, a lance of sunlight pierced the clouds and illuminated white cliffs on the coast to the far right.

The wind died down.

"Kent—this is the North Kent coast," Jameson said. "We are on the south bank of the Thames Estuary."

Frankie said something softly.

"What?" Jameson asked.

"Nothing," Frankie said. "Just a passing line from some poetry."

Rhian had heard her. Frankie said, "sea cliffs shining."

It was appropriate. Under the sunlight the white chalk cliffs of Kent did seem to shine against the dark greyness of the sea and sky. The clouds closed, shutting off the shaft of light, and the illusion was dispelled.

A ramp led down from the embankment, disappearing into the sea. A wooden flat-bottomed raft with a square bow and stern was beached there. It had high wooden sides, along each of which was attached a heavy iron chain. These ran through pulleys fixed to massive wooden pilings sunk into the ground above the high-tide mark. They looped round to disappear under the sea in the direction of the island. Two more chains ran from the back of the raft, dropping into the sea.

A squall lashed the island, reducing visibility on the far shore, but Rhian fancied she could see chains emerging from the water. They climbed into the raft. Before they were seated, the chains on the seaward side tightened and clanked through the pulleys. The chains pulled from the sea, shedding water along their length. Frankie stumbled and would have toppled over the side had Max not caught her.

"Thank you," Frankie said.

"Try not to die until the job is done," Max said, encouragingly.

Gary glared at the man, which only made Max's smile broaden into a grin.

"I know I can rely on you to look after me—at least until I am no longer useful," Frankie replied.

Nobody said anything else as the ferry clanked across the creek in a jerky motion that made Rhian feel somewhat queasy. The heavy chains damped out the raft's rocking motions, which was a bonus.

A massive head emerged from the water. Rhian had the merest impression of small yellow eyes in a slab of slate grey before yawning jaws opened and all she could see were teeth. Two shots cracked out from behind her before Gaston in the bow swung his submachine gun on its strap and let rip.

Rhian had seen such weapons fired in movies, but special effects were a pale copy of the real thing. Flame flickered from the muzzle in a continuous roar that hurt her ears. Empty cartridges spewed into the water. The hammering sound seemed to go on forever, punctuated by another double crack behind her and two loud thuds at spaced intervals. Blood and flesh exploded from the jaws and they sank back in a swirl of dark-tinged water, but not before plucking a Commission trooper from the ferry.

Max put his pistol back into his pocket. He had drawn and got off two shots before anyone else had moved. Gary calmly reloaded his shotgun, and, in the bow, Gaston clipped a new magazine onto his gun. Nobody mentioned the missing man.

At that moment, a squall hit and they hunkered down to avoid the driving rain. When it passed, Rhian was aware that something had changed. The clanking had stopped and the raft moved silently. The raft, the boat, was narrower, deeper, and the prow curved up over the water, like the Viking longships she had seen at Lundenburgh. Sunlight sparkled on the water and the air was full of birds.

Frankie tapped her on the shoulder. "There's an old friend behind you."

The stern of the boat curved up like the prow, but Rhian had eyes only for the figure holding the steering oar. It was the hooded ferryman.

"Don't pay him until we get to the other side," Rhian said, with something of a forced smile.

The long ship grounded on the shingle with a hiss like frying bacon. Frankie put a coin in the ferryman's hand. They jumped over the bow, getting their feet wet in the freezing water. Above the water line, another muddy track climbed upwards, straight as an arrow through heathland. Frankie bent down and began to scoop dirt away with her bare hands.

"What are you up to?" Jameson asked.

"Just testing a theory," Frankie replied.

"Sergeant, your knife, please," Jameson requested.

"Sir."

Gaston pulled a heavy combat knife out of a sheath on his belt and tossed it over to Jameson, who caught it one-handed. He knelt beside Frankie and scraped away the dirt. Gaston winced at the sound of steel on rock.

"There's cobblestones under the layer of mud," Jameson said.

"And there will be gravel at the edge for drainage," Frankie replied. "This is a Roman road. Can you lever out a stone and dig down?"

"I can see why he didn't use his own bloody knife," Gaston said to no one in particular.

Jameson ignored him and got to work, finding larger stones the deeper he went. He needed two hands to pull the last one free. Underneath, white cables writhed and coiled slowly around each other like giant whip worms. Bulges pulsed up and down.

"Now that's not a Roman road," Jameson said, sitting back on his heels. "So where the bloody hell are we, Frankie?"

"You gave me the clue," she replied, "you and the sea cliffs shining. This is Harty Ferry and we are on the eastern part of the Isle of Sheppy or, to be more exact, the Isle of Harty."

"Oh Christ," Jameson said. "Shternberg's people used a computer system called a Beowulf Cluster."

"And this whole area is Schrawynghop," Frankie added.

"We are all impressed by your boundless academic knowledge," Max said, with heavy sarcasm, "but is there any chance of one of you explaining for the benefit of the rest of us?"

"You read literature, Jameson, at Cambridge, while I read history at a red-brick university. The floor is yours."

"Beowulf is the oldest piece of English writing known, the Homer of the English-speaking peoples. It tells the tale of a Scandinavian hero of the Geat tribe in Sweden who travels to a far place, which is almost certainly the North Kent Saxon Shore. His task is to slay the monster Grendel that is terrorizing the Mead Hall Heorot of a Danish King called *Hroðgar*. Beowulf's longship sights land by the shining cliffs."

Jameson pointed at the chalk cliffs glowing in the light.

"Beowulf walks up a street, the Saxon name for a Roman road . . ."

"Like Watling Street?" Rhian asked.

"Like Watling Street, to Heorot, which has a paved floor. In the Dark Ages, paving meant that it was the floor of a Roman villa. They used to think that Beowulf was set in Denmark, but there are no Roman structures there, or chalk cliffs. Also, *Hroðgar*'s queen is called Wealtheow, meaning she was British, Weal being the same word as Welsh in modern English, from the Saxon Waelisc meaning—"

"Foreigner or slave, I know," Rhian said.

"Quite," Jameson said, coloring slightly.

"I would point out that we call ourselves the Cymri, the northern British," she added.

"Anyway, Beowulf slays the troll Grendel and Grendel's mother in single combat before sailing back to Sweden," Jameson moved the conversation onto less contentious areas.

"Oh great, trolls," Gaston said.

"And other things," Frankie said. "Jameson will no doubt correct me if I err, he normally does, but Schrawynghop in modern English means something like 'place in the marsh that is infested by malignant daemons.'"

"Near enough," Jameson replied.

Gaston spat, which neatly encapsulated Rhian's view. He retrieved his combat knife from Jameson.

"I half hoped we would simply to have to smash up a few computer systems, but it seems we are inside the ghost in the machine," Jameson said.

"We still could try a bit of vandalism," Gaston said, reaching down with the knife.

"I don't think . . ." Frankie started to say, way too late.

Gaston sheared a number of the pulsing cables with a quick slash. White sparklies flowed out and dissipated away on the wind. They waited, expectantly, but nothing happened.

"Okay," Jameson said. "We move on."

They made barely fifty meters before a flock of things that looked a bit like fruit bats fluttered down the hill towards them. As they got closer, it was clear that they were not really fruit bats. They were too big, for one thing, and their wings bent in all the wrong directions. Then there was the matter of their downward-pointing tusks. The tearing rip of submachine guns sounded and the bats-things fell, but their unpredictable flight made them difficult targets. Only body- or headshots took them out as hits to the wings merely made their flight patterns even more erratic.

"I'm not sure which is worse," Jameson said to Karla, firing his bolt pistol and missing, "one big pterosaur or a lot of little ones."

Gary fired calmly, each shotgun blast taking out a bat. He winked at Rhian.

"This is a lot easier than hitting clay pigeons," he said as he reloaded.

Rhian reflected that people were endlessly surprising.

The fruit bat survivors, of which there were more than a handful, fluttered on. They had nasty little scarlet eyes. There was no reason why their eyes shouldn't be red, but it was unsettling all the same.

Frankie yelled something and stretched her arms upwards, releasing a flood of green light. The fruit bats flying into it stuck, moving in slow motion. Their wings caught fire and burned with green flame. The bats fell like comets, rolling and hopping on the ground until the flames consumed them utterly. Frankie collapsed on her knees, exhausted, and the bubble of light faded. Unfortunately, there were plenty more bats.

They were so close that Rhian could hear their soft chittering cries, which became loud squeals to the wolf's ears when she transformed and bounded forward. A bat dropped to intercept her, but the wolf crushed the creature's skull in her jaws. She spat it out, bouncing immediately upwards to rip the wing off a second bat. They hit the ground simultaneously. The bat flapped its one remaining wing against the track and tried to spear the wolf with its tusks, but she sheared its neck with a single contemptuous bite.

Karla moved ahead of the wolf, faster than any human could run. Bats swarmed over her in a mass. There was an explosion of bloodied pieces. Heads, wings, and furry bodies hurtled from Karla. The last couple of bats flapped hard, trying to escape. Karla grabbed one by the legs with a clawed hand and dashed its brains out on the cobbled track. The wolf plucked the second out of the air, taking a chunk from its body.

Blood dripped from Karla's fangs. It ran down her neck and breasts and stained her hands deep red. She glared at the wolf with a terrible beauty and Rhian thought she was about to attack. A struggling bat with a broken body caught Karla's attention and she grabbed it, ripping off its head with her bare hands. She drank its blood straight from the neck.

Urged by Rhian, the wolf loped back to protect the fragile humans. She had a glimpse of Max. He smashed the bodies of two bats together until they were bloodied pulp in his hands. Frankie was on her knees trying to fend off a bat clinging to her chest, its tusks lunging at her throat. Gary was running towards her, the butt of his shotgun raised, but he was not going to make it in time.

The wolf hit the bat like an orca taking out a luckless penguin. She ripped it from Frankie and cut it in half with two quick bites. A

Commission trooper went down covered in furry bodies. He dropped his gun and put his arms up to protect his face and neck. The bats raked their tusks against his body armor. The wolf jumped straight in, jaws snapping at anything in fur until nothing moved. Gaston gazed up at her through the visor, and she smelled his fear. She jumped off, heart singing with the music of the hunt. She experienced disappointment when the last living bat was killed and dismembered.

A trooper lay unmoving on the ground, two holes punched through his visor.

Jameson held Karla, who trembled even though her claws were retracted.

"Easy Karla, focus on me, relax to the sound of my voice," Jameson said.

Max was still in hunting mode, his eyes bright metallic blue.

"Oh shit," someone said. "He's in a blood frenzy."

Rhian heard the metallic clicks of guns being prepared.

Max heard them too and moved towards the sound, towards the humans. The wolf intercepted and Max looked at her without recognition. He snarled, showing his teeth. The wolf wanted to answer in kind, but Rhian suppressed the growl. They would never have survived the bats without the help of the vampires.

Karla had Jameson to bring her out of it but Max had no one, no one but Rhian. Even if he beat the wolf, the massed automatic guns would tear him apart. Max was tough, but nothing is that tough, and Frankie had told her about Jameson's vampire-killing bolt gun. Taking a deep breath, she turned back into Rhian. She walked slowly towards Max, softly calling his name.

"Rhian, no!" Frankie said.

"For God's sake, girl, clear the line of fire," Jameson said simultaneously.

"Max, it's over. You won, Max. All your enemies are dead. Time to relax," Rhian said, stroking his face.

He looked at her, head on one side. The metallic glare slowly faded from his eyes. Max took in the weapons leveled against him and chuckled. He retracted his claws and canines, holding one hand up, palm outwards in the universal sign of *pax*.

"I am so, so, glad I kept you, Snow White," Max said. "Have I mentioned that?"

"Hmmpph," Rhian turned her back on him, eliciting another chuckle.

They resumed their trek up the hill in battle formation. Rhian found herself walking alongside Gaston.

"So, girl on the train, you are a dark horse, or should that be dark werewolf?" Gaston asked.

"I'm not a werewolf," Rhian answered truthfully. "But if it helps you to think of me as one, be my guest."

Heorot was perched on top of the ridge, surrounded by twisted, leafless trees. The wooden mead hall was rectangular with a thatched roof, from which smoke drifted although there was no sign of a chimney.

A loud groan bellowed, seeming to come from the earth itself. A mound of earth beside the hall unrolled and stood upright on two legs. Two arms disengaged from the loose soil tumbling around the trunk. Earth-covered eyelids opened to show bloodshot eyes. A mouth with fangs like a *T. rex* roared like a minor earthquake. The thing overtopped the hall, at least four meters high.

Jameson said. "Sergeant!"

"Sir?" Gaston replied.

"You and your men, full auto, the earthy looking chap with the attitude."

"Rock and roll, boys," Gaston said.

The surviving gamekeepers started firing before he had finished giving the order. Rhian put her hand over her ears to shut out the hammer of the guns. Earth flaked off the troll in strips, carved away by the streams of bullets. Gary and Max added their contribution and Grendel shed soil. The material of his body continually rearranged to maintain shape.

Grendel was smaller when the guns stopped hammering, but hardly small. He kept on coming at a slow lurch. Gaston snapped out an order and his two remaining men ran in and threw what looked to Rhian like cricket balls at the troll before diving to the ground. Concussive thumps rocked the monster, chipping off more of its bulk. Gaston changed the clip on his gun and resumed automatic fire in short bursts.

Grendel dropped to all fours and rolled over on his back. Jameson walked up to him and put two bolts between his eyes and two into the middle of his trunk. The troll's eyes winked out and he shuddered, becoming just a mound of earth again.

"That should keep him quiet for a while," Jameson said, reloading the bolt pistol. "He will regenerate of course. That's the way of trolls, but we should be long gone by then."

"A bit of an anticlimax," Frankie said. "Grendel gave Beowulf one hell of a fight."

"Beowulf only had a sword," Jameson replied. "My lads have H and Ks and grenades."

"Humans get more dangerous every year," Karla said, looking at Max.

He shrugged. "We can adapt."

"Can we?" Karla asked. "I wonder."

Gaston and his men kicked open the door to the hall and deployed inside, followed by the rest of the team.

Rhian gagged on the smell of rotting flesh. Heorot was a charnel house of scattered body parts and offal in various stages of decomposition. There was enough material here to keep an international conference of forensic scientists in work for a year.

"Christ, I knew people had gone missing, but there must be the remains of dozens here," Jameson said.

"It's London, Major. Hundreds deliberately disappear every day, hundreds more arrive unannounced from the provinces, and that's before you include the illegals living off the grid," Gaston said.

"Blood magic," Frankie said.

The worst part was that the body parts twitched with unnatural life as electrical sparks jumped from piece to rotting piece. Long, thin wire worms writhed slowly among the carnage, connecting body parts. Peristaltic waves moved slowly up and down their bodies in complex patterns.

The top half of a man's body was nailed to a wall, arms splayed in an obscene half crucifix. His chest had been sliced vertically and the ribs spread out and nailed back. His jaw hung almost off on rotting gristle. It twitched spasmodically, rattling out something that sounded like Morse code.

"It's like an alchemist's computer built for Genghis Khan," Jameson said in disgust.

"Nobody touch anything," he added, completely unnecessarily as far as Rhian was concerned. "This isn't a Hollywood bomb and it can't be shut down by cutting a few wires. Gaston, you and your people stay by the door. Frankie and I will move down the end, to the throne."

Gary, Max, Karla and Rhian went with them. Jameson looked as if he was going to object but decided against it. Rhian picked her way delicately through the butchery. The roof of the one-room building was supported by wooden columns in two lines. Heads hung from them by their hair knotted around wooden pegs. They chittered constantly, making insectoid noises.

The remains of a man in a laboratory coat that had once been white, but was now various shades of rust brown, sat on the wooden throne. Bronze spikes pinned his wrists to the arms of the chair.

"King Hroðgar's magic throne, the one place that Grendel could not despoil," Frankie said, almost under her breath. "This would be the center of the magic."

The man on the throne was dead, wireworms reaching from the floor to bury in his flesh. They probed into all orifices, whether natural or the product of decay.

"Doctor Vocstrite, I presume," Jameson said lightly.

Presumably he was trying to lighten the mood, but Rhian found the joke in bad taste. To her horror, the man's eyes opened and stared at Jameson. His mouth worked, trying to form sounds despite being filled with a pulsating wire worm reaching down his throat. At first the sounds were mere gurgles, but eventually Rhian discerned words.

The man was repeating "kill me, kill me, kill me," over and over again. His dead eyes pleaded with them.

"Not to worry, old chap. It's almost over," Jameson said, glancing meaningfully at Frankie.

She took off her rucksack and busied herself setting up her apparatus.

The sitting man shuddered and closed his eyes, to Rhian's eternal gratitude. Frankie began her spell, not bothering to put up a pentagram or circle. Rhian was not sure if they were irrelevant in the Otherworld or whether there was simply no place to draw one on the carpet of flesh. She was expecting something extraordinary in the way of magic, but Frankie just did what she always did, burning herbs and chanting. Frankie always said magic was nine-tenths willpower, and the ritual was mostly to aid concentration.

Rhian felt the buildup of charge that she associated with spellcasting. An almost translucent sparkling mist formed and rotated gently around the throne, gradually thickening into streamers of colored fog.

A bellow sounded in the distance.

"That bloody troll is coming 'round, Major," Gaston said from the other end of the Hall.

"After Grendel, Beowulf had to defeat his even more ferocious mother," Jameson said.

"Terrific!" Gaston said.

"And after that there was the dragon that finally topped Beowulf."

"Fecking great, it just keeps getting better," said a trooper, fingering his weapon.

"Be quiet, lads, and let the lady work," Jameson said.

The magical vortex whipped around the throne like a whirlpool of water marked with various dyes. Frankie pulled a pathetic little bundle out of her rucksack. It was wrapped in ancient bandages.

"A mummified cat, a powerful animal totem in Egyptian magic, to take the place of blood magic in our ceremony," Frankie said by way of explanation.

She chanted a little more, kissed the mummy, and tossed it into the vortex. It bounced off the wooden throne and lay among the carnage.

"Isn't something supposed to happen?" Jameson asked, after a while.

"Yes, I don't know. I've never tried to perform an Ancient Egyptian spell before," Frankie said slightly hysterically. "Something's wrong. I need time to think."

Another deep bellow sounded, closer than before, and it changed to howls of anguish.

"I think Mummy just found the remains of Junior," Jameson said. "Time is something we are clean out of."

"I know why the spell has failed," Rhian said, tiredly.

"Really?" Jameson asked neutrally.

They all looked at her with doubt-filled eyes. Rhian wished they were right, wished she was just a silly little girl with an overactive imagination, but she was far more than that. She was the wolf, and she knew what they didn't. She felt what they couldn't. She heard the howl of the pack over the frozen steppe.

"What is it, Snow White?" asked Max, he alone taking her seriously.

"Do you remember, Frankie, in Lundenburh when you pretended to be Freyja? You were accompanied by a raven and a wolf. Why was that?"

"The goddess Freyja is Odin's female partner of war and battles, and she controls half the Valkyrie. Odin is accompanied by two wolves and two ravens, so why not Freyja? I could only get one of each, but the Danes were predisposed to accept Freyja as having just one of each totem, as a mere goddess. Typical male sexism," she said, looking at Jameson.

"You're missing Rhian's point," Jameson said. "The cat was an Egyptian symbol. I understand why Miss Arnoux chose one, this being an Egyptian spell, but we aren't in Egypt. We're in Northern Europe, where the raven and the wolf are totems."

"Don't, Snow White, we'll find another way," Max said.

It was strange how the men understood but Frankie still hadn't got it. Perhaps she didn't want to get it.

"But we don't have a raven . . ." Frankie's voice trailed off and she gazed at Rhian in horror.

"We have a wolf," Rhian said, moving towards the vortex.

She found she wasn't afraid at all. Perhaps this was what it was all for. Why she was fated to wear Boudica's brooch, to wear the magic artifact with Morgana's wolf symbol. James' death would finally mean something and the karma would be all played out. She smiled at her friends, Frankie, Gary, even Max. In different ways, she had come to love them all, but it was time to join James. She had loved him above all. James, the one person she could not protect when he needed help. She would summon the wolf and jump into the vortex, and her death would mean something. Perhaps the saving of so many lives would wash the stains from her soul.

She closed her eyes and called to the wolf.

"Hang on a moment," Jameson said.

His hands ripped open her blouse. She opened her eyes in shock.

"Jameson," Frankie said, outraged.

He gripped Morgana's brooch and pulled hard, using his other hand to anchor the chain against Rhian's neck. A link broke with a snap and Jameson had the brooch. He threw it into the vortex. Rhian had one last glimpse of the wolf symbol before the brooch exploded in a soundless yellow flash that was brighter than the desert sun, more searing than an atomic test.

CHAPTER 28
LOOSE ENDS

"Snow White, wakey, wakey, Snow White," Max said.

Lips touched hers and Rhian woke, opening her eyes to see.

"Why is it you end up sick every time I take you out?" Max said.

"Probably something to do with your personality," Rhian said coldly. "I believe I can walk if you put me down."

Actually, that was a slight overestimate. Max had to steady her until the world stopped rotating. The Admiral's house was in flames. Gaston and his men sat on the ground, watching the fire. Karla and Jameson left the house, then Gary and Frankie staggered clear. Smoke drifted off their clothes.

Rhian realized that she had only been unconscious for a few seconds. She had been hit hardest by the collapsing magic field, perhaps because of her link to Boudica's brooch. Max must have grabbed her as she fell and carried her out of the fire.

"Um, thanks, Max," she said, reaching up to kiss him on the cheek.

He waved a hand languidly. "Life would be so much duller without you, Snow White."

"I'm called Rhian," she said, without much heat. "I am glad that is over. It is over?"

"Absolutely," Frankie said, in between coughing smoke out of her lungs. "The whole infernal engine has been wiped."

"Well," Max said, looking up at the lightening sky. "It will be dawn soon, so I must be on my way. Can I give you three a lift?"

Frankie shook her head. "Looks like it will be a nice day, so why don't we take the river taxi? A slow boat ride will do us good."

"Don't forget to post the check," Gary said.

Max smiled and waved a hand while heading for his car.

"Are you sure you don't want to rejoin The Commission, Frankie?" Jameson asked. "We would all be glad to have you back on board, wouldn't we, Karla?"

"Ecstatic," she replied, without any enthusiasm.

"I don't think so, Jameson. I kind of like being my own boss, and it will be nice to go back to locating lost cats and curing sick buildings. I'm all apocalypsed out."

"As you wish."

The three friends walked towards the river, Gary with a woman on each arm.

"You've got my number, phone," Gaston said to Rhian.

She smiled and waved a hand. She couldn't decide whether she would call him, but she would put it in her mobile's contacts list. It would sit next to "Max."

"Actually, in all the excitement, I haven't had time to tell you my news," Gary said.

"Something nice happened?" Frankie asked.

"Not really. The company management have been in touch to tell me the Swan is to close. They've decided not to refurbish but sell it off, austerity and cutbacks and all that. I'm afraid you are out of a job, Rhian."

"Never mind, I'll find another," Rhian said. "Maybe you'll want to employ me in that swish new wine bar up west you will be managing."

"'Fraid not, they are letting me go as well. Austerity . . ."

"And cutbacks and all that," Frankie said.

"Yes, but I do have some good news for you." Gary produced a page torn from a notebook. "I managed to negotiate a payment-on-results fee from Jameson. After all, you were doing The Commission's job for them. I pointed out that failure would inevitably forfeit the contract, given it would destroy London and possibly the rest of Western civilization as well, so what did he have to lose? He signed like a lamb."

"Jameson didn't mention it," Frankie said.

"I think he's forgotten in all the excitement. No doubt an invoice will refresh his memory."

Gary handed to paper to Frankie, who stared at it for quite some time.

"Is this legally binding?"

"Absolutely, I have every legal reason to believe Jameson has the proper authority to sign on behalf of his employer as a senior member of staff. Besides, do you really see them dragging this business through the courts?"

"No, indeed," Frankie said, handing Rhian the note.

Rhian skipped the text and fastened on Jameson's signature below a large figure that started with a pound sterling sign. She counted the zeros after the one, and then recounted to make sure she had got it right.

"We're rich," she said.

"Yes," Gary replied, "but how much is London worth? On another note, my fortunes are a little low at the moment, being unemployed and homeless. I wonder if the two of you could see your way to paying me a negotiator's fee, say three percent."

Dead silence.

"One percent would do," Gary said, somewhat desperately.

"Out of the question, don't you agree, Rhian?"

"Absolutely," Rhian replied.

Gary seemed to shrink. Rhian worried she and Frankie might have gone too far teasing him.

"Full partnership with one third of the assets backdated to last week or nothing," Rhian said.

"Quite," Frankie added.

"You bitches," Gary said, laughing.

"I think you got a letter wrong there," Frankie replied.

"I think not," said Gary.

"We could do with a business manager," Rhian said. "You leave the witchy stuff to us and concentrate on making money."

"Well, I do have a few ideas," Gary said. "With this bonus we could buy the Swan and do it up a bit. We convert part of the upstairs into a separate office for the magic investigation business. It looks amateur operating from home on a mobile phone."

"We would need a name," Frankie said, thoughtfully. "How about Witch and Wolf Investigations?"

Something deep inside Rhian growled. The wolf had firm ideas about hierarchical structures and her place in them.

"Wolf and Witch would make my life easier," Rhian said. She gazed fondly at her partners, her family.

"I rather like The Snow White Agency," Gary said.

"Yuk!" Rhian replied.

They walked off, arguing amiably as the Sun rose over the River Thames.

Gaston and Jameson watched Gary and the women walk away. The surviving troopers piled gear into the minivan, and Karla went to start the Jag.

"What about Shternberg?" Gaston asked.

"What about him?"

"He just walks away after causing this mess?"

"Probably. He hasn't committed any crime we could charge him with, and he's powerful protectors."

"It doesn't seem right," Gaston said stubbornly.

"We don't do what's right, sergeant. We do what we have to. You know that. Being right is for priests and politicians."

"He might try something similar."

"Shouldn't think so, he has no real connections to magic and this adventure hardly worked out well for him."

"He could have an accident," Gaston suggested stubbornly.

"It would have to be a damn good one, considering who his friends are," Jameson said, thinking about it. "Any suggestion of foul play or mysterious health problems and the SIS would have the black on us for years."

Karla hooted the Jag's horn.

"Your pet monster is getting fractious," Gaston said. "Bye Major."

Jameson climbed in beside Karla, who accelerated away with smoking wheels.

"Turn the traction control back on," he said automatically, still thinking of his conversation with Gaston. "These tires cost two-hundred-and-eighty quid each."

Karla pouted, but did as she was bid.

"What was that piece of paper you signed for Frankie's friend?" she asked, curious.

"Oh, shit!" Jameson said, remembering. "Randolph is not going to like this."

A few weeks later Rhian got a phone call.

"Jameson, Miss Jones, remember me?"

"I am hardly likely to forget," she replied. "I didn't know you had my number?"

"It took some tracking down," Jameson said. "But I have my methods."

"No doubt," Rhian replied. "But Frankie is out."

"I know, on a weekend break in Norfolk with her pub manager."

Rhian wondered if she detected just a hint of snobbery in Major Jameson's, late of Cambridge and the Brigade of Guards, tone. She still was not familiar enough with all the variations in English accents and their convoluted class system to be sure.

"But it's you I wanted to speak to," Jameson said.

"Why?" Rhian asked, guardedly.

"Have you ever seen London by night?" Jameson asked.

"Of course," she replied.

"From the air," Jameson said.

"I'm not sure . . ." Rhian began.

"Karla will be with us," Jameson said.

He obviously thought he was reassuring her, that he was not asking her out but it was a strange world where Karla's presence was reassuring.

"I'll pick you up at eight," Jameson said, taking her hesitation for acceptance and ringing off before she could refuse.

Jameson slid the Commission's helicopter through the night sky over London. Rhian sat between him and Karla in the large machine. Jameson insisted that she sit up front, where she could get a good view. She would have preferred one of the rear seats.

She fiddled with the microphone on her neck. The only way to communicate was via the intercom. It was Rhian's first trip in a helicopter, and she had not realized how noisy they were. No wonder the Queen flatly refused to fly in them.

"Do they often let you joyride in these things?" she asked.

"I'm working. I need to brush up my pilot skills," Jameson replied.

"Especially after Wales," Karla added.

Rhian waited for one of them to explain Wales but they didn't, and she didn't like to ask.

Karla had her hand on the radio. She didn't punch any buttons, but the machine flashed through a number of frequency changes anyway. It sprang to life, and Rhian heard a voice in her headphones.

"London City Tower, London City Tower, this is Cessna Light G769 at Beacon 47B requesting clearance for takeoff, destination Le Touquet."

"G769? Isn't that Shternberg's plane?" Karla asked innocently.

"Good Lord, yes. What a coincidence," Jameson said, with a grin.

"Who's Shternberg?" Rhian asked.

"He's the banker chappy who was behind all our recent problems. He put up the money that funded the unlicensed magical experiment we terminated with your help."

"I see," Rhian said.

"And you know how dangerous it is for amateurs to play with magic," Jameson said, pointedly.

Rhian didn't rise to the bait.

"I suppose he has to fly over to the Continent to start up some new rackets after his recent financial hit," Jameson said.

"Cessna Light G769, this is London Tower. You are clear to takeoff. Watch for traffic at three thousand on reciprocal."

"Confirmed."

Jameson put the chopper into a tight turn and lost altitude, watching the Cessna via the gimballed night-vision camera slung under the helicopter's nose. Rhian leaned over so she could see. The big helicopter closed rapidly on the small plane.

Karla hit the quick release on her harness. She took off her helmet and opened the cabin door.

"What?" Rhian exclaimed, making a grab for her.

Karla shrugged Rhian off, leaned out of the cabin, and looked down, watching the climbing Cessna. Rhian couldn't reach Karla, so she unclipped her own harness and slid over the seats but she was too late. Karla jumped. Rhian stuck her head into the slipstream, blinking furiously to clear her eyes.

Karla adopted the paradrop spread until she stabilized. Then she folded her arms and dived down to intercept the light aircraft like a kestrel after a vole. She smashed into the thin material on the light plane's cabin roof. She punched through with her arms, and the plane wobbled uncertainly. Karla held tight with one hand and tore a hole with the other. Wriggling, she crawled head first into the cabin.

The Cessna's nose tilted and it banked, diving towards the Millennium Dome. Before it hit, the plane reversed and plunged into the dark loop of the Thames.

Stunned, Rhian got the door closed and strapped herself in.

"For a horrible moment I thought it would crash into Tony Blair's Folly," he said, his voice sounding relieved even over the headphones.

"It's the perfect accident, a plane crash. Independent witnesses can vouch that the pilot took off alone. In the cockpit no one will find evidence of bombs or sabotage of any kind, just a dead pilot with his body broken in the impact. Shternberg's mates in MI6 can suspect dire deeds, but they won't be able to prove a thing."

"But why am I here?" Rhian asked.

"You were in this from the start, so I thought you might like to see the finish. There was no way I was going to let the bastard get away with it."

"Aren't you frightened I'll tell someone?" she asked.

"We all have our secrets, Miss Jones, you especially. Best to let sleeping wolves lie." Jameson thought for a moment. "But I should keep this secret from Frankie. She suffers from possession of an overactive conscience."

And he believes I don't, Rhian thought. She considered and discovered that she didn't give a tinker's curse about Shternberg.

She looked out over the blaze of light that was London. Streams of cars flowed down the radial roads into the city's heart like blood cells along arteries. London was still alive, thanks to her and her friends. What was a Shternberg compared to the greatest city in the world?

Jameson followed her eyes and guessed at her thoughts.

"London's beautiful from the sky at night when she's all lit up in her finery. She's a raddled old wrinkled tart of a town, a bit past her best and a little tatty at the edges, but she still scrubs up well," he said.

He raised a hand in salute.

"Here's to your next two thousand years," he said to the city.

The End